THE GIRL IN GRAY

By Annette Lyon

THE GIRL IN GRAY

BY ANNETTE LYON

BLUE GINGER BOOKS

ALSO BY ANNETTE LYON

Lost Without You

Falling to Pieces

Song Breaker

Tailor Maid

At the Water's Edge

House on the Hill

At the Journey's End

Spires of Stone

Tower of Strength

Band of Sisters

Coming Home

Paige

Ilana's Wish

Selected Collections from the Timeless Romance Anthology Series

There, Their, They're:
A No-Tears Guide to Grammar from the Word Nerd

DEDICATION

Dedicated to the thousands of Finns, both in the military and in the Lotta Svärd, who served their nation could retain its freedom. That number includes many of my relatives who served in the Winter War and the Continuation War:

My grandfather and his brother, Rudolf and Teodor Sävstrand.

Great-uncle Kemi Väinö Laurila, who died in War Hospital #34 in Rovaniemi, 21 February 1940

Three Sorvoja brothers, all great-uncles:
        Arvo, who died 15 July 1941, age of 21
        Eino, who died 20 Oct 1942, age of 20 in a field hospital
        Martti, who miraculously survived the war

ACKNOWLEDGMENTS

Each of my books has had its cheerleaders and supporters, but *The Girl in Gray* has been such a big—and long—journey for me that the number of people who have been with me along the way is significantly larger than usual.

They have been there as I researched, pulled my hair out, gained and lost confidence, and more, literally for years. They helped me find the story, pushed me to deepen the characters, and demanded that I reach farther than I ever have for anything I've ever written.

Enormous thanks to my writing group: Luisa Perkins, Sarah M. Eden, and Emily R. King, i.e. the Naked Mole Rats. *Carpe Martis!*

This book wouldn't be what it is without the amazing eye for story, character, and detail that belong to my critique partner extraordinaire, Julie Coulter Bellon. I consider it a compliment that the waitresses at our go-to restaurant kept debating whether we were sisters.

Early readers of the manuscript include Robison Wells, Luisa Perkins, Raneé Clark, Diane Freestone, Michael Gordon, and Krista Lynne Jensen. Your feedback was priceless.

Later versions of the manuscript were read and improved with the help of Luisa Perkins, Julie Coulter Bellon, Mel Henderson, and Samantha Prinster.

Thanks also goes to Eva Hesanto, who, when she heard I was writing a book about the Winter War, sent me a huge care package from Finland filled with research gold.

I'm grateful for the excitement and insight that my agent, Heather Karpas, had for this project and the way her guidance directed it. The first phone call we had, when I knew she got what I was trying to do with the story, will forever be a highlight of my life.

My parents, Melvin and Anne-Maj Luthy, read an early draft and gave me feedback, but their influence on this book goes far beyond that. Dad gave me a love of the Finnish language and culture. Mom gave me her Finnish genes and a healthy dose of Finnish sisu!

My sweet family has endured years of their mom telling stories about the Winter War to anyone who will listen, and the kids only sometimes roll their eyes. Love you all!

CHAPTER ONE

December 5, 1939—Helsinki, Finland

Sini's kitchen had seen more activity that afternoon than in the last three years. She had good reason for spending so much time there on her day off: in about an hour, Marko's train would arrive, and thirty minutes past that, he'd climb the steps to his apartment above hers.

That meant she had just enough time to add the final touches to dinner—a spread of cheeses with rye bread and crackers followed by four courses and an expensive bottle of red wine. For the main dish, she'd bought a delicate white fish caught that morning and sold by an older fisherman from the back of his boat in the harbor.

For any other guest, Sini would probably have settled for a simpler dessert—perhaps slices of vanilla ice cream topped with a dollop of jam. Something so simple wouldn't do tonight, on Marko's return from military training, especially knowing that he had only a few days before shipping off to war against the Soviets. After tonight, months might pass before they met again.

She'd missed their evenings together. Marko was her dearest friend and the closest thing she had to family. She treasured their friendship. And yet. She'd long waited for more.

One day, she thought, adding water to a pot of new potatoes. *He'll open his eyes.*

Men didn't grow close to women they found entirely unattractive. Logic said that a relationship would naturally progress, that eventually he'd develop deeper feelings for a woman he spent so much time with, right?

Unless he's . . .

No. Sini was quite sure that wasn't a problem. For one thing, Marko often talked of attractive women, and one in particular—a girl from his school days he still imagined "what if" about. Poor man.

Sini put the pot on the stove and turned it on, then checked the fish in the oven to be sure it hadn't dried out. That woman Marko still talked about, Leila, never had eyes for him. Worse, she'd married his best friend, Jaakob.

Sini closed the oven with unnecessary force. Marko deserved someone who genuinely loved him, someone who recognized his talents and intelligence in addition to his good looks. Someone like her. Tonight she'd open his eyes.

Then, after the war . . .

She bit her lip in anticipation and checked the kitchen clock. Time to get dressed, but first, she had to admire her chocolate cake one more time. She'd made the raspberry filling and ganache icing herself. The gum-paste flowers were purchased, but otherwise the cake was her creation.

She pulled on the refrigerator handle, and the door swung open. Her gaze fell not onto the smooth perfection of homemade ganache, but onto a crushed disaster. A bottle of milk had fallen over, right onto her creation. The dented surface looked little better than asphalt.

Sini held back tears. Crying over a cake would be silly, but the perfect night wouldn't happen without the perfect dessert. Not even the wine would make up for the lack. Fate held this evening in its hands—this was the night she'd bare her soul, say she loved him. She had to do everything in her power to make the night a perfect one.

She slammed the refrigerator shut and paced the kitchen—four steps one direction, four steps back—and eyed the clock.

If she hurried—if she ran—she might be able to get to the old market square hall in time to buy a new dessert and still freshen up before Marko arrived.

When she'd gone there earlier for cheeses and bread, she'd passed a stall selling the most delicious-looking chocolates and pastries. That shop was her best hope of finding a suitable dessert at the last minute.

Determined, she flicked off the stove so the potatoes wouldn't boil dry, turned the oven off as well, and covered the fish so it wouldn't dry out. Then she hurried to her apartment door, where she shoved her boots on and took her favorite hand-knit shawl from a hook, then wrapped it about her. Making sure her key was in her purse, Sini hurried out and took the building's stairs—much faster than the creaky elevator—and pushed through the outside door. She half ran, half walked to the market hall.

Freezing winter air bit her lungs, but she continued, eyes on the sidewalk, stepping on the spots with the most pea gravel for traction. She maintained a quick rhythm, thinking *Sini and Marko* as she stepped. Every so often, she reversed the order. *Marko and Sini.* That sounded even better.

She reached the hall out of breath. With purpose, she walked to the chocolatier's booth at the back. They'd sold most of their goods for the day, but through the glass, she spied a small yellow cake with piped flowers around the edge. Not quite as special as her original cake, but it would do. She'd spent most of her meager savings on tonight's dinner, and buying another dessert meant she'd be eating lean for at least a week.

Moments later, she carried the cake in a box tied with a string. No running on the return trip; she couldn't risk a fall that would destroy the cake. Despite telling herself not to let her imagination get carried away, Sini pictured Marko feeding her a forkful of cake, then pretending he needed to remove smeared chocolate from her lip as an excuse to kiss her. Her middle swooped with a thrill.

The higher your hopes, the farther they can fall. Warning herself did no good; she'd been telling herself the same thing for years.

With her gaze on the ground, she didn't notice she'd veered off course until she nearly ran into the Havis Amanda statue. She caught her balance and looked up. The fountain had been turned off and drained for the winter, but the statue still looked remarkable. A woman stood in the center, surrounded by a circle of seals that spouted water toward her during the warmer months.

Sini had learned the story behind the statue—something about a mermaid?—but at the moment, all she could think of was the May Day tradition. How new graduates of *lukio*, the secondary school academic track, wore their graduation caps that day. Anyone who had graduated, regardless of age, wore their white caps with black brim, making a virtual sea of white, with some spots of aging yellow-white marking caps belonging to older folk. Tradition ensured that Havis Amanda wore a cap too.

Sini didn't own one. Yes, she'd taken the academic track instead of attending a trade school, as all students did who intended to pursue university studies. For the first two years of *lukio*, she'd performed well despite being shuffled back and forth between two relatives' houses every few months.

A third uncle reluctantly took her in for her final year, and though she did her best to not be a bother to anyone, she didn't succeed. After a couple of months, Uncle Vesa gave her a lecture about how much she'd cost them in food and other resources, how much she owed them for taking her in.

In tears, she fled the apartment and headed to the cemetery. There, behind tall walls muffling the noises of the city, she walked the damp gravel paths that would soon be dusted with snow. She made her way past old plots and lichen-covered statues to the black marker beneath which her parents' ashes lay. Leaning down, she brushed her fingers over their names and dates. Her fingers paused over the dashes, which marked their lives. Everything that had ever happened to her parents between birth and death—childhood friends, school, courtship, marriage—happened in the span of that dash.

Sini's birth. Her first tooth. First steps.

The cemetery had long ago become a place she found solace, an escape from noisy traffic and bustling crowds. Escape from whichever relative's apartment she'd been sent to.

But on that late fall day of her final year of *lukio*, everything felt different. She remembered realizing that she didn't have to do what others demanded anymore. She was eighteen and could live her life as she wished. She needn't feel subservient and immature, like the four-year-old she'd been when her parents died, and she'd ended up at Aunt Ritva's.

There in the cemetery, Sini dropped to her knees and brushed dried autumn leaves from it. She sat back and wondered what her parents would tell her to do. How could she know, when she couldn't remember much about them? Not even what her mother's voice sounded like.

She had to decide for herself. And that was the moment she decided to claim her life as her own. She was sick of wearing clothing passed down from cousins, sleeping in cramped corners of bedrooms she didn't belong in. Tired of others telling her what her future should look like and what she should do.

No more. Uncle Vesa would get mad; the vein in his neck might finally pop. He'd probably go to the liquor store and get smashed.

Sini didn't care. Not about Uncle Vesa. Not about *lukio*. Not about anything.

After that, she stopped turning in schoolwork. Studying for tests became something she did if she had no party to attend, no friends to spend the day with. At the time, freedom and independence had been intoxicating—an emotion she'd thought was happiness.

Now, years later, she recognized that emotion as something closer to rebellion. It was what a prisoner might feel after an escape, tasting freedom for the first time. But that hadn't been happiness. In the end, those choices meant not passing her final exam. Not graduating. As much as she didn't like *lukio*, she still wished she'd passed instead of locking doors to future possibilities.

She never got to wear the white *lukio* graduation cap on May Day. She hadn't gotten a university degree. She hadn't become someone who mattered, like a doctor or a teacher or a scientist. Drunk with making her own decisions, she left permanent scars on a future that had since become her present: a girl who worked at a yarn shop. In a way, she enjoyed helping others find the perfect fibers for projects, but she'd trade her job and everything it represented to go back to that last year of *lukio*. She'd bury her pride and apologize to Uncle Vesa. She'd take her schoolwork seriously and graduate. She'd get a college degree.

In the past that could have been, she'd leave her score-counting, obligated relatives behind. That part of her present wouldn't be changed. But if she could change the rest, she would. Every year on the first of May, she'd proudly don her white cap and join thousands of others doing the same in the city streets. At a glance, everyone would know she'd done something worthwhile.

Maybe that's why Marko sees me as only a chum. Maybe he's attracted only to women who've earned a cap.

The thought had a bitter taste of truth that made her turn away from the statue and head back toward her apartment. Marko had done far more than graduate from *lukio*; he'd graduated from medical school. He'd become a surgeon.

He'd never overtly treated her as inferior. He'd always been considerate. Whether they went to a dance or museum, or even if they played chess in his apartment, he always walked her to her door. She'd once thought such behavior indicated romantic feelings, but after three years, he'd never done more than see her to her door and wave goodnight.

Wave.

Anticipation for the evening drained from her like the last swirl of water circling a drain. Sniffing, she turned her face upward, trying to dry her tears. No clouds. A worried knot formed in her middle. Clear skies often meant Soviet air raids. Clouds obscured the stars from those on the ground, but they also obscured Soviet planes' view of the city.

She hurried on, eager to get home to safety and to see Marko. The heaviness that had dimmed her excitement didn't dissipate. She'd convinced herself that tonight she would win Marko's love, or at least open a door to the possibility. With each step, however, brutal realities contradicted her hopes as if written in the air.

Silly girl, an inner voice chided. *He's never reached for your hand, never given the barest hint of a kiss.* The voice sounded a lot like Aunt Mirva's acerbic tone. Why would a handsome, intelligent doctor want a "plain, stupid girl"?

She gritted her teeth. *Marko returns my hugs.*

But they don't last long, the voice countered. *He's never even pecked your cheek.*

True. She couldn't count the times she'd hugged him, waited for something more, only for Marko to step back, then, with a wave and a smile, say, "Good night."

Each time, she'd quickly slipped into her apartment before he could note any pinkness in her face and ears—color from embarrassment as much as disappointment. He must have noticed at some point, but he'd never given any indication that he knew of her feelings. Either he was too kind to embarrass her further, or he was as oblivious as a block of granite.

I'd take an oblivious block of stone if he'll have me. She shook her head and grunted. *No more thinking like that.* She lifted her chin, put her shoulders back, and lengthened her stride. With one hand, she held the top of her coat closed. The other clutched the strings of the pastry box as she crossed the cobbled street.

Tonight would focus on the future. She'd welcome Marko home. If he was shipping out so soon that they wouldn't see each other again, she'd say goodbye, too, with a long hug. If she was brave enough, she'd peck his cheek. Let him think of it what

7

he may. If nothing else, a kiss on his cheek would mean he couldn't be oblivious anymore.

Then what? What would she do while he was gone? Perhaps help with the war effort. That would impress Marko, surely. When he returned, he'd see her—really see her. She pictured the elderly woman who came into the shop each week, and suddenly Sini knew what she could do.

The woman first came back in October, when the first rumors began to smolder about Stalin's plans to invade. She'd asked Sini for help selecting wool yarn to knit socks for soldiers, a service she'd dedicated herself to in spite of her arthritic hands.

"How do the socks reach the soldiers?" Sini asked as she rang up the purchase. "Do you give them to the Lotta Svärd to distribute?" That made the most sense; the female volunteer corps would know where the needs were greatest and have the ability to get supplies there.

"Oh, but I am a Lotta," the woman said, standing a little taller in spite of her hunched back. "You wouldn't think that of an old woman like me, would you?" She chuckled. "At my age, I'm only in the reserves, of course. During the civil war, though—oh, I was one of the most active women in the nation. Drove an ordnance truck for the Whites." She closed her mouth and nodded, clearly expecting Sini to be impressed.

She was. "You must have some amazing stories."

"Indeed. My hip is acting up, so I'll save them for another day. I'm far too old to do much, but I'll serve my country however I still can." She patted the yarn on the counter for emphasis.

"You are remarkable," Sini said. The woman had bought sock yarn almost weekly since. She must have knitted dozens of socks already.

I should renew my membership, Sini thought.

"Oh, how I hated the uniform." The woman's face had scrunched into a maze of wrinkles as she grinned. "So ugly and scratchy. And I missed being able to do pretty things with my hair. A lot of good vanity did me. Look at my hair now." She laughed, gesturing toward the smooth, tidy bun that fit the Lotta dress code.

Sini had laughed along, distinctly remembering her own thick, gray Lotta uniform, with matching wool skirt and blouse. No jewelry except for the official brooch—at least that wasn't ugly—and a simple watch. A plain wedding band was tolerated for married women.

If Sini renewed her membership, she could serve by knitting socks for soldiers too. She could do it during lulls at the yarn shop and avoid the uniform and dress code except for official meetings.

She'd joined the Lotta Svärd back in her *lukio* days, though getting the needed recommendations had been a hassle. Enough female classmates had become Lottas that she'd felt obligated to sign up. Of course, at the time, war hadn't been hovering in their peripheral vision. She hadn't expected to serve during a war, and neither did any of her classmates. Membership simply looked like an admirable thing for a young woman to have.

As she reached for the door of her building, she noticed a flyer taped to the glass. The paper was curled from moisture and cold, so it had to have been there for at least a few days, but she'd never noticed the Lotta Svärd logo.

Sini pulled the paper free and carried it inside. She'd never been religious, but the timing of the flyer's appearance felt like an act of God—or of fate, or whatever it was that guided the world.

By the time she reached her floor, she'd made her decision. Tomorrow on the way to work, she'd visit the nearest office and update her membership. Donning the uniform wouldn't be required for that, at least. Vanity was probably the biggest reason she hadn't kept her active status. But in a few days or weeks, with Marko gone, she'd have no one to impress. Going without rouge, lipstick, or earrings wouldn't be a terrible sacrifice anymore.

Finally home, she put the cake on the counter, turned the chap get ready. As she did her hair, she pondered the possibility of being assigned to one of the fronts. That was entirely possible for younger Lottas, so she should be prepared for it.

The building caretaker would need to be informed. She could pay rent in advance for several months, so he'd be more likely to hold her apartment. If he caused a fuss, she'd tell him to take his complaints to the head of the army, Marshal Mannerheim himself.

She smiled at that, then paused, lowering her arms from putting in bobby pins, and looked at her reflection—really looked at it, to see what Marko might see. She had no ugly features, precisely. She had an average face, average hair, average figure. The sum meant that she looked ordinary, plain. She took a determined breath and continued securing the twist.

If I were beautiful, would Marko love me?

Aside from her blond hair and blue eyes, she didn't resemble the mythical Nordic beauty. Her hair could be more accurately described as dingy blonde, and her eyes were blue, but so were most Nordic women's. What could Marko possibly find to admire?

I have a decent figure, she thought as consolation.

Marko cared for her; she knew that. But in the manner a brother cares for a sister. His only sibling had died of polio, leaving Marko an only child. With his mother's recent death, he had no family either. He'd taken on the role of son in regard to his mother's best friend, Sisko, who lived a few blocks away. He checked in on her regularly.

Sini glanced at the wall clock, wondering if Marko had returned yet. He might check on Sisko before coming home, but that didn't usually take long. If she didn't hear his step in the next fifteen minutes, she'd call.

Hair and makeup done to her satisfaction, Sini went to her closet and pulled out her prettiest dress—red with small white polka dots. As she put it on, she wondered whether to mention her plans to serve as a Lotta tonight. Maybe she should write him from her post, saying where and how she'd been assigned to serve.

Tonight, Marko, brilliant man that he was, would finally let Sini fill the hole that the deaths of his parents and brother had created. She would be far more than a sister.

Pearl earrings and a matching necklace finished her look. She stepped to the full-length closet mirror and turned to one side and then the other, hands on her hips. She did have a nice waist. Her hair looked elegant, almost pretty, in spite of the color. And the red lipstick made the best of her plain features. Leaving nothing to chance, she spritzed perfume under her ears.

There. He'd have to really *see* her tonight.

She returned to the kitchen to finish the meal. The potatoes were perfectly soft, so she drained them. She pulled out the fish but kept it covered. She returned to her closet and donned a pair of red heels. Still no sign of Marko. His floor was squeaky, so she always heard him walking about, but maybe she'd been too distracted to notice it. She walked to her telephone, but then stopped.

On impulse, she turned around, deciding to go to his apartment upstairs, heels and all, and invite him over. He had to be expecting dinner and waiting for her call; she'd promised to cook him dinner on his first night back from training. She took her purse from the hook by the door, key inside it, then went out and took the stairs to the next floor.

She knocked; that sounded much warmer and less formal than the buzz from twisting the doorbell. After a minute with no sound from the other side, she knocked again. Another long minute later, she surrendered to turning the key-shaped handle that rang his bell. She could hear the buzz inside, but no one answered. He wasn't home.

He'd stopped at Sisko's, most likely, and she'd needed additional help that Marko was happy to give. He'd need dinner whenever he got back. She opened her purse and removed a pencil stub and notepad, on which she jotted a note. She tried to balance her eagerness to get it written with the desire to keep her writing tidy. She discarded two notes before she felt satisfied that the third sounded neither sad nor desperate.

Marko,

I didn't forget that I promised you dinner on your return. I imagine you're hungry, and after your time at training, you can't have much that's edible at your place. I've got plenty of food for us both. Come as late as you like.

How to sign it. Love? Yours? Sincerely? She closed with her name and a small heart. *Let him interpret that as he will.*

She ripped off the page and slipped it into the mail slot. She didn't want to leave, but she couldn't stand by his door, waiting like a lost puppy, either. He'd return soon, and when he did, she'd be ready.

CHAPTER TWO

After a week of military training, Marko wanted to collapse and sleep for days. With his duffel bag over one shoulder, he left the train station, every muscle complaining. He wasn't lazy or unfit, just unused to such intense exertion. As soon as he got home, he'd take a long, hot shower.

Before that shower, though, he had an errand to do: visit Sisko. She kept the radiator turned low to save money; she'd need wood for the fireplace by now. He'd planned to drop off his duffel at his apartment then take a bundle of wood he'd stacked in a corner before training. But after stepping inside his building, he stared at the flight of stairs. His weary muscles balked at the idea of climbing them. He took the elevator to his floor, leaning against the back wall on the ride up. Despite the hunger and fatigue, he was glad to be back even for a couple of days before deploying to the Tolvajärvi sector.

He'd expected to be assigned somewhere with a lot of casualties. A surgeon like him would probably be sent to work at a hospital. That hadn't exactly narrowed the possibilities; most of the fifteen-hundred-kilometer border with the Soviet Union had seen fighting. The conflicts were focused on rail lines and roads, granted. Trains meant more food, weapons, and men. Roads were more important for the Russians, whose trucks and tanks couldn't traverse the thick Finnish forests.

Marko unlocked his door and went inside. Before the temptation to collapse on his bed could take over, he set the duffel by the door and picked up the wood he'd tied with twine before leaving—two bundles, one in each hand. Without truly taking more than a single step into his apartment, he left again, taking the elevator once more. Stairs would be even worse on his sore legs going down than up. Sisko lived only two blocks away, yet carrying the wood made his body protest, as if it knew how close he'd been to getting that hot shower and long night's sleep.

The elevator in Sisko's building bore an out-of-order sign. He glanced up the stairs, worried. Sisko's bad knees couldn't do stairs. Without an elevator, she'd been confined to her apartment. Hopefully she'd had enough food while he was gone. He didn't relish the idea of climbing five flights with a load in each hand, but there was nothing for it but to get it done. He adjusted his grip on the ropes before taking the first step.

This would be one of his last visits before he shipped out. Sisko had insisted that her neighbors would check on her, but such a fiercely independent woman would probably call for help only if she broke a hip. She'd survive on hardtack and tea for weeks before picking up the telephone and asking for help. As he climbed, he hoped the war would end quickly, with the Red Army kicked out for good.

Stalin had invaded their tiny country, but he didn't realize that Finns had an inborn strength, a quiet but powerful fire of determination burning inside them called *sisu*. And Stalin didn't know Finnish *sisu* meant they'd fight to the bitter end.

If Allied forces sent help, as many had already promised, it wouldn't come to Finns dying *en masse* as they fought for their liberty. Many countries, including the United States, had condemned Stalin's actions, even though the Soviet Union was one of the Allies in the world war. Everyone knew that Stalin's claim of needing Finnish land to defend Leningrad was baseless, that he wanted to take over another country, as he'd already taken Estonia, Lithuania, and Latvia.

The Finns just had to hold on until outside help arrived. When it did, the conflict would be over. Life would return to normal, including his regular visits to Sisko.

He reached her apartment, set down the wood, and rolled both wrists to work out the kinks. He reached for the switch on the bell when Timo, a resident in Sisko's building whom Marko had gotten to know here and there, trotted down a flight and paused mid-step, one hand on the wood rail.

Timo nodded at Sisko's door. "Why do you visit her? I'd understand if she were fam—"

Marko cut him off with a quick shake of his head. "I keep my promises." He turned back to Sisko's door, wishing Timo would leave. No point in explaining to him that if Marko didn't come, his mother's memory would haunt him until he got out of bed and trudged here through the snow anyway.

"It's nice of you," Timo said with a patronizing tone. "But your mother didn't mean for you to practically live here."

"Of course not." Marko nodded toward Sisko's door. "I must do what I can for her before I report."

Timo had to understand that much. If Timo hadn't been called up yet, he would be. They'd never been friends, but Marko sincerely hoped they'd meet again someday. That would mean they'd both survived.

"You won't be gone long," Timo said.

"I hope not." Marko was less sure on that point, but he was a realist.

The Finnish army had fewer men total—counting reserves—than the number of Russians who'd crossed the border on the first day of the invasion last week. Marshal Mannerheim needed as many men as he could get. The reserves were on notice, young and old. Marko tried not to think about how minuscule their army was compared to the Red Army. Somehow, Finland *had* to survive with its freedom intact. If it fell before help arrived, they'd suffer under the same oppression every other country Stalin had invaded ended up with.

"Got my orders," Timo said. Every conversation returned to the war. It consumed every mind for every minute of every waking hour, for everyone.

"Where are you going?" Marko asked.

"The Mannerheim Line." Timo's eyes flashed with excitement and pride. "They say it's the most dangerous because that's where Stalin's trying to break through to capture Helsinki, and the forest isn't thick there. Hope I get a hot spot."

The Mannerheim Line stretched north to south for about a hundred thirty kilometers, blocking the stretch of land between the Baltic Sea on the south and the massive Lake Ladoga on the north. The span of land was called the Karelian Isthmus, and that's where the army had to hold, even without tanks or much ammunition.

If the Russians broke through there, they'd first capture Viipuri, one of Finland's largest cities. From there, it would be an easy march to the capital—and Finnish defeat. If the Russians reached Helsinki, the war would be over. The nation would fall.

Trying to break through there made sense for the Russians. They didn't have to deal with the thick forests, swamps, and shrubbery that marked most of the border north of Lake Ladoga. Instead, the Karelian Isthmus was made of hard soil, wide spaces, and good roads. Several tanks and trucks could roll abreast with no resistance but Finnish infantry. In other words, the most important area to defend was the hardest to hold.

"The Mannerheim Line. Wow," Marko said.

What else could he say? *Good luck! Hope you don't die!*

Timo's eyes were bright with excitement. "I've heard we're mowing down Reds. It's brutal and bloody. Can't wait to kill some Russkies." He pantomimed raising a rifle, aiming, and firing, even making a noise like an explosion. Marko hoped his face didn't show disgust.

"Know where you're headed?" Timo asked.

"Tolvajärvi."

That sector covered most of the central part of the country, and it probably didn't sound as exciting and glory-filled as the Mannerheim Line. That didn't mean it wasn't important strategically.

The isthmus wasn't the only way to reach the capital; Russians could also get there by marching up and around Lake Ladoga. North of the lake, there *was* no Mannerheim Line.

Holding the Russians back around Tolvajärvi could be devastating even if the Russians didn't reach Helsinki, as many transportation hubs were located there. If the Russians destroyed those hubs, they'd essentially have cut the country in half, utterly crippling it.

The Tolvajärvi area also had harsher conditions than the Line, with heavy snows capable of burying a man, and forests so thick that only skiers could get through.

"Too bad you won't see any *real* action," Timo said with a headshake. He picked off several imaginary Russkies with his imaginary rifle. "From the Line, we'll send them running home with their tails between their legs." He laughed, slapped Marko's shoulder, and took the stairs downward two at a time.

Marko leaned over the rail and watched Timo winding down the stairway, getting smaller and smaller. The outside door opened, then shut with a clang that reverberated against the plaster walls all the way to the top floor.

"Good luck," Marko said under his breath.

Would Timo kill a lot of Russkies? Marko had been trained to use a rifle, but hoped he wouldn't be issued one. Due to a severe shortage of weapons and ammunition, not all men got rifles, even on the front lines.

The best shooters were those who'd grown up hunting deer and moose, which meant those who *hadn't* grown up in big cities. They'd be used as snipers.

His week at training had been Marko's first experience with a rifle—he grew up in a metropolitan area—and he figured he'd be given the job of helping soldiers, not shooting them. His worries were less about the weapon shortage and more about the shortage of medical supplies. He shook off the melancholy that Timo had left behind him, then rang Sisko's bell.

As the door opened, he raised his arms in anticipation of an embrace. "Sisko."

Her lined face lit up. "Marko. You're back!"

"For now," he said, hugging her gently; with every visit, she felt frailer. "I leave in a couple of days."

"Yet you still came to see me," she patted his cheek. "I couldn't be luckier if I'd had a son of my own." She peered at the floor beside him, looking for whatever he'd brought. He always had something to help make her life more comfortable. When she spotted the wood, she smiled. "You are such a good boy. Come in, come in! Let's get a nice fire going."

He gripped the ropes again, hefted the stacks, and stepped across the threshold. The familiar smell of the apartment welcomed him—coffee, cooked fish, and something else, perhaps age. He'd missed this place. When his mother was alive, he'd visited Sisko with her. As long as he could remember, Sisko had had a list of small repairs or errands needing to be done. He and his mother used to do them, and now they were his job. As she grew frailer, Marko took care of more and more.

"I haven't baked today," Sisko said, her slippers shuffling ahead of him on the smooth wood floor. "So I don't have treats for you."

"I don't have any for you either," Marko said, slipping off his boots by the door. "Hopefully the wood will keep you a bit warmer for a while. Looks like we'll have an awfully cold winter. I'll pay the building caretaker so you can turn the heat up while I'm gone." He crossed the room with the bundles, untied the ropes, then dumped the wood into the bin.

"Who are you?" a young voice asked behind him.

He turned around to see a little boy looking at him with curiosity. Marko was no good at estimating ages, but the child seemed too young to have started school. Who was he?

Marko's gaze moved to the other side of the apartment, where a woman sat at the small kitchen table. His breath—and possibly his heart—stopped for a moment.

Leila. For a second, he thought he was seeing things, but no, there she was, sitting in Sisko's apartment, with a mug in one hand.

"H-hello," he stammered. His mind had gone completely blank.

Sisko interjected. "Leila and Taneli visited me last week, but you were away then. What luck that they came back."

18

Marko managed to acknowledge her words with a nod, but he couldn't find his voice. Of course Sisko would assume that he'd be thrilled to see his old friend. For years, Marko had avoided running into Leila at Sisko's by conveniently having conflicts that kept him away whenever Leila visited her aunt.

For years, he'd tried to move beyond his feelings for Leila, worked on thinking of her with something other than passion. He'd never had managed to, not even after Jaakob's passing.

No matter how hard he tried, Leila appeared in his thoughts—and sometimes in his dreams. Every woman paled in comparison to her. At times, he believed that he still thought of her only because for the last few years, he'd lived where the three of them grew up together—Marko, Jaakob, and Leila. Every day, he walked past places with memories of the past. So when Leila crept into his thoughts—more often than he'd admit to anyone—he never pictured her as she'd looked at Jaakob's funeral two years ago. On that day, she looked thirty years older—pale and frail in a dreary black dress.

If that memory surfaced, he took a broom to it, sweeping it away and replacing it instead with the image of a laughing, smiling Leila. Even though that often meant remembering her being in love with his best friend.

When the newlyweds moved several hours east to Viipuri, Marko let the friendship drift away. That worked until they asked him to be their son's godfather. He'd agreed, of course, and attended the baby's baptism. But after that, losing touch had been simple, if not easy. When it came to Leila, nothing had ever been easy for him, though he prided himself in hiding his feelings. Jaakob died without ever suspecting.

Seeing her now rekindled every emotion he'd ever had for her, including ones he'd naively thought were starved to death.

"Goodness, Marko, is that you?" Leila said, breaking him out of his thoughts.

Had he been standing still, staring at her like some crazy person? If so, she didn't seem to care. She crossed to him, flashing the smile that still haunted him, so like the one she gave him in the fourth grade after his family moved to Helsinki from

Turku. She was his only memory of his first day at the new school.

"It's *so* good to see you," she said and hugged him.

"You too," Marko managed, holding her for a moment before reluctantly releasing her.

Leila turned to the boy. "Taneli," she said, putting an arm around his shoulders and urging him forward, "Meet my friend. This is Marko Linna. I've known him for a long time—since before you were born."

"That's a long time," Taneli said with a sober nod. The baby Marko had seen baptized in a Lutheran church could now walk and talk. The little boy seemed like a physical representation of the years that had passed.

"That's a very long time," Leila agreed, her voice mirroring her son's, but her eyes danced.

Those eyes. He'd long wished they'd looked at him the way they'd looked at Jaakob.

"Your daddy and I were friends with Marko when we were children, but a little older than you are now. Say hello."

The blue-eyed boy waved a chubby hand. "Hi." He looked like a miniature of Jaakob with Leila's nose. He should have known who Taneli was on sight.

Lowering to one knee to be on the boy's level, Marko reached out, and the two shook hands as if they were both adults. "A pleasure to meet you, Taneli."

The boy shyly pulled his hand back then buried his face in his mother's dress.

"He's wonderful," Marko said, straightening. He hoped he sounded casual and friendly even as his pulse betrayed him, beating faster and faster.

Leila stepped forward and wrapped her arms around his neck again. "It's so good to see a friendly face."

He couldn't help but hold her in return, breathing in her scent—a faint perfume he'd smelled nowhere else. Not floral and not strong. A feminine, layered scent that was all Leila. He hoped the thickness of his coat kept her from feeling his pounding heartbeat.

"I've missed you." she said, pulling away.

Were the powers of the universe giving him a final gift before he left for the war? Or was this fate's way of mocking him one last time, giving him a cosmic kick in the shins?

"I've missed you too," he said. Absolute truth, even if he meant it differently.

He probably should have kept Leila's address instead of throwing it away, but he'd thought it better to cut off contact altogether. Standing here now, her scent hanging about him like an ethereal cloud of happiness, he second-guessed that decision. At the very least, he should have asked Sisko for it.

On one hand, staying away might have been the right thing to do at the time. But Jaakob was gone now. Had been for years. Thinking about Leila that way wouldn't be wrong anymore. She'd had plenty of time to mourn. No one would fault a widow for finding another companion years later.

He'd kill me if I tried to take his wife, Marko thought. *Even from the grave.*

Leila took his hand and led him to the table. "We have so much to catch up on." She sat in the chair she'd occupied before, and he took the one opposite, which she gestured to. She wrapped her hands around a mug. Chamomile tea, if he guessed correctly. That's what Sisko always had on hand.

"Tea?" Sisko asked from the stove, as if she'd read his mind. She came up behind him with a kettle of hot water.

"Yes, thank you," he said.

"Chamomile?"

"That would be wonderful."

As Sisko put chamomile leaves into an infuser and set it into his cup, Taneli climbed onto a chair and scribbled on a piece of newsprint with a crayon. Leila watched with maternal pride while Marko watched the two of them and tried to recover from the shock of the reunion.

"So you came to visit Sisko today?" he asked.

"Yesterday," Leila said. "Or rather, we came *back* yesterday." She took a sip and lowered the mug, then added a spoonful of honey and stirred it before going on. "We visited

21

for a few days and left for home yesterday." She appeared lost in thought, staring at her yellowish tea.

Sisko had been puttering about the kitchen but turned around and looked at the two of them, saying nothing. When the silence stretched on, Marko looked from one woman to the other. Sisko gave Leila a sympathetic nudge with her elbow. "Go ahead," she said with a tender tone. "Tell him."

Unease built in his chest. "Tell me what?" he asked, worry building in his chest.

Leila licked her lips and stirred her tea some more. "Nothing happened on the leg from Helsinki to Lahti."

"But from Lahti to Viipuri?" he asked.

Her lips pressed into a line.

Marko pressed. "What happened on the second leg?"

She kept stirring her tea, though the honey was surely long-since dissolved. "Our train was . . . bombed." Even with the pause in the middle, her words came out simple and matter of fact.

"Your—it—*what?*" Marko reached around the table and looked her over, searching for injury.

"We're fine," Leila said, glancing at Taneli, clearly unwilling to upset him. He kept drawing—a Christmas tree—apparently oblivious to the conversation. "It shook us more than anything. Our car didn't get hit, but when the train crashed, we were all bumped about a bit. A lot of passengers ran out and took cover in the forest. After that, it's a bit of a blur of explosions. Flames. Screams."

Anger roared through Marko. He pushed off the table and paced the kitchen's rag rug. "That's a *civilian* line. The Russians know that."

Leila nodded grimly, her lips once more pressed together tightly.

"Stalin's targeting civilians?" Marko pushed his fingers through his hair and paced some more. "He's a monster." The idea of Leila and Taneli on the train, of how close they'd come to dying. He returned to the table but couldn't sit. "That's why you came back."

Leila nodded. She looked a little tired, come to think of it. "We hid in the trees until the bombers flew away. I don't know what happened to everyone else, but a small group from our car found a road and walked until we found help. A farmer gave us a ride in his truck to the edge of the city. Taneli and I took a bus from there."

Marko wanted to take Leila into his arms and hold her jealously, like a precious treasure, one that had almost been stolen from him. But he couldn't do that no matter how much he wanted to. He sank into his chair. "I can't believe the Russians would do something so awful."

If they deliberately attacked civilians, including women and children, what other evil tactics would they use? What chance did a small army made of decent men have against an immoral, massive force? Marko forced himself to sip some tea. Hopefully Sisko was right about chamomile's calming effect.

"So you're back from training?" Leila said, changing the subject.

"Yep. I ship out in a couple of days to Tolvajärvi. I'll probably serve at a field hospital." He still clung to that idea of not actually fighting. Assigning a surgeon to a hospital was logical.

Yet he also knew the numbers: Their army was outnumbered five to one. The ratio of Russian versus Finnish artillery, tanks, and mortars was even worse. The Russians had hundreds of tanks. Finland had fewer tanks than Marko had fingers. Chances were good that he might need to fight at some point.

Leila set her mug down, her eyes shining with unshed tears. She rested her hand on his. "I'm so glad we got to see each other one last time." Her words made something in his heart twist.

Marko turned his hand palm up and wrapped his fingers around hers. "But it's not the last time. We'll see each other again when this is over."

Leila nodded briefly and squeezed his hand. "God willing."

"God willing," he echoed, wishing he believed there was one.

CHAPTER THREE

Leila's aunt Sisko heated leftover salmon soup for Marko while she put Taneli to bed in the guest room. By the time she returned, he was finishing a bowl of strawberry kiisseli.

Leila sat beside him. "Lucky you. She made that from berries she froze last summer, knowing how much you love her recipe."

"Every drop is appreciated." Marko scooped the last of the cold berry soup.

"I'll clean up," Aunt Sisko said, taking his dishes. You two go in the other room to chat; I'm sure you have plenty to talk about. The kettle has more hot water if you want tea."

Leila poured herself some hot water, added new leaves to the infuser, and put it into the cup. She motioned toward the front room, headed that way, and Marko followed. She had things she wanted to talk about with Marko—*needed* to talk about—but not in front of her aunt. They sat on the old purple couch with crocheted antimacassars on the armrests.

"I'm glad you weren't hurt yesterday," Marko said, as if reading her mind.

"Me, too."

He'd broached the very subject she needed to tell someone about but didn't know how to begin. She curled both hands around her mug of tea. The heat warmed them as she remembered walking from the bombed train, through the frigid woods, in knee-deep snow. How the cold went bone deep.

"I feel guilty," she finally said.

"Why?" Marko asked.

She shrugged. "Before we left, Sisko begged me to send Taneli to Sweden. I stood there on the train platform, watching another mother say goodbye to her children, and I couldn't bear to do the same."

"Aren't the evacuated children already coming back?"

"Some are." She nodded, staring into her cup. "I told Sisko there was no point in sending him if he'd simply be sent back. Besides, being taken away would be traumatic for him. He's so young."

"I would have agreed." Marko rested a hand on her arm. His touch felt warm, and the weight reminded her of Jaakob. She'd never feel his touch again.

"What if our car had been hit? My son could have died because I was too selfish to send him to safety."

"Leila, no one would have thought the Reds would target civilians."

Flashes of the bombing went through Leila's mind, one after another—jolts as the train slowed and then screeched to a halt. Being thrown to the floor, clutching Taneli to protect him. Booms of explosions. Heat. Cries of fear and pain.

Knowing as she ran for the forest that behind her, wounded people were burning and dying. But she'd kept running, Taneli clutched in her arms. She hid behind a boulder and tried to be strong for him.

That entire night, and now that entire day, she'd fought her emotions—first for Taneli's sake, and later for Aunt Sisko's. But with Marko, she couldn't maintain the façade—didn't need to. Fear, worry, and sadness pressed against her chest; she clamped her lips together in her usual way of trying to compose herself.

"The truth is . . ." Tears burned behind her eyes. She swallowed. "I didn't send him, and he could have died. Instead of protecting him, I was selfish."

"You are the most *selfless*—"

"No, Marko, I'm not," Leila said, cutting him off. "I couldn't bear to be alone after losing Jaakob. With my training,

I should have been able to save my own husband, and when he died . . . I can't bear the thought of losing my son, too."

"You're a nurse, not a miracle worker," Marko said softly. He brushed some hair from her shoulder. "No one could have saved Jaakob."

Tears finally escaped down her cheeks. "That's what I tell myself, but my heart won't believe it." She swiped at her tears, annoyed at them. "Keeping Taneli with me almost killed him. And that time, it *would* have been my fault."

Her shoulders started shaking, and Marko pulled her into his arms. She rested her head against his chest as her emotions tumbled out. She wept for Jaakob. For her sweet little Taneli. For how he might have died. How, if he had, she'd have blamed herself for the rest of her life.

After some time, Marko stroked her hair and whispered, "Tell me more about how you got back."

Sweet Marko, trying to help her feel better by talking about what *had* happened instead of what *could* have. She lifted her head, noting the wet spot she'd made on his shirt, and wiped her face. He seemed reluctant to let her go.

"Many people with us were very kind." The memory made her smile a little. "One man—Matti—offered to carry Taneli on his back because the snow was so deep. Before long, Taneli insisted that he was too tired to hold on. So Matti asked if Taneli knew the old myths—"

"He's your son," Marko interjected. "Of course you've told him the old stories."

"You're right." Leila chuckled. "So Matti said, 'Pretend you're Ilmarinen plowing the field of vipers. I bet you're as strong as he was.' It worked, of course." She chuckled a little at the memory. Actually chuckled. She was feeling better already. "Boys always have to prove how strong they are."

Marko smiled. "You'd be surprised at how far we men go to impress women we love."

She looked toward the guest bedroom and hugged herself. "I don't know how I'd survive without him. But—" Blinking only released more tears.

26

"But?" Marko prompted. He brushed away another strand of hair that had escaped her bun.

"Sisko's right. I must send him away until after the war. He's just so young. He won't understand. I'd be ripping my soul in half, trying to live with half a heart. I can't do it, but somehow, I must." She pushed her fingers through her hair and closed her eyes. "I'm not making sense."

"You make a lot of sense." With a thumb, he wiped some of her tears.

Somehow, telling Marko about the crash felt right, and talking about what had happened gave the events less power over her, so she went on.

"There was a young couple," Leila said. "She was pregnant, but none of us realized she was in labor until we reached the farmhouse."

Marko tilted his head, the medical aspect no doubt piquing his interest. "What happened?"

"Fortunately, we got to ride in the back of the farmer's truck, but it was a long way, and she progressed quickly. I delivered her baby about an hour outside the city."

"Wow." As a doctor, Marko could certainly appreciate the situation: the potential complications, the heightened emotions of the parents, and much more. "How are the mother and baby?"

"Doing well when we parted. It was a girl." Leila's brow furrowed as she remembered the feelings that had come over her as she'd watched the new parents cradle their baby, how their faces had glowed despite the darkness, freezing temperature, and bumpy ride.

Leila had witnessed a sacred moment of family and life and love. "In that moment, I saw our future—I saw what we're fighting for. We must stay free. If Finland falls, we lose everything. I watched that new little family with love and hope and possibility in their eyes. *That* is what this war is about. Family, love, peace, joy. The things that are worth the most." She dabbed at her eyes again. "We can't let Stalin take them from us."

A single tear fell from his eyes as well. Sweet Marko. He always had been a good person. She looked into his face, deeply grateful for the chance to see such a dear friend when she needed it most.

"Thank you," she said, cupping his stubbly cheek with her hand. "For staying late to talk with me. I'm sure you're exhausted."

He lifted a hand to hers, pulled it away, and kissed her palm, gazing into her eyes. After several seconds, he finally said, "Anything for you, Leila."

CHAPTER FOUR

December 6

A door banged shut somewhere in the corridor outside her apartment, waking Sini with a start. She looked around groggily to gain her bearings. She looked down at herself, sitting at the kitchen table, still in her dress and pearls. Judging by the black marks on her forearm, her mascara had smeared horribly. Her neck ached; she stretched it as well as her shoulders.

A pot sat on the stove, and a dish of fish beside it. She blinked to clear her vision. Right. She'd made dinner for Marko's homecoming. Sometime after nine, she'd eaten alone, but she'd left the stove and oven on low for another two hours, thinking that Marko had to be home soon. He'd see her note and come down. If nothing else, he'd be hungry.

But he didn't. At some point, she'd turned the stove and oven off. The food had completely dried out. She'd held out hope for a telephone call or a quick chat at the door with an apology. She'd read a magazine to pass the time.

She remembered quickly flipping the cover of two soldiers marching in full gear. Images of war wouldn't help her forget why the night mattered, how she might have missed her opportunity to see Marko again.

The inside of the magazine wasn't much better; almost every page had something about the war. She found other images from around the world and tried to distract herself with them—the Eiffel Tower receiving a new coat of paint, Gandhi, a rock outcropping along a shore somewhere, comic strips, a crossword puzzle.

The paper and ink still seemed steeped in war. Her hand had stilled at a photograph of government leaders at the Viipuri train station. The caption said that it had been taken on their third trip to Moscow for negotiations with Stalin. Back when people believed the madman could be reasoned with.

Other pages had references to the war but were less overt, like the short piece about Jean Sibelius' patriotic hymn, *Finlandia*. But even the full-page advertisement for books, which featured some sixty covers in rows, had the cheerful suggestion, "Give Books to Your Soldier Boys!"

The magazine had been too depressing to keep reading. She'd blown her nose several times. Checked her face in the bathroom to see whether her tears would be detectable. She'd still been thinking in terms of *when* rather than *if* he came.

The reminder of the previous night made her stomach sour. Her hand went to her head, which pounded like a locomotive slamming into her skull. Had she drunk a lot of wine and forgotten about it?

She leaned forward and rubbed her scalp. Nausea came in waves. From hunger, surely, but mostly because she knew the truth now: she wasn't good enough for Marko. She didn't possess what he wanted in a woman. If she did, then something would have happened between them over the years. A man and a woman couldn't spend so much time together without *some* spark—unless he viewed her as he viewed his male friends, a platonic buddy. A chum who happened to wear skirts.

Sini lifted her face, noticing more dark smudges on her arms. After licking her thumb to see if the odd stains would come off, she realized that some of it was black ink from the magazine.

She was frustrated at herself, at Marko, and at the stupid magazine that couldn't even sell books without bringing up war. She grabbed the magazine, folded it in half, then marched across the kitchen and shoved it inside the trashcan. The resulting sense of satisfaction lasted but a fleeting moment. Her stiff neck and back still complained, and her head felt even worse, likely because she'd stood too quickly.

She opened the cupboard with the aspirin bottle, swallowed a tablet with water, then checked the clock. Eight thirty-three. She glanced out the window—still dark. In another hour or two, the dim winter sun would hover low in the eastern sky then skirt the edge of the horizon until it sank in the west in the afternoon. With her fingers, she tried to comb her hair but realized it was wild and misshapen. She truly was pathetic.

She attempted to think through her morning routine as if she'd woken in bed instead of at the kitchen the table in her best dress, waiting for a man who never came. If she hurried, she could still reach the yarn shop in time to open the doors at ten o'clock. She tamped down the disappointment growing in the pit of her stomach and headed for the bathroom, ignoring the dried fish in the ceramic dish.

He must have a good reason for not coming. The thought appeared as a surprise, unasked for, unwanted.

Stop thinking about him, she ordered herself and shakily made her way down the hall. *It's not as if you won't see him again. Marko won't deploy without saying goodbye.*

She gripped the sides of the bathroom sink and stared at her gaunt face as if she could demand an answer from her reflection, something to explain why she never seemed to attract any men.

Would he leave without a goodbye? A years-long friendship wasn't enough to elicit the slightest bit of romance. He probably didn't think of her as a close friend, either.

The smudges under her eyes said she needed to wash off last night's makeup. Then she'd address the tangle of hair; hopefully it was salvageable without a wash, as she didn't have time for drying and styling. She washed her face, angrily scrubbing her face as if doing so would also scrub away whatever was broken in her.

When she dried her face, it was swollen and tender, but pink—clean. Before dealing with her hair or makeup, she went to change clothes. On the way out of the bathroom, she glanced at the front door and noticed a small white rectangle on the floor—a folded piece of paper that had been slipped through the mail slot. Her hand trembled as she stepped forward, bent down, and picked it up, knowing without looking at it that it had to be from Marko.

Sure enough, it bore his angled script in blue ink. She didn't open the note right away. Would it be sweet and wonderful? Or distant and cool, something she could use to steel her heart against its magnetic influence drawing him to him again?

She took the note to her bed, where she sat, took a deep breath, and flipped it open.

Dearest Sini,

Typical. He had no inkling what *dearest* meant to her.

I visited Sisko tonight. She had two visitors—a dear friend and her child. Do you remember my school chum Jaakob? His widow is Sisko's niece. I hadn't seen her since his funeral years ago. I ended up staying at Sisko's longer than usual.

Of course he did. Sini lowered the note to her lap. This "dear friend" was the love of his life. Did he really not remember how often he spoke of Leila to her? Of course he'd stayed with Leila late into the evening. Sini felt as if a vise in her chest were tightening around her lungs.

I didn't get home until quite late. I'm sure you're asleep. Thank you for thinking of me. Perhaps we'll have a chance to see each other before I report. I have much to do before then, but I would enjoy one last dinner together.

That sounded dreadfully final. Friendly—even polite—but nothing else. Had she been awake when he came home? She wanted to say yes, of course, but the fact that she didn't see the note until this morning said otherwise.

32

I hope my medical training will make a difference to our men. May God keep you safe until we meet again.

Odd phrasing for an atheist. From many of their late-night conversations, she knew that he didn't believe in God, and he knew how she *wanted* to. Would they meet again? If so, under what circumstances? A knot stuck in her throat as she read the last line.

Yours,

Marko

No, he wasn't hers. Not in any way that counted.

She'd never met Marko's dream woman, had never seen a picture of her, and had only his glowing descriptions with which to conjure an image. If he were to be believed, Leila was at least as desirable as the Maid of the North from the *Kalevala*, the national epic. The Maid of the North always had a powerful wizard seeking her hand.

Sini didn't need a graduation cap or university education to figure out that Marko would spend as much time with Leila as he could before he deployed, not with a neighbor from downstairs.

She imagined what it would be like to see Marko off at the train station, if she were given the opportunity. He'd give her a friendly hug, setting off butterflies in her stomach. She'd want to kiss his cheek, but mightn't dare. He'd gaze lovingly—not at Sini, but at Leila, who, in her imagination also stood on the platform. If he had his way, he'd say farewell to *her* with a long, lingering kiss, a torture Sini would have to endure, somehow.

No. It would not—could not—be that way.

Sini crumpled the note and threw it across the floor. Fighting tears, she tilted her head back and looked at the ceiling, refusing to cry over him.

His bedroom was directly above hers. Was he still there, sleeping? Had he gotten up? She didn't hear his typical morning movements, the squeak of floorboards above her closet, the sound of water in the pipes. Maybe he'd already left for the day.

If only she could see into his mind, know his thoughts and feelings. Then she'd know whether he'd written the note out of pity, or whether he really cared about her, even as a friend. Whether he genuinely hoped to see her again. He'd penned awfully nice words, but were they anything beyond nice words? She knew the answer and had through years of denial.

He doesn't care about me even as a friend, not really. I've been a source of free dinners, a partner to pass an otherwise dull evening with. Nothing more.

If she vanished from the earth, would he miss her half as much as she'd missed him during his training? He probably wouldn't notice her absence until he wanted a homecooked meal. He might go a week or more before noticing. The realization hurt—it stabbed—but in an odd way, it was a good pain, as if someone had lanced a boil and released the pressure from a chronic infection.

An apartment door banged somewhere in the building. What if it was Marko coming down right now to say his final goodbye? He couldn't see her like this. She tiptoed to the door and peered through the peephole. The elevator passed her floor, heading down with a plump elderly woman visible through the gaps in the accordion-like gate.

Sini rested her forehead against the door, relieved. But then she scowled at her reaction. Why should she care if Marko saw her like this? Who was he to dictate her emotions?

She swiped her cheeks to remove any trace of tears. Time to stop letting others decide how she felt and what she did. Time to make her own future, not have it chosen for her by someone else.

Her entire life, other people had decided what she did. Her relatives used to decide where she lived, which schools she attended, what she wore. Aunt Ritva had even gotten her the job at the yarn store. The only major life decision Sini had made on her own was slacking off on her secondary studies, and look where that had gotten her.

She pushed off the door, resolution fixed. Pacing her small apartment, she thought through her plans. Saying goodbye in a note would be wise. Not in person.

She'd slip an airy, distant note through Marko's mail slot and say goodbye to him.

Stop, pivot, pace.

In time, she'd reach a point where she wouldn't react to his presence, but that day lay in the future. To maintain control over her life and her heart, she needed distance.

Pivot, pace.

After the note, then what? He might not report for a week or two. She wouldn't be able to avoid him entirely for long, probably only a couple of days. They'd spent enough winters in this building to have developed some Christmas traditions. What if he was still here as the holiday approached? He might assume he was still invited to Christmas Eve dinner.

And I might not be strong enough to say no.

She paused and hugged herself, puzzling out how to maintain distance from Marko. Moving was unrealistic. Finding a new place could take weeks, and by the time she managed to move out, the point would be moot; Marko would already be gone. Depending on what happened during the war, she might not ever see him after that.

What if Marko died? An odd sensation struck in her chest—tragedy at the thought of him dying, but also the tiniest fleck of relief at the idea that she might not see him again. She shook her head, feeling like a horrible person. She didn't want him dead—she didn't want anyone dead. She just didn't want to have to deal with Marko ever again, at least, not until she'd reached the point where he couldn't stir the coals of the very emotions she needed to extinguish.

I don't want to have to see Marko ever again. At least, not until I can move past him.

Her feet resumed their pacing. How to maintain control of her heart when she had no control over when Marko deployed?

The answer showed itself like a spotlight illuminating a hidden but crucial piece of the puzzle. Her steps slowed and then stopped, and a grin spread across her face.

I'll volunteer for active duty. It won't matter when he reports if I already have.

Yes. She'd stop at the Lotta Svärd office on her way to work, renew her membership, and request an assignment. With the decision made, she marched to her closet and flung the door open to get ready for the day.

For now, the idea of completely ridding herself of all feelings for Marko seemed impossible, but she could do everything in her power to try. If she ran into him even that very day, she could behave differently because she was going to serve the country. She would have a duty to focus on, spend her energy on. She wouldn't have time to wallow over a man.

She took off her dress and replaced it with a simple one of navy blue, appropriate for both work and the Lotta Svärd office. She'd stop there on her way to sign up for whatever they needed help with.

With her dress buttoned and smoothed, Sini hurried to the bathroom to finish getting ready. She wanted to leave the building with the upper hand, and if Marko knocked on her door to visit, she didn't want to be inside.

She smoothed her hair into a simple bun and fastened it with hairpins, creating mental lists of items to do. She had enough in savings to pay rent for four months. Active Lottas weren't paid, only given food and lodging wherever they happened to be sent. With four months' rent, she could leave right away, if they had a place for her. She'd tell the store owner, Meiri, to find a replacement.

Sini pictured herself leaving fast, leaving a note for him, and avoiding an awful goodbye. A thrill of anticipation zipped through her at the thought of being the one in control.

Ready at last, she wrote the note quickly so as not to obsess over the words. Her sole object was to make this goodbye quick, breezy, and not sentimental.

Marko,

Thank you for your note. I hope Leila and Sisko are doing well. In case we don't cross paths again, I wish you safety and luck wherever you are sent to serve.

Sini

She looked over her words, rereading them three times before reminding herself to not analyze them. *I don't care how he reacts.*

Thoughts of Marko in romantic terms had become almost a reflex. Breaking that habit might well turn out to be as hard as overcoming cigarettes had been a few years ago. She folded the paper and wrote his name across the top, knowing she'd need continual reminders to stop caring.

A glance at the clock told her that she didn't have time to dawdle if she wanted to stop at the Lotta office on her way to work. She quickly put on her boots, coat, and earmuffs, then slipped her purse over one shoulder and returned to the kitchen for the note. Hanging onto a small thread of courage, Sini headed upstairs on tiptoe to avoid making noise. If she wanted to be the one steering the train of her own life, this needed to be her last contact with Marko until after the war.

At his door, she listened for any sounds to be sure he wouldn't come out suddenly, though she'd heard nothing from his apartment all morning. She opened his mail slot slowly to keep it from squeaking. The note shook as she held it out, and at first she couldn't let go. Temptation reared inside her to knock for a chance to talk to him for a few moments. Maybe hug him. Speak her true feelings.

He loves Leila. The thought returned like a record with a scratch, hopping back to the same spot over and over. *Leila. He loves Leila.*

Her fingers opened, the note slipped through the slot, and Sini hurried down the stairs without a backward glance.

No more pining for a man who didn't care. No more competing with a phantom. No more pity. If she didn't reclaim her life today, she'd lose the nerve. She pushed the building door open, and the freezing morning air hit her hard. Instinctively, she lowered her chin for warmth, only to realize she'd left her scarf behind. She considered going back but quickly discarded the idea. She'd left the note, and now she needed to stay away for the day. If she went back, the temptation to see Marko might win. So she burrowed her chin into her coat collar even further and headed toward the nearest Lotta Svärd office, trying to ignore the nipping wind.

When she reached the office, she paused and wondered if she should have come in her Lotta uniform. Her membership wasn't active, so hopefully regular clothes wouldn't be frowned upon. The fact that she'd let her membership expire might be a bigger issue. Her bun and minimal makeup would serve as testament of her willingness to make the required sacrifices.

She headed inside, where she found a middle-aged woman at a desk in the familiar gray wool skirt and blouse with a white collar. The wool was practical; it was warm and almost never wore out, plus, it hardly wrinkled, so it almost always looked neat. The downside was that any woman wearing it looked shapeless and plain.

"May I help you?" The woman's steely gaze made Sini want to run back outside.

Instead, she swallowed and lifted her chin; this woman would not see Sini Toivola cowed. With feigned confidence, she stepped forward. "I'd like to help with the war effort," she said, trying to sound proper. "I haven't been as active as I should have been in my chapter, but the country needs every willing hand, so I am here to renew my membership and serve."

After her speech, she took a breath so as not to pass out and reminded herself to unlock her knees. Collapsing onto the wooden floor was a real possibility, one that wouldn't exactly provide the kind of first impression she wanted to make of a strong volunteer.

The woman's brows drew together. "You are a Lotta?"

"I am," Sini said, glad she could say so. She took a seat across the desk then dug into her purse for her membership card. To her dismay, her membership had expired not only a few months past, but more than a year ago. She blushed as she handed it over. "I regret letting my membership lapse," she said sheepishly. "But I'm eager to volunteer. My references are still current, and—"

"Yes, yes," the woman said, taking the card and waving her other hand as if active membership didn't matter after all.

Maybe it didn't. Maybe the military was desperate enough that they would take any girl, regardless of previous membership or references. She doubted the last part, especially because the woman seemed to be studying Sini, taking inventory of her character and worthiness.

At last the woman set the card on the desk and slid a notebook in front of her, on which she transcribed Sini's information.

Hoping to correct any bad first impressions—and break the awkward silence—Sini spoke. "I'm a good knitter. Fast, too. I also sew, if that's a needed skill." She clutched her purse on her lap. "Of course, I'm willing to go anywhere and do anything."

The woman glanced up and said, "Hmm," before returning to her notebook.

Sini waited nervously, perched on the edge of the chair, waiting for the woman's verdict. Sini *had* to serve. What other option did she have besides slipping back into the pitiful life she'd vowed to escape?

Volunteering on the front lines, even dodging Soviet bullets, would be easier than trying to stop caring about Marko.

No, she *needed* a change, a big one, so that she'd create a new life where Marko had no part—not even a needle's width of room for him. That meant leaving as soon as possible as a

Lotta Svärd. She'd found a way to do something that mattered where her lack of education had no bearing. The thought brought a small smile to her lips.

The woman set her pen down and clasped her hands. "What other skills do you have?"

Sini thought quickly, unsure what other skills the woman might be looking for. "I'm a hard worker at whatever I set my mind to, and I'm willing to learn."

The woman scowled and held out the membership card, which Sini returned to her purse. Did that mean she wouldn't be able to help? Or was that the woman's natural facial expression?

"Hmm." The woman opened what looked like a long recipe box. Inside were rows of cards that she flipped between. She put on a pair of reading glasses then flipped from one section to another, pausing here and there. At last she shifted her gaze to Sini, looking over her glasses at her. "Do you cook?"

"Yes," she said eagerly. "I've never cooked for large groups, but I can learn. I'm quite good in the kitchen." At least, Marko had said so often. Had he been sincere, or had he complimented her because he enjoyed having dinners he neither had to pay nor cook for?

The woman tapped a section of cards. "We need assistant cooks and general support in a few areas."

"Sounds great," Sini said eagerly, then, "What does 'general support' mean, exactly?" Did it mean guard duty? She'd heard rumors that some Lottas were armed at guard towers that spotted incoming bombers. Would she be driving ordnance shipments? She'd heard of Lottas doing all of those things and more. She quietly hoped she'd go to a factory like the one she'd read about in Tampere, where Lottas sewed white camouflage suits for soldiers to wear while navigating snowy forests on skis.

The woman removed a section of cards and set them on the desk. She took off her glasses, placed them beside the cards, and clasped her hands again. "In addition to your primary assignment in the kitchens, the camp staff would rely on you for any other duties they require as needs arise. You could do any number of things—clean latrines, gather wood, shovel snow between tents, help with the wounded, mend uniforms, clean weapons, and so on." Her hand twirled in the air as if that explained the whole of it.

"I can do all of that," Sini said with an enthusiastic nod. She had no fear of hard work; she'd spent many summers as a child working on Uncle Heikki's farm. They hadn't been happy summers, but they'd taught her that she could do hard things, like milking cows after being kicked by them. She'd gotten a couple of dinner-plate-sized bruises from that.

"Good." The woman replaced her glasses and picked up the cards, tapping the bottom of them against the desk so they settled into a tidy stack. "We've received requests from a few areas. Let's see . . . Suomussalmi, Kollaa . . ." She raised her gaze over her glasses again. "That's a terribly dangerous place right now. Where else? Oh, yes, Tolvajärvi . . ." The woman pressed her lips together in consideration. "It's difficult to know where and how the war will shift, and therefore where the greatest needs will be. One area needing much support today may not need it in a few weeks, and vice versa."

Again the woman tilted her head back and studied Sini, who felt as if her soul were being weighed and measured. She sat taller, with her shoulders back, like a soldier. "The Tolvajärvi sector. Yes, that's right." The woman scratched Sini's name into a column. "A field hospital in that area needs support. I'll make the arrangements. That is, assuming you're available. How soon can you get your affairs in order?" She picked up the black receiver of the telephone on her desk but didn't dial, waiting for a response.

This was all going too smoothly; Sini hardly dared hope that she'd continue to be so lucky. "I can leave tomorrow."

"Perfect." The woman made an additional notation then began dialing a number. "Report at the train station at eight o'clock tomorrow morning. Your ticket and further instructions will be waiting for you."

Knees jittery with relief and excitement, Sini stood. "Yes, ma'am."

"Be sure to wear your uniform," the woman said sternly, now waiting for someone to answer her call.

"Of course." No matter how ugly she looked in it, Sini would gladly don her uniform.

"And *no* makeup."

"Yes, ma'am. I'll abide by every rule."

"You may go."

"Thank you," Sini said before leaving. "Truly."

She headed for the door in a haze of disbelief. What exactly had she just done? Was she sure that serving in the war was what she wanted? She'd never been impulsive—with the exception of her last year of *lukio*, and that hadn't ended well. Her second impulsive act of her life was even bigger. She'd signed on to work in a war zone. Had she gone mad?

Sini rode the tram to the yarn shop with the shocked haze still hanging about her. But when she took a break for lunch, she felt better. When she told her boss, Meiri, about her need to take a leave of absence, and Meiri supported her entirely, Sini felt even better. For the moment, she didn't fear what lay ahead of her. Her actions that morning were a victory.

During lulls in business, she tried to knit, but nervous anticipation about reporting soon meant that she couldn't hold her needles steady, and she kept dropping stitches. By early afternoon, Meiri suggested she go home early to prepare for her departure. She gave Sini a big hug, as if they might not meet again.

Perhaps we won't, Sini realized as she headed for the door.

Sini must have left the yarn shop a thousand times, but this was different; she didn't know if she'd ever return.

After boarding the tram, Sini looked out the back window as the yarn shop disappeared around a corner. She sighed and sat against her seat, feeling as if the shop itself were a friend she'd said goodbye to. Sini leaned her forehead against the chilly glass of the tram window and closed her eyes.

For better or worse, from this moment forward, her life would be drastically different.

CHAPTER FIVE

December 7

Marko walked along as part of a long snake of two dozen men newly arrived in the southern part of long, multi-fingered Tolvajärvi Lake. He was assigned to the 2nd Battalion, 16th Infantry Regiment. The arrivals had a good distance to walk to reach camp.

I'm part of an infantry regiment. Marko had to keep reminding himself of that because his mind refused to believe that he wouldn't be working in a hospital.

Lugging his duffel through ankle-deep snow, he focused on the winding white path of road ahead instead of what he might be facing soon. Today had been a rest day for the battalion. Tomorrow might mean fighting. The thought brought an uneasy sensation crawling up his back. He jerked his shoulder to shake it off. It didn't work.

Their bus had broken down after leaving the rail stop at Ilomantsi. The rest of their gear would be brought along to camp later, but they couldn't sit and wait for repairs. Something about radio communications getting knocked out. No one needed to explain why sitting in a frozen metal box for hours was unwise. Reaching camp meant a hot meal and hotter coffee, then sleeping in a dry tent with a stove. Staying behind meant succumbing to the White Death.

Marko's toe caught a rock, sending him stumbling into the next man. He regained his balance in time to avoid landing in the deeper snow at the side of the road.

"Sorry," he said, taking a step back.

"It's nothing," the other man said, waving it away. He looked back at Marko and slowed until they walked side by side. He nodded at the lightening sky, where the lavender-gray of dawn was gradually replacing the black curtain of night. "At least we can see where we're going now."

"Yeah," Marko agreed. The curving forest road had been little better than a maze for a blind man. "I'm Marko, by the way. Marko Linna."

"Tofferi." When Marko raised one eyebrow at the unusual name, the man explained. "My mother is Irish, so I have an English name."

"Tofferi . . . Christopher?"

He nodded—about the only real gesture they could make as they carried their gear. "Nice to meet you. Wish this all were at a better time of year. Miserable season for war. How do you think Stalin expects either side to find the other when it's dark most of the time? The man's a lunatic."

Marko grunted in agreement. He'd asked that very question during training and had heard an earful about shutting up and getting back to work. The few daylight hours would be the most dangerous. Most Soviet air raids and reconnaissance flights happened then because darkness made many missions dangerous.

He hadn't dared ask his commanders how their own small air force was managing. The Finns didn't have air bases and landing strips located in convenient places. The Soviets, however, had a base in Estonia, a short flight away across the Baltic. Their planes crossed the water, dropped their bombs over Finland, and returned with time left over to relax with a smoke. Meanwhile, the Finns had already been forced to use creativity and their native grit, their *sisu*.

He assumed the air force functioned somehow, but he didn't want to know specifics. So far, every time he'd learned something new about the defensive efforts, the country seemed more doomed than before. The huge number of Russian soldiers and supplies compared to the Finns' was enough to make even a man with *sisu* shake in his boots. The papers said that the Mannerheim Line soldiers had faced hundreds of *tanks*, on foot, without antitank training.

Logic had dictated that Stalin and his unlimited resources would quickly win. He'd promised victory within days. Yet here Marko was, arriving on the front more than a week after the initial invasion, and the fighting was no closer to an end.

"The Russians have been lied to, you know," Tofferi said.

Marko glanced at Tofferi, then returned his attention to the road so he wouldn't slip. "How so?"

"My uncle and his family were evacuated from Sortavala. He sent his wife and two children ahead, but he stayed back to burn the farm."

Marko nodded. The Finns had a history of being invaded by one neighbor or another, and they often burned property so invaders couldn't possess it. Some farms had been burned and rebuilt multiple times over generations.

"The Russians arrived before my uncle left," Tofferi went on. "Said the Reds couldn't believe their eyes."

"They weren't surprised to see the fires, were they?"

"That wasn't the surprise." Tofferi lit a cigarette and blew out a stream of smoke.

Marko wished he had a cigarette for the warmth. "So . . . what *did* surprise them?"

Tofferi took a drag, held it in, then slowly blew out. "They think they're coming to free us from oppression." He grinned at the ridiculous idea.

Trying to make sense of Tofferi's claim, Marko kept walking. Shortly after declaring independence from Russia in 1917, civil war had broken out. Some Finns, who called themselves the Reds, wanted a communist government. Naturally, they were supported by the Soviets. In the end, the other side, the Whites, who wanted a republic, prevailed. In the intervening years, Finland had become a stable, if not rich, country, with an elected government. The people generally had a good standard of living and were happy. Tofferi's words made no sense.

"Free us from what oppression?" Marko asked.

"That's the lie. Russian commanders tell their men that we poor Finns need saving from our own leaders." He punctuated his next statement with the glowing tip of his cigarette. "Oh, and when they march into our cities, they expect a hero's welcome, complete with parades. With *marching bands.*"

Marko laughed with a grunt. "Rather, they'll be met with rifles aimed at them."

"Exactly. My uncle says the Russians stood there, mouths open as his house burned. Said it was a nicer house than anything they'd ever lived in. They're shocked that we already have food, clothing, shelter, fuel—everything they thought they'd come to give us."

"Good," Marko said. "If they know they have nothing to offer, then this will end soon."

"Doubt it." Tofferi took another drag. "Their army won't let word spread. My uncle says some of them have been forced to fight—they've marched to the frontlines with their commanders following behind, rifles at their backs to be sure they fight."

"Hard to believe." Marko wasn't sure which part he referred to. It all seemed crazy.

"With their numbers, they should have broken through by now," Tofferi said.

"But our lines are holding." Which didn't make any sense. Everything Marko learned made the war seem futile, yet they hadn't fallen yet. It seemed like nothing short of a miracle. What other explanation could there be for the Russians' being held off for even a day?

Careful. That sounds religious. Marko might have been baptized as a baby—the only reason he'd been allowed to be Taneli's godfather—and he'd gone to some Christmas and Easter services over the years, mostly with the grade school. That didn't mean he believed any of it.

Marko thought through everything he knew of the war. How Stalin blamed the Finns for the aggression even with clear evidence showing that his forces fired first. The grossly outnumbered Finnish army with their lack of supplies and proper training. Bombings that had already killed innocents, like civilians on Leila's train.

If God existed, he couldn't be benevolent; of that much, Marko was certain. If Finland happened to get God's help, it would be for the sake of a deity's personal entertainment. Watching Stalin rage at what was supposed to be a quick win might make a god chuckle, as if he were amused by a comedy show on the radio.

"Why do you think the Reds haven't won yet?" Marko asked.

"Because they're being forced to fight. They have more men and better weapons, but they aren't fighting for something they believe in." He tapped his chest with his fingers. "We have our homes and families to protect. We stand to lose traditions and history—maybe even our language." He dropped the cigarette stub and crushed it with his boot.

"And our freedom," Marko added, nodding. "You're right. We have a reason to fight." He hoped that putting their all into defense wouldn't mean dragging out inevitable defeat, but he couldn't imagine winning this war, unless the Allies stepped in.

The men walked in silence during the rest of the sunrise— if one could call it that. With the way the sun skimmed the horizon in December, a day was little more than extended dusk. Snow squeaked beneath their boots with each step. Tofferi's words of home and family had turned Marko's thoughts to Leila and her little boy. They deserved to be spared Stalin's tyranny. Young Taneli should grow up free.

A man with a cause dear to his heart had more fuel for courage than anyone fighting on threat of death. If Finland had any chance of holding on until Allied help arrived, *that* was where it lay: in fighting to retain their freedoms.

As they walked in silence, Marko wondered about Tofferi. Was he lost in thoughts of his own loved ones? Did he have a girlfriend or wife back home? Was he a father? What, specifically, was *he* fighting for?

Finally, they reached the camp, such as it was. The road was lined with trucks painted white, and beyond them stood dozens of white tents. Not until he drew closer did he note wisps of smoke curling above them from stoves inside. Everything was white, the perfect camouflage against snow, which made the deep green pines stand out in sharp relief.

Marko couldn't tell how big the camp was; the tents blended in so well that he couldn't guess at the number. Their group was directed to a man wearing a white snowsuit and holding a clipboard. He looked young, with bits of regular civilian clothing showing at the collar and cuffs of his jumpsuit instead of a uniform. His dark knit cap bore an army badge recently sewn on by hand.

When Marko announced his name, the man said, "Fourteen," and nodded to the left. Marko picked up his bag and headed that direction. A movement to his right made him slow his step. A soldier was leading an officer, purportedly to his quarters, but they were headed toward what looked like a mound of earth, branches, and shrubbery. The young soldier in the lead reached out toward the mound—and opened a door.

Only then did Marko realize it was a camouflaged bunker. The officer went in, the door closed, and he went over to peer at the structure—concrete walls covered with branches and snow. If it had fooled him from a few meters away, it had to be invisible from the air. The door opened again. As an officer left, Marko peeked inside. The walls were lined with reindeer fur. He whistled. The room had to be downright toasty.

Tofferi passed and clapped a hand to Marko's shoulder as he went. "Come on. Our tents are this way."

Marko hefted his bag over his shoulder and followed, trudging through the path others had made through knee-high snow. They reached a group of eight-sided tents and noted numbers on the doors. Nine. Ten. At last, fourteen.

Home sweet home, he thought, and stepped inside.

To his surprise, the interior wasn't particularly cold. It wasn't warm, either, but tolerable. He'd be able to sleep without much trouble. A few reindeer pelts hung on the walls as in the bunker. The air felt a bit stuffy, but he didn't mind if it meant warmth instead of arctic freeze. Several cots filled the tent, arranged like spokes on a wheel, with a stove for warmth in the center. Judging by the duffel bags and lockers at the heads of the cots, all were in use but two on the opposite side.

He addressed a young man lying on one of the cots. "I'm new," he told the boy, then gestured toward the empty cots. "Is one of those mine?"

"If you're Linna, yes," the boy said. "The other one is for Eskola."

Marko walked around the stove and set his bag on the floor beside an empty cot, wondering if he could lie down and take a nap. Before he had a chance to sit, the tent flap opened and another soldier entered, identifying himself as Eskola. The boy and Marko both pointed at the last cot. After Eskola had set his bag down, the younger man stood.

"Come with me," he said. "I'm supposed to show you around camp."

A brief tour led Marko to the latrines, office, supply tent, camp headquarters—which was in a bunker like the one he'd seen earlier—and finally, the mess hall.

"Hungry?" the soldier said, looking over at Marko and Eskola as they followed. "With so many shifts, someone always needs to eat."

Inside, Marko got hot pea soup, which, to his delight, had the traditional bits of ham. Hard rye bread and a slice of cheese rounded out the meal.

"When you're done," the soldier told them, "report to tent three for orders."

"Will do," Marko said. Eskola nodded agreement as he chewed bread.

The soldier left them, but even with someone nearby, Marko's sense of being utterly alone remained. A handful of other men ate too, chewing bread, eating soup, all without talking. They looked haggard in body and spirit.

He was seeing the future. Within a couple of weeks, he'd have rings under his eyes, a drooping mouth, slumped shoulders. He'd eat one bite after another not because the food tasted good but because it would keep him alive another day.

He stirred his soup and ate some, trying to forget that he'd been sent to fight men instead of heal them. He wouldn't be sewing wounds; he would be inflicting them. The thought made his food taste like tar.

After he finished, he returned his dishes and tried to find tent three. He got lost twice—the path and trees all looked alike—but eventually he found it.

The camp was still alive with far more activity than it had been when he'd arrived. Before Marko could enter the tent, the flap moved and two men with a commanding presence stepped out. He instinctively saluted and stood at attention. One man bore the markings of a colonel.

Is that Talvela? He was over the entire sector, but Marko hadn't thought he'd ever see the renowned military leader.

The second man, a Lieutenant Colonel, turned to him. "Are you Linna?"

"Yes, sir," he answered, still at attention.

"I was looking for you. Go see the quartermaster for a snowsuit and skis. At twenty-three hundred hours, report to the amphitheater with your supplies."

"Yes, sir." Marko noted more people about, moving with purpose, as if getting ready for something important. "May I ask what the assignment is, sir?" He hoped it wouldn't involve him shooting anyone on his first night.

"Do as you're told. Get your suit and skis. Bring your gun and ammo and report when you're told to."

"Yes, sir. Sorry, sir." He saluted again, starkly aware of how unmilitary-like he'd behaved.

The men walked off without another glance, and Marko's salute slowly dropped. He wanted to call out that he was a prestigious surgeon. He couldn't, of course. He'd been brought to the front as an infantryman. He had to obey orders. That was reality.

He looked around, wondering what the night would hold for his company. With orders to meet an hour before midnight, they were certain to get a nighttime assignment. He'd have a white snowsuit and skis, a rifle and ammunition. He'd be ordered to . . . what?

He found the quartermaster's tent and got his gear. The wood skis felt heavy as he carried them. At his tent, Marko leaned his skis against a nearby tree and went in. He crossed to his cot, sat, and put his head between his hands. Tonight he might have to kill. A pit of nausea burned inside him.

He couldn't stop imagining himself raising a rifle, aiming at a man instead of a target.

Pulling the trigger.

Could he do that?

CHAPTER SIX

December 7

The train ride felt both eternal and too fast for Sini. With every pine zooming past, the physical distance between her and Marko grew. She deliberately detached her heart, picturing the chugging train breaking the connection between her and Marko one kilometer at a time. The pain was cathartic, like peeling a scab and seeing new, pink skin where a deep wound had been.

Deep scabs leave scars, she thought, gazing at the view, a blur of dark trees dusted with snow.

Images of her night waiting for Marko to come kept appearing in her mind; it all seemed pathetic now.

But she'd taken her life and heart back. She'd made the decision to remove herself from Marko and heartbreak—literally.

Did that make her more or less pathetic?

Someone as inexperienced in such matters as she couldn't say, but she felt stronger already. Even if Marko had no idea about any of it.

The day's travels—several train legs and a bus—had stretched into what felt like a week. She closed her eyes, hoping to get some rest. The jolts and bumps would prevent restful sleep, but perhaps she'd doze a little.

Just as she reached the place between wakefulness and dreams, the brakes squealed. Sini sat up and steadied herself on the seat beside her with her hand. The train slowed and jerked her backward, then crawled to a complete stop.

Birches, pines, and spruces stood out as individuals now, each prettier than the last. No sign of a city or factory or a bustling population. The sight reminded her of going to the family cottage during the winter. Uncle Heikki and her father cut a big hole in the ice at the end of the dock. They'd heated their sauna, which was about thirty meters from the lake. Sitting in the wood-paneled room, they let the heat seep into their bones. Then, to cool off, they ran along the short forest path to the dock, where they jumped into the lake through the hole.

Now Sini gathered her suitcase and joined the queue of passengers. She grew antsy, as if leaving the car would mean leaving the ghost of her past behind. When at last she stepped from the train and frosty wind hit her face, she breathed in the arctic air. Her next stop was the hospital camp where she'd cook and clean and do whatever else was needed. She'd do important work. She'd matter.

A man in uniform barked orders. His handlebar mustache twitched with each word. "Come along! Come, come! This way." He held an arm to his left. Nothing but trees was visible from here, but such views could be deceiving; a huge lake, a caravan of army vehicles, or an entire army, could be a two-minute walk away, hidden behind the dense forest.

Growing up, she'd felt safe in the woods, as if the trees and undergrowth were a blanket of protection. Now, she squinted at the forest with suspicion. If it could hide her from bad things when she was a child, it could hide enemies now. She clutched the collar of her coat with one hand and hefted her suitcase with the other. She picked her way across the ice, following the others. They had to be going the right direction; the mustached man stopped yelling instructions and took up the rear.

After a few minutes, Sini had to lower her suitcase and switch hands. They reached a road, a white ribbon winding between trees, snowbanks on either side, and gravel on top to provide traction.

Around the next bend, the bus came into view. A red cross was painted on the side; this was probably an ambulance. The rest of the vehicle was painted white—likely another reason she hadn't spotted the bus earlier. She knew of the thousands of white snowsuits and capes made for the soldiers, but she hadn't considered that white camouflage would extend to other things. It made sense, of course, and it was comforting, too. A Soviet plane flying directly overhead would be unlikely to spot a white bus against a white road. She glanced at the sky and then continued along the road again, a little less anxious than before.

She should have figured out the white camouflage, of course. The Finns had to use every advantage they had. They could navigate forests and hide in them. Finnish children grew up cross-country skiing and snowshoeing. Every child spent much of their lives outside and knew how to read the landscape.

Stalin didn't have the same understanding of the elements. Neither did his commanders, let alone his infantry. Who would have thought that thick forests would be an advantage? The Russians would have to work to learn half of what the Finns knew of the forest simply by being raised in it. Hopefully that advantage would buy them time until the promised foreign aid arrived. In addition to weapons and other supplies many countries had promised men to fight. Little David could use the strength of increased numbers against the Soviet Goliath.

For the first time since hearing about the invasion, Sini breathed easy. The war would be over soon. The moment America, England, and others arrived, Stalin would be sent away with his tail between his legs.

The idling ambulance belched exhaust. They walked to the bus by dimming sunlight. The pretty, if brief, sunset was already fading. Sini enjoyed sunsets, but she'd come to appreciate colorful ones more of late because those were created by clouds. Tonight's display of pink and orange sunset meant plenty of clouds and a night without an air raid.

As they approached the bus, it shuddered and then went silent.

"Hey," the mustached man called. "Get that engine going. We can't afford to have it freeze on us."

The driver got out, wearing a fur hat with flaps hanging from the sides. Without acknowledging the officer, he went to the rear of the bus and opened a door there. He pulled out a wooden crate—a makeshift step stool. Eyelids half shut, he gestured for the Lottas to board.

"Did you hear me?" the officer demanded. He marched over to the driver. "Turn it back on."

The driver looked at the officer, arms folded with annoyance. "The engine's been running for fifteen minutes. It's plenty warm."

"Not for long," the other man spat. "It can freeze solid in minutes, and if that happens, we'll all be stuck out here."

The driver made a show of slowly lighting a cigarette. The officer's face turned a mottled red; he clearly expected others to respect military protocol.

"Look," the driver said after a drag, "don't lecture me. I've seen engines freeze more often than you have. I know my vehicle. I've got a good fuel mix in there that takes longer to freeze. We're running half empty. Do you want to run out of fuel? Great way to ensure we're stranded."

The officer's jaw clenched. "You must—"

"No."

The veins in the officer's neck bulged as the driver continued. "I'm telling you; it'll stay warm enough for a bit. If we haven't left in fifteen minutes—" At the officer's widened eyes, he held up one hand. "Ten. If we haven't left in ten minutes, I'll start it again."

The officer made a show of raising his left wrist, pushing up the cuff of his coat sleeve, and checking his wristwatch. "I'll be counting."

"Fine," the driver said. "Just remember that she's half empty. Someone was supposed to fill her tank before I left camp but didn't. We'll be lucky to make it back as it is." He nodded toward the Lottas. "If the new medics and Lottas get hypothermia and frostbite, I'll let you explain to Major Elomaa back at the camp. He probably won't be thrilled." He flicked ash from his cigarette. "Just a guess."

The mustache checked his watch again. "Eight minutes." As he turned about, he noticed Sini watching the conversation. He narrowed his eyes at her, and she quickly dropped her gaze, adjusting her scarf as if she hadn't been eavesdropping. The line ahead of her moved, and she closed the gap between her and another woman.

When it was her turn, she climbed onto the crate into the bus. She slid her suitcase under an empty bench and sat down. This was less comfortable than a train, but trains weren't painted white. She preferred the bus.

As the bus filled, the close quarters warmed. A woman sat beside Sini but didn't acknowledge her. Instead, she stared forward with a pinched expression. Her skin looked sallow, her eyes weary. She clutched a bag on her lap.

Her bearing said she didn't want to be talked to. Sini understood not wanting to draw others' attention, so she didn't introduce herself. The two of them would likely get to know each other soon enough. The same held true of everyone else aboard the bus. She'd spent the entire day with these women, mostly in silence. Yet they would be sharing their lives and what would no doubt be difficult times.

The driver closed the rear door. A moment later, he climbed into the cab and started the ignition, which leapt to life. The vehicle jerked forward and gained speed, bouncing over the uneven, snowy road.

With the back of her mitten, Sini wiped condensation from the window beside her. All she could see was more snow, ice, and trees. The landscape didn't fly past as it had on the train. Many pines had no branches close to the ground. Someone her height could stand straight beneath the tree, with the lowest branches beginning above her head, the whole tree rising high into the sky. The effect was a white landscape broken by hundreds of brown columns, and above them, impossibly thick greenery.

The twisting road could have been anywhere in Finland; she'd traveled plenty just like this one. But today she noticed its beauty contrasted with the ugliness of why she was driving past the green arms reaching for the sky.

After about an hour, the heater stopped working. The body heat from passengers helped, but eventually Sini's fingers and toes felt like icicles ready to break at the slightest movement.

When they reached camp, it was fully dark. They received tent assignments, then dragged their suitcases and bags to their quarters. Sini couldn't make out much around her beyond general shapes. Several trucks lined the entrance, some running without a driver. After hearing the argument with the officer earlier, she suspected that someone had the job of running engines periodically to keep them from freezing. As she moved into camp, a big shape appeared on her right. A large tent, or maybe several.

In the distance, a thin, scarf-like trail of smoke rose above the trees. The mess hall, perhaps? A door slammed nearby, and someone approached—a man roughly her age. A flashlight lit his way, but at the sight of the new arrivals, he paused.

Sini pointed at the trail of smoke dissolving into the sky. "Is that the kitchen? That's where I report tomorrow."

"Kitchens are over there," he said, pointing to her left. He jerked his thumb toward the smoke. "That's the one piece of heaven we have out here."

Understanding dawned on Sini. "Sauna?"

"One of three." He grinned. "You didn't think we'd fight a war without them, did you?"

"Of course not." How truly heavenly a sauna would feel about now.

"You'll get a turn soon."

"Can't wait," she murmured.

He chuckled in understanding and continued his trek through the darkness.

Standing there in the cold, with moisture seeping into her boots, and likely into her suitcase, Sini yearned to slip into a sauna. Whenever her turn came, she hoped she'd have it to herself for a few minutes, though she'd likely have to share with other women. Even if it was crowded, she'd get to sit on a wooden bench, close her eyes, soak in the heat, and, for a few minutes, escape winter, the war, and the thoughts of Marko that kept popping up like mushrooms after a rainstorm. She'd be able to sit and *be*.

Heaven, indeed.

The noise and jostling around her reminded Sini that she needed to find her tent. She followed the others, and after a few tries, identified the correct tent, which was mostly round, looking almost like a miniature circus tent. Lugging her suitcase behind her, she went inside. The interior was small but warm, with a small stove in the center offering heat. A pipe reached to the center of the roof, ventilating to the outside. A woman sat on a cot near the entrance.

"Won't the enemy see the smoke?" Sini asked. But as soon as she spoke, she knew it was a silly question. Even up close, she hadn't noticed smoke—only a little from the sauna and some from what might be the kitchen.

The woman looked up from writing in a notebook. "It produces heat but very little smoke. I'm Katri."

"I'm Sini."

"A nurse?"

Sini shook her head. "My official assignment is 'general support,' but I believe I'm mostly assigned to the kitchen." She looked around at the cots, wondering which of them was hers. "I thought I'd be assigned to a clothing factory. I didn't expect to come to a field hospital."

"You'll learn to expect the unexpected out here," Katri said, setting her notebook aside and pointing across the way with her pencil. "Those two cots next to each other are empty. And that one, and the one on your right. You're here first, so you can choose."

"Thanks."

This would be her home for the foreseeable future. On one hand, the tent seemed barbaric. Her building at home had a pretty salmon-colored stucco on the outside, and even her apartment had beautiful lines, like the archway between the main room and the kitchen.

Her quarters weren't pretty in any way, but they were serviceable, which, she supposed, was more important. Reindeer pelts lined some walls, to keep in more warmth, she realized. Nothing used to build a camp in the middle of the forest would be by accident.

The tent felt far more comfortable than she'd expected. All bundled in her winter gear, Sini was starting to sweat a little. The air smelled a bit stale, but she'd take that over frigid temperatures.

She walked past the foot of four cots, stopping beside one of the two neighboring empty ones. She took off her coat and laid it on the second one. Each spot had a scratchy wool blanket and a thin pillow. Two other Lottas from the bus came in chatting, and their arrival sent a whoosh of cold air inside that raised goose bumps on Sini's skin.

She and the other new arrivals had barely gotten their suitcases opened when a hurried knock sounded on a tent pole by the opening.

"Come in," Katri called.

The flap opened, and a soldier appeared. His military badge was obviously sewn by hand to his cap. A rifle was slung over his shoulder. "All medical personnel are needed in the surgical tent—now!"

Every other woman got moving—abandoning suitcases, throwing coats back on—and hurried out.

Sini, apparently the only Lotta in this tent who wasn't medical personnel, stood there, alone in what now felt like a very large, very empty, space. Should she stay and unpack? No, the nurses and doctors would need food after a rush of casualties, which was what she assumed had happened. She put her coat back on, abandoning her suitcase as the others had. Though every bone in her body yearned to lie down and sleep, she couldn't give in to the temptation.

She hadn't been given a direct order, but when did a true Lotta need one before doing her duty?

Sini pushed the tent flap open and stepped into the cold, dark night. She'd find the kitchen, where she'd help make food to strengthen the medical personnel so important to the war.

CHAPTER SEVEN

Night of December 7–8

The bustling of other members of the company got Marko moving. Before donning his jumpsuit, he added wool socks, a sweater, and a coat over his thermals. The white suit went on last. He zipped it, then put on his boots, hat, and gloves. With his gear added on top—knit cap, rifle over his shoulder, pack with ammo, binoculars—the white suit didn't seem like much camouflage.

His suit didn't have a hood and cape; those extras went to machine gunners and snipers whose jobs required more time spent in the open. But that didn't stop Marko from wanting a cape so he could blend in more.

As a group, the men gathered their skis and poles. He really looked at his skis for the first time and only then realized they had no foot bindings. Another soldier noticed Marko's confused expression.

"They're made that way so you can stop, hop out, shoot or fight, and hop back on."

"Ah. Thanks." The skis' construction made sense for getting off them in battle, where a split second could be the difference between life and death. But how well would they stay on *while* skiing?

He followed the others to a clearing, where dozens of men already stood in ranks and files. Aside from a few lanterns, the night was pitch dark. Marko looked up; stars gave some light, but not much. Neither did the sliver of moon. Once they left camp, they wouldn't use flashlights or lamps for guidance—those would reveal their presence. But in the darkness, someone could ski off into the wilderness and freeze to death or be killed by Russkies.

Two companies made up the gathering: the 9th Company in addition to the 4th. Marko guessed that combined, they numbered around one hundred fifty or so. A lieutenant colonel—the same man Marko had seen earlier—paced on a raised wooden platform.

As the men settled into position, the commander stopped and looked over the group. Someone else called attention. Marko snapped his heels together, chin up. The commander had an easy, confident bearing, which was oddly comforting.

The newspaper and radio reports had been grim; the Finns weren't doing well by any measure. They'd lost too much ground, and lines were close to breaking in several areas. Worse, they had yet to secure anything remotely resembling a success. Yes, they'd held off the Soviets longer than anyone had expected, but a break somewhere was inevitable.

When? Days? Hours?

Someone whispered that this was Lieutenant Colonel Pajari, who had volunteered for tonight's mission.

More whispers from the men in the back. "I heard that Colonel Talvela wanted to lead, but Pajari said he knew the area better."

"Yep," another replied. "Pajari fought in this area during the civil war. Besides, he's a Jaeger."

A Jaeger. Wow. They were the best of the best, military leaders trained long ago in Germany. Mannerheim was a Jaeger too, as were many of his commanders.

"Tonight we take down a Russian battalion," Pajari called over the men. "Follow orders, stay quiet, and you may be part of our first victory."

To call his words bold would have been an understatement, but he spoke with assurance, as if a win tonight was a foregone conclusion.

"Another commander will be leading a second team that will probably be within earshot. Pay no attention to them. We'll cross the Tolvajärvi Lake then attack the Russian camp stationed on the other side."

Palpable worry zipped through the ranks, but Pajari went on, relaxed in tone. "On the lake, we'll be in the open, but we'll also be able to travel faster. Rest assured, no Soviet aircraft have been spotted in the area, and no one expects us to be there. You'll receive further instructions as needed."

He gazed left, right, and left again, over the men. His voice lowered, but his words still carried. "I cannot overstate the importance of this mission. The Soviet army has had too many victories, while we have suffered loss after loss. This is our chance to raise morale throughout the army—along the entire border, along every front." He punched a fist into the air. Then he inhaled deeply, as if preparing for his final words.

"Tonight, the Russians finally get a taste of who they're dealing with. We have men who have been hunting all their lives. Some of you can drop a moose at a hundred meters and can easily drop Russkies at half that distance. We need your skills."

Pajari touched the inside of a fist to his chest for a moment then scanned the assembled men again, a motley group of ages, professions, and training. Marko did too, looking side to side without visibly moving.

For a flash, he considered requesting a transfer to a medical assignment of some kind. But he knew better than to attempt that before completing his first significant order. If Pajari was right, this raid could help the army in untold ways. What kind of soldier wanted to avoid such action?

They're trying to destroy us. Killing is justified.

A major named Forsman stepped onto the platform. "As we travel, be sure to spread out on your skis; give everyone room to move," he said. "We travel in silence. No talking of any kind. Stay with your company."

His snarling tone sent everyone scrambling. Marko felt like a schoolboy trying to avoid detention. He dropped one ski and then the other onto the snow. In the relatively brief time he'd been a doctor, he'd gotten used to others speaking to him with respect. Having someone else view him as lesser, and demand deference from him, felt jarring. Even as a medical student, he'd garnered more respect than he'd gotten since reporting for duty. In the army, he mattered no more than the youngest, lowliest private.

I have a job to do. And I'll do it.

Shortly before midnight, Marko moved out with the 4th Company, followed by the 9th. They proceeded slowly at first. As soldiers spread out, Marko had more room to move, allowing him to push one pole into the ground and then the other, skiing with long strides.

As they swished through the forest, their ranks blurred and reformed. They wove around trees while navigating thick woods. Marko hadn't skied in years—possibly not since *lukio*—but the technique returned quickly. His arms and legs moved smoothly, gliding him along.

But he quickly grew tired; while he'd stayed active over the years, biking and running on city trails, he was no longer a teenager, and skiing used muscles unused to working this way.

Younger, stronger soldiers breathed easily while he huffed. Marko wished he could check a clock to see how long they'd been skiing; it felt like half an hour, but might have been only ten minutes. The experience had an unreal quality to it, everything from the puffs of breath to the weight of the rifle on his back.

How had the world turned upside down?

Why hadn't the rest of the world stepped in immediately to stop Stalin?

Judging by the whisper of skis around him, the others had found the same rhythm. Those like him, who hadn't skied in ages, had reverted to their experiences as children.

The thick darkness made seeing much impossible. He could barely make out the silhouettes of others' white suits. Only the swishes and heavy breathing confirmed that he wasn't alone. Too bad they didn't have a full moon.

On and on they went. Each time Marko's lungs and body cried to stop, he kept himself moving with thoughts of the tens of thousands of enemy troops who had already invaded their land, and of thousands more ready to follow. The Soviet Union's population was hundreds—thousands?—of times greater; they had unlimited access to weapons, troops, and other supplies.

One moment, he was confident that the Allies would step in against one of their own. They *had* to condemn Stalin's actions and send aid—and do so with more than the weak letter FDR had sent to both countries, basically telling them to be nice. The next moment, he was sure that within days, the Finland he knew would exist no more.

But we won't surrender, even if it means losing our country, our culture, and our language.

Marko gritted his teeth and skied harder, keeping his focus on the skis of the soldier in front of him to be sure he followed the right path. His eyes had somewhat adjusted to the dark; he could more easily tell the difference between skis, snow, and white snowsuits.

They reached the lake and stopped to rest in the cover of the trees. Marko leaned against his poles, breathing hard. The exertion helped him stay warm, but if they sweated too much without getting back to camp soon, damp clothing could freeze them.

Shaking off the possibility of dying out here, he looked over the lake. Visibility was much better across the expanse; dim starlight and the thin moon glinted off crystals on the ice-covered surface. He squinted ahead, trying to guess the size of the lake. He'd seen a map, so he knew it was long and thin, running north to south. They'd be crossing the narrow direction on the southern tip, west to east.

All too soon they were off again, this time under stricter orders to remain silent while in the open. As predicted, no Russian planes flew above them, but enemy snipers or spies could be hiding anywhere. Marko skied again, pushing off the shore onto the crunchy ice. Rock-sized pieces of ice made balancing unsteady, but when he got farther from the shore, the ice smoothed out. Once he nicked another soldier's ski and nearly crashed in a heap but managed to regain his balance.

His arms ached and his lungs burned even worse from cold and exertion. He doubted he could go much longer, but he couldn't let himself think of stopping. Not yet. Not if even older men than he could still ski. Besides, they had to be close.

At long last, those ahead reached the far shore and maneuvered their skis onto land. Pajari gave a hand signal. One of his officers repeated it, and the signal was passed along silently. The group went up a slight hill into more forest. Marko's legs shook beneath him, but being once more in the cover of trees was a welcome relief.

In the distance, a flickering orange light cut through the night. Were his eyes deceiving him? He blinked several times. His fellow soldiers did the same; everyone looked confused. After skiing for so long in darkness, they had to squint against the bright light.

The men stayed at the base of the small hill while Pajari went ahead. Staying low, he crawled to the top a bluff, where he peered over the top. He returned a few minutes later, wearing a wide smile.

"It's a delicious target," he said, then, to his commander, "Spread the men along the bluff, then wait for my mark."

Marko and the others crawled up the hill. They stopped at the ridge of the bluff in a long line. As Pajari had done, he lay face down and slowly lifted his face enough to see the target. Several massive bonfires blazed in full view, made of what looked like whole trees stacked atop one another.

Pajari wasn't kidding when he'd called the Russian camp a "delicious" target. Had someone told Marko that the Russians would do something so foolish, he never would have believed them. But there they were—Russians being ridiculously stupid by announcing their precise location to their enemy.

Around each fire, rings of Russians held their hands to the heat, turned to warm their backsides, and rotated front again.

Thick clouds of smoke billowed skyward. Marko wondered why he hadn't noticed the scent earlier.

The fires were the size of bonfires lit for Midsummer Eve celebrations, the one night of little or no darkness, depending on how close you were to the Arctic Circle. Marko had never seen such enormous fires in the winter. The sight was disconcerting, like finding snow in July. It didn't fit.

Grand fires should be a sign of happy summer times, not a winter of death and carnage.

Tonight, these Russians had marked themselves for death. Their men looked like the rings on a target, with the fire as the bull's eye. By using a foolish method to stay warm, they'd signed their own death warrants.

Marko looked from fire to fire, unable to believe it all, even though he was seeing it himself. An entire battalion stood below them, ready to be wiped out.

The Russians couldn't be so foolish . . . could they? The largest, and supposedly greatest, army in the world had to know how to keep warm without signaling their positions with bonfires. They might as well have radioed their coordinates to Marshal Mannerheim.

What if this is their way of luring us into an ambush?

He looked behind him into the trees, looking for Russian snipers. The two companies had skied right past those trees and across the lake before that, in plain sight. All without a single enemy bullet. If the Russians were planning an ambush, and if they had brains in their heads, they'd be hiding their real force somewhere else, maybe in the forest behind Pajari's men.

Again, though: wouldn't the Russians have attacked if the two Finnish companies had skied right past them?

Maybe they were as foolish as they looked. An entire battalion of Russians would be destroyed, and they wouldn't know until it was too late. Uneasy, he turned his attention back to the bonfires, waiting for orders.

Muffled sounds came from all around; he tried to gain his bearings and shake off the sense of being watched. Soldiers along the bluff readied their weapons, mostly rifles, but a dozen or so automatic weapons, brought on sleds that had been pulled by skiers.

Those with white capes and hoods donned them. Once more, Marko wished he had a cape and hood, but then banished the thought. Anyone with a cape would be expected to pay for it in lives taken.

Marko got his rifle into position. The barrel seemed to tremble, and only then did he realize his hands were shaking. Not only from the cold, either. He slowly loaded the weapon, hoping he wouldn't have to fire it.

Too bad the wizard from the old tales wasn't real, or Väinämöinen himself could return, sing one of his magical charms, and conquer the enemy.

Behind them, Pajari walked along the line, whispering commands, giving praise and encouragement.

How can he be so confident with only 150 men?

Doubts notwithstanding, Pajari's bearing continued to have a calming effect. The lieutenant colonel must have already considered the possibility of Russians lying in wait, so if he was still calm, perhaps the raid would succeed. Maybe the Russians really were as incredibly foolish as they appeared.

Weapon loaded, Marko unsteadily lay against the hill and leveled his sights at one of the bonfires. He swallowed, his mouth dry as ash.

"Prepare to fire, but hold," Pajari said in a hoarse whisper, repeating the phrase every few meters so everyone would hear. "Fire on my command."

Marko waited, staring into one of the fires to avoid looking at the faces of men about to die. He blinked, only to realize he'd blinded himself by staring at the flames. He blinked several more times to rid his vision of spots.

After several minutes, weapon fire erupted in the distance, jumpstarting his heart like an old car jolting to life. Were Russians upon them after all? The others on the bluff looked around and gripped their weapons, waiting for orders, fingers near their triggers. Many turned back to Pajari, ready to flee if given the order.

Marko forced himself to keep facing the bluff, ready to fire, but not because he wanted to shoot. Because he had a feeling that if he saw the spooked faces of the soldiers near him, he'd panic too. So he held his position, stomach heavy, as if he'd swallowed a bucket of granite.

At last, Pajari spoke. "What you hear is a feint attack, a distraction to ensure that this camp doesn't believe they'll be under fire."

He paused and walked a few paces, and Marko listened to the booms and rifle shots in the distance. They were from fellow Finns. Feeling more optimistic, he faced the camp again, but this time studied their faces.

Just as their commanders had hoped, the Russians had grown alert on hearing the sounds of a nearby skirmish—or so they thought. They milled about, but in an anxious way, moving stiffly, every man with a weapon at the ready.

After a few minutes, when no sign of attack came their way, they relaxed. Many lowered their rifles. Most returned to a fire to warm themselves. Murmurs of conversation, along with occasional laughter floated to the two companies on the bluff. The feint attack had done its job; the Russians thought the Finns were fighting elsewhere. If they'd been at all concerned about an attack earlier, they weren't any more. Even the few guards who'd been standing watch pulled back and joined those warming themselves.

The Russians were sitting ducks. Fools.

This really was an ambush on the Russians, not the other way around—or would be, as soon as Pajari gave the signal. The sounds from the feint attack gradually quieted. Still Pajari waited.

Minutes passed; how many, Marko couldn't tell. At least twenty. Muscles in his arms started to cramp, and his knees felt like ice cubes. At last Pajari gave the signal. As one, the men fired, not in a scattered or chaotic way, but taking deliberate shots. Fingers stiff from the cold, Marko gripped his rifle and aimed at a Russian below. Before he could do anything, the man dropped. Marko lifted his head and looked over the bluff.

Below, Red soldiers were falling, one after another. More and more, dropping like birds from the sky, creating red puddles below them. Bile rose in Marko's throat.

He aimed at a man's chest and forced himself to remember his training, to think of the torso in his sights as nothing but a target on the shooting range—a dummy, maybe, wearing a uniform. Anything but a person of flesh and blood—with a life.

His finger squeezed the trigger slowly, evenly. When the bullet finally fired, the recoil slammed into his shoulder. The shot met its mark; the man dropped to his knees. Marko couldn't move as he watched a dark stain spread across the soldier's chest. He drooped forward, catching himself on his arms before even they gave way, and he went limp, face-first to the ground. The snow below him changed colors as a crimson stain spread around the fallen Russian.

Marko stared, motionless, nausea clawing at him over what he'd done.

Below, Russians frantically raced for cover. Many grabbed their weapons and looked about for the enemy. Hadn't they noticed the bright yellows and oranges of muzzle fire above them?

When Pajari called off the attack, Marko felt relief but wondered about the order. Once again, he looked over snowy bluff. Below, the Russians were actively looking for the source of the attack, so Pajari wouldn't give them any more flashes of muzzle fire to betray their location.

Marko's attention returned to the man he'd shot, lying prone in the snow, motionless.

Killed? Oh, God, no.

Russians continued to dart here and there. They grabbed weapons, searched for cover, all in a chaos that made additional clear shots impossible, even if Marko's entire body hadn't started shaking, even if Pajari hadn't ordered them to stop.

The two companies remained silent, watching, transfixed, as Russian muzzle fire flashed below.

"They think they're being attacked from the forest," the man beside Marko whispered.

Sure enough, what soldiers were left below were frantic, looking about, shooting at signs of movement, often shooting blindly into the darkness. If they killed anyone, it was their own men. And all as they attempted to defend themselves against their attackers, but did the Finns' work for them.

Pajari gave another signal, which was passed down the line. The soldiers ducked below the ridge. Marko held his breath, certain that someone would realize what had happened. They'd figure out where the fire had come from, climb the bluff, and take down the companies that were part of the night's raid.

He looked along the line to his right and then to his left, expecting to see someone injured. Everyone seemed fine. Not a single bullet had been shot at the bluff as return fire. Even so, he grew anxious to leave. The longer they waited, the more likely the Russians would wise up and give chase.

Was their mission complete? He doubted it, as they hadn't wiped out the camp. After what felt like an eternity, the commander gave another signal—time to leave. He raised his head and peered over the snowbank, needing to see what they were leaving behind.

Russians littered the ground. Bodies lay strewn among the trees, firelight lighting the faces of the dead that revealed pain, shock, and terror.

Marko stared, half amazed at the power and accuracy of his fellow soldiers. Half horrified at the slaughter. Sick at the realization that not all of the dead were from Finnish bullets. Instead of looking up and seeing their muzzle fire, the Russians had run into the trees, hoping to hide, only to mistake one another as the attackers. Those left appeared to be firing at each other.

All they'd had to do was look up. They would have seen the bluff ablaze. Unbelievably, dozens of Russians still shot back and forth through trees, from behind boulders, at one another.

The skirmish of Russian friendly fire was at once wonderful and horrific. Marko wanted to cry *and* cheer, to mourn the dead *and* celebrate.

Most of all, he needed to vomit.

71

Shots pinged and popped below in a continual barrage. The fires cast eerie shadows; Marko felt as if he could see the dead men's expressions, their mouths forever open with shock, faces twisted in pain. How many were dead? How many were slowly bleeding to death? How many could he save if he could go down to their camp and treat them?

He knew what would happen to those men who were wounded but not yet dead. In this arctic temperature, bleeding would slow. In other situations, that would be cause for hope, but for these men, it only meant bleeding out more slowly. It meant possibly dying of hypothermia before they could bleed out. It meant a longer, slower, more painful death.

His throat felt as if a meatball were stuck in it. He gripped his weapon as if it might somehow save him. His attention unwillingly returned to the one soldier he'd shot. Despite the slaughter below, Marko could easily find him. He was short, with red hair. Right before he collapsed, the bloodstain on his chest had spread.

He came to take our freedom, he reminded himself. *I did my duty.*

Team captains whispered firm orders to get back on their skis. Time to make their escape undetected while the Russians remained distracted. And dying.

They moved slower now that the one-sided battle was over and the adrenaline in their veins was burning away. Marko checked the ridge, searching for any Finnish casualties, still unable to believe that they'd ambushed a Russian camp and gotten away without a single injury. Every Finn was on his feet.

Marko put one boot and then the other into his skis and followed his company out, led by Pajari. Soon they were heading back the way they'd come, through the woods toward the lake. But instead of crossing the lake as before, they turned south to go *below* the lake this time, then curving northward back to camp. A different route, likely to avoid detection, though no one informed the ranks as much.

His skis, combined with those of the soldiers around him, created a soft, humming chorus as they went through the trees. With the mission over, their pace slowed considerably, and

Marko's body protested with fatigue. But as they drew farther and farther from the bluff, the ranks grew louder. While they weren't having conversations, they no longer held back heavy breathing, and at times, they even exchanged a few hushed words.

Ahead, a sharp cry cut through the stillness. Marko knew the sound—pain. Had someone been wounded after all? Did someone escape injury earlier, only to fall and break a leg on the return trip?

Everyone slid to a stop. Did they have a medic with them? He hopped out of his skis, picked them up, and, holding them as well as his poles, he ran toward the cry ahead. With little moonlight, he couldn't see much, but a small lantern suddenly turned on, piercing the velvet night and revealing a cluster of men.

No order came, but something about the silence made Marko move as quickly as he could through the dark, stepping over shrubbery and fallen logs to reach the huddled group where the sound had come from. When he reached them, his instincts were confirmed: someone lay on the ground with labored breathing.

"I'm a doctor," Marko said, purposefully *not* calling himself *Dr. Linna*, because in the army, he was still nobody, and referring to himself with the title of doctor might be taken as a lowly soldier trying to appear more important than he was. "Can I help? Does anyone have first aid supplies?"

The men huddled in a group moved aside, revealing a man on the ground. Someone had draped a coat over him. A soldier had removed his own coat, on this brutal winter night? For whom? The answer came like a blinding muzzle flash. The man had to be a commander. Marko squinted, trying to make out the man's face, but shadows made identifying him by sight impossible.

"I need some light," he said as he knelt. He held out a hand, and someone put a flashlight into it. The light flashed across the uniform and markings, but Marko aimed the beam onto the man's face first.

Pajari.

"What happened?" he demanded of the man across from him. While waiting for an answer, he checked the colonel's pupils with the flashlight. Normal. Pajari blinked on his own and shifted, indicating that he was still conscious. Marko looked him over for signs of trauma—blood or scrapes, limbs bent at odd angles. Bullet holes in his snowsuit. Nothing.

"*What happened?*" he demanded. "Someone tell me. *Now.*" All worry about military protocol and whether he'd offended someone were gone. He had to help this man.

"He just—collapsed," said a man on the left. "Fainted, I think."

Marko touched the lieutenant colonel's forehead—clammy and drenched with sweat. Skiing could account for some of the sweat, but not the clamminess or the obvious pain. Marko reached for the man's hand and pressed two fingers to the wrist. The pulse was racing, though he'd been lying flat for several minutes.

A possible diagnosis came to mind, but he didn't want to commit to it yet, not without ruling out other possibilities. A heart attack in the middle of a snowy wood didn't bode well.

"Did anyone see signs of distress *before* he collapsed?" Marko demanded of those in the circle. "Did he trip? Hit something like a tree? Did he trip a boobytrap?"

"No, nothing," the man said. Several others concurred.

He'd known the answer before asking the question; he just hoped he'd missed something. The Russians had run into plenty of Finnish boobytraps so far, but to his knowledge, they hadn't planted any.

He leaned over Pajari's form. The man's eyes were closed, and he seemed to have lost consciousness. "Sir?" Marko tapped his cheek firmly. "Can you hear me?"

No response. Then Pajari lolled his head to one side and might have bobbed forward. An unconscious movement, or an intentional answer? Marko tried again, gently shaking his shoulder. "Sir?"

Pajari groaned, his face a mask of pain. Marko aimed the flashlight away so the beam wouldn't shine directly into his eyes. "Where do you hurt?"

"My chest . . . Can't . . . breathe . . ."

Marko pressed his ear to Pajari's chest then straightened and mentally went through the signs of myocardial infarction. The lieutenant colonel's symptoms could be explained by the strain of the mission itself, and yet . . . they could also be explained by a heart attack.

One flicker of memory clinched the diagnosis: Pajari had put a fist to his chest before the raid.

"Did he complain of chest pain earlier today?" Marko asked.

"He mentioned indigestion," someone said.

Not indigestion, just the first symptom of what was to come. The fact that he'd lasted through the mission defied logic.

What did Marko think he'd be able to do now? No doctor ever trained for how to do surgery on the snowy forest floor.

"I have . . ." Pajari took a breath. "A bad . . . heart." He closed his eyes, brow furrowed. "It's been . . . bad . . . for some time." Several more breaths. He grasped Marko's arm, locking an intense stare on him. "I *had* to do this mission. No one else could. Had to . . . for Finland . . ."

The two men communicated eye to eye. Everyone else seemed to melt into the darkness, and for that moment, only the two of them existed. Pajari had served in this very area during the civil war. He knew the landscape better than anyone else in the military. Choosing him for this mission made perfect sense. It might not have succeeded with anyone else in command.

Marko now understood the sacrifice Pajari had been willing to make in hopes of keeping his country free. He'd led this specific mission under cloak of darkness, across kilometers of snow, under great pressure and strain, to wipe out an enemy camp.

And he'd done so with the full knowledge that this mission, even if all went perfectly, could kill him.

"We'll get you fixed right up, sir." Marko called orders to those around him, first to a few men, who quickly fashioned a stretcher out of supplies on hand—ski poles, blanket, and rope. For the rest of the trip, he was pulled by two men on skis.

Two officers, though not as familiar with the area as Pajari, had a general idea of how to get back to camp. Marko stayed at the lieutenant colonel's side the whole way, checking him for any signs of his condition worsening.

He had no medical supplies here, so he could do nothing for the commander beyond giving him water and aspirin, which he had in a little metal vial he kept in his pocket in case of a headache. He hoped that would ease the pain, at least.

After some time, with Pajari's labored breathing still filling the night, he reached up from the makeshift stretcher. Marko called a halt to those pulling it. After hopping off his skis, he knelt by the commander, who looked him in the eye.

"What is a doctor doing in a combat unit?"

"I—don't know, sir."

"I'm glad you're here." He took three shallow breaths. "This is probably my last mission—I'll have to retire now. But I'll make sure you get transferred where the military can better use your skills."

Marko wanted to weep with relief. No more shooting. No more killing.

"Thank you, sir."

CHAPTER EIGHT

December 11
Tolvajärvi Sector, Field Hospital

Hours in cold water left Sini's hands chapped and cracked. She set another scrubbed potato aside and stretched her back before taking the next one from the pile, which never seemed to shrink.

Her first days in camp had been busy and hectic. So far, she'd been given only kitchen duty—a job that didn't mean cooking three meals a day but having food available around the clock. No matter which shift someone worked, they could eat.

The most important aspect of the kitchen, according to Raisa, the head cook, was the virtually smokeless stoves that lined one wall of the square, concrete kitchen. She'd explained that the stoves were critical for keeping the camp hidden from Russian aircraft. In contrast, Russian field kitchens were large and smoky, a fact that had already proven helpful in the Finnish effort. Several camps had been bombed after being identified by cooking smoke alone.

Sini had worked mostly on meal preparation—chopping vegetables, stirring deep pots of soup and stew, checking the fuel and flames on the stoves, and washing dishes. She hoped to be given serving duty more often, in the front part of the building, where the job didn't involve cold water. Serving came in waves, so out front, she could even rest sometimes. Only twice had

Raisa given her a serving job, ladling soup made of root vegetables and pieces of sausage into waiting bowls.

Both times, she'd been on edge. She'd watched the mess hall's door, and every time it opened, her heart jumped and her middle lurched. Would Marko enter?

It never was Marko. Of course not.

The fighting spanned hundreds of kilometers. Yes, she was at a field hospital, and he was a doctor, but there were hospitals, including school buildings adapted for the war. Marko was bound to be assigned somewhere like that.

The odds of being at the same camp were ridiculously small, but her mind couldn't convince her nerves of that fact. She'd believed she could run away from thoughts of him, but they'd followed like a relentless dog.

Now the back door opened. Raisa appeared and held it open. Pilvi entered, hefting a bag of flour. She lugged it to a corner storage area, set it down, then sat on it. "Did you hear? Two new doctors arrived."

The scrub brush slipped, nearly taking skin off of Sini's cracked thumb. Stout Raisa shut the door and grunted as she walked past Sini, who looked over at Pilvi on the sack of flour and feigned indifference.

"Oh?"

"Good thing, too," Pilvi said. "The last two days I've had serving shifts, everyone's been talking about how we're losing ground and getting more and more casualties. Something has to change, or else . . ." She widened her eyes to communicate the seriousness of the situation.

Sini hoped that more doctors meant more troops to fight off the Russians. She tossed a potato to the side and grabbed another. Every joint in her fingers ached the way she'd heard old *mummos* complain about arthritis—just holding a potato hurt. She'd never appreciated her comfortable job in the yarn store. In the store, she might have a hand cramp if she'd knitted too long, but she could take a break.

If peeling vegetables wasn't enough, the cracks on her knuckles turned her one escape—knitting socks for the soldiers—into misery. She'd had to set aside a pair of blue socks she'd started until her hands healed a bit; the wool scraped across her chapped skin something terrible.

If one of the new doctors is Marko, and working in the kitchen means I'll see him . . . Well, then she'd happily scrub a thousand more potatoes.

No, she was supposed to leave him behind. In her past. She didn't want him here.

But as she rinsed off the newly scrubbed potato in the tub, she made a promise: after the war, she'd go at least a year before so much as looking at another potato.

Pilvi went about stacking plates to take out front. Sini eyed her, wondering how to learn about the new doctors without revealing how much she cared about the information.

"How . . . old are the new arrivals?"

With a laugh, Pilvi set a few more plates atop the stack and turned to Sini. "Lottas don't fraternize." Her teasing tone prompted a laugh from Sini. Was she so transparent?

"I was just curious." She shrugged. "Forget ages. What are their names? Or is that classified information?"

Pilvi's smile widened. She seemed to enjoy the implication that she was good at getting information. She flirted something fierce, so even with her hair in a tight bun, wearing a shapeless uniform and apron over that, without a bit of makeup, men responded.

So much for not fraternizing.

Only one man here had tried to flirt with her—and he couldn't have been over eighteen. He looked closer to boyhood than manhood.

"They're both from Helsinki," Pilvi said. "Dr. Eskola and the handsome one is . . ."

Sini scrubbed and pretended disinterest. After stacking five more plates, Pilvi remembered. "Ah, yes. Dr. Koski."

A combination of relief and disappointment made Sini's stomach heavy. Good. She didn't need him around to distract her from work anyway. Even so, her nerves bounced around inside her, making them shake. She set the brush and potato aside and clasped her hands to stop it. If anyone asked about the trembling, Sini would say her hands were cold.

Truth, if only part of it.

"Sini," Raisa called from her desk in the other room.

"Yes?" She quickly returned to her work.

Raisa entered the prep area, brushed her forehead with one wrist as if she'd been the one scrubbing potatoes for an hour and was perspiring from the effort. "You're needed in the infirmary."

"I'm—what?"

"We can spare you for a few hours. Kuusinen can take over." Raisa nodded at Pilvi.

"But I haven't been trained—"

"Hurry."

"Yes, ma'am." Sini handed over the scrub brush to Pilvi, who eyed the remaining potatoes with dismay. Sini mouthed *Sorry,* and reached behind her to take off the white—and rather wet—apron.

Raisa grunted in acknowledgment and returned to her desk.

Sini rinsed her hands to get off any potato juice, and winced. Maybe she could ask for lanolin from the medical supplies. She patted her hands dry on a washcloth then put on her coat, hat, and mittens.

Outside, her boots squeaked in the snow with each step. When she reached the infirmary, she braced herself, took a deep breath of icy air, then stepped inside the tent. The smell of disease came over her—infection, plus burned and rotting flesh. She covered her mouth with her coat sleeve and willed her stomach to quiet. She would have preferred a night in the arctic cold to five minutes with such a smell. But the soldiers in rows of cots, many moaning in pain, softened her heart. They were unable to so much as walk outside to get a breath of fresh air.

For my country, she thought. *I have plenty of* sisu. *I can do this.*

While the tent was relatively warm, with several stoves; no one would freeze in here. She saw no doctors, and once more the familiar combination of relief and disappointment flashed through her. A pretty nurse stood at the other end, her blonde hair swept into a classic twist. Sini's hand strayed to her sad knot of a bun. Even in an ugly Lotta uniform, that nurse was easily one of the prettiest women Sini had ever seen.

The woman noticed her, smiled, and held up a finger to indicate she needed a moment. After writing on a patient's chart with a pencil, she came over. "Did the kitchen send you?"

"Yes."

The nurse wore a half smile, which put Sini at ease. Her genuine kindness drained Sini's envy about her looks. "I'm Nurse Kallio. And you are?"

"Sini. Toivola." What was the proper way to introduce yourself here? They were near the same age, though something in the nurse's face indicated a deeper maturity, perhaps life experience, or hidden sadness.

"Glad you're here," Nurse Kallio said. "The others were called into emergency surgery because of a rush of new casualties. Leave your coat and things on the hooks by the entrance and join me over there." She indicated a cot about halfway across the room. Sini quickly took off and hung her winter things before joining her.

"Where are you from, Sini?"

"Helsinki."

"I grew up in Helsinki," the nurse said with another smile. "I've lived in Viipuri ever since I got married, though." She turned to a tray of instruments covered by a white cloth. As she removed the cloth, Sini noted the simple gold band on her left hand. The tray below had silver instruments in a line like shiny soldiers. "They're sterile; don't touch them. Hold the tray near me so I can reach what I need."

As the nurse turned to the patient, Sini studied the tools, with no idea what many were for. *On second thought, I don't want to know.*

Nurse Kallio sat on a chair, scooted toward the patient, and turned to adjust the position of the tray. Sini did her best to hold it just so. The nurse gently removed the dressing on the patient's shoulder wound. The smell in the tent had already bordered on unbearable, but the moment the bandage came off, the stench increased tenfold. Sini looked away and breathed shallowly through her mouth, willing the roiling nausea away.

Nurse Kallio folded the bandage and set it on a separate tray she must have put on the cot earlier. She took a bristled brush and bowl of water from the same tray and gently scrubbed the wound. "Removing any dying flesh is critical," she explained. "That's the only way to prevent gangrene."

She worked with obvious care, yet the soldier grimaced and held back cries of agony, his entire body tense. The pitch of his voice made Sini's knees uneasy, but Nurse Kallio never lost her expression of calm concentration. Sini found another chair near a neighboring cot. She nudged it closer with her toe then lowered herself onto it.

She then opted to distract herself with conversation. "So, um . . ." Shallow breath. She glanced at the gold band on the nurse's finger. "Is your husband serving in the war too?"

The nurse's movements stopped. She closed her eyes briefly then shook her head before resuming her work, lips pressed together.

"I'm sorry; I shouldn't have pried."

"Don't apologize." Nurse Kallio's hand brushed the soldier's arm—not at his wound, but he tensed again anyway. "You're doing well," she soothed. "We're almost done. You're healing nicely. You'll be playing baseball soon enough, just wait and see."

The soldier returned a weak smile. He was obviously trying to breathe evenly and calm himself, but even his toes betrayed his nerves—bent and braced under the blanket. Nurse Kallio took another clean cloth from the tray and soaked it with what looked like isopropyl alcohol from a bottle. When she pressed the cloth into the wound, the man arched his back, fists clenched, his groan deep.

The tray shook; Sini lowered it to her lap so the instruments wouldn't tumble to the floor. How could the nurse work, knowing she was practically torturing the man? Yes, to save his life, but even so. Sini's respect for her rose with every second.

At long last, the hard part was done, leaving the soldier breathing fast and sweating heavily. Sini breathed easier too. Nurse Kallio gently bandaged the wound. Sini helped cut gauze then tried not to look at the wound until she was certain that the fresh bandage covered it.

The soldier opened his eyes. "Could I have some morphine?"

The nurse's hands paused in their work, and for the first time, her expression flickered with something akin to sadness. "Our supplies are very low, but I'll see what I can do."

"Thank you," he said, closing his eyes.

I could never scrub a man's wound like that, even if it meant saving his life, Sini thought.

She stole a glance to her right as she held the loose end of the bandage and Nurse Kallio pinned it in place. Did she ever collapse in tears when no one was looking?

Nurse Kallio returned with aspirin, not morphine. She helped the soldier take the tablet and swallow it with water. She wrote on the chart at the base of his bed, then nodded toward the other tray, the one with the discarded bandage covered with blood and pus.

"That needs to be disposed of. I'll show you where."

The thought of handling something so vile, even for a moment, made Sini shrink. Nurse Kallio picked up the tray of instruments and motioned for Sini to follow. No time to delay or succumb to fear. Sini took the tray with the old bandage, and walked, chin lifted, gaze averted. In an adjoining room, she was instructed to dump the tray's disgusting contents outside in a metal container. She hoped everything in the container would eventually be burned.

Sini obeyed, and when she returned, Nurse Kallio gestured to a spot on a table near a machine, where she'd already placed her tray. "Trays go there. It needs to be sterilized before being used again. You'll want to scrub your hands." The nurse washed hers first, and Sini followed, using lye soap to rid herself of blood and germs. The soap stung, but she scrubbed anyway. After drying off, she waited for her next assignment.

Nurse Kallio had opened a cupboard along one wall, revealing shelves filled with bottles, bandages, gauze, cotton balls, and more. Sini went over, but when the nurse spoke, her words had nothing to do with the cupboard.

"My husband would have served . . . if he hadn't died from pneumonia two years ago." She stared into the cabinet as if seeing the past inside it.

Sini lowered her voice to a reverent whisper. "I'm so sorry."

The nurse sighed. "The worst part of the war is being separated from our son."

"Is he with family?" Sini asked.

She shook her head. "My only family is an elderly aunt. He's in Sweden. My poor, sweet Taneli." She blinked back tears while arranging rows of bottles.

The facts Sini had learned since first walking into the infirmary started snapping together, like pieces of a jigsaw puzzle. A young widow. A young son. A nurse. An aging aunt.

The love of Marko's life had not been sent here, had she?

Nurse Kallio began showing how to catalog and inventory the supplies, but Sini had to be sure. "What was your husband's name?" she asked, interrupting an explanation about how to tell the difference between various bottles of fluid. Sini had to know who this kind, capable—and beautiful—woman really was.

Nurse Kallio lowered her arm from a line of iodine bottles. She took a breath—in, out. "His name was Jaakob."

The room tilted. "Is your first name . . ." Sini licked her dry lips. "Leila?"

A surprised smile changed the nurse's face, and she cocked her head. "How did you know?"

Because for years, I've heard Marko pine for you.

Because I've imagined you a thousand times.

She decided to go with the generic, "A friend of mine is also one of yours. Marko Linna?" She hoped for a denial. Maybe this happened to be a widow with the same common name—as well as the beauty and nursing skills and kindness he yearned for.

Leila's face lit up. "Marko is a dear friend. We've known each other since I wore pigtails. He was Jaakob's best friend. He's a good man."

"He is," Sini managed. She wanted to hate Leila, but Sini couldn't find it inside her. During Sini's school years, she would have admired someone like Leila Kallio. As an adult, she was the kind of woman Sini would want as a friend. She couldn't even be envious of her beauty, not when Leila didn't hold herself like one of those women who strutted about, knowing they were gorgeous. No, Leila had a simple, elegant beauty. Sini had thought that no one could look like anything but a lumpy sack of potatoes in a Lotta uniform, but Leila was proof to the contrary. A rush of swirling snow and two nurses came in from outside.

Leila turned to them. "Back already?"

The nurse nodded. "Many of the wounded were determined to be well enough to handle a train ride, so they were sent elsewhere."

"I guess I'm not needed here anymore," Sini said. Too bad, really. She liked Leila—and she had no desire to return to scrubbing cold potatoes. She looked to Leila to be sure.

The nurse nodded and said, "I can manage. Thank you for your help."

"Of course." Sini gave the nurse a respectful bob from the knee.

She turned to the tent exit, only to remember that her coat and hat were on the other end. Bracing herself, she went back into the recovery area, but the second time wasn't as bad. She put on her winter things, wondering just how many times she'd hope to be near Marko before the war ended. Hundreds already. Hopefully she could squelch the thoughts before the number hit the thousands.

She'd wondered about Leila for years, yet the possibility of being assigned to the same camp had never occurred to her. The one and only Leila, who was genuinely all of the things Marko claimed her to be.

Everything I'm not.

As Sini trudged through the snow toward the kitchen, she couldn't help but compare herself with Leila and come up short in every respect.

When she reached the kitchen and opened the back door, she found Raisa's assistant, Sirpa, walking her way, a small crate of food in hand. She stopped and grinned. "Heard you went to the infirmary tent. Isn't it awful?"

"It is," Sini said simply.

The other Lotta eyed Sini, still in her warm clothing. "Here. You take this meal to Bunker D," she said, pushing the crate into Sini's hands.

"W-why?"

"You're already wearing your winter clothes."

"Sini, go," Raisa called from her office.

Sini didn't have to be told again. Not that she enjoyed being out in the snow, but the longer she stayed away from those potatoes, the better. Sini looked at the crate's contents. "This isn't much. Is only one officer doing the interrogation?"

"It's for the prisoner. He's starving, literally."

"Oh. And Bunker D is . . ."

Sirpa pointed, giving directions, and Sini headed that way. She took a breath of frigid but clean air as her boots tromped rhythmically in the snow. The sun was up, though hanging low as it did all winter, but it was bright enough that they had no need yet of flashlights. Good thing, because she probably couldn't have carried one *and* the crate. Doing so at night would have been asking for a twisted ankle or worse.

Sini's brow furrowed. "Oh." She stared into the box, which held a serving of stew—every meal was hot and had plenty of protein. Heat and protein: whether a person had them or not often meant life or death in these conditions.

Two elements that the Russians' diet reportedly lacked.

As she walked, searching for Bunker D, she wondered at the meal. The officers wanted this prisoner to live? To be comfortable? That didn't sound like war.

The crate Sirpa had prepared had several pieces of rye bread, not hardtack, which lasted almost forever, had little nutritional value, and tasted worse. Each slice of bread had been slathered with butter.

To round out the meal was a glass of *kalja*, a traditional homebrewed beer that had little alcohol. Sirpa must have filled it from a keg perched on the edge of the counter.

When she reached the correct bunker—more of a cabin, built of logs and camouflaged on the top with greenery—she shifted the box to one arm and knocked.

The door opened, revealing three Finnish officers in a semicircle before a young man—the Russian who'd been taken prisoner. The Russian looked older than she'd expected. His face was gaunt, his hair thinning, his back and shoulders hunched.

The officer holding the door open leaned against it, looking oddly relaxed. He blew cigarette smoke toward the doorway, but it hit Sini in the face anyway. She coughed.

"I—have food?" She hadn't intended it to sound like a question, but the tone reflected how she felt. Unsure, scared of the officers and their sidearms. And at the same time, a burning hatred for the middle-aged man in the chair.

"Very good," the officer said, stepping aside. "Come in."

Sini stepped inside. One moment her breaths were white puffs, and the next, her hands were thawing. Fur-lined walls made a stuffy but cozy room. As she passed the officer at the door, she read his nametag: Ahonen.

The semi-circle of officers parted, giving her a clear path to the prisoner—the first enemy she'd seen. One of thousands upon thousands who'd invaded their home and threatened their freedom. Her fingers tightened around the box, the corners digging into her hands. The pain helped her look outwardly composed.

Ahonen gestured toward a desk beside the prisoner. "Put the food over there."

"Yes, sir." She quickly crossed to it and unpacked the box. As she lifted out each item, she concentrated on not trembling. Could the Russian hear her pounding heart? She could certainly feel it thrumming against her ribcage like a frightened hare.

I'm safe, she assured herself. *He can't hurt me. He's disarmed, and these officers will restrain him if he tries anything.*

She withdrew the glass of *kalja* last, setting it on the wood surface with a slight thud. Lifting the empty box, she looked up—inadvertently right at the Russian. He eyed her with a haunting expression that would be forever seared onto her soul. She held the box to her chest and took a step to leave, but another officer raised a hand, stopping her.

"Give him the soup."

Did he expect her to spoon feed the prisoner? He wasn't bound, so that seemed unlikely. Even so, she nodded and returned to the desk. She lifted the bowl. The weight of the prisoner's gaze never left her. She paused a moment before rotating slightly and holding the bowl out to him. She deliberately kept her eyes on the bowl—the cooked carrots and onion and potatoes and parsnip and rutabaga—on the steaming broth and specks of floating pepper. When he didn't move, she inched the dish closer—and looked at him.

He stared at the soup longingly, as if it were a river of gold he would never possess. He then tore his gaze from the food and looked at each officer in turn, as if needing someone to give him permission to eat. Or maybe he worried it had been poisoned.

She almost wished it had. For a fleeting moment, she felt an unwieldy temptation to dump the hot liquid into his lap. Yet the yearning in his gaunt face wouldn't let her. His expression seemed to say that he wouldn't mind dying if it meant he had a full, warm belly.

When Ahonen nodded at him, the prisoner slowly raised his hands to the bowl. His skeletal wrists and fingers had angry dark spots of frostbite. The sight made Sini gasp. Only then did she let herself truly see him. How his uniform hung on his body like a boy trying on his father's clothes. His sunken cheeks. The dark circles under his eyes not from age, but hunger and the elements.

The more she looked at him, the younger he seemed. She tried to imagine him with full cheeks and rested eyes, a full head of hair, and a body that filled out a healthy man's clothing.

He could be as young as twenty-five, she thought in shock, stunned at the realization when she'd assumed he was twice that. A few weeks of war did that?

She reached for the dishcloth and unfolded it, revealing the day-old rye. The Russian swallowed some soup then set the bowl onto his lap. He reached for a slice of bread and devoured the whole of it in a few bites. He couldn't have hardly tasted it as he gulped it down.

Getting captured saved his life.

Yet he fought for Stalin. He was the enemy. If given the chance, he'd kill her and everyone else in the room.

So why did she feel a thread of sympathy and compassion for him? He could have killed hundreds of Finns. He deserved to die.

And yet. Those eyes. Those cheeks. Those fingers.

He's the enemy. Sini tried stoking the fires of hatred in her breast but found only embers that were not so easily provoked.

Confused with the emotions crashing inside her, she held out the glass of *kalja.* He greedily drank the whole thing without stopping. A part of her felt *glad* to have helped give him some relief. And she felt guilty about helping ease a Russian's pain.

Nothing about this war made any sense.

He abandoned the spoon on the desk, lifted the soup to his lips, and drank the rest. With the food gone, he sighed as if he'd already died and entered heaven.

"You are dismissed," one of the officers said to her.

She hurriedly repacked the crate with the dishes and cloth then turned about and looked around the room, from one officer to the next, as if someone could give an explanation that would set everything right that had been knocked askew.

But their attention had returned to the Russian. They all appeared to be in good humor, as if they'd rescued a starving dog. An officer lit a cigarette then handed it to the prisoner. Wasn't that tantamount to giving him a weapon?

Sini's mouth opened slightly in surprise. She managed to gather her wits and ask, "Anything else I can help with, sir?"

"Not now, thank you," the officer in charge said. His nametag read Elomaa. "We'll call if we have further requests."

The prisoner took a long drag then leaned back in the chair. He relaxed and stretched out, looking taller than before. He might as well have been in a bar in Leningrad.

A city she'd hoped would be destroyed. Except now that she'd seen this Russian . . . he wasn't a faceless enemy. He was a man, with emotions like any Finn's. She couldn't reconcile any of it in her head.

Were his parents still living? Did he have a wife waiting for him, hoping he'd return? Children? Siblings?

Eyes burning, Sini bobbed at the knee in deference to the officers. Ahonen opened the door again, and she hurried through. The cold slammed against her like an icy wall, filling her lungs with frigid air, a shock after the warm interrogation room.

When the door closed behind her, she looked back at the wooden bunker and held the box tight to her chest. She hated the man she'd just fed. He represented everything Stalin was trying to strip her nation of—hard-earned freedoms won after a century of Russian oppression.

The man was a filthy, evil Russian.

Then why did she pity him? A single tear escaped one eye and trickled down her cheek. She shook her head adamantly, refusing to let any more fall. She'd keep herself busy, not let herself think about the frontlines. She'd do her duty by accomplishing anything asked of her. She'd focus on the camp and forget that anything outside it existed.

He's in this camp too.

She gripped the box harder and angrily stomped through the snow, back to the kitchen. Inside, she put the box beneath the bread counter then just stood there, staring at the concrete wall and hoping the others in the square room wouldn't bother her.

How could the officers be so kind to a man they could easily justify putting a bullet through? Such thoughts made Sini's head begin to pound.

Sirpa turned to her. "I brought food to a prisoner last week and didn't want to do it again. I'm sorry if it was too hard. I probably should have warned you."

It had been hard, but not in the way Sini had expected. She raised her chin toward Sirpa. "Why are we so good to them?"

She smiled grimly. "After a Russian is captured, he's no longer our enemy, just another poor soul who needs help." She shrugged. "Or so Major Elomaa says. The directive comes from above him."

The concept circled Sini's head like a mosquito that wouldn't go away. She was quite sure that other countries didn't act like this during war. She hadn't been in the bunker long, but from what she'd seen, the prisoner had been as surprised by the meal and cigarette as she had.

"I should have gone, Sini, I'm sorry," Sirpa said. "Next time, if there is one, I'll go." She clenched her jaw as if repressing a wave of anger. "I just can't see a Russian without wanting to spit in his face."

Sini nodded in silence, understanding all too well. "Looks like the potatoes are done. I'll go wipe the tables in the dining area."

She dunked a dishcloth in a tub of warm, soapy water, wrung it out, and escaped the kitchen. Wiping one table after another, she tried to work off the hate, anger, confusion that were moving through her like thick tar, threatening to suffocate her.

Sini worked so feverishly that she finished quickly, so she wiped the tables again—anything to use her nervous energy. She tucked a loose piece of hair behind one ear and noticed Sirpa standing by the door. Sini stopped wiping and stood.

"We're better than the Russians," she said simply. "That's why we're good to them. I still hate them. But I understand why we treat them as we do. We can't lower ourselves to Stalin's level. He is nothing better than an animal. If we act as he does, we'll become monsters, too."

Sini twisted the dishcloth in her hands. "You're right. We *are* better than that." She nodded in the general direction of the bunker. "He probably didn't ask to fight. He may have loved ones at home like so many of our men. But he's here now in a frozen land he wasn't prepared for, and he almost died."

"He's one of the lucky ones," Sirpa said. "He got caught."

Lucky to be a prisoner of war. So strange.

"I suppose we're some of the lucky ones too," Sini said. "To be born here instead of there."

CHAPTER NINE

December 13

Leaving the operating room, Leila untied her cap and mask and tossed them into the laundry bin. She slipped her arms out of the bloodstained surgical gown, and the door opened. A soldier walked in, trailing snow across the floor, which would soon be a soggy mess. But before she could say anything, his quick breaths caught her attention.

"Are you sick?" She walked toward him to feel his forehead.

"I'm fine." He stepped out of her reach. "A nurse is needed on the front, right away. A truck is waiting to take you as far as the road goes. You'll ski the rest of the way."

Leila's tired brain wouldn't think clearly. She almost asked why a nurse, but then guessed why. Her shift in the OR had ended when another nurse relieved her, but plenty of wounded waited for surgery. None of the surgeons could leave right now. "What's happened?"

"It's Dr. Komulainen—he's assigned to one of the first-responder stations. This morning, he went to some injured soldiers on site, but then he was wounded."

This young soldier likely worked at the same first-responder station, where others did their best to stabilize the injured before they were transported to a field hospital by train or ambulance.

"So just one man?" Leila confirmed. He nodded. She thought through the details as best she could "I haven't eaten in hours. I'll need food and water to take with me."

"A Lotta in the kitchen is preparing food for both of you."

"Good. Wait. What do you mean, both of us?"

"She's coming as support." The soldier crossed to a high shelf and pulled down several large backpacks bearing red crosses. "Here. Come with me to the quartermaster. You'll need a snowsuit and skis. You can ski, right?"

"Of course," Leila said, taking the pack.

"While you're there, get a suit and skis for Lotta Toivola."

"I will." She followed the young man outside and into the darkness. "What's her first name?"

"Sini, I think," he tossed over one shoulder.

The girl who'd helped her the other day. It would be good to see a familiar face. They lapsed into silence, largely because Leila's mind spun with possibilities about where she was headed and what she'd need to do.

Would Russians snipers find them while they were out?

No. She could not think such things; they would only distract her from her work. She'd be more likely to make a mistake and put Dr. Komulainen's life at risk.

Stay focused. She could do that for her little boy. *For Taneli.*

Leila tried to empty her mind of the unknown and dangerous possibilities ahead as she followed the boy to the quartermaster. She knew it as they approached; several men stood outside, putting white snowsuits over their coats.

"What do you need?" the quartermaster asked of the soldier.

"Two suits and two sets of skis." He hooked a thumb Leila's direction. "For her and another Lotta."

The man reached for a snowsuit from a stack behind him, shook it out, and held it up to her. "Looks about right." He tossed it at her.

"The other Lotta is about the same size, I think."

The man grabbed a second suit from the same stack and tossed it to the young man. Leila stepped away from the tent and began putting on her suit. She stepped in, one foot after the other, then pulled it upward, slipping her arms into the sleeves before zipping it closed. She swung the medical pack onto her back and adjusted the straps. The young soldier came over and handed her a set of skis.

"Thanks," Leila said, taking them just as Sini Toivola appeared. The Lotta wore a backpack of her own, which Leila assumed contained food and water. She already felt weak and unsteady. Eating something soon would help.

The soldier tossed Sini the other snowsuit. "Here. This is for you."

She caught it. "Where are we going?" she asked, looking at him and then at Leila, who shrugged.

The answer came from one of the men closer to the tent, who'd already suited up. "Kivilä."

A village near the border. Leila's brow furrowed. "Kivilä evacuated weeks ago, and no fighting has been reported there."

Residents of every town near the border had been evacuated within days of the invasion. Many had been burned to the ground by their owners.

"No, no fighting right now," he said. "But you never know. We boobytrap any building still standing. Gives the Russkies a surprise. If they do anything—settle onto some hay to sleep, open a cupboard, even use the outhouse—they trigger explosives." He grinned, teeth shining in the glow of lanterns. "Those who don't get injured get paranoid. Remarkably effective."

"I'm sure." Should Leila be proud or horrified?

What could the tiny nation do but fight in unconventional ways? Any Russian death that didn't cost a Finnish lives—or dozens of them—was to be celebrated, right? The idea of war continued to turn her world upside down.

"We weren't done rigging the traps," Pertti said, putting on a snowsuit of his own. "Another team went out today to finish, but a couple of men set off our own traps. The others are being brought in by skiers on blankets, but one man's still out there, and he can't be safely moved without more support. We need a Red Cross sled at least—and a professional."

"Let's go," an officer named Sinisalo said in a deep voice. "We're wasting time." His skis in hand, he led the way toward a truck waiting for them on the road in the distance.

"Coming," Pertti answered.

Sini had gotten her suit on and replaced her backpack. Carrying their skis, poles, and packs, the women followed, neither saying a word, but staying together. They climbed onto the bed of the truck, and soon it jolted to a start then rumbled down the bumpy, icy road.

"Could I eat something?" Leila asked Sini. "I've been working for hours."

"Of course." Sini removed her pack and unzipped the top. She pulled out a paper bag of jerky, some hardtack, and a canteen. They ate without speaking. The engine was so loud that they would've needed to shout to hold a conversation, but even if it had been quiet, Leila wouldn't have wanted to talk.

Finally the truck shuddered to a stop. Sinisalo stood and motioned for them all to get off. "Move out!"

A minute later, they were stepping into their skis. Sini and Leila glided into the forest, following Sinisalo and a few other men who'd come along. With a faint moon and stars to show the way, they maneuvered around trees and brush. Leila settled behind a soldier who seemed to know his way. Leila relied on his shape to avoid getting lost.

Before long, her lungs and muscles protested every movement, but she kept going; a man's life might depend on her strength. She focused on each movement—pushing with one leg and then the other, the opposite poles digging into snow.

After several minutes, Leila slipped into a rhythm with her movements and her breathing, and her mind drifted to what lay ahead. What kind of boobytraps had injured several men—and one so terribly he couldn't be moved? An explosion, probably. She might have to deal with burns, shrapnel, puncture wounds.

All of the things she didn't see after the train was bombed but could have.

Should have? Perhaps this was fate's way of punishing her for not going back to help the injured. *Don't think. Just ski.*

But crowding out the guilt invited other thoughts she couldn't bear: Taneli's tear-streaked face as the train pulled away, palms flat against the window, taking him to safety—but in his mind, simply taking him away from his mother. She tried desperately to think of something else—or to empty her mind altogether.

At last the forest thinned, and they entered what was left of the town. They went down what had recently been a main street, with businesses flanking both sides. At least half of the buildings were charred, with little standing beyond some blackened timbers to show where they'd once stood. Leila could only guess what they'd been. A single building had a readable sign, blackened by smoke.

The first word was illegible, but the second read *bookstore*. Leila sighed. What literary treasures were forever gone? She hoped the owners had taken some of the books with them, but other necessities—clothing, blankets, food—likely took precedence.

The farther they went, the more burned buildings they passed. In the distance, near the edge of the forest, she made out the remnants of a barn. Were the animals still safe, or had they died in the fire? Before it?

As the group skied close to the other side of the town, they moved into a tighter formation and didn't speak, as if they all knew they were closer to the enemy. Sinisalo lifted his radio, pulled his scarf from his mouth, and spoke quietly.

"We're in Kivilä, on—" He strained to find a street sign and gave up. "What looks like a main street. Church on one corner as you described. Where are you from here?"

Garbled instructions replied. Sinisalo acknowledged receipt and clipped the radio onto his belt. "Left here. We're almost there."

The quiet of the town felt almost loud, filling Leila's mind with the cries from the train passengers. A fist seemed to be clenching her heart. She tightened her grip on the poles and focused on the ground in front of her.

The group stopped suddenly, making Leila trip and Sini fall into the snow.

A soldier standing guard was holding up a hand. "Stop. Say, 'steamroller,'" he ordered Sinisalo.

Sini, back on her feet, brushed off some snow and leaned in to Leila. "What on earth do steamrollers have to do with anything?"

Before Leila could answer, Sinisalo grunted. "You know me, Korhonen."

"Say it. And hurry. They need you."

"Fine. *Höyryjyrä.* Now let us through."

Leila leaned in to Sini and explained. "That's the easiest way to weed out Russians pretending to be Finnish. Only natives can say those vowels correctly."

"Interesting," Sini said with a nod. "*Höyryjyrä* doesn't sound Russian, that much is for sure."

"Yeah," Leila said grimly. "It's been . . . effective." The word made her think of the boobytraps. She'd heard men in the infirmary talking about the code word, and how Russian spies had been shot on the spot after attempting—and failing—to say it right.

Satisfied with Sinisalo's pronunciation, the soldier stepped aside and pointed out the correct house, wooden, and one of the few unburned. The exterior was stained with smoke. Leila guessed it used to be white.

In front of the house, the group hopped off their skis, and the women ran inside. Leila was suddenly grateful to have another woman with her.

They were led through the house to the kitchen in back, where a man lay on the floor. Sini reached the kitchen threshold before Leila. She stood there as if she'd been struck dumb. Leila stepped beside her and peered into the room. Sure enough, even an untrained eye could tell that an explosion had gone off, perhaps when a soldier reached to open a cupboard to set a boobytrap, only to set off a trap already placed there. Whoever had set off the explosion couldn't have been foolish enough to be searching for dishes or food, unless he was Russian. In which case, she wouldn't have been called to help.

Sini sucked in a breath. She stared at something on the floor, eyes wide. Leila looked in the same direction and found the wounded man. His face was an angry red. From burns, no doubt. His cheeks and forehead were scraped—possibly from flying debris, like wood. He didn't appear to have any serious wounds—his chest, abdomen, and legs had no visible bleeding or tears in his uniform. Perhaps this wasn't the soldier she was supposed to help. He didn't look critical.

But the first man, who'd led her the way into the kitchen, beckoned. "Hurry. He's fading."

Leila nodded, squeezed past Sini, and knelt beside the man. She felt for his pulse—weak, but there. "Dr. Komulainen, can you hear me?"

"Yes," he said between his teeth. "I . . . hurt."

"Burns are painful. I'll take care of them as best as I can out here, and we'll get you to the field hospital quickly." She took off her backpack, gesturing Sini to join her.

He should have all of his vitals checked, but without proper equipment, Leila couldn't do much.

She pulled off her thick mittens with her teeth, winced at the biting cold, and pressed her fingers to his carotid artery. She could feel nothing, perhaps because her fingers were half numb. But the man was conscious, clenching his jaw against the pain. He definitely had a pulse, even if she couldn't feel it.

She pulled out a stethoscope from the bag, huffed against the metal end to warm it, then slipped it under his uniform and pressed it to his heart. There it was—not a strong heartbeat, but not as weak as she'd expected. She draped the scope around her neck and tried to think. This was nothing like nursing school or a hospital.

As she searched through the backpack, trying to catalog what supplies she had and what the soldier would need, the man who'd led them into the house cleared his throat. "What do we do with his hand?"

Leila found a bottle of isopropyl alcohol and took it out, glad it didn't freeze easily. "I'll treat his hand too. Is it burned?"

"No," the soldier said. "His hand is . . . over . . . there." His odd tone made Leila look up. "Nurse, what do we do with it?"

She followed where he pointed. A pale lump lay on the rug, bright red and white on one end, fingers on the other. Despite her training, bile rose in Leila's throat. She covered her mouth to not retch. She imagined her strict nursing teachers lecturing about maintaining control. How nursing took grit and brains and a take-charge attitude.

She reined in her shock and turned to her patient. The man's nose was turning white—probably early frostbite.

If he'd had an entire hand blown off, why wasn't there more blood?

"Wrap it in a cloth and pack it back to camp."

The soldier obeyed, wrapping the hand in a cloth and taking it elsewhere—something Leila and Sini both breathed a sigh of relief over.

Leila's training told her that a tourniquet was crucial in times like this to prevent someone from bleeding out. This man was hardly bleeding at all, but she followed her training anyway, searching in the backpack until she found a cord that was surely intended to be used as a tourniquet.

Cord in hand, she turned to Sini, who look perilously close to slipping into shock. "I need your help," she said, and she did, though she hoped that giving Sini a job to do would stave off shock.

"Kneel on the other side of him and hold his arm off the ground so I can tie it off." She purposely didn't refer to his arm as a stump. The Lotta crawled to the other side of the man and gingerly raised his arm off the floor.

She looked at the ceiling. "Sorry. I can't look at it."

"You don't have to," Leila said, slipping the rope into place. "You're doing great."

As a nurse, she didn't have the luxury of looking away. She'd seen a lot of awful things. Being at a first-responder station, Komulainen had surely seen even worse.

They carefully lowered the man's arm to his chest, and then Leila couldn't help but look into his face. If he lived, he'd be sent home. Losing a hand would be hard for anyone, but a one-handed man couldn't be a surgeon.

He may curse me for saving his life.

"Can you hear me?" Leila asked Komulainen, but his face remained twisted in agony.

If he was lucid enough to hear her, he was in too much agony to respond. He needed some kind of pain relief, or the trip back to the camp hospital might kill him. They couldn't wait, either; frostbite could lead to infection, nerve damage, and possible amputation of his arm. Time to get him out of the elements. Maybe into a sauna.

Hoping the backpack had something to ease the pain, Leila rummaged through the supply backpack again. She found three ampules labeled *morphine*, and was suddenly grateful for the man's steady heartbeat. She wouldn't have dared give him the medication if his pulse was weak.

But when she tilted the bottle, her face fell. The medication was frozen. In other circumstances, she'd have held a vial against her underarm to thaw them. She'd heard of medics doing that in the field. But after skiing, she'd perspired enough that removing layers to reach her armpit would put her in danger of hypothermia and frostbite too.

She handed an ampule to Sini. "Put this in your cheek. Don't bite. It needs to melt."

Sini took the small glass container and popped it into her mouth between her cheek and teeth. She grimaced at the cold. Leila braced herself and put one in her own cheek as well.

This man needed to be transported soon, and the journey wouldn't be quick without morphine. As they waited for the vials to thaw, Leila looked him over for other wounds, removed pieces of wood and disinfected the sites, all while puzzling over the situation.

Why hadn't Komulainen bled much?

She looked at the soldier who'd taken away the hand. "How long ago did this happen?"

"Two, three hours ago." He looked paler, likely from wrapping a piece of human flesh and then tying off the stump it used to be attached to. He was lucky the rug wasn't soaked with blood. That would have made the scene much worse.

The answer to the relative lack of blood hit Leila suddenly. Cold temperatures slowed the circulatory system. That had to be why he wasn't bleeding out. Hypothermia and frostbite were very real dangers—they could lead to infection and death—but for now, they'd spared his life. She'd never imagined that winter itself could act as a tourniquet.

She pulled her ampule out of her mouth and tilted it. Only a little liquid. "Is your ampule thawing?"

Sini pulled it out of her mouth and held it out. Again, some liquid, but not enough. Back into their cheeks they went.

Leila returned to removing small pieces of debris. Sini looked increasingly pale. Most people weren't used to seeing things like blood and bone—or human flesh lying under a table.

"You look faint," she told Sini. "Go lean against the cupboard."

Sini nodded and crawled away, then, leaning against some drawers, closed her eyes and breathed deeply.

While they waited for the morphine to thaw, Leila opened the alcohol bottle. She tipped it against a gauze bandage, then dabbed the antiseptic on the areas most likely to get infected, including some minor wounds on his face. Komulainen groaned at each touch, sucking air between his teeth.

This would be easier if he were unconscious. Leila tucked some stray hair behind an ear before returning to work. Nursing wasn't supposed to be practiced in a freezing country house in the middle of nowhere.

She checked her own ampule again and found a little more medication. "Let's give him what we have," she said. "It won't be a full dose, but hopefully it'll be enough to take the edge off."

Sini returned, holding out her vial. It had more liquid than Leila's. She'd have no way of knowing exactly how much she was giving him between the two vials—not much—but it might ease his pain a little.

She loaded a syringe with as much of the medication as she could. Komulainen groaned as the cold fluid went in. A moment later, he relaxed a tiny bit.

"Thank you," he whispered hoarsely.

Leila felt tears prick the corners of her eyes but fought them back. "You're doing great, doctor. Let's get you back to camp."

She pulled a thin, wool blanket from the backpack. "Help me cover him," she told Sini.

The two of them tucked it around him. "All right," Leila said, finding the soldier again. "Get him on the sled. We're heading back."

"You aren't going to remove the bigger splinters?" Sini asked. So she'd noticed the bigger pieces of debris, some as wide as a thumb.

"Only the little ones out here. Anything big needs to come out under controlled conditions."

"And these are far from controlled," Sini added. She didn't look quite so white anymore. This girl had more *sisu* than Leila had given her credit for.

"Exactly."

The soldier watching everything went out and barked orders to get the sled ready and for a few men to come carry Komulainen out to it.

She and Sini followed them, found their skis, and stepped into them as their patient was carried out by two men and carefully laid on the sled.

"I wonder if he has a family," Sini murmured.

Now that the time for being the nurse had passed, Leila's self-control fled. She leaned against the fence and shook. "Oh, God. Did I do enough?"

Sini gently turned Leila to face her. "He'll be fine," she said, pulling her into a hug.

Leila hugged her back with surprising strength, holding tight to Sini's coat. Cheek pressed against the rough wool of Sini's coat, she wept.

CHAPTER TEN

December 18

Due to some transfers both in and out of camp, Sini was reassigned to a new tent with several nurses. After her evening shift, which consisted of more knuckle-bleeding dishwashing and vegetable peeling and chopping, she headed back to her new tent, with a flashlight to show the way. At the entrance, she stomped her boots, then quickly entered, closing the flap tightly before much warm air could escape.

The tent was empty save a woman sleeping in the cot next to Sini's. Moving quietly so as not to wake her, Sini went to the stove and held her hands to it. They quickly warmed, so she removed her scarf and hat. She had her coat half unbuttoned when she stepped toward her cot and, with the narrow beam of her flashlight, recognized the sleeping woman. She'd know that strawberry-blond twist anywhere.

For a brief flash, the old envy fought for space in her chest, but was quickly overshadowed by the fact that Leila had proven herself to be both kind and capable. She'd done nothing to hurt Sini.

She got ready for bed, putting on thermals and a pair of woolen socks she'd knitted, then climbed into her sleeping bag. Once settled, she clicked off her flashlight and lay on her right side, facing Leila in the dark. Without more light, she couldn't make out much beyond a dark shape, but Sini didn't need to see Leila to know she was there.

Thoughts of the past flared again. Sini tried to force the feelings of inferiority from her mind, but exhaustion combined with late hours were cruel; they made her mind go in circles, like knitting a sock, round and round, eternally. She cursed whoever invented two o'clock in the morning. Nothing good ever came of it. Knowing she needed sleep, Sini shifted to her other side, her back to Leila.

Through the quiet, a cry rent the air. Sini bolted upright, only then realizing she must have fallen asleep. She tried to orient herself, make sense of the screaming that had morphed into whimpering. Then sobbing. A woman sounded bereft.

Leila?

Forehead wrinkled with concern, Sini unzipped the sleeping bag and swung her legs over the side of the cot. She reached out toward Leila but stopped before touching her, unsure. Would Leila be embarrassed at being awakened like this? Angry?

The cries softened, but now she whispered, "Taneli, oh, my boy."

Leila's cot creaked, as if she was trying to rock back and forth. She was clearly having a nightmare, and anyone would welcome being woken from that. Sini touched Leila's arm. No response. Sini gently shook Leila's shoulder.

"Nurse Kallio?" No response. She tried again. "Are you all right?" Sini shook her shoulder a bit harder. "Leila," she said louder, "Leila, wake up."

At last Leila jolted awake and sucked in her breath. "What—" She raised her torso, leaning on her elbow, and looked side to side, as if trying to gain her bearings. She smoothed back some hair that had escaped the twist. Sini couldn't make out more than vague shapes, but Leila's movements seemed confused and disoriented. She sat up all the way and rocked back and forth, moaning; she wasn't fully awake.

Sini could sit still no longer. She unzipped Leila's sleeping bag, so she'd have more freedom of movement, then helped

Leila turn so her feet dangled off the cot. She breathed hard, as if she'd been running. Sini sat on Leila's cot beside her and slipped an arm around her shoulders.

"Taneli," Leila moaned. "Oh, my boy. My boy." Leila's quiet sobs gradually increased until they racked her whole body. She shook her head again and again.

Was she awake or still dreaming? Sini couldn't tell.

"Leila?" she whispered. "It's me, Sini. Are you all right?"

The nurse took a sudden breath and lifted her head, looking around. "I—oh." She smoothed her hair back with both hands and looked at Sini. "I'm so sorry. I was dreaming—" Her voice cut off, and she stifled another cry without finishing the sentence.

Sini debated what to do and say. She pulled her arm back. "Do you want to talk about Taneli?"

"How do you know his name?

"You kept saying it, just now."

"Oh." Leila hugged herself. "I miss him so much. And I worry . . ." She covered her eyes with one hand. "Every night I dream about him. Sometimes it's saying goodbye at the train station. Sometimes it's him being killed by a bomb on a train." She wrapped her arms about herself. She said nothing more, and after a few minutes, Sini wondered if she should return to her cot. But Leila spoke and leaned in to Sini's arm. "Maybe talking about the dreams will make them stop."

"All right." Sini felt entirely inadequate for being such a confidante but wanted to help.

"We were on a train that was bombed, Taneli and I. We escaped, but not everyone did. That's when I knew I had to send him away. He could have died that night. But when I brought him to the train station, and he had to get on a train—without me—he was frightened." She turned to Sini, though their faces were in shadow. "He's only three. He couldn't understand why we were going back to the train station. I didn't dare explain too soon—that would have made him even more afraid. And he would have cried, and then I wouldn't have been able to go through with it." Leila took a deep breath that stuttered on the way out.

"How awful," Sini said. "For both of you."

"I felt as if I were delivering him to an altar for sacrifice, but no angel would come to stop me. I told Taneli he was going on an adventure. He thought we were going together. I prayed with everything in my heart that he'd understand that I was sending him away *because* I love him. But—" She breathed shakily through tears. "I worry that—"

Sini rested a hand on her back. "That what?"

"That he'll think I sent him away because I don't love him. And that he'll forget me." She shook her head. "I can't bear the thought of getting my sweet boy back, but being a stranger to him. What if he hates me? What if he doesn't remember Finnish?" She covered her mouth with both hands.

Grief from Sini's childhood thrummed behind a wall she'd erected in her heart long ago. The accident that took her parents hadn't crossed her mind in a long time. Now she struggled to find words of comfort and said the only thing she could be sure of. "He'll remember you."

"How can you be so sure?" Leila's voice held a thread of not hope, exactly, but the desire for it.

To keep her voice steady, Sini had to take a moment to gather herself. "My parents died when I was quite young. They were hit by a truck while riding their bikes."

Leila gasped quietly. "That's terrible."

The accident was so bad that Sini hadn't been allowed to see their bodies. She'd long wondered over the decision made by her aunts and uncles to not allow her to see her dead parents. Yes, she'd been young, but at four, that kind of closure might have helped.

"I was very young," Sini said, "a little older than Taneli, but not by much. I still remember them."

"Really?" Leila said, her voice pleading for the glimmer of light she so desperately needed.

Sini clasped her hands in her lap and braced herself to temporarily tear down the wall that she'd built around those memories. Merely saying the word *parents* had formed a knot in her throat. "I was four."

She knew nothing more of Taneli and could think of no way to comfort Leila other than to share her own experience, as painful as it was. "I remember some things from much earlier than the accident, when I was only three."

At that, Leila's tearful face lifted to hers. "Like what?"

The question hung in the air. Sini's chest pinched. Telling the first part had rattled her emotional wall enough to set loose both pain and joy alike. Speaking what little she'd already shared had tempered the tender, raw edges. Perhaps speaking more would have a soothing effect for both her and Leila.

"I remember my mother," Sini said.

"You do?" Leila spoke in a reverent whisper, as if Sini was about to reveal something sacred.

She supposed she was. "I remember helping her set the table at our summer cottage." Images of the past flashed through her mind as if someone were flipping a deck of cards in her mind, showing the colors, numbers, and suits in rapid succession. "Having sauna every night in the summer. In the afternoon, we'd gather fallen birch branches to make *vihtas*. I'd hold the bunches while she tied them off. In the sauna, she tapped my back gently. It felt so good. Every time I use a *vihta*, the smell alone brings me back to my mother." She chuckled to herself at a memory and then shared it. "I tried to use the *vihta* myself, but it was too heavy. Even holding it with two hands, I could barely lift it."

Though they now sat in a tent in the middle of a wintry forest, she could almost feel the dry heat of the sauna turning wet with billowing steam whenever her mother helped her ladle water onto the hot stones. What she wouldn't give for one more time in the family sauna. Her uncle had inherited the cottage from her father, and she'd rarely been back. Her apartment's tiny sauna, scarcely big enough for one person, wasn't the same.

"Do you remember anything else?" Leila asked.

"Berry picking." Speaking of those times didn't hurt as much as it used to. "We'd pick them in the forest in the morning and eat bowlfuls with fresh cream. If we'd gathered enough berries, my mother made a pastry for later. Blueberries were her favorite. Tiny wild strawberries were mine. Dad said he didn't have a favorite, but Mom knew he preferred lingonberries and cloudberries, so she tried to find and bake pies out of those, too. At home, we always had a jar of cloudberry jam for him."

Sini stared into the darkness of the tent wall. Sometimes the memories lingered on one image long enough for her to savor its sweetness.

"My mother taught me to ice skate," Sini said. "I'd heard that children ice skated at school, and I worried that I'd be the only one who didn't know how. So she took me to the rink at a park every day for weeks. I had a pale-blue coat with white fur around the cuffs and sparkly snowflakes embroidered on the pockets. Mom hated covering her head because it mussed her hair, but she brought me to the rink anyway, knit cap and all, for hours. I loved it when the tip of her nose turned pink. I still remember her coat: dark blue, with tan fur around the hood."

Speaking of her mother brought sadness, but it lacked the bitter sting of not belonging to anyone, of being shuttled between relatives. Those pains would always linger. But at that moment, those deep aches lingered in the background.

Maybe it was because she had an interested and compassionate listener. Maybe because she was recalling the stories to comfort someone else who was suffering.

Maybe this is what friends do for each other. Sini's eyes misted at the thought.

"Tell me more," Leila said.

"On the ice, she stood in one place and put me on her right side. Then she guided me into skating a number three on one skate—my left hand, then both, then my right when I ended on her right. I got pretty good at it."

"And you were so little when she passed," Leila said.

"Yes," Sini said quietly. She held out her hands and could almost feel her mother's touch.

"Maybe Taneli will remember something of me, too. I packed him a handkerchief with my initials embroidered beside three pink roses. I sprayed some of my perfume on it too, in case that might be a comfort." She sniffed and sighed. "But a handkerchief might be too feminine for a boy to carry around."

"No, it's perfect." Sini said. She turned, pulling her knee atop the cot to face Leila, who did the same, so the two could look each other in the eyes. "He'll want something that reflects you. He'll keep that handkerchief forever, years after you're reunited, and after he's grown. He'll be able to have it in his pocket without anyone knowing about it, but it'll be there to comfort him. And while you're apart, he'll hold that handkerchief close and breathe you in. He'll think of you every day."

Leila made a sound—one almost happy, and at least not as miserable as before. "He also has a photograph of me and his father on our wedding day. Maybe he'll remember what I look like, too."

"I'm sure he will," Sini said.

For a few seconds, Leila said nothing, and Sini wondered if she should share more memories. But then Leila went on, as if her own emotional wall had been torn down, and her thoughts and feelings began to spill out.

"We had to write the children's important information on a card, and as I pinned it to his coat, I saw soldiers getting ready to leave. They looked so young—just boys. There I was feeling sorry for myself, while I was about to save my son's life and other mothers were sending their sons away to die. One mother held her son's face between her hands." Leila held out her hands as if acting out the memory. "'Be strong and brave,' the mother said. 'And come home to me. Promise.' She had tears rolling down both cheeks, and so did he. He promised, hugged her one last time, and got on the train." Leila sniffed and shook her head. "They both knew he couldn't keep his promise. Their faces said so. That boy will probably die on a field somewhere. Maybe he already has. But Taneli is alive, and he's too young to fight. I should be *happy*. I have no right to cry over him."

"You have every right," Sini said. "Of course you're grieving. Pain is pain. You can't compare one person's hardship with another's." A moment of silence followed. Had she said the wrong thing?

"Thank you," Leila whispered. "I pray he isn't heartbroken. I can't stop thinking of his wide eyes when he realized he was going without me."

Sini listened intently, wanting to know more about Leila and her son. To be the kind of person Leila wanted to turn to in times of trouble, telling her these things not just because Sini happened to be there when the bad dream arrived.

"I told him that I couldn't let anything happen to the person I loved most, that he was worth more to me than a ship full of gold, but he didn't understand." Leila wrung her hands. "I told him I loved him, over and over, and to never forget it. He said—he said he loved me too. And then he wrapped his chubby arms around my neck and cried. It broke me."

Sini could almost feel the crushing weight.

"A woman came to take him, and he wailed. He cried my name and stretched his arms toward me as she carried him away. He kept yelling, 'Let me stay, Mama! I'll be good!' I wanted nothing more than to run after him and take him back."

"But you didn't," Sini said. "Why?" She knew the answer but sensed that Leila needed to speak the words.

"Because I love him. Keeping him in danger would have been selfish." Leila let out a breath that sounded like a sardonic laugh. "And a little bit because Jaakob would be angry if I didn't keep our son safe. After the train pulled away, with his little face pressed to a window, tears streaking down his cheeks, I collapsed on a bench. Part of me died on that platform."

She cried again, and Sini couldn't help but cry with her. Leila leaned in and hugged Sini.

The tent flap opened, and with it a flashlight beam entered. The two women broke apart, unwilling for their private moment to become public. Sini stood and returned to her own cot. They both slipped into their sleeping bags as the nurse who'd entered rummaged through her belongings and got ready for bed. When the light turned off, Sini felt a slight movement and opened her eyes. Leila was facing Sini's cot.

Sini lifted her head expectantly. "I can go get you an aspirin if you need one." Crying often gave her a headache. Maybe the same thing happened to Leila.

"I wanted to say thank you. Not many people would be so kind and comforting, especially toward someone she hardly knows."

Sini couldn't help but smile. "I feel as if I've known you for a very long time. But you're even better than I'd heard." She purposely left out Marko's name.

"I'm so glad I have a friend out here," Leila said. Then she settled back onto her pillow.

Long after Leila's breathing turned deep and even, Sini lay on her back, awake, staring into the darkness and marveling.

She called me her friend.

CHAPTER ELEVEN

December 22

Sini counted herself fortunate that, after spending some of the night awake due to Leila's nightmare, she'd been able to sleep in a little; she didn't need to report for duty until ten o'clock. Even so, fatigue pulled at her as if her cot had a force of its own, extra gravity demanding that she stay in bed.

She managed to get ready for the day and then headed from the tent to the kitchen, still only half awake. She glanced at her wristwatch, glad that she wouldn't be late—she'd arrive a few minutes before ten, when the winter sun had finally crested the horizon. The winter solstice had just passed, which meant that days would begin to lengthen again, if only by a few minutes a day.

The days would get longer and longer until the summer solstice in June, when nights would be as light as the days were dark now. In the middle of winter, however, it was hard to believe that winter's iron grip would ever be released by spring.

Unlike some mornings, when she had to use a flashlight to find her way from her tent to the kitchen, she had both hands free and was able to hug herself with both arms in an effort to ward off, the chill. When she reached the building's back entrance, she stomped her feet of snow just as the door swung open.

Raisa came out dragging a trashcan. "Ah, there you are. You still have your coat on, so you take this to the dumpster." She didn't wait for an answer, though had Sini been alert enough, she might have pointed out that Raisa had put on a coat for the job. Instead, the cook went back inside and pulled the door closed.

Sini stood there, cold and achy, every centimeter of her body yearning for her sleeping bag. The smell of the garbage jolted her to full wakefulness. She scrunched up her face and brought a coat sleeve to her nose.

Nothing to do but face the nasty chore so she could warm up indoors. She pushed the lid on hard to keep anything from falling out. If she kept the metal can behind her, the stench might stay away from her nose.

With both hands behind her back, she grasped one of the handles and pulled the can. She made her way slowly across the slippery path. Again she was glad it wasn't dark, so she didn't have to manage a flashlight while picking her way across snow and ice.

The can caught on something and tilted; Sini scrambled to steady it so nothing would spill. With the can upright, she heaved a sigh of relief. Dragging it didn't work. Fatigue and cold had worn her to the bone; the idea of getting her dress and long underwear soaked in snow was intolerable. The longer she stayed out here, the more likely that would happen.

Reluctantly, she clutched the handles, turned her head to the side, and lifted the can. She shuffled along the path to make sure she didn't slip, keeping her boots on the ground. It reminded her of the times she'd told Leila about, ice skating with her mother so long ago. Back when she didn't despise cold and darkness.

Because of those memories, she used to like winter. Not anymore. Now she wished for a nighttime snowstorm not for the magic of freshly fallen snow but because a storm would prevent air raids. Now she hated winter.

The flyer seeking Lottas had promised satisfaction for a job well done, a life of patriotism and pride. Somehow, dragging rotten fish bones and other refuse didn't feel particularly meaningful.

I'm one small cog in a large machine. The reminder had become a habit, a way to keep herself from regretting her decision to volunteer. Her work supported the soldiers as they fought to keep their country free.

Even dumping garbage matters. But that fact didn't change the sense of loneliness she still felt. She thought of Marko less and less often, but that didn't mean she'd found contentment.

Last night, while comforting Leila, she'd finally felt needed.

She felt useful the few times she'd helped in the infirmary—anything she did there felt meaningful—it counted for something. Despite her initial aversion to the sounds, smells, and so much more, she was glad for the chance to work there periodically. She'd seen soldiers, so young they were practically boys, trying hard to look stoic and brave.

She'd sat with young husbands and fathers and listened to old men who should have never been called to fight for their country again after having fought in the civil war, and before that, the war for independence. Those older men made her heart ache; they were the ones truly sacrificing. After so much service, they should have been able to live out their later years in peace.

Most liked to tell her stories from their other war experiences. They were intimately acquainted what war with the Soviet Union meant, including their slim chances of returning home to their families. They'd fought anyway because, as several of them insisted, freedom from tyranny mattered more than their own lives.

She'd been honored to care for such men, to comfort them, to listen to those who needed a compassionate ear, someone to weep with them.

Amazing how experience could change perspective. Her first time in the infirmary had been a barrage on her senses with so much human suffering. She'd wondered how Leila could work there day after day.

Sini understood now, at least a little. She'd come to care about many soldiers. They were men in pain. Men with hopes, dreams, and fears. She no longer saw merely rows of cots. She saw individuals. Cleaning a wound became an act of kindness.

At times, Sini still wondered how Leila could focus on her work while being apart from her son, but Sini was beginning to guess the reasons. Leila never gave a partial effort; she gave everything or nothing. Naturally, she'd pour her soul into tending to the wounded.

Leila was religious, so maybe she hoped that if she cared for others, God would somehow make sure her own son was cared for.

At the dumpster, Sini lifted the can, which no longer seemed so heavy or distasteful. On her toes, she tipped it into the large metal container. When she brought it down, her mittens had something slimy on them.

She set the can on the ground and looked for a spot in the snow to clean them off. She hadn't been disgusted at the muck; she felt a strange bit of pride in that. Even so, she needed to wash off her mittens with clean snow. She'd do a better job with soap later, but a good scrub now would keep them from getting too smelly.

She walked past the dumpster, purposefully going beyond camp to be sure the snow was clean. Too close to the garbage area, traces of old food could have reached the snow, which would make her sick. Some patches of snow were dusted with gunpowder carried there by the wind. She avoided those spots.

Nurses in her tent told stories of soldiers who'd tried easing their thirst with snow, only to wish themselves dead later. Gunpowder poisoning sounded horridly painful.

Having left the shoveled paths behind her, Sini moved through knee-deep snow. The bottom of her skirt was covered in sparkling white, and she could feel moisture seeping into the tops of her boots. She'd have to hurry back to the kitchen and get warm again or risk being wet and cold all day.

She dragged her feet a little to make a clear path to follow back. Even in short distances, in the midst of thousands of identical trees, it was easy to lose all sense of direction. A low-hanging sun that cast few shadows and barely arced through the sky didn't help with keeping a sense of direction. Her camp had found more than one Russian soldier who'd died of exposure, likely after getting lost.

A few days ago, a truck had mistakenly brought three dead Russians into camp. One was in a sitting position and seemed to be looking at something on the ground. Another would eternally be about to light a cigarette, and the third still held a pair of binoculars to his unseeing eyes. All three looked alive, as if they could move or speak at any moment. But they were as solid as ice.

"This is a hospital, not a morgue," a captain had snapped at the apologetic driver.

Sini would never forget the sight of the truck pulling away, the bodies still in the positions they'd died in. She'd had more than one nightmare about it.

As far from camp as she dared venture, Sini found a patch of snow with no evidence of footprints, shell casings, or gunpowder. Nothing but unsullied, pristine white. Dreading the chill, she quickly pulled off her mittens and scrubbed them. Ice crystals scratched her bare skin.

I'm a small but important cog. A Lotta keeps herself clean. I cannot serve if I'm sick. The reminders helped a little, but what she really needed was the warmth of the kitchen. *Others have it worse,* she reminded herself. *Like Leila. She suffers more than she lets on.*

By the time Sini woke up that morning, Leila had already left the tent. In a way, that had been a relief. She wasn't sure how Leila would feel about what had happened, whether she'd be embarrassed to have shared such private things with a Lotta who worked in the kitchen.

Sini had wished for a friend, someone to ease the loneliness, and after last night, she had a glimmer of hope that Leila could become that friend. Who would have thought that she'd *hope* to become friends with the woman she'd once envied with every breath? Sini shook her head in wonderment.

Feeling as clean as she could get, Sini shook the snow from her skirt and coat, glad the wool repelled some of it. She looked around and felt a welcome peace at being by herself in the middle of nature. Not lonely. Peaceful. The busyness of camp didn't reach her here. In the darkness, she could almost pretend that this was a Christmas school break, and she was spending it at her uncle Heikki's cottage. She closed her eyes and tilted her head back, breathing in the cold, clean air, letting peace wash over her. She knew the feeling would be temporary, so she was determined to relish it while she could.

With a sigh, she opened her eyes and looked at the sky, which was mostly dark, though the promise of dawn had shifted it from pure black to deep purple.

No clouds. She sighed again, not from pleasure that time. So much for peace. She hated that such a mundane detail meant worry—a clear sky could literally mean death. Hopefully one day, a clear sky would return to simply being a clear sky.

She was about to turn back to camp, but something caught her notice—a dark spot in the sky. Thinking she'd imagined it, or it was a bird, she stopped and looked at it. The spot was definitely moving. Not like a bird, and not like a plane, either.

She heard the hum of a motor and found another object, one that looked like a plane. It was low enough for her to make out the basic shape, and it didn't appear to be a bomber. Maybe just a Russian plane doing their supposed "routine patrols," which everyone on both sides quietly acknowledged were reconnaissance. Thanks to the army's camouflage efforts, a Soviet pilot would be hard pressed to spot the camp.

The plane disappeared, and Sini's attention went back to the other, smaller spot in the sky. It made no noise that she could make out, and it moved downward. As a precaution, Sini stepped backward into the cover of trees. Curiosity kept her there. She'd have plenty of time to raise an alarm if needed.

The object resolved from looking like a smudge into the silhouette of a person—legs, arms, head. A man. A parachute released and expanded. The plane hadn't dropped a bomb; it had dropped a person.

As the Russian drew nearer, Sini held her breath and stepped deeper into the shadows of the trees, glad for so many evergreens to hide her presence. This was an enemy with weapons and training and . . .

She looked back toward the dumpster, hoping someone else had seen the parachute too and was coming—security officers from camp headquarters. But she saw no one. Only the messy path she'd forged. Her stomach knotted. Camouflage wouldn't stop an enemy spy from following her prints, finding her in the trees, and then walking right into camp.

She swore under her breath and lifted her skirt, debating which way to run across the clearing and back to camp. The parachutist seemed to move faster now; if the sun had been up, she would have been able to see his face. And he was close enough that if she ran, he'd notice her movement and follow. What would he do to her?

She peered through the branches and decided she'd stay hidden if possible. She'd watch him, then report him.

When? After he follows my path to camp?

She didn't dare cut through the forest to get back; she'd get lost. She had to cross the clearing, which he was clearly aiming for. What were the chances he'd be able to shoot accurately when they were both moving, and it was still mostly dark out? How quickly could he get out of the chute to follow her? She didn't want to learn the answers to any of those questions. She braced herself against a tree as if she were the one falling.

Watching his descent, Sini had an equally horrible and hopeful thought that his parachute might catch on the trees. He'd freeze to death, tangled in the lines, if the impact didn't kill him first. She'd be able to fetch help. Guards would come, get him down, and interrogate him.

He was close enough now that she could make out some of his features—short, pale hair, a strong jaw. Why would a spy be dropped here? Was there some strategic advantage to spying on a military hospital she hadn't thought of?

Unless he'd been dropped off course, and wind carried him even farther from his intended course. If she could get lost from her own camp, how easy would it be for a Russian unfamiliar with the landscape to get lost?

Maybe he was supposed to drop onto the frozen surface of Tolvajärvi Lake. She imagined that missing a long but narrow target would be easy.

He must be terrified. The sympathetic thought came out of nowhere and vanished as the parachute collided with a high branch. With a loud crack, it broke off and dropped to the ground, taking the man with it. He landed with a thud and spray of snow. The momentum of the parachute carried him forward, but his feet were stuck in the snow, so he fell face first. A surprised noise escaped him, and then he was silent and motionless.

Sini's heartbeat roared in her ears. Had he noticed her? Was he unconscious? If so, she could run for help—maybe. She'd have to go right past him, though. If he was alive, he could catch her before she reached the other side of the clearing. Or shoot her.

He shifted, moaning again.

Alive, then. What do I do?

Groaning, he pushed himself up with his arms then sat back on his knees. He worked the clasps that kept the chute attached to him. His hands were clumsy, fumbling. He grunted in frustration and tore off his gloves, then tried to free himself again, with no success.

He muttered something in Russian. Judging by the tone, he was using words she would have blushed at. His voice made him real—as human as she was. Yes, he was also her enemy. But right now, he wasn't trying to kill anyone.

Branches clung to the chute, keeping him in place if he couldn't release himself. At the rate he was going, he wouldn't free himself. He'd die right here, in front of her, from the cold.

Killing the enemy made sense intellectually when it meant a faceless mass of guns and tanks run by Stalin. But this man looked about her age. He could have been a classmate. He had emotions. He was flesh and blood.

And if she let him die, she wouldn't be able to live with herself.

Summoning her courage, Sini stepped from the trees into the clearing. One step and then another gradually brought her within a stone's throw of the man. The little light available was enough to make out his face. Her heart pounded, and she got ready to run or scream for help.

The Russian must have heard her, because he glanced up and jerked with a start. He'd paled and backed away on his hands and feet, crablike. When he hit a trunk and a tangle of cords, both holding him in place, she ventured forward.

"I'm Sini," she said, pointing to herself and speaking slowly. He probably didn't know Finnish, and she certainly didn't know Russian.

He looked about rapidly as if trying to find an escape and she were the threat instead of the other way around. His anxious response gave her confidence. She took another step forward. He braced himself as if waiting for her to attack or draw a weapon. She pointed at herself again.

"Sini. You are . . ."

He stared at her finger pointing at him, his chest rising and falling rapidly. He answered with a single word. "Nikolai."

Sini smiled broadly at her success. "Nikolai," she repeated. She gestured toward the buckles and mimed opening them. "May I help?"

He looked from her hand to the clasps then slowly nodded. Sini worked on keeping her smile in place. In the cold, the expression felt false, as if her face would freeze, and she wouldn't be able to stop smiling until she thawed out by a stove.

When she reached him, she paused, and when he didn't pull a weapon on her, she reached out and worked the buckles, pondering her next step. He'd need shelter and food. One of the camp officers would need to interrogate him; perhaps a colonel, like Talvela, who commanded this sector. Or Commander Pajari, who'd recently pulled off a late-night raid that leveled hundreds of Russians. Rumor said he'd be promoted to colonel thanks to his raid, a small part of the larger Tolvajärvi effort—a part that had increased morale throughout the country.

She wished she could ease the Russian's fears, tell him that Finns didn't torture prisoners. Granted, Finns could be vicious when their lives and liberty were on the line. She'd heard about the so-called Sausage War from a few weeks back, when a company of Russians breached the line in the middle of the night—something that could have cost the Finns the entire war.

Instead of completing their mission, the starving enemy got distracted by the smell of sausage soup cooking on a mobile field kitchen stove. Orders forgotten, they headed straight for the soup and stuffed their faces with it. The delay allowed the Finns to regroup. Reports said that the battle raged throughout the night and was horrific—not the "civilized" fighting of guns at a distance, but brutal hand-to-hand combat with knives and bayonets, and, in the Finns' case, anything else they could get their hands on—chairs and filing cabinets from the offices, pitchforks from the quartermaster, anything.

A single two-man team had killed dozens of Russians. One shined a bright lantern, just long enough for a nearby Russian to stop and stand still like a frightened deer. Only a moment, but enough for the other to shoot the soldier dead with a single bullet. They did it again and again.

Brutal and bloody. By necessity, yes. That was the reality of war. But *hearing* such things never made them real. Seeing them was something else, like the frozen Russians from the other day, who could have been mistaken for mannequins in a department store window.

Nikolai watched her as she worked, never looking away from her face. She nervously looked up, and their eyes met—his strikingly blue ones contrasting with his pale hair. She blushed, unable to look away. He reached to help with a buckle. That broke the link, and she returned her attention to the chute. At last it released. He took one arm and then the other out of the straps and stretched.

Now what? She knew only two Russian words: *no* and *truth,* the latter being the name of their newspaper, *Pravda.*

She straightened and brushed off her skirt. She could have sworn that ice crystals were forming on her cheeks. They both needed to get out of the cold. She stepped back from the now-freed parachute jumper.

"Come," she said, motioning for him to follow. "I can get you food." She mimed spoon and bowl.

"N-no." The word began hesitantly but ended firmly.

She sighed and rested her hands on her hips in thought. Now what? He didn't act threatening. If anything, he was nervous, even though he was much taller and stronger than she was. She posed no threat to him.

She didn't think he'd shoot her in the back if she left. But if she left to report him, he'd run off and get lost before any guards could find him. Realistically, he'd die in the woods, but he might spy on the camp and get some information out before succumbing to the elements. None of that seemed like something a Lotta should settle for. He had to come with her.

She mimed eating again. "I can get you food. Come."

His eyes narrowed, and he shook his head. He tensed but didn't move, just studied her warily. She wanted to slap his ears like an old grandmother would a foolish child. Didn't he realize he'd die out here in that silly cotton uniform of his? He didn't seem to have a radio or other way to contact his superiors, and he'd clearly landed off course.

He was shivering—near hypothermia, probably. She could get food to warm him from the inside out. Despite the snow, she dropped to her knees to look him in the eye.

"Why not?" she asked in frustration. A puff of white came out with her breath.

He searched her face. His jaw worked, and his eyebrows came together, a sign of a big debate happening inside him. "The Finnish army tortures prisoners. Kills them."

Sini was so stunned to hear her own language that she didn't argue. "You speak Finnish?" Her brain refused to accept it. A soldier in a Russian uniform, who was clearly Russian, speaking her language?

"My mother is Finnish. She was born in Oulu. We spoke Finnish at home."

"Ah." What must it feel like attacking his mother's homeland? "But we don't torture or kill prisoners. You'll be safe."

Would he be safe, though? A vast number of possibilities existed between the poles of torture on one side and safety on the other. What would Elomaa think of a Russian dropping from the sky? Maybe the army handled spies differently from other POWs—maybe spies did get tortured. Her doubt must have shown, because he pulled back, hesitance renewed in every feature, every movement.

"Come with me. I'll get you food and dry clothes. If you stay out here, you'll freeze to death by morning." She was so glad she could explain. Sini reached out a mittened hand as a show of friendliness.

He considered her words then finally nodded. He didn't take her hand, but he got to his feet then brushed off his uniform. The fabric was soaked through and the pant cuffs were stiff, frozen. That was the kind of uniform the Finnish army used during the summer. Never in winter.

Reports had said that Russian soldiers didn't have proper uniforms, but she'd assumed that was hyperbole. Stalin really was insane enough to send men to war in the dead of winter, wearing thin cotton trousers. Her ugly Lotta top and skirt provided far more protection.

"Will you hide me?" he asked.

"Will I—what?"

His pleading gaze held hers. Sini opened her mouth to say no, of course she wouldn't—couldn't. But he stepped closer. Only then did she realize his full height; nearly two meters. He could easily overpower her. If he felt his life was threatened, or if she didn't cooperate . . .

Oh, how foolish she'd been. He had a rifle, but he surely had other weapons in his backpack or hidden in his clothing. What had she gotten herself into? Adrenaline raced through her body.

"I'll die," he said. His frightened eyes shifted something inside her.

She remained cautious, but not terrified. His eyes begged for mercy, and his bluish lips sent a pang of sympathy through her. "Come with me," she said again, this time as she might try to comfort a child. "We don't hurt prisoners. You'll see."

"Don't let them arrest me." He reached out and touched her shoulder. Her eyes darted to his hand, so close to her face. She held her breath, expecting him to grab her, shove her, somehow force her to obey.

Instead, his touch asked, making no demands. His hand was so big it engulfed her shoulder. If she'd dared, she would have taken off her mitten again, reached up, and touched his hand, felt his skin. This was a man who was lost, cold, and hungry. Something in his eyes assured her that he meant no harm.

He isn't my enemy.

Stalin's men weren't kind to any Finnish soldiers. They weren't humane. She could show Nikolai that Finns were better than that. For a few hours, she'd ease his mind and assure him that he would be safe. And then she'd report him.

"Hide me until I can find a way to escape back across the border. Some men were supposed to meet me at my landing point, but . . ." He shrugged and looked around. "I'm clearly not in the right place. I have no way to contact them . . . just . . . help me. You have to."

Sini's toes tightened nervously. She couldn't promise to hide him for any significant length of time, but he'd managed to earn a little of her sympathy. Partly, no doubt, because he looked Finnish and spoke Finnish. She had to remind herself that he wasn't fighting as one of her countrymen.

If he'd been born and raised on this side of the border, he would be fighting on their side. Then he'd have a wool uniform. He'd don white coveralls and ski through forests to defend against Russians. Instead, he had to fight for Stalin's evil designs.

Sini glanced back toward camp. Could a Lotta be court martialed for aiding the enemy? She could get into so much trouble.

Maybe she could find somewhere for him to sleep, but keep him restrained somehow. She'd have to figure out how to get him out of camp undetected—and across the border. An old compass might be enough for him to find the way. If she succeeded, he'd be gone in twenty-four hours, and no one would be the wiser.

"Fine," she said. "I'll try."

CHAPTER TWELVE

Nikolai's face softened with relief. He took a step forward to follow Sini. He wore no gloves or mittens, and his fingers were icy cold, surely turning blue, but she couldn't make out the color in the dim light.

"Thank you, Sini. My mother thanks you too. And my father, may he rest in peace."

Unexpected compassion tugged at her heart, and with it, a flash of another mother and child: Leila and Taneli. Families were not so different across enemy lines.

"This way," Sini said and headed back through the snow.

As they walked, she purposely skirted the edge of camp to avoid being spotted. The whole way, she considered her options even as she picked their way through, this time without her flashlight to remain undetected. Now that she no longer worried that he'd attack her, she focused on what to do with the Russian soldier—spy? Could she actually find a way for him to escape back across the border? Should she convince him to reveal his presence at camp headquarters? Should she turn him in without his consent?

Surely he'd be safe in that circumstance—fed and warm and clothed. How best to turn him in without getting herself into trouble or making him feel cornered and betrayed? Maybe that was the kind of situation that would flip a switch inside him, like turning on a machine. He might attack anyone who tried to imprison him.

She glanced over her shoulder and gave him a smile, noting his height and build again. He might be able to kill some of the guards in camp before being subdued, if given the opportunity. What if he did? Would it be her fault?

I should turn him in right away, she thought, but couldn't quite believe that the decision would be for the best.

She couldn't break her word to Nikolai. Granted, he fought for soulless Stalin, but promises meant something to *her*. In all likelihood, she'd be forced to tell someone about him, and sooner than later. But for now, what was she to do?

She glanced back at him again. What had his mission been? For all she knew, she might be playing into some Soviet strategy. On the other hand, he didn't seem to have a two-way radio or any supplies other than whatever his small backpack held, which couldn't mean more than a little hardtack for food. The thought of asking him for his rifle and then attempting to search him for any other weapons turned her stomach.

Even a good man, when faced with a threat to his life, would defend himself.

For the moment, for his sake as well as for her own safety, her goal was to keep him from feeling threatened.

She ducked under some tree branches and stepped over a fallen log. Keeping her balance in the dark proved tricky here. Wordlessly, she glanced back again, hating that her eyes always went from his face to the shadowy shape of his rifle. He could have weapons tucked into his belt or pockets. A blade or two hidden in boots or pants pockets.

As they drew near camp, Sini quickly decided what to do. She'd take him to the underground food-storage cellar, a dugout that kept food cool without freezing it. That's where they stored vegetables, flour, oil, sugar, cans of smoked fish, and more.

She took the trip to the dugout regularly, and now as she pictured the space, she tried to come up with a way to hide him there. Rearranging some of the bags of sugar, flour, and oats into a semblance of a wall might work, at least for a few hours. And a few hours might be all she could manage. She wasn't on duty around the clock, and who knew how often others went there. She could be the one who made trips there on her own shift, but others could easily go to the dugout and find him when she was off duty.

Behind the kitchen building, they continued to a spot tucked behind a small grove of pine trees and spruce.

"There," Sini said, pointing toward a short incline that led to the door of the food storage dugout.

"Wow. I did *not* see that," Nikolai said, staring at the camouflaged storage room.

Most of it was underground, but the dugout had a partial roof covered by trees and snow, making it blend right into the landscape unless you knew exactly where to look.

"You Finns are smart," he added as they reached the incline leading down to the door.

His words made Sini's step come up short. Would hiding him here help the Russians? This year's brutal winter—the White Death, many were calling it—had killed more Russians than Finnish bullets had. Maybe she was walking Nikolai into a place where he'd learn how the Finnish army was surviving the bitter cold. Information he could pass on to the Soviet army.

Maybe he knows Finnish because he's a trained spy, not because of his mother.

No, his accent was too good for that. At least, she thought so. She was tempted to ask him to say *höyryjyrä*, as the guard had demanded as a test when she and Leila went to Kivilä.

She kept moving, but the toe of her boot caught on something—a root or rock beneath the snow. She fell face-forward, landing on the hard ground. One arm and the side of her head smacked against something—a branch or rock. Without much light, she wasn't sure what had happened, only that stars burst into her vision, and she gasped from the pain.

Nikolai dropped to his knees beside her. "Are you hurt?"

He knows where the dugout is. He'll tie me up, steal our food, and run.

But he didn't. He was freezing and soaked—his lips were tinged blue now, but he stayed by her side. "How can I help? Can you walk, or should I carry you?"

She blinked a few times to clear her vision, and let his words settle in her mind. He'd offered to help her? When she shifted, Nikolai was there, helping her to a sitting position as she regained her bearings.

"I'll have some bruises," she said, rubbing her arm and the side of her head. "But I think I'm fine."

He gave her a smile; he looked even more handsome with it. She liked how the corners of his eyes crinkled. He held out a bare hand. "Let me help you up."

Sini took his hand, and he gently eased her to her feet. She steadied herself on his arm, feeling lightheaded for a moment, partly from the fall, but also thanks to a heightened awareness of Nikolai's presence, so close his breath warmed her cheek. She looked up—and up and up, it seemed—to meet his face. His smile softened as he gazed back.

"Th-thank you," she said, still holding his hand, reluctant to let go.

"You're welcome. And thank *you*."

Sini could have stayed there all day and night as a new kind of warmth coursed through her. When the silence stretched, she nodded toward their hands. "The gloves you had before. Were they homemade?"

He nodded. "I must have dropped them."

"I'll go back later and see if I can find them for you."

"Thank you. My—mother made them for me." He seemed about to say more, but emotion clung to his throat instead.

"Of course," Sini said, cheerfully, as if she hadn't noticed.

His mother would have known what kind of winter he would face; she'd lived through many herself. "She must love you very much."

"Yes, she does." His smile dropped, and his brows drew together. "She's an amazing woman. I worry about her, though; she got sick a few months ago, and she's never improved. She always wanted me to see her homeland, but . . ." He looked around them and gestured at his rifle. "This wasn't exactly what she had in mind." He attempted a chuckle.

Sini rested a hand on his upper arm—the muscle beneath his sleeve was thick and firm and strong. Her middle flipped over. "She'll get better," she said—an attempt at comforting him, despite knowing nothing about his mother's condition.

He reached across to take her hand in his, then clasped it. "I hope you're right," he said, giving her hand a squeeze. Too bad this wasn't another place and time. Someday, perhaps, she'd find someone in Finland like Nikolai.

Silence settled over them again, but one that felt easy and natural. Her intellect argued with the feeling. This was a stranger, a Russian, a soldier, possibly a spy. And here she was standing at the edge of a camp for a Finnish army hospital. But he didn't *feel* like a stranger or a Russian. He didn't look like a Russian, except for his uniform. He didn't talk like one. Or act like one.

He shivered, pressing Sini into action. "You're freezing, and you must be ravenous. Come."

She walked the rest of the way down to the dugout but didn't want to release Nikolai's hold on her hand to open the door. He must have caught her looking at their entwined hands, because he winked and squeezed hers. A pleasant buzz erupted in her chest, spreading until her insides vibrated.

This is no time to be getting carried away with an infatuation with the enemy, she lectured herself.

But he's not my enemy, she thought as she released his hand. With both hands, she pulled the heavy wood door open.

Doesn't matter who he is. I can't let myself get caught up in another man who doesn't return my feelings.

If ever there were a man with whom a future relationship was doomed from the start, a Russian soldier in the middle of a war was it.

He followed her inside, and then she pulled the door closed behind them. Sini took a flashlight from her coat pocket and shined it so they could get their bearings. She swept the beam around the space, analyzing the room, trying to decide how to reorganize the supplies subtly enough to not raise suspicion but enough to hide Nikolai. The area seemed smaller than it used to.

The two of them stacked boxes and bags. They rearranged crates of vegetables and cans of fish, all to create the illusion of a wall but with a gap for a hiding place behind it. They stood back to observe their work. The room looked much as it had. With luck, anyone noticing a change would assume it was the result of new shipments or someone—maybe even a Lotta like her—who had simply decided to organize the food storage differently.

She led Nikolai around the false wall to a spot in the corner where they'd even created a "chair" from two sacks of flour. "It's not fancy, but I think it will work."

They'd purposely put the gap he'd be hiding in next to a narrow slit at the top. The gap at the ceiling had a bit of glass to let in some light from the roof without allowing the elements in.

Nikolai entered into the hiding spot, which shrank when filled with his large frame. He sat on the flour sacks and looked around. He wouldn't have much room, but hopefully the space would keep him safe and alive.

Unless he was found. Or until she turned him in.

"Nikolai . . ." Sini walked over and managed to sit beside him on the flour sack, which proved to be a bit of a squeeze. "I don't know how long I can hide you here. If someone finds out—" How best to phrase this? "It would be best if they didn't discover any weapons on you."

His seemed to be thinking hard, as if her words tumbled over one another in his head, along with their implications. "You're right." He took the rifle off his back, lifting the strap over his head, and handed it to her. "Here."

She held it out in front of her as if it were a live grenade. "Any others?"

"Just my knife." He lifted the side of his coat to reveal a leather sheath on his belt with a short blade, the kind her father and uncles used for everyday chores like cleaning fish. The leather sheath was obviously Finnish, as was the knife—the handle was carved reindeer antler. This man really did straddle two worlds.

"Keep that to open cans," she said, nodding at the knife. She stood and smoothed her thick, wet skirt, then made her way around the dugout, trying to decide what he could eat now that wouldn't be missed and wouldn't spoil once opened.

She picked up some canned fish—it was one of the few things in something other than a large sack, a crate, or huge can. But then she wrinkled her nose, realizing that the smell of the fish would give him away. She looked around—sacks of flour, sugar, beans, dried peas—so much that couldn't eat directly. Finally she settled on some hardtack.

"Here," she said, bringing him a stack in hand. "Not the tastiest meal, but better than trying to eat straight flour."

Nikolai took the food and bit into it eagerly. "Right now, it tastes like manna."

She chuckled. "You have awfully low standards for food."

"I'll worry about flavor another day," Nikolai said. "For now, I'm grateful to have something to put into my stomach."

He took another bite, and some hard crumbs fell down his chin. He caught the biggest pieces against his shirt then smiled at her, his voice turning somber. "Thank you. Really. You saved my life."

"Glad I found you." Sini felt her cheeks heat and was glad the dugout was dim so he wouldn't see her blush. She took a step toward the door. "As soon as I can, I'll bring more food, some dry clothes, and a blanket." She reached for the door but then hesitated and turned back. "If someone finds you, speak Finnish. That will be the best thing you can do. Tell them your mother is Finnish."

"I will," he said, and his matter-of-fact tone made her believe him.

Once more she intended to go, but she had to give him more advice. "If someone questions you, say *höyryjyrä.*"

He raised an eyebrow. "Um, why? I can't operate a steamroller or—"

"It's a code word. Russians can't say it, only native Finns can. If you can, that alone could save your life—especially if I can get you a Finnish uniform to wear instead of that." She gestured toward his Soviet clothing.

"I'll remember," Nikolai said. "Thanks."

She breathed heavily with relief. "I'll return as soon as I can." She left, closed the door, then headed back up the incline.

CHAPTER THIRTEEN

Sini half walked, half ran across the slippery path to the kitchen. However long she'd spent with Nikolai was surely *too* long. Raisa would lecture her, then assign Sini extra jobs, insist she work longer hours, and who knew what else. Unless she could invent a believable explanation for why a quick errand to the camp garbage dump hadn't been quick.

The trashcan. She couldn't go back inside without it. What had she been thinking? She pitched forward and caught herself on the door then whirled around, fishing her flashlight from her pocket to light the way back to where she'd abandoned the trashcan.

When she finally returned to the kitchen, she tried to slip inside without being noticed. The door hinges squeaked when she pulled it open. She peered through the gap at two Lottas working inside. Raisa wasn't visible, but she was probably in her office. Sini opened the door the rest of the way and slipped inside—or tried to. The trashcan bumped the frame, and then the door itself *thunked* against it too.

Only Pilvi, who was chopping onions, glanced over, and only briefly. Sini replaced the can in the corner then took an apron from the hooks on one wall and, as she moved to the sink, tied it on. The kitchen always had dishes to wash, and if she got right to work, perhaps no one would ask where she'd been.

"Sini?"

At the sound of Raisa's voice, she stopped in front of the sink. "Yes?" she said, hoping she could avoid turning around.

"Before you finish the dishes, would you check on the stoves? They're probably running low on wood."

Was that all? With relief, Sini turned from the sink. "Right away."

Raisa just nodded, not even looking up from her clipboard before turning and going back to her office. She must not have realized that Sini had only just returned from dumping the trash.

That realization made the rest of Sini's shift not exactly comfortable, but at least less scary. Knowing that her absence had slipped under the others' notice was a definite lightening of her worries, but her middle still had a niggling uneasiness.

Did I do something wrong? Sini thought as she opened a stove door and stirred the embers with the poker. *He's lost and hungry.* She added wood, closed the stove, then moved to the next one. Nikolai hadn't said a loyal word about Stalin. But he was still part of the Soviet army.

He's practically Finnish, she argued back to herself as she tested the heat of the second stove.

I did a good thing. He would have frozen to death. Helping a fellow human was the right thing to do.

But for the rest of her shift, she couldn't quite convince herself that helping him in *secret* was something else entirely.

The guilt wasn't enough to keep her from watching for scraps of food she could slip into her coat and skirt pockets to bring to Nikolai. It wasn't enough to stop her from thinking through how she'd get a blanket or fresh clothes to bring to him.

And it certainly wasn't enough to keep his handsome face from returning to her mind again and again.

When her shift finally ended that afternoon, daylight was gone. She left the kitchen with a lightness in her step and a little thrill going through her that she'd managed to smuggle out so many things for Nikolai: a bottle of milk, rye bread, boiled potatoes wrapped in wax paper, and a little butter. She hadn't been able to sneak away any meat; she'd try again tomorrow.

At the dugout, she carefully opened the door so it wouldn't squeak, then slipped inside and closed it behind her. She turned on her flashlight, rounded the fake wall, and there he was, looking nervous until he could make out her features. Then he smiled, stood, and offered her a seat on the flour bags. He'd added a third to the stack.

A gentleman even here, she thought, sitting. The beam of her flashlight was trained ahead of her, lighting the dirt floor at his feet. She dug into her pocket and held out the milk bottle. "Here."

He sat beside her, and their legs touched. She was acutely aware of how his shoulders were so much higher than hers, how broad his chest was, how . . .

She wedged the flashlight between a couple of sacks of flour, then unloaded the rest of her booty from her pockets.

As Nikolai watched, his stomach gurgled loudly. He took the rye bread and bit it. "Mm. Thank you," he said as he chewed.

She pointed to the milk bottle, which he'd set by his boot. "Keep that. You'll need it later."

Nikolai raised an eyebrow. "Why?"

"For, um . . ." Her cheeks heated.

Stop blushing. It's a biological function.

"For when you need to . . ." More blushing. Disloyal cheeks.

"Ah," he said with understanding—and a slight laugh.

She'd made him laugh. A warm tingle of triumph shot through her chest.

"I'll be sure to keep the cork so I can close it after. Then what do we do with it?"

"Maybe we can dig a small hole to the surface where you can slip it outside for me to take away. Or I'll take any bottles whenever I come, or . . . We'll figure it out." She wanted to change the subject. She really wanted to stay and talk to him, get to know him better.

Nikolai shoveled bites of cold potato into his mouth, rolling his eyes with pleasure as if they were caviar. "Thank you," he murmured.

"Of course," she said, then retrieved the flashlight and stood to leave.

But he stood, too, and touched her arm. The simple pressure on her coat sleeve sent her heart racing again, and she paused in her step.

"I don't know your full name."

"Sini Toivola."

He leaned closer and reached for her hand holding the flashlight, covering her fingers with his. She swallowed against the pattering of her heartbeat. With the beam raised, it spilled onto her face. Nikolai looked into her eyes. "Sini—blue. Good name for someone with your eyes. And Toivola—that means 'place of hope,' I believe? I like that."

"Thanks." She felt alive and wanted to stay, but at the same time, her instinct was to flee, to hide and figure out what was happening inside her. She'd gone completely mad by hiding a Russian. She'd never known how to flirt with or behave around men she was attracted to, and now, in the middle of war, she had no idea how to behave around or what to say to a Russian.

"I, um—good night." She turned to go, and he released her hand. She turned off the flashlight and turned to the door.

In the darkness, he called to her. "Sini?"

Her name on his tongue shot a thrill through her chest. "Yes?" She couldn't see him, but his voice was clear.

"Could you stay a little longer?"

"I really need to leave."

I don't want to go. I need to tell someone about you. I need to find you a blanket and clothes.

He gestured around himself. "Thanks again," he said. "For all of this."

"You're welcome, Nikolai." She went to the door and opened it, feeling warmer than she had since the invasion. "I'll find a way to get you more supplies, but is there anything specific you need?"

Why did she always fall into talking about practical things even when her heart was nearly to bursting over something so far from logic as to be on the opposite pole?

"Well, there is one thing."

"Oh?"

Nikolai grabbed his backpack, which looked even smaller than before. He reached inside the heavy canvas and withdrew some papers, followed by a couple of pencils. "I'm not that good," he said, unfolding the papers. "But this is something I enjoy. It'll be dark in here much of the time, but—"

"I'll try to find some candles or a little lamp or something you can use," Sini interjected.

"That would be wonderful," he said. "Though you'll have to check from outside whether the light is visible through the door."

"Or through there," Sini added with a nod to the upper part of the wall beside them. "Though we can probably cover it with something. Cracks in the door will be trickier." She looked from the window to the door, then realized she was doing it again—being overly practical in a moment that called for more than that. "I'm sorry. I interrupted you. You were saying?"

"I'm not great, but I enjoy drawing. It's a good way to while away the time during war, when so much of what you do is wait, wait, wait."

"Especially now," Sini said with a wan smile. She leaned in to look over his arm at the drawing on top of the stack of what looked to be about four sheets of paper.

The sketch was a forest scene, one he'd surely seen versions of ever since he'd come to war. Spruce and pine, birch trees that were skeletal without their leaves. Snow-covered shrubs. Two reindeer. And a sun hovering above the horizon, ready to fall beneath it. Somehow he'd captured not only the details of the scene, but the emotion, too—a combined awe and sadness.

"That's amazing," Sini said.

He chuckled. "You're just saying that because I'm an armed enemy trooper, and you want to stay on my good side."

Sini playfully nudged him with her elbow. "Nah. I don't pretend to like art even when a Russian's opinion hangs in the balance. If I didn't like it, I'd say so. In fact, you've got the moss wrong on the trees—it should all be on the same side. The south side."

"You are so Finnish."

"What does that mean?"

"You speak your mind."

Sini wasn't sure if they'd veered from flirting to something else. She searched his face, trying to know what he was feeling. "Are you calling me *rude*?" Hopefully she hadn't just offended him.

"Some people might call it *blunt*. I call it *honest*."

She returned her gaze to the paper. "Well, I guess that's true. I am honest. To a fault, sometimes."

Nikolai moved the landscape scene to the back of the stack, revealing a portrait of a man—a soldier.

"Wow," she said. "His eyes have a story in them." She pointed to the others. "May I?"

He handed the papers to her, and she took her time looking at his drawings. He must have spent hundreds of hours on them—adding more details, shading, starting a new image in a corner here or along a margin there.

She tilted her head, marveling at how he'd captured the sparkle of moonlight on snow with nothing but a pencil. "Looks like you could use more paper."

"That's exactly what I was going to ask for."

"I think I can manage that," Sini said. "Some pencils, too?"

"You read my mind."

That's a first for me with a man.

She felt completely comfortable with Nikolai—a man she'd met that morning, who was technically the enemy, but felt like a friend. Yet she felt as if she knew him, that she didn't have to pretend to be someone she wasn't. She didn't have to pretend to be whatever his version of Leila was.

And he claims to like my blunt honesty.

Maybe she could put off turning him in for a few days, maybe until after he'd drawn her.

CHAPTER FOURTEEN

December 24—Christmas Eve

For the last two weeks, the hospital had been on constant alert, with battle after battle in the area. Though more than a week had passed since the recapture of the Hirvasharju Hotel, the hospital hadn't recovered from the stream of casualties and depleted cupboards. Entering the supply room of the surgical tent, Leila took off her scarf and coat and hung them up before heading to the shelves to take inventory, so she'd know what to order on the requisitions form.

She opened the first cupboard, one that not too long ago had been stuffed with bandages and gauze of various sizes. Now the shelves were nearly bare. Another cupboard had been stocked with isopropyl alcohol and hydrogen peroxide, but only two bottles of each remained. Analgesics were in even lower supply. She made notes of it all on her clipboard.

During the height of the recent battles, she would have panicked at how empty the closets had become, but action in the area had tapered off somewhat. If the number of casualties didn't spike again, they would be fine. Leila wished as much but didn't dare hope for it.

The recent bloody, costly battles along this front were all part of a larger campaign that had led to the Finns' first real victory. And while that success was celebrated, no one believed for a moment that it meant the country was safe.

Danger yet lurked along the border, especially to the south, where the Soviets were still working to break through the Mannerheim Line. If they did, they'd march on, claim the capital, and all would be lost.

She moved to the next cupboard, which was filled with dingy but clean towels and sheets. New ones—and a much gentler soap—would be nice, but such things were luxuries and therefore out of the question for now.

Word said that the regiments in the area would be able to defend the land they'd retaken. If so, and the number of casualties dropped, maybe she wouldn't be needed, and she'd get sent home. What if, in a few short weeks, she could hold Taneli in her arms again?

She tried not to raise her hopes, but she couldn't *not* think of Taneli on Christmas Eve. As she counted syringes, she couldn't help but remember the traditions she'd carried on from her childhood.

Would Taneli's Swedish foster family give him presents tonight? Without Aunt Sisko's famous Christmas dinner, would he be sad? He'd always loved finding the almond in the rice pudding. Someday he'd figure out that Aunt Sisko always put one into his bowl, but as of last year, he thought he'd simply been lucky.

Did Swedes celebrate with ham and rice pudding? They celebrated St. Lucia's Day, of course, as Finns did, so he'd already had one familiar tradition this month.

The lines on the inventory form blurred; Leila clutched the clipboard to her chest and willed away the tears. She couldn't let them fall. Not yet. She'd let herself think about her boy tonight as she prayed for him before bed. After that, she'd lock away her tears and worries once more so she could continue being Nurse Kallio.

Kallio—rock. I sure don't feel like one now. Not when the world shifted continuously under her, not when she didn't know what tomorrow might bring. For centuries, Finns had had their own culture, traditions, and language, but they'd been ruled by either Sweden or Russia. Twenty-two years ago this month, they'd declared their independence. Leila was older than her country was, but her people were much older.

Would the border shift again in Russia's favor? Would the Finnish people be left without a country to call their own, without freedoms Stalin didn't expressly give them?

We haven't fallen yet, she thought, stubbornly wiping tears from her eyes with the back of a finger. And we've had a victory on this front. *We can win.*

But could they? Without the promised Allied help, they couldn't win. So far, no meaningful support had arrived.

Leila closed another cupboard as the outside door opened and a flurry of snow came in. Unwilling to let another person see her weak, Leila shifted so her back was to the door as she moved to the next cupboard.

The other person closed the door, stomped off snow, then spoke. "I've come to help." It was Sini.

Leila relaxed. "That would be great." She held out the clipboard, which Sini took after hanging her coat and scarf. Something in her bearing made Leila take a second look. "You seem mighty cheerful this afternoon."

Sini blushed and shrugged one shoulder. "It's been a good day. We're past the winter solstice at last. Days will start getting longer again. That's something to be happy about."

"Sure," Leila said slowly, turning back to the cupboard. "And there's the Tolvajärvi victory to celebrate too."

"Definitely." Sini frowned at the pencil. "I never thought I'd miss pens, but I really do."

"So do I." Leila couldn't hold back a smile. Ink froze, so they had to use pencils instead.

"Pencils make me feel like I'm back in primary school." Sini peeled off a bit of wood to expose more lead.

"Is that how you sharpened them?" Leila asked, nodding at the pencil.

Sini looked at it and laughed. "Not how I was taught to, but how I often did anyway." She peered onto a shelf that held clipboards and other office supplies. "Looks like we have plenty of pencils. Do you think I could borrow a couple?"

"Go ahead. We have supply problems with just about everything else, but not with pencils, I don't think."

Sini pocketed a few, then returned her attention to the form. "Now, where were we? Syringes?"

Something had happened to Sini, and Leila wanted to know what. She folded her arms and raised her eyebrows. "I recognize that look. It's the one I wore after Jaakob first kissed me."

Sini's cheeks flushed bright pink, but she focused intently on the clipboard. "I don't know what you mean." Even her neck and ears were coloring.

Taking inventory could wait a minute. Leila sat on a nearby bench and patted the surface. Sini sat mechanically, her knuckles turning white as she clutched the clipboard.

"So who is he?"

Sini's eyes widened, and she shook her head vehemently. "No, there's—"

Leaning in, Leila whispered, "I won't tell anyone that you're fraternizing with a soldier." Fraternization was grounds for a Lotta's dismissal. She wouldn't do that to a friend. Besides, Leila needed something light and fun to distract her, and talk of Sini's crush on a soldier might be just the thing.

"Well . . ." Sini cleared her throat. "The truth is . . . I'm *not* fraternizing . . . with a soldier." She returned to picking at the pencil lead.

"You're admiring each other from afar?" Leila said with a nudge. "If you ever want to talk about it, I won't tell. You can trust me."

"I—" Sini's voice cut off as she looked at Leila then lowered her gaze again, almost as if she were guilty of a crime.

"Finding a soldier attractive isn't anything to be ashamed about," Leila said. "Neither is flirting with one."

A hesitant smile and flushed cheeks returned to Sini's face. Trying to contain her grin, she bit her lip and nodded. "Nothing can come of it, of course. I doubt he sees me the same way. Men never have."

"Oh, that can't be true," Leila said. "You're pretty, you're smart, and you're a hard worker. Any man would be crazy not to notice you and want you on his arm."

Sini searched Leila's face as if she'd lost her mind. Then Sini shook her head and laughed. "Oh, that's—that's so funny."

"What?" Leila asked, genuinely confused. "I meant it."

"I know." Sini said, shaking her head. She wiped her eyes. "You don't know what it's like . . . you really don't."

"What are you talking about?"

"I bet you've always had boys chasing you, even in first grade." Sini's voice softened into a more somber tone. "You don't know what it's like to wish—to yearn—that a special boy, or a certain man, would see you that way. You—" Her voice caught, and she lowered her face to her lap. "You *really* don't know what you're saying."

Leila sat there, stunned, completely confused as to what she'd said to spark such a reaction, or why Sini would say such things. "I'm so sorry. I didn't mean to offend you, I—"

"No apology needed." Sini stood. "Let's inventory." She returned to the open cupboard.

Leila remained on the bench, staring at her. What had just happened? Why wouldn't Sini look at Leila? Had they gone to school together, and Leila had forgotten? There was definitely a detail she was missing, but what? Sini spoke of Leila's past as if they'd known each other a long time. It made no sense.

She thought back to her nightmare a couple of weeks ago. How Sini had calmed her and spoken words of comfort. She'd thought they'd found a kernel of friendship, but then what would upset Sini so much that she didn't want to speak?

"I'm sorry if I offended you," Leila said. "I honestly didn't—"

"I've lived in the same apartment for several years now," Sini said, interrupting but not turning to face Leila. "I live directly below a man who is handsome and smart. Funny. Loyal. We're good friends. I've spent years hoping that our friendship would become more."

"How do you know he doesn't want more too?" Leila joined Sini at the cupboard but moved slowly, as if approaching a wounded cat. "Maybe he's too shy to say anything."

"No, he's not shy." Sini laughed bitterly and finally turned around. "His heart is already taken. He often talks of the woman he's been in love with for years. And it's *not* me." Sini licked her lips and went on thoughtfully, picking at the tip of the pencil again.

"How can you be sure?" Leila asked.

Sini chuckled through her tears and hugged herself. "Do you remember the day we met? How we have a mutual friend?"

Sudden understanding came over Leila. "Of course. Marko." She looked into the cupboard without registering what it contained. "I didn't realize he was in love with anyone."

"He's been in love with the same woman for most of his life," Sini said. "She married his best friend."

The pieces fell into place in Leila's head like the tumblers of a lock. Her head came up with a start as a mental door opened with understanding. She heard a gasp, and after her hand flew to her mouth, realized the sound came from her. As the truth sank in, she lowered her hand.

"Are you sure?"

"Quite sure," Sini said. "He often told me about how beautiful and wonderful you are."

"Stupid man." She muttered under her breath. "You must hate me."

"No, I don't," Sini said. "You *are* wonderful. I've seen for myself that you're kind and smart. You're *so* good at what you do. You're obviously a wonderful mother. On top of all that—as if that weren't enough—you *are* beautiful." Sini smiled and shrugged. "Honestly, when I first got here, I wished I could hate you. But how can I hate someone so *nice*? You've become a friend to me—the only friend I have out here. That means more than you'll ever know."

Leila's brow still wrinkled with concern. "I had no idea."

"I know. There's no reason Marko would have mentioned me. I'm just his downstairs neighbor." She sighed, but the hint of a smile appeared. "Being away from him has been good for me. I had a moment today that I admit was rather enjoyable. I might have imagined it, but I thought someone showed a *little* interest in me. And it felt . . ." Her voice trailed off, and she smiled broadly. She picked at the pencil tip and shrugged, blushing again.

"I hope this guy has more between his ears than Marko," Leila said.

Had the fool really kept a candle burning for her all these years? Why had he never said anything?

And why did I never see it?

Now that the truth had been laid bare by Sini, the signs seemed obvious to Leila: the small acts of kindness, the long talks. Even that night sitting together on Aunt Sisko's couch, when he'd kissed her palm and said he'd do anything for her. Her entire past looked different now.

Leila took the clipboard from Sini and set it on a shelf. She took Sini's hand and dragged her back to the bench. "Tell me all about the secret man who likes you."

"Who *might* like me," Sini hedged.

No one was operating in the other room, no calls of incoming casualties had arrived, so for the moment, the two of them had privacy.

"Tell me everything you know," Leila said. "I want to hear everything."

"I don't know much about him," Sini said hesitantly. "His mother was born in Oulu."

"And?"

"He's tall. Broad shoulders. *Very* nice build. And he has the most gorgeous blue eyes."

Leila had every intention of drawing as much of the story out as she could. She had plenty to make up to Sini, wrongs she hadn't known about but which she was determined to make right. Sini's entire being seemed to glow as she spoke of her mystery man.

That was a start.

CHAPTER FIFTEEN

Night of December 24–25

Christmas Eve supper, typically the largest and grandest meal of the holiday, had been humble. It was also Sini's first without Marko in three years. The camp kitchen had served ham—canned, not baked—but with the traditional hot mustard. No carrot casserole, but they'd made a rutabaga one. That was about as fancy as a row of stoves in an indoor field kitchen could do. The casserole burned on the bottom, but to Sini, it still tasted like ambrosia.

At first she wondered why this Christmas Eve felt peaceful—almost happy—compared to the last several. Then she realized that she hadn't worried about how she looked or what Marko would think of her or her cooking, not for a single moment. No wonder even a simple rutabaga casserole had tasted so good.

Now *that* was freedom.

She'd added a pat of butter and shook some salt onto the top for extra flavor and finished off her serving, enjoying every bite.

Christmas morning, Sini stirred one of the large pots of rice porridge, a food usually served for a holiday dessert. Today it served as breakfast. She shook a jar of almonds over the pot, then stirred the nuts in.

Tradition held that the lucky person who got the almond would have a happy year. As she stirred the thick mixture and watched the nuts disappear into it, she wished that the superstition were true—that she or someone else would have a lucky year simply by finding an almond.

Of course, if it had been real, pouring dozens of almonds into a single pot would have been a cheat; just about every serving would have an almond, and some would have several.

She was tempted to pour in the entire can of almonds, as if that might help Finland beat the Soviets, or at least that more nuts would mean that the doctors would be able to keep more wounded soldiers alive. Heaven only knew that they could use all the luck they could scrape up.

As the last almond disappeared beneath the surface, she made a wish, as if she were blowing out birthday candles, that the extra almonds would indeed bring luck rather than tempt fate to send the opposite. In that moment, she almost believed in the luck. After all, Nikolai still hadn't been found, and how could that be due to anything other than luck?

She hadn't figured out a way for him to get back over the border safely, and she certainly hadn't had the heart to turn him in. But she knew full well that he was less and less likely to remain hidden, and no amount of wishful thinking over almonds would keep him undiscovered indefinitely.

All of the front lines had heated up with action in recent days, along many sections of the border, especially near rail lines and roads. Though this area would still be active, the camp wasn't as busy as it had been, as casualties were more heavily concentrated in other areas—especially along the Karelian Isthmus. As a result, some of the medical personnel had begun to be transferred elsewhere. The camp wouldn't be disbanded, but it had begun to shrink.

A smaller camp meant fewer mouths. At first, Sini was glad for that; the food storage would last longer. But with each trip she took to the dugout to fetch a sack of sugar or flour—and bring whatever she could to Nikolai—she was keenly aware that Raisa wasn't ordering as much food to replace what had been eaten. Fewer mouths also meant less food storage was needed. And that made hiding Nikolai harder by the day.

Sini took a break from stirring long enough to reach into the almond bottle on the counter and sneak one into her mouth. She bit down hard, as if doing so would mean that she'd consumed any luck it held.

The first almond is the lucky one. No matter that she'd just invented the rule.

Using dishcloths to protect her hands, she grabbed the pot handles and carried it out front to the serving table, where she exchanged it from an empty one with Annika, another Lotta, who dipped her ladle into the new pot. Two doctors entered as Sini headed back to the kitchen with the empty pot, and the men's conversation carried to her.

"True," one said, "but Kolla can't hold much longer. We need another victory."

Sini stepped through the kitchen door but stayed just beyond the threshold, listening. Whether from a deep-seated need or from morbid curiosity, she didn't know, but she felt an urgency to hear the latest news of the war. She hadn't been able to read a newspaper or magazine in days, and her new tent didn't have a radio.

"What about the Hirvasharju?" the other doctor said as they approached the serving table. Sini heard clanking as the men each took a bowl from the stack.

"Sure, recapturing the hotel was *technically* a victory," the first conceded. "But at what price? Many lives lost. In some cases, their sanity was lost."

"Which is as bad as death."

"Or worse," the first countered. "Do I have to remind you—"

"No," the second jumped in quickly, cutting the first one off. "I know we're outmanned and outgunned. But we've finally regained control of some areas now. Some areas that have seen a fair amount of fighting are quiet now. All I'm saying is that it's possible we're wearing them out."

Sini found herself twisting the dishcloths she'd used to carry the pot. She hoped he was right, but deep down knew that their side couldn't win so easily. Or at all, really.

The first officer snorted. "*Quiet* isn't necessarily a good sign. The Russkies are planning something. Just wait and see. They aren't anywhere near done with us."

The clunk of the ladle sounded as Annika served their porridge, and Sini heard them move to the other end of the mess hall to eat. She walked to a nearby counter, where she smoothed the dishcloths and folded them. No sense in thinking about other areas of the war. She knew better than to listen to such speculation.

From where she stood now, she could no longer hear the officers' continued debate anyway, so she returned to work, tackling a mountain of dirty dishes.

As loudly as she could, she washed pots and bowls and spoons and stacked them in wide drying racks above the sinks, but no amount of noise kept the truth from her thoughts, and truth always brought dread with it: The Mannerheim Line was the only thing keeping Stalin from the capital. If the Line fell, so would Helsinki. If Helsinki fell, so would the nation.

She'd never been to the Karelian Isthmus, but she'd heard about how it had the fewest trees of any part of the border as well as the least amount of swampland. She couldn't quite imagine what the landscape would look like without either a city, or forest and water everywhere.

But along the Mannerheim Line, Finnish infantry faced Russian tanks, which could drive side by side instead of following a twisting forest road. With so much additional Soviet firepower, the Mannerheim Line naturally needed more men, more ammunition, and the only artillery the army had. The Mannerheim Line was their strongest defense, but even it might not be enough.

She understood why more and more men were being sent south to that neck of land. Her Lotta side knew the necessity of the decision, but she couldn't help worrying that they'd have more transfers out of camp.

For two weeks, no one had discovered him—a feat unlikely enough to make Sini believe in miracles. But she wasn't foolish enough to assume he'd stay hidden if the food storage emptied much further.

Raisa appeared from her office. "Could you get a start on tonight's soup?"

"Of course," Sini said. She checked the chalkboard that listed upcoming meals, then went to a shelf to get several cans of fish for the soup.

If we get through this war free, with Nikolai undiscovered and safely across the border, I may start believing in miracles.

She gripped the can opener more aggressively than needed as she opened it. For days, she'd hoped that focusing on her work would keep her distracted. The strategy hadn't worked at all.

From the stove, Pilvi called for Sini to bring another pot out front. Sini left the can on the counter and fetched the pot of rice pudding. She checked the pitchers out front to see which needed to be refilled with milk, and while she did so, she heard one more bit of conversation. The officers had dropped off their dirty dishes in a bin near her and turned to leave.

"It can't all be happy coincidence and *sisu* that's gotten us this far. It's a miracle we've lasted this long, and you know it."

The word *miracle* echoed in her mind. *I'm not the only one thinking like that.*

She was vaguely aware of the door slamming in the other room, of the half-open can in the kitchen, of the heavy pot she was supposed to bring to the table, of her aching feet. But she didn't move, just stared at the counter and questioned everything.

Was this war a miracle? If so, it was a pretty miserable, hideous one, with unthinkable suffering. Yet so many things had happened that defied any other explanation. Again and again, small groups of Finns—handfuls, really—had held off *thousands* of Russians. Mannerheim himself hadn't believed some of the numbers until he'd seen the weapons and ammo collected from the dead.

If there was a God, Sini reasoned, He cared for her country, but not for individuals. Certainly not for her.

He hadn't cared when she was a child, when she'd been passed between relatives like a ratty dog. In her teen years, she hadn't mattered enough to garner God's notice, when her *lukio* classmates paired off, but she never went on a single date. And He certainly hadn't helped during her many years of yearning for the love of a man or for something other girls seemed to have naturally: a best friend.

Maybe if she'd gone to that private girls' school, she'd at least have had a best friend. She'd heard some relatives whispering about how her mother had wanted that for her, but Aunt Ritva and Aunt Mirva wouldn't hear of spending money on tuition.

Maybe if she'd finished *lukio* and gone on to a university, she'd have a best friend and a man who loved her.

So many maybes.

The can's top gave way. Sini gripped the edge to pry it off, mad at herself yet again for not finishing. How many thousands of things had she missed out on because she'd abandoned her studies? Thousands of opportunities she could only guess at. She twisted the lid, trying to make the last bit of metal break. Impatient, Sini yanked it and felt a sharp stab. A thin red line bloomed on her thumb. She swore before putting her bleeding thumb in her mouth to ease the sting. Should she go see a nurse? She'd been given some immunizations when she'd reported on the day of her departure. Was tetanus among them? What were the chances of getting an infection?

She looked at the cut; it didn't look all that deep, but it was bleeding a lot. She grabbed a clean dishcloth and pressed it to the wound as Leila had taught her.

Leila's a friend. The thought sounded like someone else's voice. With the cloth pressed against the cut, Sini leaned backward against the counter. Even with the sting of the cut, a smile parted her lips at the reminder of Leila—the closest friend Sini had ever had.

They weren't best friends in the typical sense, of course; they'd known each other a short time. And Leila probably meant more to Sini than Sini did to her. Besides, Leila was the type who'd probably had ten or more "best" friends as a girl, and undoubtedly had one now, too.

Sini still imagined their friendship continuing after the war—and the image didn't seem like an unattainable dream. That counted for something.

Maybe after the war, God willing, I'll have Nikolai, too.

She smiled wider, both at the thought of being with him, and at the irony of bringing God into her vision of the future.

Her middle warmed just thinking of Nikolai. Something special had started to grow—slowly—between them. Each time she brought him food or other supplies, he insisted she stay awhile. By the light of the tiny window near the ceiling, or sometimes a candle, they talked and talked.

He asked about her, questions no one had ever cared enough to be curious about. She'd gotten used to his arm about her shoulders. She, Sini, felt entirely comfortable and natural with a man's arm around her.

He may do that to keep us warm, she thought. *But it could mean more.*

Now, whenever she imagined her future, Nikolai was in it. If dreams could come true, if there was a God, then somehow, she and Nikolai would be together after the war. How, she could not fathom, but she had to hold on to hope.

How strange that in the middle of a horrible war and such suffering for others all around, she'd found the friendship and love she'd dreamed of all her life. She lifted her gaze to the ceiling as if she could see a heavenly throne and mouthed, *Thank you.* The closest thing to a prayer she let herself say in the moment.

She turned back around and emptied the can into a pot, still smiling. Who would have thought she'd find friendship—and more—in a hellish war?

CHAPTER SIXTEEN

December 25—Christmas Day

Before Sini's shift on Christmas Day, a fellow tentmate, Marianne, had returned from her own shift in the camp main office. She sat on her cot and opened a Christmas care package. Sini watched with a bit of interest and a lot of wonder—not quite envy at not having family who would send such a thing, but something near it.

Marianne pulled out a notebook and laughed. "My mother still thinks I'm going to be an artist someday, all because I loved to draw when I was in primary school." She tossed the sketchpad onto her cot. "Anyone want that?" she asked as she looked into her box and pulled out jelly candies—the green ones Sini had loved as a girl.

The candies didn't capture her attention this time, however—the sketchpad did. She nearly jumped across the circular tent to claim the book. Not just any notebook, and not loose sheets of paper, but an actual sketchpad, with the kind of paper intended for drawing.

"Here. You can have these, too," Marianne said, then handed a small rectangular tin out for Sini.

She took it and read the writing on it: inside were six drawing pencils of different hardness. "This is wonderful," she said, taking both the pad and the pencils. "Thank you."

"No problem," she said, and continued rummaging through the care package she'd received for the holiday.

"Thank you," Sini said, heading back to her cot.

"Merry Christmas." Marianne tossed a smile at Sini and continued working through her package.

"You, too."

Marianne had no idea how much she'd just improved that Christmas.

When it was time to leave for her shift, Sini hid the pencils in her coat pocket, but the sketchpad, though small, was too big to fit into any of her pockets, so she held it under her coat and walked to the kitchens with her arms folded, holding the book shape close.

The kitchen was a bit more energetic than usual, surely due to the festivities. Raisa, however, was grumpier than usual—surely due to imbibing a bit too much during her own celebrations the night before.

As she had for the last few days, Sini volunteered to make dugout runs any time someone so much as mentioned a possible trip there. She often brought back additional kitchen supplies to lower the odds of anyone else making a trip when she wasn't on duty.

Each time, Sini dropped whatever she was doing and jumped to volunteer, often opening the door to go outside before her arms had slid into her coat sleeves. Once outside, she ran the whole way there, scarf waving behind her, so she could stay an extra minute or two without raising suspicions. Inside, she shared whatever food she'd stashed into her coat and skirt pockets.

She was able to make two such trips during her shift, but she didn't give Nikolai the art supplies yet, only some food and a bottle of milk. She'd wait until after her shift to visit him, when she wouldn't be rushed.

After she left the kitchen, she slipped the sketchpad out from behind some cutting boards, where she'd hid it that morning. She held it under her coat again and headed to the dugout.

After finding Nikolai, Sini had asked for permission to bring some candles to the storage area. Raisa agreed, likely to keep Sini so willing to make the trek to the dugout.

Out of caution, Nikolai hadn't used the candles much. Any light seeping through the door cracks could mean he'd be found. Besides, he didn't want to risk a fire or being overtaken by fumes.

The day after the candles, she'd brought him a flashlight that had been left under a table in the mess hall. With so much snow and darkness, losing such items wouldn't raise many eyebrows, and neither would someone being unable to find them.

Batteries weren't as easy to come by as she'd expected, and while they didn't produce poisonous fumes, a flashlight was still dangerous. Even blocking the window wasn't a guarantee that a crack of light wasn't leaking to the above-ground world, so he kept his use of the flashlight to a minimum as well.

Over the last three days, she'd also found him a coat left behind by a soldier who'd died, two blankets from the infirmary, and a pair of old socks. The sudden loss of minor supplies from various parts of camp had been noticed by a few people, making her extra cautious moving forward and making Marianne's gift that much more welcome. The pad and pencils were exactly what Nikolai wanted, and not a soul would miss them.

Walking to the dugout, Sini listed the items she'd already given to Nikolai and felt an odd mixture of pride and guilt over her success. And yet.

She was pilfering supplies her country needed and giving them to the enemy. At least, that's how it would look to an outsider. Her step slowed, and she looked over the camp. No. The country was suffering, was on the verge of falling, but not because a Lotta had taken a flashlight and a few other minor things no one had been using anyway.

Sini reached the dugout and opened the door with only one hand to keep the sketchpad from falling. When she'd gotten inside and secured the door, she whispered, "It's me."

As usual, he didn't come into view on hearing her call; they'd agreed that he should stay hidden until she rounded the corner. She walked to the side of the dugout where he hid. Turning the corner, she reached out and supported herself against the logs that lined the wall.

The full moon cast a silver beam through the little window, lighting up the side of Nikolai's face. He was smiling at her. "Merry Christmas," he said.

"Merry Christmas." Sini stepped forward, still holding the sketchpad under her coat with one hand as she made her way toward him.

He stood and held out a hand, a smile brightening his face, which made him look even more handsome. She'd never seen him like this—at ease, peaceful, happy. "I have something for you. A gift."

"You do?" Curious, she crossed to their bench of flour sacks and sat on it, not removing her coat yet—not until she'd given him *his* gift.

He bent his knees and reached between two crates, then withdrew the same stack of papers he'd shown her before. He looked from the page to her and back again, then separated the top paper from the stack and held it out to her.

Curious, Sini stood and took the paper, stepping sideways toward the window and lifting the paper so moonlight would spill across it and she could make out what he'd given her—a drawing. More specifically, a portrait of a woman from the waist up, reaching out as if beckoning the viewer to follow. Her Lotta uniform was unmistakable, as was the watch on the wrist of the extended hand. It was a picture of *her*.

Sort of. This was a beautiful woman with strength and intelligence behind her eyes, none of which Sini felt she could lay claim to.

"This is amazing," she said. "You didn't have a picture or anything."

He tapped the side of his head. "Didn't need more than what I have in here."

"You took a few liberties," Sini said, still looking at the drawing. She wished she did have some smooth skin, such perfect cheekbones and a nose that angled elegantly.

"I didn't do you justice," Nikolai said. "I could do better with the model herself sitting for me. But I'm out of paper, so that will have to wait."

"Hm. I may be able to help with that." Sini set the picture atop a crate that served as Nikolai's nightstand, then reached into her coat and withdrew the sketchpad. "Here. Brand new. For you."

"Really?" Nikolai took the book and stroked the cover, then opened it and flipped through the pages, breathed in the scent as he fanned the paper under his nose. "This is perfect. Thank you."

"I'm not quite done yet." She reached into her coat pocket and withdrew the tin of pencils. "These will do a much better job than the stubs of pencils from the infirmary."

With almost a reverence in his movements, Nikolai took the tin and opened it. He held up each one to the moonlight and smiled more broadly with each one. "Thank you. Truly."

"I have an idea," Sini said suddenly. "Come here."

She jerked her head toward the door and headed that direction. Nikolai quirked his head in confusion, but she waved him forward. "It's late, it's dark, and most of camp is drunk, enjoying sauna, or playing cards. I know a spot in the woods where you can stretch your legs a bit and get some fresh air." She headed toward the door.

"You're sure it's safe?" The only times he'd been outside were for very quick trips to relieve himself in the way a bottle wouldn't suffice.

She grinned at him. "No more dangerous than harboring a Russian soldier in a storage cellar."

She walked up the incline and looked around, holding her hand out to Nikolai as a signal to stay hidden until the coast was clear. Sini looked about but saw and heard no one. "Come!" she whispered. "This way."

Clutching the sketchpad, Nikolai followed her. She closed the door quietly then hurriedly led the way into the woods. They were soon up to their thighs in snow, but she pressed on, remembering a big gray boulder they could sit on.

They moved wordlessly, the only sounds that of their clothing swishing against the snow with each step. When they were a good hundred meters from camp—but still close enough for Sini to find her way back—there was the boulder.

"Here," she whispered, and climbed onto it.

He did the same. When he sat beside her, he put his arm around her shoulders. The gesture was entirely natural now. Sini leaned her head against his shoulder.

They sat there for several minutes in silence, enjoying the untouched winter scene before them, lit by the full moon shining through the trees.

"Isn't it beautiful?" she whispered.

"It is," Nikolai agreed. "Feels like home."

"I hadn't thought of Russia having a landscape like ours, but it makes sense. Leningrad isn't *that* far from here."

"That's not what I meant," Nikolai said. "I mean, parts of Russia do look similar, but I miss Finland. In many ways, it's my real home."

Sini lifted her head enough to look at his face. "I thought you grew up in Leningrad."

"I did, mostly. We spent my first six years here, in Oulu. Being back in Finland really feels like coming home."

She rested her head against his shoulder once more and retraced the thoughts she'd had on her way to visit Nikolai— how she'd felt like a compassionate, good person on one hand and a traitor to her country on the other. How others would see her as a traitor.

But she couldn't see Nikolai like that. As far as she was concerned, he was Finnish. Just unlucky enough to have lived most of his life in Russia. Unfortunate enough to be sent to fight Finland as a Russian.

"I wish my father had been able to immigrate to Finland," Nikolai said after a moment.

"Did the Soviet government forbid it?" she'd asked.

"He never tried, so we'll never know. He wanted to."

"But?"

"But he had a good job, and we lived in an apartment we didn't have to share with another family. He was afraid of losing all of that." With his arm still around her shoulders, he began thoughtfully stroking her shoulder with his thumb.

"But if he'd come, he and your family would have had that and more," Sini said.

"That's what my mother said." He chuckled, and Sini wished she could see his expression even as she rested in his embrace, feeling his heartbeat against her cheek. "He was intelligent. A physicist working for the government."

"Oh, I'm sure he could have found a very good position here at a university or a lab or something."

"I'm sure you're right." Nikolai sighed. "But he worked for the government, and let's just say that Soviet leaders aren't known for be willing to give up something they see as a valuable asset. His work was largely with the military. The government needed him, and they feared he'd share their secrets with their enemies if he ever left."

"Goodness," Sini said under her breath.

Nikolai murmured in agreement and continued. "He received threats that warned him not to try to defect, or he'd be charged with treason. We stayed because of what he was sure they'd do to me and my mother if we went back to Finland."

A hand flew to Sini's mouth. "I can't imagine . . ." Her voice trailed off as she tried to imagine a young mother trying to manage in a strange country, a strange language written with a different alphabet, and living in fear that the government might decide to do away with her and her son.

"Papa told her to take me back across the border, but she refused. Especially after he was arrested. She felt certain that if she left Leningrad, she'd never see him again."

"Did she see him while he was in prison, then?"

"No." He let out another big sigh. "At least, not yet. He was arrested fifteen years ago. They wouldn't tell her where he was being held. For all we know, he could be at a workcamp in Siberia. Or, he could be . . . dead."

The last sounded difficult for him to get out. Sini raised her face to his and placed a hand on his leg. "I'm so sorry."

His eyes looked glassy as he stared into the distant trees. "Before I left for the war, she held my face and cried, saying that she should have taken me back, but now I had to fight my own people."

Sini took his hand from her shoulder—it was freezing cold, so she held it between her hands.

"Can you imagine if my mother and I *had* returned when my father said we should? I might have still ended up right here in this camp with you, but in a Finnish uniform."

"Maybe," she said thoughtfully, doubtfully. He showed her affection and seemed to like her, but that was likely because she was the only woman—the only person—he had contact with right now.

"Then again, if we'd come over the border back then, I probably would have been assigned somewhere else. It's thanks to my mother staying in Leningrad that I met you. I wouldn't be here in this camp otherwise." Nikolai's voice had grown warm. He leaned his head against hers. "Seems like a pretty great way for fate to make up the loss, don't you?"

He turned his head and pressed his lips to her hair. Sini inhaled with her eyes closed, memorizing everything about the moment so she could recall it later, relive it again and again.

"Can I draw you?" he asked suddenly. "Before we both freeze." He laughed.

She tilted her head to gaze at the moon. "Sure."

He took the tin of pencils from his trouser pocket and removed one from it, then moved an arm's length away from Sini and told her how to sit, where to hold her hands, how to tilt her head so the moonlight would give him the right play of light and shadow.

By the time he finished, and they got him safely back into hiding—a close call thanks to someone getting off kitchen duty right as she closed the dugout door—Sini had no idea how long they'd been outside. She didn't feel the cold as she normally would have, and she nearly floated back to her tent, now holding something else safely under her coat: two pieces of paper, each bearing a portrait of herself done by Nikolai.

Sini saw Leila on the way back to the tent. Her friend eyed Sini. "You look awfully happy right now."

"I am quite happy right now," Sini said evasively. "It's been a good Christmas."

Leila gave her a quizzical look. "Because of the mystery soldier you're not fraternizing with?" Her tone made it clear that she didn't think that fraternizing was a bad thing at all—and that she assumed Sini was doing that very thing. So far, Leila hadn't guessed that the object of Sini's interest was Russian.

Leila smiled knowingly at Sini before they entered the tent. "I hope you get to end your happy Christmas with sweet dreams of your friend."

"I hope so too."

But as Leila went into the tent, Sini's smile dropped a little. If Leila ever learned of Nikolai, their friendship would be over.

CHAPTER SEVENTEEN

December 26

As Sini wiped counters in the kitchen, she counted the minutes until her break. As soon as the final minute had ticked past, she untied her apron, not wasting a moment.

"Taking my break," she called to Raisa and the other Lottas. Casually, she hung her apron on a peg and put on her coat, pockets heavy with food.

After pushing through the doors, she held her hands against her pockets so their bulges wouldn't give her away, and her coat wouldn't swing, sag, clank, or rattle. She had two empty bottles and one of water today. The empty ones would serve as his makeshift lavatory for today.

She'd thought of the idea thanks to her uncles, who'd once talked about using bottles for such a use while on hunting trips. As a girl, she'd been disgusted by the idea. But at ten, on a long drive to Rovaniemi with Uncle Vesa's family, she'd been envious of the ease with which he and his sons could relieve themselves—an envy that grew when he refused to let her stop for bathroom breaks. From the back of the car, she wished that girls, too, could simply pee into a bottle. They'd managed to slip him outside a couple of times at night for the *other* biological function a bottle couldn't address.

This was the fifth day she'd been bringing bottles and food to Nikolai. That morning, she'd found him a shirt and a knit cap to add to his supplies.

She could hardly believe it had been nearly a week, yet she'd gotten into a familiar routine. Noting extra items lying around had become second nature. In addition to food, water, and empty bottles, she brought soap and washcloths to wash with to reduce any body odor that might give him away. She rather enjoyed visiting him right after he'd washed.

After each visit, she made a quick trip to the garbage to dispose of the used bottles, making sure they were covered with other trash. Old bottles weren't thrown away, but saved to be made into Molotov cocktails. Sometimes she felt a twinge of guilt over throwing away perfectly good bottles; Molotov cocktails were one of the few weapons their side had found success with. With such a weapon shortage, the state liquor board started donating bottles to the cause. And she was throwing them away.

She assured herself that there were too few bottles coming from this camp to matter at any of the battlefronts, though she had no evidence of that either way.

Today, Sini had also brought chocolate, which Leila had received in her aunt's care package and shared with Sini. Of course, even Fazer chocolate tasted sweeter when shared.

When she reached the dugout, she stepped onto the hard floor. To her left stood the flour sacks she'd stacked to look like a wall. Nikolai spent most of his time in the small gap between the sacks and the wall.

Normally, as soon as she entered, she lit the lamp, then called out to him, so he'd know who was entering. This time, she didn't dare use the lamp; no one had sent her on an errand, she was off shift, and lamplight leaking through the tiny window or through the door could draw attention.

She headed around the false wall. Night had fallen, so she couldn't see much. In spite of her care, her toe caught the edge of a crate. A shock of pain went through her; she had to hold back a cry as she stumbled and caught herself on a sack of onions. Deciding that cries of pain would draw more attention than a sliver of light, she pulled out her pocket flashlight, intending to turn it on just long enough to gain her bearings.

The beam revealed Nikolai stripped to the waist, doing pushups, his hands braced on the flour sack she'd often sat on with him. Rather, he *had been* doing pushups. He held the position, his every muscle tense, as if waiting for an intruder to leave. He looked over and sagged with relief.

"Oh, good," he said. "When you didn't call out . . ." He didn't need to finish the thought. Nikolai faced the floor again as he pumped out ten more pushups. His arms and back flexed with the motion. The slight beard suited him—it had a hint of strawberry.

Sini couldn't help but stare—and want to pinch herself. How had she gotten so lucky as to spend any time with a being so perfect? He looked as if he'd descended from the legendary Ukko, leader of the gods.

Nikolai finally stood, picked up his shirt, then wiped his shining face. Coming to her senses, Sini clicked off the flashlight; it had been on too long. Even through the thick darkness, her mind could still see his perfect torso—broad shoulders, sculpted chest, trim waist. The underground room was cool, but not freezing, so she could understand how, after vigorous exercise, he'd take off his shirt.

How often has he exercised, and I've missed it? The question made her cheeks grow hot. Moonlight through the window was enough to make out general shapes. Thanks to her few seconds using the flashlight, she knew the path, so she walked forward.

Nikolai continued to wipe himself down. "Any chance you could find another bar of soap soon? It's almost gone."

"Already stashed another one for you," she said, walking toward him. "I'll bring it tomorrow." She stopped half an arm's length away. She wanted to reach out, touch his chest and stomach, make sure this wasn't an illusion.

"Didn't think I'd see you again tonight," he said, his voice husky. Was that emotion? Or was he simply whispering for safety?

She tried to shake off the shiny cobwebs that his physique had draped over her mind. She'd already come today; what excuse could she give for a second visit? That she'd missed him and didn't want to wait to see him until morning? That was the truth. But that would sound pathetic.

Nikolai saved her from having to answer by taking her hand and leading her to the flour sacks. They'd shrunk from being sat on so often. It had become a sofa of sorts for them. And a gym of sorts for him, apparently. She turned to the false wall and pulled down a new bag of flour.

"We need new furnishings," she said, trying to keep her voice light.

"We?" he said from right behind her, making her arms break out in goose bumps.

Oh, no, no, no. What was I thinking? I may be nothing but a friendly face and a source of meals, yet I sound as if we're a couple living together.

Yet they were genuine friends. Perhaps nothing more. She knew how that worked. But at least they were that much— friends. The secret hope that they'd become far more, that he'd feel for her what she already felt for him . . .

All a foolish dream, but she couldn't stop herself from feeling that way.

"Let me do that. Those are heavy." In a single effortless motion, he took the sack and laid it atop the compacted ones. Sini wished there were enough light to see his muscles flex as he did it. "There," he said, turning to her. "Now we have something more comfortable to sit on." He didn't sound annoyed or worried. What, then? Amused? But in a good way.

Her worries began melting, warming her from the inside out. Nikolai sat on the stack and patted a space beside him. Normally he scooted to the far edge. This time it would be a snug fit. She didn't mind at all.

With her heart rate going crazy, she felt hot, so she slipped off her coat. With it draped over her arm, she withdrew the supplies, set them beside the false wall, then squeezed next to Nikolai. She breathed in deeply, trying to relax. The effort failed; her heart fluttered like the patter of a machine gun.

Even after exercise, he smells good. A warning bell went off in her head like an air raid siren. *You're opening yourself to getting hurt again.* Of course he didn't see mousy Sini the same way she viewed him. How could he? He existed in the realm of legends, while she lived quite firmly in the plain reality of earth. She meant food, shelter, and safety. Of course he'd be friendly, perhaps even flirt. Currently, she was his only human connection.

But she couldn't deny a connection. Moments they seemed to communicate without words. Her day off when she'd visited, he'd held her close as they talked for hours. Could he have pretended for every single minute? *Something* of their time together had to be real.

Even if most of it had been an act, she couldn't find it in her to care much. She'd never been treated like this. Besides, even if he could contact his superiors, she had no information to share with him, no matter how much he made her swoon.

Nikolai glanced at his chest. "Oh. I, uh, should probably put this on." He raised his undershirt, balled in one hand. His uniform shirt lay nearby on a bag of potatoes.

She opened her mouth to say that no, he needn't bother, but couldn't get a word out. He slipped the shirt over his head and tugged it down.

What about Marko? she thought suddenly.

What about him? she argued back, annoyed at herself for having such a reaction, almost like a reflex. She owed Marko nothing. She took his mental image and ground it into nothingness like soldiers did with spent cigarettes, twisting the toe of their boots in the snow. Time she let herself think about another man, even a Russian one. Even if a future together was tenuous at best.

Nikolai slipped his arms into his uniform shirt and sat beside her again, not buttoning it over the undershirt. He took her hands. His were still warm from exercise. "You're cold."

She rested her head on his shoulder and closed her eyes, enjoying the feel of his big hands warming hers. She could have stayed there, content, for hours.

"What brings you here?"

She looked at her coat, now on her lap, felt the Fazer bars, which she'd left in the pocket, and lifted her head to tell him about the chocolate. And there was his face, oh so near. His gaze caught and held hers.

After a beat, during which she was certain he could hear her racing heart, she managed, "I came . . . to . . ."

Nikolai's eyes drifted to her lips. A jolt of anxiety went through Sini.

I didn't come to throw myself at you. She wanted to say it; she wasn't that kind of girl. But if he *wanted* to kiss her . . .

His eyes met hers again, now hinting at a smile. One eyebrow rose in silent question—asking permission. She swallowed against a tightness in her throat and reminded herself to breathe. After she managed two quick nods, he tilted his head to one side and drew nearer. But then he paused, as if wanting to be sure. What if he wouldn't kiss her after all? Anticipation erupted into a flame. She wanted to kiss Nikolai. The world, with all of its problems, vanished, leaving the two of them in the shadows, suspended in time. She nodded again, slower this time, so there would be no misunderstanding. She hadn't intended for this to happen. Hoped for it, perhaps . . .

For another moment, which felt like an eternity of torture, Nikolai looked toward the door and lifted a finger to his lips. Sure enough, there were footfalls. How had she *not* heard them?

The steps retreated, but Nikolai and Sini remained silent and motionless for a little longer. At last Nikolai shifted, and his gaze returned to hers. This time, he leaned closer, his lips so near she could feel an electric zing pass between them. She wanted to reach up, pull him close, but something held her back. She would wait for *him* to kiss *her*.

At last, he closed the distance. He softly pressed his lips to her lower one, then moved to her upper lip, kissing it so tenderly that she nearly melted like chocolate in the sun. He pulled back, eyes searching hers in the dim light. At last, their lips met fully, both satisfying and feeding her inner fire.

Sini threaded her fingers through his hair, so blonde it almost glowed in the dark. She closed her eyes, consumed by the moment. He held her, kissed her, again and more deeply. She held him, felt his chest against hers, and kissed him back.

When he pulled away, she trembled all over. Neither said a word. Sini pressed her hands to his chest and smoothed his shirt as if it had wrinkles, but really to feel close to him, to feel his heart beating fast, like hers, beneath her palm.

He put his hand atop hers, pinning her palm to his chest. "I probably shouldn't have kissed you."

She was about to protest, but a voice called in the distance. "Sini? Sini, where are you?"

Someone was looking for her because she hadn't returned to the tent. Maybe it was Leila. Or Raisa. It didn't matter who.

"I need to go." Sini stood and fumbled with her coat. She turned to leave, but Nikolai grabbed her hand. She turned back questioningly. He was little more than a silhouette; she couldn't make out his expression. She squeezed his in return, then remembered the chocolate. "Here. A gift." She pulled it from her coat pocket and tossed it. Somehow, he caught it in the dark. She wouldn't miss the chocolate; she'd just been given something even better.

She found Raisa, who was looking for her with a question about how many pounds of potatoes were left in the dugout. Sini gave her a quick answer then went back to her tent, only then letting herself grin over the memory of Nikolai's kiss. She'd have to explain her absence—and smile—to Leila and the others. One look at her ridiculous smile, and they'd think she'd lost her mind.

Not my mind, she thought as she turned on her flashlight to light the way. *But perhaps my heart.*

CHAPTER EIGHTEEN

December 29

The weeks since Pajari's raid had been the longest of Marko's life. After tending to the commander during his heart attack, he'd been rewarded with a transfer to a medical position. He'd assumed that meant a surgical hospital, not a first-responder station. He couldn't have been sent closer to the front unless he'd been assigned to be a plain old medic.

After Marko got his orders, he read them several times, as if the words would change on the page.

"Do good work at the aid station," a lieutenant said, "and maybe you'll get a hospital post."

"Maybe," Marko muttered, folding the papers and shoving them into his coat pocket.

Pajari had said that someone with his expertise should help the cause by saving the wounded. Didn't that mean more than patching up men in hopes that they'd reach a field hospital alive?

Maybe I can ask Pajari for a new assignment, he thought, then scoffed at the idea. *And maybe the summer solstice will appear in December.* That was as likely.

He was driven to an aid station at the northern tip of Tolvajärvi Lake. It was still part of greater Group Talvela, named after one of the highest-ranking generals, whom Pajari reported to.

The aid station proved to be a nightmare. Calling his living quarters a ramshackle hut was generous. Supplies consisted of little more than antiseptic and bandages. They had nothing to effectively treat the hypothermia that killed as many as infection did. They often warmed men with blankets so they wouldn't freeze to death, while trying to balance the opposite danger of warmth increasing circulation, making a soldier bleed to death.

On particularly lucky days, they received small amounts of morphine. While it didn't save lives, it eased the anguish a little, and that helped Marko from wanting to run into the woods and scream to get away from it all.

But they often went a week or more without a new shipment. No matter how much or how little morphine they had, no matter if they had casualties or hours without any, the cries of agony echoed in his head around the clock and likely would for the rest of his life.

He dreaded arrivals and the inevitable sight of clenched jaws and desperate moans. The sounds frayed what few nerves he had left by the time any morphine was thawed enough to use. Men writhed, crying for death, begging him to kill them, to end their misery.

Eventually, of necessity, he grew as numb as the toes in his boots, functioning as an automaton. If compassion threatened to bubble up, he shoved it back down. Emotion would break him, make him useless as a doctor.

The aid station consisted of three other men, but he never asked about their medical training. If they were surgeons, too, then he had no hope of leaving this hell hole. He loaded men onto ambulances, which were repurposed trucks and busses. He performed what they euphemistically called "improvised medicine"—stabilizing casualties, even the grossly wounded, as they were able, though with little hope that they'd survive the trip to a hospital.

Where Marko deserved to be.

More than once as an ambulance pulled away, he'd wanted to jump on board, then beg to stay at whatever hospital it arrived at, promising to do anything they asked. But that was all fantasy, of course. If he left his post for a hospital, he wouldn't be allowed to operate. Instead, he'd be court martialed.

So he worked through one of the coldest months on record. He rarely had complete feeling in his hands or feet, and he hardly slept. At last, someone noticed his efforts—a captain with a deep laceration in his thigh, which Marko had the time and supplies to stitch properly. That kind of thing was the closest to surgery he'd gotten.

"I'll put in a good word for you," the captain said. "It's a waste to the army to have you here." Marko hardly dared hope the man would remember his promise, or that if he did, that his word would have any effect.

But finally, an unfamiliar man arrived to take his place, with new orders for Marko. He read and read the words to be sure he wasn't dreaming. But yes, it was true. He'd be assigned to a hospital down south, near the Mannerheim Line, but first, he'd spend a week or two training at another field hospital.

"Driver's waiting to take you," the new arrival said.

"I leave now?" he asked, head coming around with a start. He hurried to his cot and threw his few belongings into his duffel bag. After slinging it over one shoulder, and without a goodbye to the others, he raced through the snow to the idling jeep and jumped inside.

The truck ate up snowy white kilometers, taking him farther from the nightmare he'd endured. As the distance between him and the aid station increased, he began to relax. Compared to what he'd seen and had to do, a hospital sounded like a dream, even one near the Mannerheim Line.

The driver wasn't talkative, leaving Marko to gaze at the scenery as they bumped along. It was always the same: snow- and ice-covered roads, thick forests of pine and other evergreens on either side of the white road. They could've driven the same road in a loop, a dozen times, and he wouldn't have known. Wouldn't have cared, either. This was far preferable to the hellish weeks he'd endured.

Part of him, the idealistic young surgeon who'd been ready to change the world with his hands, wondered if the compassionate side of him would ever thaw so he could be a feeling doctor again. Maybe with time. For now, his emotions were by necessity locked behind a thick wall of ice, where they'd stay until the war ended. He'd figure out how to melt the wall later.

Somehow, a few unwelcome emotions remained on this side of the wall: despair, hopelessness, fear. A reluctant acceptance that war was his existence. A future without war was hard to imagine in anything but vague terms.

The only spot of warmth he'd felt at the aid station had been in the wee small hours of the morning on nights he'd woken not from screaming soldiers begging for a bullet between the eyes but from utter quiet. A few times, he'd lain awake and comforted himself with thoughts of Leila. Picturing her face, imagining her voice, had kept him alive—had kept him human.

Now he relaxed into his seat and closed his eyes, tamping down the worry that a field hospital would be as bad as, or worse than, the aid station. The hospital behind the Line, which was under the worst of the artillery bombardment, would bring new atrocities he could only guess at, but at least he'd be able to use his surgical skills.

The jeep finally rumbled to a stop, and Marko got out. Carrying his duffel bag, he followed the driver and another man who met them and led the way, along with two other newly arrived doctors to their quarters. They passed a few camouflaged wooden bunkers, which would surely be warmer and safer than the old hut.

His quarters turned out to be one of several large, eight-sided tents like the one he'd stayed in when assigned to Pajari's raid. He stepped inside and walked to the small stove in the center to warm his hands. He looked around. This tent held more cots than there had been men at the aid station.

The rest of the day was a blur: unpacking, eating, being shown around the operating room and equipment. He wanted to collapse on his cot and sleep for days, but new wounded came in, so he scrubbed and operated with the others. Removing twisted bits of shrapnel from a soldier held a satisfaction he'd long waited for.

After closing his last patient for the day, he looked over his work. The stitches were straight and even, like a row of soldiers. The boy had lost a lot of blood, and despite a transfusion, would need another. Chances were high that he wouldn't make it. Marko had assumed that cases this severe were sent by train to hospitals in outlying cities, where they had access to more equipment. A few hours in the OR had taught him that serious injuries were too common for all of them to be sent far away by train.

He finished, then really looked at the soldier lying on his table—unconscious, stripped of his uniform. He looked child-like. How old was he? Surely a teenager.

This was Stalin's handiwork.

The bastard.

The anger Marko expected to build inside him was tempered by the wall of ice. He sighed and left the OR at the same moment a nurse came in to help move the patient to the infirmary.

As she passed, he had the strongest sense of déjà vu. He stopped and looked over his shoulder, but with the woman's surgical cap and mask in place, he couldn't make out much besides her height and hair color. Something about her, though . . . she'd even smelled like Leila. But she could be one of thousands of Finnish women.

Ridiculous. He grunted, annoyed at himself, then went to the dressing area, where he dropped onto a bench, exhausted.

He'd loved—and longed for—her for years. But he never thought he'd start seeing her in random women. What was next, hallucinations? With the stress of war, that was a possibility. He'd heard stories of commanders losing their minds in the middle of a losing battle—and believed every word of them.

Being deprived of sleep for weeks, seeing unimaginable horrors up close—all of that tended to wreak havoc on one's mind. So a nurse resembled Leila from the back. He had to stop thinking about her so much. That was why he saw her everywhere.

He tossed his surgical cap into the laundry bin and scrubbed his arms in the sink, hoping he'd be able to collapse into a dreamless sleep.

CHAPTER NINETEEN

December 31

As the fighting intensified along the Mannerheim Line, more medical personnel had been transferred south. That meant Sini found herself assigned to the infirmary more often, which she'd come to dread, and not only because of the sights and smells. She'd learned to tolerate them a little better than before, though after a shift around disease and infection, she had to force herself to eat supper. Infirmary shifts meant a day of nausea.

Spending time with Leila certainly improved matters, but Sini had a gnawing worry in her middle whenever she was in the infirmary, something that had nothing to do with the sounds of soldiers in pain or the sight of gangrene. Every minute she spent in the infirmary was a minute she wasn't assigned to the kitchen staff. Every hour that ticked by was one when someone else might have gone to the dugout.

She constantly worried that Nikolai would be discovered by another Lotta, though her imagination offered her scarier possibilities: what if an officer found him? The two men would certainly end up killing each other.

Almost as worrisome was the additional challenge of getting food and supplies for Nikolai—a much more difficult task now that she no longer spent her days around food and drink.

Out of necessity, her visits to Nikolai had become less frequent, but an hour rarely passed, even as she took temperatures, wrote on charts, and dispensed medications, without her strategizing when and how to visit him next, what she'd bring him, and how she'd smuggle the items into her pockets—and enough for more than a day, in case she couldn't visit the next.

The best chance to smuggle food out of the kitchen was during the nightly shift change, when there was more traffic going in and out of the kitchen, and especially when the supervisors switched and the one arriving mightn't know if Sini was supposed to be in the kitchen at that hour. She could slip in without being noticed. She did her best to make Nikolai's meals hearty, adding apples, rolls—anything she could find to tide him over until whenever she could bring him more.

Meanwhile, she became adept at washing and dressing wounds, emptying bedpans and doing many other jobs she would have thought impossible only a month before. She'd never have guessed that a handsome Russian soldier would provide ample distraction even from the infirmary.

On her shift today, New Year's Eve, she carried a bedpan to the outhouse—a job she didn't think she'd ever get used to. Last New Year's Eve, she'd enjoyed cocktails, melted tin horseshoes that were then dumped into a bucket of cold water to foretell her luck in the coming year. She'd been rather distracted by Marko. This year, she was distracted by a man, yes, but a different man.

She stepped into the outhouse and breathed through her mouth as she dumped the bedpan.

The action felt oddly similar to dumping the little pools of melted tin into the water bucket. What had the shapes of the tin predicted for this year? She couldn't remember, but last New Year's Eve certainly hadn't foretold anything about serving in a war, meeting the woman Marko was obsessed with, or finding herself falling in love with a Russian.

She hurried back to escape the biting cold, wondering why she'd ever wanted to escape the kitchen. She'd much rather have cracked knuckles and cold hands from peeling unending piles of potatoes than empty bedpans.

Besides, when she got those cold hands, she had more opportunities to have them warmed by Nikolai's warm ones.

More than once she had to catch her balance as she slipped on patches of ice. She was far too distracted; couldn't she navigate a path without her mind drifting to Nikolai? Her step caught a slick spot, and she landed unceremoniously on her backside. At least she'd fallen *after* emptying the bedpan. She laughed quietly to herself and got back to her feet.

The image of Nikolai's eager face awaiting her arrival, of his smile when their eyes met, the feel and taste of his kisses, all sent a warmth through her that even snow and ice couldn't penetrate.

See, Marko? she thought victoriously, stomping her boots outside the infirmary door. *I don't need you.*

She went inside, and as she disinfected the bedpan, she pointedly refused to think about *why* Nikolai cared for her. Whether he would've kissed any girl who'd hidden him and brought him food. Whether his affection was an act. The memory of his touch, his kisses—sometimes cupping her cheek with one palm, his fingers supporting the back of her head—were enough to make her believe he cared for her as much as she did for him, that she meant more to him than a way to survive.

At least he's aware that I'm a woman. That's more than I can say of a certain man.

Nikolai had been in the dugout for well over a week—far longer than she'd expected, and much longer than she'd thought possible. They'd managed the occasional visit outdoors in the middle of the night when fewer people were awake. He'd slipped into the woods for a few minutes so he could stretch his legs and get some fresh air. Sini stood watch to be sure the camp sentries wouldn't spot him.

She put the cleaned bedpan on a shelf and washed her hands. One of the other Lottas, Mia, entered from the infirmary, rubbing one hand across her forehead as she crossed to the linen closet. "We had a nice lull, but we were just radioed that more casualties are on their way." She counted out several bedsheets from the stack, then added, "Of course this happens after we've lost half the medical staff."

"Why here?" Sini asked. "Aren't we full?" She peered through the small window in the door to count empty beds.

"We're full," Mia said. "I'll have to push the cots closer together to make room for more, but we'll probably end up with men sleeping on the floor."

"Need help making beds?" Sini asked.

Though she hated aspects of working on the medical side of the camp, she always felt useful there. Anyone could peel potatoes and haul flour; not everyone could change bandages, sterilize instruments, or administer shots, all skills she'd recently gained. She'd also learned the names of most of the equipment and knew not only the names of medications but what they were for. Sometimes she felt like a real nurse and thought that maybe she was smart after all.

At night after a long day, she sometimes drifted off to sleep with thoughts of attempting a university education after the war—of becoming a nurse. Then the next time she faced oozing pus and bandages caked with dried blood, she reconsidered.

Yarn shops were peaceful, happy places, and they even smelled nice.

Mia brushed back a stray wisp of her hair then picked up the stack of sheets she'd counted out. "I've got things under control here, but Päivi sent word that they need help in surgery."

"I'll do the beds, then. You go to the OR."

The other Lotta held the sheets closer as if hugging them and shook her head. "You go."

"I'm not a surgical nurse," Sini said.

"I'm not any kind of nurse, either." Mia took a backward step toward the infirmary. "They probably just need someone to sterilize instruments and fetch supplies. With so many wounded." She was probably right, and that wouldn't be too bad.

"All right." Sini had used an autoclave to sterile instrument several times.

Outside, she felt the wind kick up, sending her heavy skirt to one side. She pulled her coat tighter at the neck and picked her way toward the white surgical building, which had a red cross on the side. At the door, she paused. Even working in a room near surgeries would be unnerving. If she were Catholic, she'd cross herself. She needed something to calm her twisting insides.

She entered the side room where medical personnel dressed and scrubbed. After hanging up her coat, she found a tray of instruments that appeared to have been washed—thank heavens—so she put them and other items she found into the autoclave to be sterilized. When it was full, she closed it and turned it on. She rechecked everything, not wanting her incompetence to cause someone a life-threatening infection.

That done, she crossed to a table with a clipboard to record what she'd done. She took the pencil, which was attached to the clipboard by a string, and wrote *autoclave*, and her initials and time next to the word. The next page on the clipboard had a list of things needing to be done. She was reading through the second page when the door from the OR swung open.

"Good, you're here," Päivi said, holding her hands up to keep them sterile. She must have opened the door with her hip.

Sini pointed to the autoclave. "I just got that started. Should I do laundry next?" Blood-covered scrubs filled the post-op bin.

"We need you in there." With a slight backward jerk of her head, Päivi indicated the operating room.

Sini's stomach soured. "But—"

"Hurry," Päivi said impatiently. "We need more hands. We have some surgeons who just arrived, but not enough nurses to assist. Three just got off shift and are probably sleeping. If I wake them now, they'll be useless later."

Not long ago, the infirmary had nearly done Sini in. Surgery would be a thousand times worse.

How can anyone expect me—

Sini forced her thoughts to cut off before arriving at specifics. If she let herself imagine organs and wounds, she'd pass out before walking through that door.

"I'm not a nurse," she said, wondering if Päivi had forgotten that detail. No one could think it a good idea to send a Lotta without medical training into surgery. The idea of standing beside a man who was cut open chilled her, as much as if someone had injected melted snow into her veins. She'd rather empty a thousand bedpans.

She'd grown tougher since first helping Leila, but she'd only recently stopped feeling queasy at the sight of needles. How would she stay standing if she had to watch scalpels cut through skin and muscle? She'd probably have to assist a doctor while he searched for shrapnel fragments embedded in flesh. She could already imagine the clink of metal—shrapnel dropped into a cup that she held.

"Scrub up," Päivi said, her tone turning irritated. "Hurry."

She turned toward the door, but Sini caught her sleeve. "First, I'd better check to see if Raisa needs me in the kitchen." A weak argument, and she knew it.

To her credit, the nurse smiled sympathetically. She took a step closer to Sini, hands still raised so they wouldn't touch anything. "You'll be assisting, not suturing or administering anesthesia or anything like that."

Sini remembered sitting across from the old woman at the Lotta Svärd office. *I promised to help however I'm needed. And now I'm needed in surgery.*

After a nervous swallow, Sini managed, "I'll be right in."

"Good." Päivi smiled; Sini could tell by the way her eyes crinkled above her surgical mask. "You've seen us scrubbing, right?"

"Yes," Sini said, hoping her voice didn't sound as terrified as she felt.

Päivi gave a few instructions anyway. "Put on a surgical gown first. Be sure to scrub everywhere—between your fingers and under your nails, too. Be thorough but quick." She disappeared, the door swinging behind her.

Sini stared after her, unmoving. *You have* sisu. *Do it.*

She went to the cupboard that held the surgical gowns, caps, and masks. She'd laundered and folded them but never thought she'd wear them. After donning a set, she moved to the sink. While she scrubbed, the words she'd spoken at the Lotta Svärd office repeated themselves in her mind like a chant, or a prayer.

Anything for my country. Anything for my country. Anything for my country.

When her hands and arms were pink and sore, she released the water pedal. She held her hands in the air as Päivi had, then nudged the door with her hip and stepped into the operating room.

Päivi met her with a pair of rubber gloves. "You're on table six."

To avoid seeing the operations underway, Sini kept her gaze on the floor as Päivi led her to the correct table. Bloodstains of various sizes and shades covered the cement floor. Her stomach turned. The smells of antiseptic, blood, and other things she couldn't identify assailed her nose. Clanks, snips, orders, and other noises created a disturbing symphony.

Päivi stopped at the foot of a table, prompting Sini to look up. "Nurse Hesanto has been working tables five and six. She'll be glad to pass one of them along to you."

Sini found Nurse Hesanto, who nodded. "Thank you so much for coming. I'll answer any questions you have."

"Where . . . what . . ." Sini had so many questions that she could hardly put words to any of them.

"Stand over here," Päivi said, walking to a spot on the far side of the table, by the wall. Sini walked over, looking desperately at Nurse Hesanto.

"I'll be on table one," Päivi said. "I'll check on you when I can."

"Thank you." Sini doubted her voice carried past her surgical mask; she'd made the mistake of glancing at the patient, and now she couldn't tear her eyes from the open abdomen.

Päivi spoke, addressing the surgeon at Sini's table. "Here is someone to assist you, Dr. Linna. She's not a nurse, but she's one of the best Lottas we have."

The meaning of Päivi's words took a moment to connect in Sini's mind, but when they did, her head shot up. She stared at the surgeon across from her. He wore full surgical gear, so only a little of his face was visible. His eyes were narrowed as he studied the belly of the unconscious soldier on the table.

"Thank you," he said offhandedly.

Sini knew that voice. She didn't need to see the brown hair under the cap, didn't need to remove the mask, to recognize the arched nose and the probing eyes. The mask concealed his chin, but she knew that if someone took it off, she'd see a cleft there, something that appeared only when he concentrated, as he was now. Even without hearing his voice, she'd have known that furrowed brow, those short, dark lashes. She gripped the table and gaped at Marko, waiting for him to look at her.

Päivi looked about to walk away, but then her eyes narrowed, and she turned to face Sini full on. "You look pale. Are you all right?"

"I'm a little lightheaded," Sini said in barely more than a whisper.

The other nurse grabbed a metal chair from the corner and placed it beside Sini. "Sit. Put your head between your knees."

Sini obeyed, and Päivi went on.

"Breathe deeply. Good." She gently rubbed Sini between her shoulder blades. The lightheadedness gradually passed, but Sini kept her head down. How to prepare herself to not only work beside a soldier who was hovering near death, but also to assist Marko?

She'd happily thought of him in only vague, disjointed terms since finding Nikolai. But now Marko's name and presence, even when he was utterly unaware of her, sent her reeling.

CHAPTER TWENTY

Hearing Marko's name was definitely a shock, but the excitement and thrill she waited for never came.

Päivi continued rubbing Sini's back. "Your color is returning nicely."

Perhaps, but under these circumstances, pink cheeks didn't mean that she was any less likely to pass out.

"Take another minute or two, and then get to work. I'll check on you when I can." With that, Päivi left, returning to her table.

Sini felt the loss immediately and wished Leila were there. On the heels of that thought, came another. *But if she were here, Marko's attention would be on her. Our attention needs to be on the patient.* That included hers.

She slowly straightened in the chair, and when she felt steady enough, stood, keeping her gaze on the floor. Steadying herself on the edge of the table, Sini slowly lifted her eyes to him. He remained intent on his work, picking out shrapnel with what looked like a large pair of tweezers, sometimes suctioning or shifting positions to avoid casting a shadow on the patient.

I should be suctioning, holding a pan out to catch shrapnel, adjusting the angle of the light . . .

Long seconds passed. He hadn't given any indication that he recognized her. Had he not heard her name or noticed her arrival? Was she entirely unrecognizable in surgical garb?

He's oblivious. As always.

"Nurse," Marko called over his left shoulder to table four. "Blood pressure."

After handing a tool to the surgeon at table four, Nurse Hesanto hurried over to take the blood pressure of the man on Sini's table.

The thrill and excitement—an odd mix of hope and fear—that had awakened inside her at hearing Marko's name and seeing him again now faded, as they always did. This time, the feeling vanished faster.

For years, when the hope left, an equally familiar but far less-welcome set of emotions arrived: disappointment and dread. They settled in her middle with a heaviness that felt like tar, as if her joints were made of black, sticky pitch.

The dark feelings had always come, though the reasons varied. Like the time he promised to take her to a fancy restaurant and forgot. Whenever he said he'd call but didn't. Every time he talked about Leila, though he never just *talked* about her. He gushed about her, raved about her. Especially any time he indulged in too much to drink.

On those nights, Sini had let herself drink more than was good for her, too. The warm buzz made his pining easier to bear. Not painless, but at least not torture.

She'd felt those heavy things a thousand times before, and now she braced herself for them to return. But this time, after the quick, almost instinctive burst of hope had flared and then extinguished itself almost as fast, she felt nothing. Nothing toward Marko. Nothing at all.

And that sent a wave of relief and happiness through her so unexpected that she nearly laughed right there at the surgical table across from him.

"Ninety-three over sixty," Nurse Hesanto said as she removed a blood-pressure cuff. She laid it on a tray and returned to her table.

"Good," he said.

"How can I help?" Sini asked. Her voice sounded more confident than she'd ever heard it.

He looked up as if ready to give an order, but did a double take. His eyes squinted, and his brow smoothed out, and his cheeks pushed against his mask; he was smiling. She hated that she knew him so well.

"Sini Toivola, is that you?"

"Sure is." Her old self would have lowered her eyes and studied the tray of tools. The old Sini might have had her vision swim and blur as she fought tears.

She wasn't that person anymore.

"Fancy seeing you here." His tone was friendly but distant, as he might address a random acquaintance he'd bumped into while shopping for expensive shoes or ties at Stockmann. This was not how you spoke to a close friend you'd spent hundreds of hours with. Not how you'd address someone who you'd shared your innermost feelings, hopes, and dreams with.

We were friends, she thought, but mentally shook her head against his dismissive tone, which she'd seen him use with people he wanted to impress but hardly knew. *We were nothing more, but we* were *friends.*

"Suction," Marko said, and she complied. Her movements were smooth and easy. Her hands didn't shake or tremble. She could look at him and not care one whit what he thought of her. She cared more about the patient on their table and making sure she did her job well.

For several hours, they worked across from each other. More than once, their hands touched, something that even through gloves, would have sent her stomach flipping and swooping as if the two of them were on a date, and if he were trying to hold her hand.

She felt nothing but the accidental contact of a surgeon's glove. Out of boredom, her mind reviewed how he'd greeted her.

Fancy seeing you here, he'd said, in the same tone she'd heard him use with a waitress at a restaurant.

I'd never talk to him like that. Cheerful formality—that was what it was. A contrived friendliness. She took pity on her old self from only a matter of weeks ago, the woman who would have cried herself to sleep if Marko had ever spoken to her so flippantly.

Not so long ago, she would have been loath to have him see her in her Lotta uniform, homely and boring after weeks of stress and poor sleep that led to dark circles under her eyes and acne across her forehead. She didn't care if he noticed any of that.

Nikolai has never seen me with civilian clothes or makeup.

"Clamp."

She held out a clamp then suctioned more blood. *I always thought that fate had a sick sense of humor,* Sini thought. *This time, it's perfect.*

As the hours went on, and one surgery followed another, she became adept at offering instruments handle first, and a few times even anticipated his requests.

Nurse Hesanto checked on Sini less and less often, and once complimented her on how quickly she'd learned.

"Thank you," Sini said. "It helps that I learned some things in the infirmary with—" She choked back Leila's name, and her eyes darted toward him as he stitched—much more slowly than the others. "I've been taught well by all of the nurses I've worked with."

Did Marko know that Leila was in camp? If not, Sini wasn't about to be the one to tell him. More importantly, did *Leila* know that *he* was here?

At last they finished. The patients had all been carried out, and the surgical staff filed into the side room to remove their surgical garb. Sini stretched her back and looked around as if coming out of a daze. The experience had drained her. She'd learned a lot and had even managed to look at several wounds without fainting or growing nauseated. But now she needed food.

Nikolai, she realized suddenly. *He must be starving.* She checked the clock on the wall. She'd planned on going to see him two hours ago.

Marko took off his blood-covered smock and tossed it into the bin. Sini followed suit, dropping hers in at the same moment he added his mask and cap. Their hands touched, and as before, she expected the old feelings to flutter through her middle with a thrill coursing through her body as fast as lightning.

Instead, she felt a sadness that she'd wasted so much time on someone who would never return her feelings. She thought of Nikolai, and *then* the swoop went through her, along with a deep yearning for his touch. Her heart began to race. How fast could she realistically get to Nikolai?

Marko went to the sink to wash. "First time?"

"Clearly," she said with a chuckle. She needed to wash, too, but rested on a bench while some of the others cleaned up first.

Eventually she finished and headed outside with Marko and Nurse Hesanto, who put a hand on his arm and said, "I'm going to get some coffee and dinner. Care to join me?" She glanced at Sini and seemed to remember only then that she was present. "You, too, of course," she added, but without the flirty femininity.

"I'd love to," Sini said. "Thanks, Nurse Hesanto."

"Call me Marja."

"All right . . . Marja."

They walked to the mess hall, mostly in silence, with his flashlight as their guide. In the quiet, Sini's mind ran overtime. Why was she going to the mess hall with Marko when she wanted to get to Nikolai?

Marko's sudden appearance in her life seemed to be a sign that she needed to somehow close that volume and move on. Would having dinner with him in the mess hall resolve the old feelings? She didn't think so.

When they reached the mess hall, Sini sighed. "On second thought, I'm too tired. You two enjoy your dinner."

Nurse Hesanto's eyes narrowed as if she wondered what Sini's strategy was. Sini just smiled back; she had no strategy, only freedom.

"Are you sure?" Marko opened the door of the mess hall and gestured for the women to go ahead.

Sini held back. "I'm sure. I need the sleep."

Marja sailed past him on her way inside, pausing just long enough to say, "It's sure nice to have new doctors here."

"Unfortunately, I won't be here long," he replied. "I'll be heading to the Mannerheim Line soon. Now that will be exhausting."

Sini stepped backward and lifted a hand to wave goodnight, but his voice stopped her. "It's good to see you again, Sini." He used the tone of the Marko she knew. "Real good."

This was her friend. Whoever he'd been trying to be before, he was back now. Unless the other version was the real Marko. Would he continue to vacillate between the genuine, warm version of himself and the arrogant, distant one?

"It was good to see you, too."

Their eyes held. She stood there, waiting for something. For him to speak? Give her a hug? She wasn't sure, but for the first time in years, she didn't worry about what he wanted.

He moved to go inside the mess hall, but Sini stopped him, wanting to have even a brief exchange with the real version of her old friend. "Marko, wait."

He paused and looked back expectantly.

"Old friends need to say hello with a hug at least, even in a war zone."

"You've changed," he said. "I can't quite put my finger on how, but you've definitely changed." He looked almost . . . impressed. He opened his arms, and she gave him a brief hug.

She breathed in his musky scent mingled with antiseptic. Memories rushed back, both happy and sad. She braced for her feelings to rush back. All she could think of was how, though Marko's scent was familiar, she'd rather hug Nikolai. She'd known him for such a short time, but he felt more like home to her than Marko ever had.

Marko went inside, and the door closed behind him. She had Nikolai now. He was waiting for her. He cared. She'd known Nikolai for so little time, yet in some ways, he knew her better than Marko did after years of friendship.

Nikolai cared for her more than Marko ever had. More than he ever would. She was realizing more every day that she was good enough for someone, and that Nikolai was the only man who mattered to her.

Someone came up from behind and opened the door to the mess hall, a man who held it open, waiting for her to go through.

She gave him a nod of acknowledgment. "Thanks, but I'm not going in right now. I have somewhere else I need to be."

CHAPTER TWENTY-ONE

Sini hurried into the darkness, heading straight for the dugout, needing to see Nikolai. She didn't see anyone along the way—good thing, because she couldn't have borne a delay. She needed to see him, talk to him, hear him, touch him.

As soon as she reached the dugout, she looked about to make sure no one was around. Heart beating faster now, she opened the door and slipped inside. She reached into the darkness and found a broken broomstick tucked into a corner. She braced it under the door handle so no one could open it from the outside.

Then she hurried toward Nikolai's hiding place. "It's me," she said in her usual loud whisper.

A sliver of moonlight filtered through the window. Nikolai's silhouette appeared in front of it. "Sini." He sounded relieved, maybe even happy to see her.

Wait. Was Nikolai glad to see her because he was hungry and assumed she'd brought him food?

"Oh, no. I forgot your dinner. I'll—"

"Stay." He walked over and reached for her shoulders.

"You must be starving," she said, but melted into his embrace without any real protest.

"I've saved some food here and there for times you might not be able to come. In fact, I still have that chocolate bar. It should be shared."

She relaxed even more in his arms and took a deep breath, grateful for the calm and warmth she felt near him. The extent of her fatigue after hours in stressful, unfamiliar surgery began to wash over her. Nikolai's embrace, and the resulting peace flowing through her, was so different from the anxious energy that used to accompany her interactions with Marko. Had *always* accompanied them until tonight.

"I had to help in the OR for hours and hours. And then I hurried over, forgetting to stop for food, because—" She wouldn't speak of Marko. He didn't deserve that. Sini lifted her head just enough to kiss a spot on Nikolai's neck. "I had to see you." She hugged him tighter as if he might vanish. Without a word, he rested his cheek against her head and smoothed her hair back to her bun. She closed her eyes and just breathed in his touch.

"I *had* to see you," she repeated, wanting to add, *I had to feel you, too.*

"I'm glad you came," he whispered.

"I needed you tonight. I—" She buried her face in his shoulder and tried to keep back the tears threatening to fall. Several tumbled onto his shirt anyway. She closed her eyes and clung to him. "I just—I need you."

"It's okay," he said, stroking her hair again. "I'm here."

She nodded and pulled back slightly, wiping her cheeks. Without another word, Nikolai took her by the hand and led the way to his hiding spot. The moon was nearly full, so she could make out the layer of flour sacks along one edge that he used as a makeshift bed, off the cold ground. He sat on the end of the sack and gently tugged on her hand. Sini sat beside him. Her heart pounded at his nearness, yet he slid closer and stroked her cheek, wiping away the last of her tears.

He lay back, and she did the same, coming to rest with her head on his chest, her shoulder fitting perfectly under his arm, as if they were puzzle pieces made for each other, joined at last. She rested her other arm on his chest; Nikolai put his hand over hers and stroked the top with his fingers. She melted inside, wanting this moment to last forever, knowing it could not. Dreading the time it would end.

"How will we find each other?" she whispered, absently rubbing a button on his shirt. "After the war?"

He continued stroking her hand. "I don't know, but we will." He lifted her hand to his lips and kissed it, sending warm tingles down her spine.

Nikolai had hugged her before and kissed her before, and most of those times, she'd simply enjoyed the moment. Tonight was different. She focused on every second, committing every touch, smell, sound, to memory so that no matter what happened—if she and Nikolai were separated, if she never loved another man again—she'd forever have the memory of this moment. She'd be able to recall this man, whom she'd come to love so quickly and fiercely.

Nikolai kissed her hair. "Don't worry; *I'll find you.*"

She lifted her head and looked him straight in the eyes, which were darkened with deep-gray shadows. "How can you be sure?"

"Helsinki may be a big city, but I'm sure a former spy could find a pretty Lotta who served in the war, especially if she's living in the same apartment. I already memorized your address." His face softened into a smile, but it seemed stiff, as if he was trying to convince himself, too.

"But what if you can't get back across the border?" Sini asked. "My address would mean nothing then, and I'd have no way of finding you. What if my apartment building is bombed, and I have to live somewhere else—in a different city, even? What if Stalin sends you to a Siberian workcamp as a traitor? What if we can't exchange letters across the border? What if—"

His fingers traced up her arm, cutting off her words and sending another delicious shiver through her. He brushed some stray wisps from her face, combing his fingers through her hair and likely mussing her bun. He leaned in. She closed her eyes and waited to feel his kiss. Instead of feeling his lips on hers, they pressed against her right eyelid—soft, gentle—then her left.

Her right temple. Left temple.

Right cheek. Left cheek.

Just below her left earlobe. Kisses followed along her jawline, and by the time he reached her mouth, she yearned for the feel of his lips on hers.

But he didn't kiss her lips for long. Instead, he paused in kissing her altogether. She opened her eyes. He was gazing at her. They both smiled before he finally closed the distance. His touch was soft, but she returned the kiss with hot intent. He responded with equal intensity.

As she raked her fingers through his overgrown hair, ran her fingers across his stubble, the dugout melted away along with her worries, like snow in July.

Nothing existed but the two of them, right there in that moment in the near darkness.

Her hands traced down to his chest, where his muscles pressed through his uniform. She could feel his heart racing under her hand, a twin to the drumming in her ribcage. Holding her face with both hands, he pulled back. He wiped tears from her cheeks, and only then did she realize she was crying. Happy tears.

He smiled broadly. "Trust, me, Sini. I'll find you. I won't stop looking. No more worries. Everything will work out." He wiped away more tears and kissed each of her eyes one more time. "Do you believe me?" he asked, pressing his forehead to hers.

Slowly, Sini nodded. She didn't quite believe, but oh, she wanted to, more than anything. To believe that his government wouldn't keep them apart. That their dreams of a life together could become reality. That when this war ended, they'd be together, and they'd raise a family. And someday, the two of them would walk along Esplanadi, admiring the immaculately landscaped trees, sculpted shrubs and flowers, and sculptures of famous Finns.

One day, she'd slip an arm through his as he pushed their baby's carriage on their way to a coffee shop or to the open-air market, where she'd buy fresh fish and berries for dinner.

And Nikolai would belong with her, in his mother's homeland.

His fingers traced her brow, her cheek, but worry kept her from fully enjoying his touch. After the war, would he be viewed as just another Russian? An enemy, an object of hate?

The last thought shattered the fantasy of their future together. As they kissed, she mentally grasped at the dream, trying to figure out what parts of the dream might be possible. Nikolai spoke Finnish pretty well. He didn't sound Russian.

He could change his name to something that sounded Finnish. Or they could pretend he came from Sweden or another country. Yes. That might work. She resurrected the vision of their lives together and clung to Nikolai just as intently as she did the images.

Determined to hold on to the dream, she pulled his face closer, kissing him with a passion she hadn't known she possessed. Her fingers combed through his hair again, pressing their bodies together as if somehow she could drink him in and make him a part of her forever. Her breath quickened, and something inside her felt ready to explode.

Nikolai ended the long kiss but sprinkled in several shorter ones. She didn't want him to stop, and even tried to keep the kisses going, but he pulled away slightly and ran the back of his fingers along her cheek. She closed her eyes as they traced the side of her neck. She expected him to cradle her face again, but this time, he traced the skin at the edge of her collar. The movement was slow and deliberate, as if one wrong move would break a priceless antique he needed to protect.

At last he resumed their kiss, and she leaned toward the motion as he stroked her neck, then her back, where his hand moved like velvet butterflies. He returned to the front of her scratchy blouse, where his fingers found her collar and his thumb stroked her collarbone under the fabric. She opened the top button, which let him reach the skin directly. His finger gently slipped into the gap.

Without letting herself think beyond the moment, she reached for the next two buttons and opened them. There. He had more access, without so much scratchy wool in the way. He pulled the wool back a few centimeters and looked at her with what she imagined was a deeper question in his eyes.

A man desired her. Wanted her.

She hadn't thought *that* far, but suddenly, her answer was a resounding yes. She nodded. Her frame felt weak from nerves, but they were eclipsed by the passion roaring through her for this man.

Fingers shaking, she opened a third button. Then a fourth. A fifth. Each was easier than the last, giving her more confidence. This was what she wanted. Nikolai made pleased noises, gradually moving his touch across her skin—across her collarbones, and down, down, until one hand cupped her breast, his thumb stroking it. A new sensation, one she'd never felt, erupted inside her, so strong she almost had to stop him so she could catch her breath.

Her fingers trembled too much to open the last buttons; Nikolai undid the rest for her, kissing her all the while. She started on his buttons instead. She'd felt his defined muscles many times and now couldn't get his shirt off fast enough so she could touch them, caress him, taste them. Feel his bare chest pressed against hers.

He tugged the bottom of his uniform shirt free from his pants, then slipped off one sleeve and the other before tossing the shirt aside. In a single fluid motion, he pulled the tight undershirt over his head, revealing thick cords of muscle across his chest and arms. The sight made Sini catch her breath, and it sent another rush of desire through her—followed by a sense of inadequacy.

Nikolai was about to see her body—really see it. Yes, in near darkness. But he'd see enough, and feel the rest—plenty to know that she wasn't nearly the specimen of perfection that he was.

He drew her scratchy blouse open, and the shock of cool air on her torso made her catch her breath. Before she could cover herself or tell him to look away, he kissed her again. His fingers traced her shoulder, her arm, her hip.

197

"You are so beautiful," he murmured, kissing her neck. He moved to her shoulders, arms, chest, never once letting go.

For the first time in her life, Sini felt beautiful. Desirable. Loved.

She slipped off her sleeves and skirt, then peeled off her thick stockings along with her undergarments, somehow managing to keep her lips on his most of the time. He followed suit, unbuckling his belt and removing his trousers.

Then they both paused, as if fully realizing what was about to happen. The hesitation lasted only a moment; he reached for her, and she willingly went to him. They lay on the flour sacks as before, the same and yet entirely different.

Despite the chilly air, Sini had never felt such warmth, such love.

Nikolai caressed her body—her arm, ribcage, waist, thigh. She moved closer and kissed him with all of the love she had, knowing that she was about to truly make *love* to this man, becoming one in a manner she'd lost hope of ever finding.

No matter what happened tomorrow and beyond, for this moment, he was hers.

CHAPTER TWENTY-TWO

January 1, 1940

By the time Marko finished his rounds, bone-deep weariness had set in. So had despair, which was amplified with each explosion in the distance. He couldn't let himself think about how, with each mortar, lives were lost. Finns' lives lost. Their bodies torn and burned.

He could personally help only so many, and of those in his care, not all would survive. Thousands had already died in the frozen hell of the conflict. Now that the constant stream of men coming straight from the battlefield wasn't parading past him, emotions he'd carefully pushed aside started to creep back. He started having nightmares about the aid station, when all he could do was slow the worst of the bleeding or disinfect a wound, hoping to prevent gangrene. Sometimes, he was the soldier on the litter, begging for death.

But he wasn't there anymore. He was at a small field hospital, and his shift was over. He could go back to his cot and rest. He put on his coat and scarf, reminding himself yet again that if he let himself think too much about his patients—as men with parents, siblings, spouses, children—he'd fall apart completely. Like the commander who, so rumor said, had run straight for Russian tanks in a sudden, desperate madness. He was desperate for a sleep too deep for dreams, but he hadn't had a restful night in weeks.

It wasn't full dark yet, so he didn't take out his flashlight for the bitterly cold trek to his tent. He yearned for a cot but would never complain—those at the front worked shifts every bit as long. A warm tent and sterile scalpels were luxuries he should appreciate.

Yet fatigue affected everything. His gait had become slow, and his boots often dragged instead of lifting with each step, so at times he tripped on tree roots or rocks, nearly sending him to the ground. He even blinked slowly, as if his eyes actively resisted any effort to keep them open.

But if he were to lie on his cot now, he'd either sleep with restless nightmares, or he'd lie awake, second-guessing his work in surgery.

How many lives do I have on my hands?

With his shoulders hunched against the cold, Marko's boot caught on another rock in the path. He pitched forward, and someone exclaimed, reaching out to help him regain his balance.

"Sorry. I'm—so clumsy," he mumbled, then looked over at the woman beside him and thought that the exhaustion had made him hallucinate. "Leila?"

"It's good to see you." She smiled and patted his arm, which she still held. "One of the Lottas told me you were in camp. You look tired."

"I am." He stomped his boots to keep his feet warm, something from his school days that had returned as naturally as breathing. When he was a boy, he'd done the same thing before coming into the apartment building so he wouldn't leave wet tracks on the steps. Back then, he'd stomped off snow several times a day, whether coming home from school, a hockey game, or sledding with friends. Innocent times long gone.

Leila gave him a big hug, which he could hardly feel through their layers. He wished he could hold her slim figure in his arms without the coats. That he could hold her hand without thick gloves or mittens in the way. That it were summer and he could stroke her hair under the midnight sun.

"I'm so glad you're safe," she said, stepping back from the hug.

He could hardly believe that Leila was here, right in front of him. He'd just touched her, held her. She was real. "I didn't know you'd signed up with the Lotta Svärd." He pointed to the pin on her uniform, though with her entire outfit, there couldn't have been any doubt.

Leila turned to face the sunset and shrugged. A sliver of winter sunlight was still visible. "Just doing my duty."

"How's Taneli?"

At that, she closed her eyes tightly, and her lashes trembled a bit before she opened her eyes again and answered. When she spoke, her gaze remained straight ahead, intent on the horizon. "They tell me he's with a kind family . . ." A tear trickled down one cheek. "I hope so."

He turned to look at the fading sunset, too, not daring to speak and risk saddening her further. Leila hugged herself. Under other circumstances, he would have put his arm around her—done something to comfort her. But she and her thoughts seemed far away, so he held back.

Another time.

He used the silence to admire her profile and wonder at his luck at being near her during such an awful time—near the girl he'd loved since before they were grown. Though her hair was pulled into a bun and hidden under a knitted hat, he could picture times when her golden curls had hung past her shoulders. When something made her blush back then, she'd lower her face, and a lock of hair fell into her eyes. He'd loved making her blush.

So many years later, this wasn't how he'd imagined ringing in the New Year, but seeing her again at a hospital in the middle of the forest was far preferable to the aid station.

She was as beautiful tonight as she'd been at sixteen, when she, Jaakob, and Marko had spent entire days together. A time or two, she'd even donned boys' hockey skates to keep up on the rink, saying that figure skates were for pretty tricks, not speed. In the summer they spent hours walking beaches in the twilight of a sun that didn't set until well into the night, planning their futures.

At some point, Leila and Jaakob began planning their future together—just the two of them. Marko featured prominently in their imaginations, of course. One day, he'd be Jaakob's best man, and later, their children's godfather. The couple would always live near him, and they'd spend holidays together. His children and theirs would be as close as cousins.

On May Day, they ate traditional funnel cakes and got too drunk to remember much. On Midsummer Night, they danced under the midnight sun as bonfires blazed offshore. On Christmas Eve, they ate ham that Leila prepared to perfection.

If he'd been completely truthful with himself, Marko could have seen the hints as far back as third grade saying that Jaakob and Leila would end up together. At first Jaakob threw snowballs at Leila—a clear sign that he had eyes for her. He threw them too, for the same reason, but it was Jaakob she grew angry at, to the point of tossing his hat into a tree and marching away, nose in the air as she tried to hide a tiny smile.

Years later, she insisted that she'd truly hated Jaakob at the time of the hat incident, and perhaps she had. But over the next winters, Marko noticed their interactions more, always aware of how Leila behaved and wishing that Leila would like him better. A few times he'd even prayed in case there was a god, like the minister said over the PA at school once a week in his devotionals.

Over the years, he'd thought that Leila's infatuation for Jaakob had ended, and that she might be seeing him in a new light. That was especially true when she confided her heartaches. He assumed that was a good sign, until their first year of secondary school, when a fellow classmate, Sirpa, had pulled him aside and explained.

"Girls don't tell their crushes about their problems." She tossed a thick red braid over her shoulder. "Trust me. To her, you're a *friend*, not a *boy*. And a friend is all you'll ever be."

Shortly after that conversation, he noticed Leila and Jaakob holding hands under the table and flirting relentlessly. They sat so close that a sheet of paper couldn't have fit between them.

Sirpa eyed Marko from across the table, one eyebrow raised as if to say, *See? Told you so.*

He'd looked away and focused on his food with an intensity normally reserved for hockey games. Sure, he'd worried that this was coming, probably for much longer than either Jaakob or Leila. And good old Sirpa had warned him that he didn't have a chance.

Marko would never have wished death upon his best friend. But Jaakob was gone now. And Leila was here. He was a doctor, she a nurse. They had so much in common, and not only careers in medicine: years of shared experiences plus hundreds of the same likes and dislikes. He and Leila could have a future now; he was certain of it. Coming to her camp in the middle of the war? That had to be a sign. Was she still mourning Jaakob too much to consider another relationship?

If anything good could come of this conflict, perhaps finding love together was it.

Leila turned from the dim light and tilted her head at him. "You look pensive. What are you thinking about?"

He recoiled at the idea of answering. He wasn't ready to bare his soul. He decided on a half-truth. "I'm thinking of the time we paddled out from the beach and—"

"Flipped the canoe," Leila finished. She tilted her head back in laughter, sending out frosty puffs of breath. "I forgot about that. It was your fault, you know." She elbowed him then began walking, and he found himself following.

"It was *not* my fault," he countered. His body seemed to find new energy. "You dropped that flower into the water and then insisted I get it back for you."

Willing to do anything for Leila, he'd reached out so far from the canoe that it tipped, sending them into the frigid, salty ocean. Somehow, Jaakob managed to get the boat upright and climb inside, then help Marko in—carefully, so it wouldn't flip again. The two of them then lugged aboard a drenched Leila. At the time, he'd been sure she knew he loved her. How could she not have known? *He* was the one who'd reached for the flower, not Jaakob.

She smiled now, perhaps at the memory of that day. "Can you believe that was almost half our lives ago?"

"Seems impossible." He looked skyward. Stars were just starting to come out. He still wasn't used to seeing so many—thousands more than were ever visible from the city. At the sky's darkest, it looked as if someone had spilled diamonds across the expanse. One thing he'd learned from being in the elements so much was that the more stars visible in the sky, the colder the temperature plunged. And, of course, it meant air raids, and therefore more casualties and work for him.

"As a little girl, I loved clear skies, especially when we went to my grandmother's summer cottage." Leila's forehead crinkled unhappily. "I hate them now. Probably always will." Her face struggled with emotion. "The train bombing happened on a night just like this one." Leila spoke in almost a whisper. "I was so sure the Russians wouldn't bomb a passenger line."

"Everyone thought the same thing. Anyone sane would. Targeting civilians is a war crime."

She lowered her chin and sniffed. "Aunt Sisko was right. I should have sent Taneli to Sweden earlier."

Her eyelids pressed closed, and a tear slipped down her cheeks in spite of her obvious efforts to be strong. Marko pulled her into his arms, hoping to mend the crack that the war had created in this priceless vase that she was. She stepped into his embrace and wrapped her arms around his neck. As he stroked her back, she clung to him, sniffing through her tears.

"You are a wonderful mother," he whispered into her ear. The touch of her forehead on his neck—the one spot where a tiny bit of skin was exposed through the layers of scarf—spread warmth to his chest.

"Thank you," she whispered. "I wish I could believe that in my heart."

He kissed the top of her head—and wanted to kiss much more than that. *Not now,* he warned himself. *Not yet.*

She let go and looked into his eyes, tear tracks on her cheeks. Her mouth quivered, and she raised a mitten to cover it.

Marko couldn't abide her tortured expression. He took her hands in his. "You made the right decision. Taneli is lucky to have you as his mother."

"Oh, I hope so. I often wonder what Jaakob would want me to do." Her eyes searched his, as if trying to find an answer in them.

"He would want you to do exactly what you did." In an attempt to lighten her mood, his mouth quirked into a smile. "And you know I'm always right when it comes to Jaakob."

She lifted one eyebrow, along with one corner of her mouth—a victory. "How can you be so sure?"

"I knew Jaakob before you did, remember." He shot her a smile, which she returned, along with another playful elbow nudge.

"By two months. That hardly counts."

His voice turned more serious. "If all goes well, you'll be reunited with your boy soon."

"I pray you're right," Leila said, hugging him again.

As they stepped apart, he tilted his head to one side, curious. "You've never been the praying type."

She looked at her mittens. "Well, war changes things—changes people."

She was right about that. Even her face had changed. It had sharper angles, more pronounced cheekbones. Shadows under her eyes.

He nodded. "Yes, it does."

CHAPTER TWENTY-THREE

January 2

After that first night with Nikolai, everything had changed, not in any way an observer would have noticed. She brought him food and drink, they exchanged a few kisses, and then she floated along the icy path to the infirmary. She hadn't slept much over the last few days—she couldn't, not when memories kept her awake.

Happy memories, for once: of Nikolai's kisses, his body pressed against hers . . .

This morning, as she headed to the infirmary, she stumbled wearily and yawned. Normally she craved sleep and grew cranky without enough rest. But she didn't mind now, when her fatigue was from remembering and reliving every moment, every touch, with Nikolai. She walked along and pictured how he'd looked the first time she found him without a shirt on, and her veins heated anew.

Such a man had looked at her with desire. He'd acted on that desire. He loved her.

She slipped on some ice and tried to catch her balance on a tree but landed in a bank of snow. Some got into her boots, which meant having wet socks for her shift. Yet as she clambered to her feet, she merely laughed and brushed off what snow she could. Who cared about wet socks when she had love?

She looked at her snow-covered boots and suddenly marveled. She knew she'd be cold and wet today. And she'd laughed about it. A zing shot through her, picking up the pace of her heart. Was this what true happiness felt like? If so, she'd never truly been happy.

She continued her way, more slowly now, making an effort to hide her smile so as not to invite questions from others. The snow sparkled like a rainbow as the morning sun hit it. She paused to look at the beauty. Dawn had created millions of scenes like this, but Sini couldn't remember ever seeing anything so beautiful.

In the distance, a hare darted across the snow, visible for only a flash as it bounded between trees, but long enough to interrupt her thoughts and bring her back to the reality of duty and shifts and winter. Arms around her torso to keep herself a little warmer, she kept walking, but the pensive mood stayed with her.

Have I ever really lived? The question both thrilled and troubled her. Thrilled because she felt as if she'd been born blind, and now she could see. Everything from before Nikolai seemed gray, but the world suddenly had brilliant color.

Somehow, even in a war zone, even with the freedom of her nation hanging by a thread, she'd never felt more alive. Thoughts of what the future could hold hung in the back of her mind. The very real possibility of living under Stalin's iron rule. Being torn from Nikolai. The two of them unable to find each other after the war. With the force of an icebreaker on the ocean, she shoved the thoughts from her mind. The only thing she knew about happiness was the present.

I'll live in the present for as long as I can. She reached the infirmary and went inside. She signed in—technically a minute late, but no one seemed to notice. Nurse Mia glanced up from the cupboards, where she was folding laundry piled in a large cloth bin.

"Big changes happening at the front," she said, snapping a sheet before folding it. "Shouldn't have any new casualties today."

207

"That's great," Sini said, unbuttoning her coat. Mia held up a finger, making Sini's hands stop on the third button. "What?"

"Without any new casualties, you're assigned to the kitchen."

"Oh. That's good." Sini redid her buttons. The kitchen meant no smells or sounds of the wounded. More importantly, it meant more access to food for Nikolai, though it might also mean red, angry skin tonight. She wound the scarf back about her neck. "Permanent reassignment?"

"Raisa says it depends on what happens on the front, how the army is moving and where the battles are." Mia settled a perfectly folded sheet onto the shelf and pulled a new one from the bin. "For now, she's expecting you."

"Happy to help where I'm needed," Sini said—and she meant it, too, which felt both wonderful and odd at the same time.

She headed for the kitchen, ordering herself to *not* stop at the dugout on the way. She'd already visited Nikolai—and only a few minutes ago. If she gave in to the temptation, she'd almost certainly stay with him longer than she could explain away with the excuse of not knowing of the change in her assignment.

Halfway to the kitchen, a man approached along the same narrow path. Sini glanced at him just enough to know when to step aside so they wouldn't collide, but the sight of this particular man made her stomach feel hollow.

Marko. She debated taking a detour around some other tents but decided that he probably wouldn't even notice her. She was just another Lotta. If she tugged her scarf a little higher, over her mouth and nose, he wouldn't be able to see enough of her face even if he looked right at her.

The old Sini would have sought him out, found a reason to "accidentally" cross paths, even though she'd long known, even through her cloak of denial, that nothing would bring the two of them together.

Someone else finds me attractive, she thought defiantly. *And I love Nikolai.*

Why was she thinking of him anyway?

She took smaller, slower steps, as Marko drew closer, and she waited for the rush of nerves and excitement he'd always elicited. She felt nothing. Not excitement. Not even the old dread that had begun to surface back home at the thought of seeing him. Dread that he wouldn't care. The ache in her chest that always came after greeting him.

For the first time in memory, she felt nothing for Marko after the initial surprise had passed. No pain, no longing, no ache. She searched her heart and tried to find the wounds he'd left there. They'd scarred over; they weren't entirely gone, but they no longer hurt.

I don't love him anymore, she thought with no little astonishment. *If I ever did.*

He walked right past her, never looking her direction, and nodding politely as he brushed past. She turned and watched him go until he entered the infirmary.

I don't love him. She stood there, stunned. *I don't hate or resent him, either. I'm not mad. I feel . . . nothing.* She took a deep breath and let it out in a huge whoosh, as if the burdens she'd carried were leaving her body with the air.

Just as the Finnish army had had a small victory last month in the Tolvajärvi campaign, Sini had her own victory. Marko no longer had any power over her.

She put her hands into her coat pockets and returned to the path. When she passed the snow-covered roof of the camouflaged dugout, a hot wave of emotion hit her, as if she'd walked into a hot sauna. Marko might not hold power over her—something she could cry with relief over—but someone else did.

That power had firmly shifted to someone else. Any kind of love carried risks—and loving a Russian soldier during war was nothing if not risky. But she'd happily give him control of her heart again.

And again, and again, forever.

Sini spent her shift not scrubbing or peeling vegetables—thank heavens—but cutting ham into cubes for the gravy that would go over boiled potatoes. She raised the cutting board over a pot and used the knife to push another pile into the pot.

As she wiped her brow with the back of her wrist, she noted a bright blue spot out of the corner of her eye. She looked over at blue yarn visible from her coat pocket—a pair of socks she'd finished last night when unable to sleep.

She set the cutting board and knife back on the counter and reached for the dish towel to dry her hands on. All day, she'd been debating what to do with the socks. She could knit up to four pairs of socks a week, and until now had always handed them over to the quartermaster to give out to a soldier who needed them. She had plenty of yarn; she wouldn't need to request more for some time.

But these socks felt different. She'd knitted them after everything had changed. Every stitch had been made with thoughts of Nikolai in her head, emotions in her breast that she hadn't known existed. They represented love and belonging. Freedom.

Leaving Nikolai after that first night had been one of the hardest things she'd ever done. She'd found the strength only because she knew that staying would endanger them both. She'd be noticed missing from her cot, a search would be launched, and they would be found. Nikolai would be bound and taken away.

Every night she yearned to go to him, to hold him and kiss him. To be held and kissed and caressed. But she couldn't leave the tent at night without arousing suspicion. So she knitted instead. Last night she knitted an entirely new sock and finished it. That was the second sock of a pair, so she did the finishing work—wove in the ends of both socks—then held them up. She was getting faster.

Now, in the kitchen, she eyed the flash of blue. She'd poured her longing for Nikolai into those socks. By all rights, they belonged to him, though they'd been made with yarn from the Finnish army. She closed her eyes and pictured blue ribbing peeking over the tops of Nikolai's boots, the wool stitches keeping him warm. Her own ribbing that created the elastic for the cuffs.

She'd give the socks to Nikolai. A meager gift, yes, but one made with her own hands, one he could take with him until they were reunited after the war. A gift that would last longer than a meal.

"Ham ready?" Raisa called.

Sini startled and turned toward the door leading to Raisa's office. "Almost." She returned to her work and remained diligent until Raisa's office door had closed. Then Sini's hands slowed, and her mind drifted again to the socks. She pictured herself giving them to Nikolai. His face lighting up.

He'd made her feel things she'd never known she could, things that left warmth and joy in their wake—not pain.

If she could just see Nikolai right now. Every millimeter of her body wanted to run to the dugout and hold him—be held *by* him. She checked the clock; thirteen minutes until her shift ended. She reached for another ham and set to chopping it, glad that they had meat for the troops. Glad that she could bring meat to Nikolai. No matter what Sini did, everything returned to Nikolai.

Raisa reappeared several minutes later, having finished some paperwork, and now rushed about, giving orders, checking stoves and workstations. When she went to inspect the new loaves of rye bread, Sini quickly placed a few slices of ham inside a cloth napkin, then slipped it into one of her skirt's front pockets, which she'd kept unbuttoned for this very reason.

Sini angled herself away from Raisa so the bulge would be less noticeable. No matter how many times Sini took food to Nikolai, she worried about getting caught. To think it had all started as a way to reassure a scared man.

The truth was that landing in enemy territory had saved Nikolai's life. He was no longer a scared man she was kind to. He'd become a part of her, and she would do anything to protect him.

That meant not just bringing food and water, but finding a way for him to escape and safely hide until the war ended. Maybe he could find a friendly old *mummo* in a cottage who hadn't evacuated, a sweet old lady who'd house him until he could safely go to a city. Someone who wouldn't turn in a young man in need who could also do work for her. One she'd trust because he spoke Finnish.

Sini hoped to steal a uniform for him from the quartermaster, perhaps when delivering more socks and asking for more yarn. Nikolai could wear a uniform and hope a half-deaf *mummo* didn't hear his accent.

But assuming they could get him a uniform, how would he escape camp undetected? How would he find a safe place to stay? The worry gnawed at her, growing stronger and displacing joy. She had to keep him safe, even if it meant punishment later.

Could a Lotta be court-martialed? Would she be put in prison for aiding the enemy?

I'm not helping the enemy. I'm helping a good man who was unlucky by being born on the other side of the border. Stalin gains nothing from this. Nikolai's blue eyes and blond hair came back to mind. *He's not my enemy. Not with those eyes.*

She bit her lip to stop herself from smiling; if Raisa or another Lotta saw her grinning like a fox, they'd suspect something and would demand to know what was going on. She looked surreptitiously in both directions. Everyone's attention was on their work. Sini tried to relax and finish with the ham.

She slid the last into the pot, which she covered and brought to the stove. In the last minutes of her shift, she joined Suvi, a Lotta cutting potatoes and chatting with Tanja, who was scrubbing dishes at the sink. The three other Lottas in the square room discussed the invaders and how illogically the war had played out so far. Sini listened and chopped, glad for the distraction.

"The Reds have plenty of tanks and ammunition, and unending numbers of men," Tanja said from the sink. "But their leaders have no sense. They're stupid or mad."

"Exactly," Suvi said, gesturing with the point of her knife. "You'd think a country with a place as cold as Siberia would know how to keep its army from freezing to death."

Annika added water to the yeast she'd poured into a small bowl. She leaned back against the counter and stirred the mixture with a fork. "You'd think they'd understand how colors work so they can avoid being spotted."

Tanja laughed at that then wiped a stray hair from her forehead with the back of her wrist. "How did they only recently realize that painting trucks and tanks white might be a good idea in the winter? A child could have figured that out earlier."

The Lottas laughed, but Sini really did wonder. Why didn't the Russians know better? Even now, Russian soldiers rarely wore white, while one of the Finns' first preparations was to make as many white snowsuits as possible. Maybe Stalin's ego and overconfidence had blinded his judgment. Sini listened on, the cogs in her mind turning.

"At least we have a few advantages," Tanja said. She set a dried plate on a stack with a clank. "And we're making the most of them."

"We are at that," Suvi said with a nod that moved in rhythm with her knife. "And on top of that, we have *sisu*. Russians will never have a bit of *sisu*."

The knot of worry returned to Sini's middle, tighter than before. *Not even* sisu *will be enough if the West doesn't step in to stop the madness.* How long will it take them? It's been over a month.

Worry made the meat in Sini's pocket feel heavy, pulling at her skirt. She checked the clock again—four minutes. Could she leave early? Suvi had the potatoes well under way. Only one person could fit at the sink at a time. Raisa would have no one but Annika make the bread.

Could Sini claim that she'd been called to help at the infirmary and simply leave early? She'd been called to help there often enough. With her shift almost over, Raisa wouldn't expect Sini to return. She could walk toward the infirmary until she was out of sight of the kitchen, then double back to Nikolai. She casually turned around and leaned to the side to peer into Raisa's office. Empty.

"Anyone know where Raisa is?" Sini asked, trying to keep her voice light.

"She went to double check how many cans of fish are left," Annika said, then checked the clock. "You're almost off, but before you leave, would you get another bag of flour from the dugout? The bin's almost empty, and I'm so tired. I meant to ask Raisa to bring one back, but I forgot to before she left."

Raisa had gone to count cans of fish. In the dugout.

Don't panic, Sini told herself. *Plenty of people have gone in there without finding Nikolai.*

He was expecting her soon. Would he be on guard?

"I don't know what's taking her so long," Annika said. "I thought she'd be back already. Would you mind?" She glanced Sini's way but then did a double take. Her eyes narrowed. "Are you sick?"

But Sini couldn't move. Raisa had gone to the dugout and should have returned by now.

What if she'd found Nikolai? What if she hadn't returned to the kitchen because she'd gone to camp headquarters to report him? What if Nikolai was being interrogated right now?

What would happen to him?

"I'll—I'll go," Sini stammered, though her mouth had gone dry. For once she was glad for the thick skirt; it hid her trembling knees. She grabbed her coat on the way to the door.

She hurried toward the dugout, hoping—praying—for Nikolai's safety. *God, if you're there, then you helped me hide him. You can't let him be found. Help me get him out of here.*

In the dim light, a figure moved toward her—Raisa, alone. Relief washed over Sini so intensely that her knees nearly unhinged. Raisa must not have noticed anything untoward, because she merely nodded and asked, "Shift over? Have a good evening."

Sini watched her go until she could no longer make out Raisa's figure, worried she'd suspect something and return with questions. Sini waited nervously until well after the kitchen door closed. When it didn't reopen a few minutes later, Sini clasped her hands to calm her nerves and walked to the dugout. She felt the bulk of the socks in her coat pocket—and a renewed urgency came over her to give the socks to Nikolai. She had an uneasy feeling that her time with him would be over soon. She had to give him the socks and plan his escape as soon as possible.

Flights of dreamy happiness had lulled her into a false sense of security, but Raisa's delay had slapped her solidly back to reality. Nikolai could be found at any moment. The one good thing in this hellish place would end, and he might be killed in the process.

She slipped inside as quietly as she could. As always, she shoved the broom handle in place. It wasn't a secure locking system, but it would keep someone out for enough time to get Nikolai hidden.

"It's me," she said quietly. Without the use of a light, she picked her way around the sacks, bags, and crates. The top of Nikolai's face appeared by the dim light from the tiny window.

"You're safe!" She flew to him, and he enveloped her in his arms. "I was so worried when Raisa came down."

"I think she suspects something," Nikolai said.

Sini looked at him, her eyes wide. "We have to get you out of here." She turned to pace and think, but he reached for her and drew her close again. His strong arms eased her worries, if only for a moment. She could breathe again.

"We'll figure something out," he said.

She nodded and hoped he was right.

He tilted her chin up and kissed her, long and soft, and her insides warmed. The haze of bliss began to descend, so she pulled away, knowing she needed to speak before she lost all sense.

"I made something for you," she said suddenly—and louder than she'd intended. She put a finger to her lips as if shushing herself. After withdrawing the socks, she held them out. "I made them for you," she said, this time whispering. Before he could take them, she snatched them away and held them behind her back. "But I'll need another kiss as payment."

"Gladly." He kissed her again, longer this time, until she had to catch her breath. She put the socks into his outstretched hand, and he held them up to the window. "They're blue."

"A pretty blue. Or rather, a *masculine* blue."

"It's the blue in your flag."

She hadn't thought of that. "I didn't mean anything by it," she said in a rush. "It was the only yarn I had at the time. I didn't mean to offend—"

"They're not red," Nikolai said. Like the Soviet flag.

"I'm sorry." She reached for the socks, feeling stupid for not realizing what blue would mean to Nikolai. She'd take the socks to the quartermaster after all. Maybe she could request another color. Maybe brown or green . . .

"I love them." Nikolai fingered the yarn thoughtfully. "My mother would approve."

Sini relaxed. "I suppose she would."

She still felt a tiny bit guilty about using yarn intended for a Finnish soldier's socks. Would some Finn lose his toes to frostbite because she'd given his socks away to a Red?

No, not to a Red. To Nikolai. Whose mother was Finnish.

She doused the hint of guilt and gave him a flirtatious smile. "Let's put those socks on you." She took his free hand and led him toward the sacks-turned-furniture.

She sat first, and Nikolai followed, so close that their bodies touched from shoulder to boot. He leaned nearer, seeming to take in her features hungrily.

"I don't see your beautiful face in the light nearly often enough," he said, whispering so faintly that each word was a mere breath. He reached over her shoulder and placed the socks on a crate. "If you don't mind, I'll put them on in a few minutes."

"Not at all," she said, breathless.

He cupped her face between his hands and kissed her. She wanted as much of Nikolai as she could get. Their time truly was limited. She vowed to savor every second as if it were their last. She let her worries and fears slip away and let herself be consumed by the moment.

CHAPTER TWENTY-FOUR

They lay in the darkness, covered only by their coats for warmth. Sini wasn't sure how long she'd been there, but the dugout had grown full dark. She shivered, and Nikolai rubbed her arm to warm her. Then he brushed a lock of hair from her eyes. She could fix her bun later. Knowing she needed to leave soon, she leaned her head against his chest. He held her close, kissed the crown of her head, rested his cheek on it.

She sighed happily. "I wish we could stay here forever."

"Me too," he said, then chuckled. "Although in better accommodations."

Worry over the future—of his, especially—returned, pushing away the joy and reminding her that they weren't suspended in a fairy tale. Rather, they were walking a dangerous line that could mean life and death. She closed her eyes and slipped her hand around his waist, wanting to hold him, feel his realness while she could. Whatever it took to keep him safe, she'd do it.

Nikolai must have sensed her sudden tension, because he leaned back slightly. "What's wrong?"

She didn't look in his eyes. Instead, she reached over and stroked the coat she'd found for him. "We need to get you out of here." She pushed away slightly, trying hard to resist the desire to stay in his arms.

For his sake, I must be practical.

Nikolai hadn't been captured; he'd been sent to spy on the Finns. The POW she'd seen in the log bunker had been near death, starving and frostbitten. Nikolai was healthy, warm, and fit—he'd be seen as a threat. The army would assume he'd been spying on them the whole time. A spy could be shot without a trial. Any Russian spotted near camp could be.

She shuddered. Nikolai must have assumed it was from the cold, because he handed her uniform to her. "This will help."

They dressed quickly. Seeing Nikolai pull on the blue socks brought a wistful smile to her face. She tucked in her scratchy blouse. "We may be able to hide you in an ambulance after one leaves empty, but that won't get you far. You'll still need a safe place to hide, and a way to get there." Despite her efforts to be practical about the matter, she heard a tremor of worry in her voice.

Apparently, he did, too. "Come," he said, pulling her into his arms. "Everything will work out."

"I couldn't bear losing you." Tears pooled in her eyes, spilled over, and traced paths along her cheeks. "I need you to escape right away. If something happens to—"

"Nothing will happen to me," he said, stroking her hair. "Nothing."

She grabbed his hand mid-stroke. "Don't."

He furrowed his brow, clearly confused.

"Nikolai, we can't pretend that your capture isn't a possibility." More tears trickled down her face. "And I love you too much to risk your life." She couldn't say how he'd likely be killed if caught, but they both knew that it wouldn't be pretty.

Nikolai cradled her face with both hands and wiped her tears with his thumbs, which slightly dulled the stabs of fear in her chest, if but for a moment. He leaned in and pressed a kiss to her forehead. "Let's make a plan—including how we'll meet after the war."

"Thank you," Sini said, sagging with relief.

Between the two of them, they'd find a way to get him out of camp and to safety. They'd plan a way to be reunited. In a few months, they'd be together. She took a steadying breath then smoothed her hair back as she looked around for something to write on. "I should find a pencil and a notebook."

"You'll be missed if you don't get back soon. Let's think on it tonight and plan tomorrow."

"Perfect," she said.

He kissed her again, short and sweet. She squeezed his hands, then left and made her way back to her tent.

As she approached, she heard a flurry of tense conversation inside. Had transfer orders come? Was she getting reassigned? If so, she'd have even less time to get Nikolai out of camp than she'd thought. She'd been right to insist on coming up with a plan to get him out sooner than later. She stomped her boots and went inside, where she tried to appear relaxed as she went to her cot, all while listening to the women.

"You're joking," Leila was saying. "How could that have gone unnoticed?"

"So close to camp, too," Katri added.

Not transfers, then. Yet their tone put Sini on edge. "What went unnoticed?" she asked as she sat on her cot. She tried to sound light and airy, but sure she sounded tense, like yarn on a beginner's needles—too tight to work, ready to snap.

Leena had started taking out her bun. She removed a few hair pins from her mouth and leaned forward. "Marika—camp secretary; you know her, right?—found a *Russian parachute*." She sat back, clearly pleased with the shock she'd provoked. Sini felt her face paling.

How could she have been so stupid as to forget about the parachute? She should have gotten rid of it by dumping it into the trash and covering it with other garbage. Her jaw was hanging open; she snapped her mouth shut, making her teeth click.

"Is a Russian division nearby?" she asked, but she knew the answer: no. She just couldn't think of what else to say.

Heidi piped up, eager to be in on informing Sini. "Some Russian spies tried parachuting behind the front lines. We don't have the same security as a combat division would, which must be how a spy landed undetected." She leaned forward as Leena had. "The snow behind the parachute is undisturbed—no old footprints. Nothing."

"Nothing?" Sini asked hopefully.

"They did find some indents in the snow that could be footprints." She lowered her voice for the next part. "They lead right into camp." A collective murmur swept the tent. When the sound died down, Heidi continued. "No one has found any Russian, dead or alive."

Katri nodded in agreement as she folded some clothes. "So we probably have a spy somewhere in camp. Likely armed. I'm scared to death."

I didn't take his pistol, Sini thought with a sinking feeling. *I haven't seen it since bringing him to the dugout. Oh, no.* If he shot to defend himself, he'd be filled with lead. How many foolish mistakes had she made?

"When do they think he landed?"

Leila answered this time. "A couple of weeks ago, at least."

Their gazes caught—Leila's held terror. Sini wanted to reassure her that Nikolai posed no threat. She couldn't do that now, so she tried to ease her tentmates' fear another way. "He probably froze to death somewhere in the woods."

I fed him food meant for our soldiers. I stole a coat for him. A blanket. Made him socks with army wool.

If he was found, would the socks be recognized and tied back to her? Dread pooled in her middle like acid. She quickly composed her face. No one seemed to have noticed her reaction.

"He *could* be dead." Leena said doubtfully. She set some bobby pins on her footlocker and ran her fingers through her loose hair. "But a search party around the perimeter found no body, and no evidence of someone trying to survive—no fire pit, no shelter. Mark my words, he's in camp. They've already increased security, and as soon as it's light, they'll search every tent, bunker, and closet. Don't worry; they'll find him."

Katri slipped a sweater over her head. "I overheard Major Elomaa talking about it in the office. He's thinks someone in camp is helping the spy."

"No . . ." Sini's voice trailed off. What else could she say?

"It's hard to believe," Katri said, "but we have a Red sympathizer among us. I'm guessing one of the older officers, someone who fought in the civil war for the Red side and wishes they'd won."

Sini smoothed her stiff skirt. "Did Elomaa say what would happen to the spy—or the sympathizer—if they're caught?"

"When," Leena corrected.

"Of course," Sini said offhandedly. "When."

"He didn't say exactly." Katri pulled a pair of thick socks from her footlocker. "The spy will probably be shot on sight, though. If the sympathizer is lucky, he'll get a trial."

"And if they're not lucky?" Sini asked.

"They'll be thrown into a cell." Katri shrugged as she slipped on one sock and then the other. "Or get shot right along with the spy. I don't know how it all works, but wouldn't that be a sight?"

The women continued their speculation. Who was the sympathizer? A surgeon? A guard? Where was the spy hiding? Maybe he was in the infirmary, pretending to be a Finnish casualty. He could have hurt himself, gotten hurt parachuting, and put on a Finnish uniform.

Sini lay down and turned onto her side, boots, coat, and all. A mountain of fear seemed to be crushing her chest, stealing her air, freezing her lungs. Katri and Leena had no idea that they were inflicting pain on her. She couldn't tell them to stop talking about the Russian in camp. She couldn't explain, even to Leila, why she was suddenly crying. In their shoes, she'd have said the same things, with the same curiosity and incensed worry.

But she wasn't in their shoes.

She stared at the blanket on the next cot, trying to breathe as the horrifying knowledge washed over her. In a matter of hours, Nikolai would be found. Tomorrow was too late for making plans. Anyone with half a brain would know to check the dugout early in their search.

Nikolai might raise his arms and plead for mercy—in Finnish, so they'd know he wasn't entirely Russian, not entirely enemy. Just unlucky enough to be born across the border.

But, no.

During war, no one looked for reasons to be merciful. Nikolai would be riddled with bullets. In the warmth of the dugout, he'd quickly bleed out.

Then the search would turn to the sympathizer. They'd seek out names of those with access to the dugout. A couple of questions was all it would take to learn that she'd visited the dugout more than any other Lotta. That she'd volunteered at every opportunity to make the trek to it.

She'd be arrested. If she was lucky, she'd be shackled and taken to a cell. If not, as Katri had said, she'd be killed as a traitor.

We'll die apart instead of living to old age together.

Tears burned her eyes and dripped onto her pillow. She breathed through her mouth so her stuffy nose wouldn't give her away. Eyes closed, she pressed the heels of her hands against them, but the barrage of worries and possibilities—all horrible—didn't subside. Images of death, dying, and blood flooded her mind. A sharp pain radiated from the base of her skull, shooting to her right eye. She heard herself whimper as she rolled onto her back and covered her face with her hands. The conversation about the Russian spy continued around her with all kinds of speculation. If someone noticed her tears, she'd blame them on a very real headache; she felt as if an icepick were lodged in the back of her head.

"Why would a spy be sent here?" someone said. Sini didn't bother raising her hands to see who spoke. "A hospital wouldn't have military secrets."

He went off course. Sini wished she could say it.

"Elomaa will learn what intelligence he was after," someone else said. Maybe Leena.

"Hmm. Do you think they'd torture him?"

Sini's eyes flew open. "Torture?"

"Only if he doesn't give us his secrets easily," Leena said. "I don't know if they do that. I was just guessing."

222

A new possibility unfurled in Sini's mind—that they might want Nikolai alive. The other women in the tent stared her direction, surely confused by her sudden reaction to the suggestion of torturing a spy, followed by the half-smile that replaced the worry.

Sini didn't care what they thought. She scooted to the edge of her cot, heart pounding with hope. "If they manage to capture him without a struggle . . ." What could she say without giving herself away? "Do you think they might interrogate him instead of shooting him?"

They'll feed him. Take care of him. And he'll live. Sini almost cried with relief.

She ignored the icepick and bit her lip. Instead of listening to any more of the conversation, she thought hard to figure out what she should do. How could she get him captured safely—and not killed? She'd rather suffer a life sentence for harboring an enemy than suffer with the knowledge that he'd died because of her.

Nikolai had two weapons she knew of: a pistol and a hunting knife. She'd seen him use the latter as a tool, but now wished she'd taken both.

I have to tell Major Elomaa about Nikolai—tonight. Before a search party stumbled onto him. Before the worst could happen. Nikolai had gathered no Finnish intelligence—she was certain of that. She doubted he had anything of value to share from the Soviet side, but if Elomaa *thought* he did . . .

Sini stood, still wearing her coat, hat, and scarf, and quietly moved toward the tent opening, past chatting women who glanced her way but gave her little heed. She secured the flap behind her. She pulled out her flashlight and hurried to camp headquarters, where she'd betray the only man who'd ever loved her.

The thought halted her step. If she continued, everything would change, not all for the better. She wouldn't have control over how Nikolai was treated. He might die anyway.

If I put this off at all, I'll lose my nerve. Nikolai will definitely lose his life.

Summoning her courage, she walked the path. In the distance, a sliver of light showed through a crack in the wall of camp headquarters. She heard intent voices but couldn't make out words. At the door, she paused, the weight of what she was about to do pressing against her chest, stealing her breath again.

Do it. Do it now.

Sini fisted her hand and raised it to the door. Her trembling arm hung in the air for a moment before she could force herself to knock.

CHAPTER TWENTY-FIVE

Almost as soon as Sini knocked, the door opened, making her jump. The man on the other side made a shooing motion. "Lotta business can wait until morning." He moved to close the door, so she stuck her boot in the way and spoke in a rush as loudly as she could.

"I know about the Russian."

The voices quieted as quickly as a radio being turned off. The man opened the door wider, revealing Major Elomaa at the far end of the room. He scooted his chair back and stood behind a wooden desk, arms folded, eyes narrowed. "You know more than the rumors going about camp?"

"Yes." She couldn't breathe. "I—" Her voice cut off. Now that she was here, she didn't know what to say.

"Come inside," he said impatiently. "You're letting in the cold."

Sini stomped her boots and went in. The door swung closed, and someone latched it securely behind her to seal in the warmth of the room. The air felt thick with tension, the air muggy.

Elomaa rounded the desk and leaned against it. "All right. What do you know?"

Sini's knees trembled. *Be strong. For Nikolai.*

She took a deep breath and lifted her chin. "I know where he's hiding."

The room erupted, men talking over one another. Some yelled questions; others argued. Major Elomaa pounded his fist on the desk. After the room quieted, Elomaa folded his arms again and regarded Sini with a stare that could have felled a reindeer. "I suggest you tell us everything you know."

With a nod, Sini tried to moisten her mouth, but it felt as dry as a sauna. The major raised his brows impatiently.

She licked her lips, trying to think of Nikolai and the fact that she was doing this for him. "I was taking out kitchen trash," she began. "And I saw a Russian parachutist landing near camp."

The room watched and listened. No one looked ready to shackle her—yet. Perhaps she could get through this with partial truths and save herself, too.

"He landed quite close to camp. He was scared. His uniform was cotton, and I knew that if he stayed outside like that, he'd die." When the room stayed silent, all eyes on her, her voice gained strength. "I tried to tell him that we don't torture prisoners." She turned to one of the officers she recognized from the POW interrogation. "I've seen how we treat them— we're kind and humane. But he was terrified. I didn't want his death on my hands."

"And?"

She cleared her throat. "I planned to get him warm and fed and then report him."

"But you didn't." Elomaa's voice had an edge to it. His words were not a question.

Sini glanced around the room, feeling a sudden increase in tension and anger toward her. "I planned to report him. I did. But first, I hid him. Brought him food and water."

Several men looked ready to pounce, their faces red. One demanded her arrest. Unsure and scared, she looked to Elomaa. He held up a hand, which quieted the room again, then nodded for her to continue.

"I meant to turn him in, I swear." She prayed that her voice and face wouldn't betray her. "He's been hiding for several days now." No need to say exactly how long. "He isn't an intelligence risk or a danger to anyone."

An officer to her right snorted. "Naïve girl."

"I didn't know what to do." That was the truth. Sini lowered her head. "The longer he was there, the more confused I became. I know now I should have come straight to you."

"Yes, you should have," Elomaa said. "So where is this Russian?"

"Half Russian. His mother is Finnish. Sir." She should have mentioned that first. She clasped her hands and waited. Would talking more help or hurt Nikolai's chances? "His mother was born in Oulu, and he speaks Finnish almost as well as a native." She prayed to a God she didn't quite believe in, begging for them to believe her.

Elomaa walked across the room, hands behind his back, narrowing the gap between them. "Sounds like you know this spy well."

"We've had several conversations." She found herself gripping the sides of her coat.

Elomaa strode back to his desk. "Where is he? I assume he's still in camp."

"Yes. Again, I apologize for not reporting him sooner. It was wrong—"

"*Where. Is. He?*"

Sini's heart leapt to her throat. "In the food-storage dugout. Behind the sacks and barrels on the left by the window." The energy in the tent multiplied; all of the officers seemed alive and eager to act.

"Listen!" Sini cried. They looked at her in surprise, as if the last thing they expected was a woman to give an order. "He couldn't have gained any information from us, but he may have information about the Soviets that could benefit us."

Elomaa grunted impatiently. "What are you saying?"

"Take him alive. He's armed. If you surprise him, he'll try to defend himself."

Her words seemed to settle into everyone's minds as if they understood what she wasn't saying: that surprising the spy would also mean his death, and with it, the loss of any information he had that might help their side. Sini held her breath, hoping no one would call her bluff—that Elomaa would want to interrogate Nikolai.

The major stroked his chin. "You can visit him without arousing his suspicions?"

"Yes."

"Do you know where he keeps his firearm?"

"I think so."

She thought of a gap between two barrels of beans, which Nikolai made a point of never closing. He'd never said his pistol was there, but she'd guessed as much.

Elomaa addressed an officer to his left. "How many men on security can you round up at this hour?"

"Four, at least," the man said.

"Good. Bring them here. I'll send some men to keep watch outside the dugout until your men are ready to arrest the Russian. I'll order a truck to prepare to take him away."

"Yes, sir." The officer made a respectful salute, whipped about, and left.

Sini tried to speak, but her voice left her again, so it took an extra attempt. "Sir, where will he be taken?" When Elomaa didn't answer, she tried again. "I beg you to tell me. Where?"

"Away," Elomaa said pointedly. "You don't think that a Lotta who has violated camp security—and possibly betrayed our country—would be given such information, do you?"

"No, sir," she said. "May I ask what will happen to me?"

He took a step closer and eyed her with one arched eyebrow. "We'll decide that later, *after* we verify the truth of what you've told us."

"Yes, sir." She bobbed at the knee this time to show respect.

The next quarter of an hour became a blur, with men racing about and shouting orders. Sini was ordered to sit on a chair in the corner. Waiting, unable to do anything, felt like a unique brand of torture.

Four men on security detail reported to Elomaa. He spoke to them in tones quiet enough that she couldn't make anything out, but she knew he was talking about her, at least in part, because at one point, the men eyed her as if trying to read her soul. What did they see, a traitor?

For the first time the question swirling around the tent entered her heart: *Was* Nikolai a threat?

Chills raced up her arms and down her back. She gripped the sides of the folding chair and focused on a knot of wood in a floorboard. After a moment, Elomaa barked an order. One of the soldiers strode toward Sini, stopping when his boots reached her line of sight.

"Come." When she looked up at him from her chair, he grabbed her arm and yanked her to her feet.

Elomaa left. The rest of the security detail followed, with the soldier still pulling Sini along in the rear. She tried not to cry out in pain from the grip around her arm. In the sudden darkness, she couldn't see the path. The soldier at her side didn't let her choose her pace, either. She stumbled on a slick patch of ice and pitched forward. Instead of landing on her knees, she found herself dangling from his iron hand as if she were a rag doll.

"Get up!"

She scrambled to her feet and prayed she wouldn't fall again. He gave her arm another yank and moved on, leading her like a farm animal. His strides were much larger than hers, and he seemed to be deliberately taking big steps to make keeping up harder for her.

I'm not a traitor, she wanted to say. *Don't treat me like a dirty Russkie.*

Three lanterns appeared ahead. They lit the path but also cast foreboding shadows. Though she couldn't see far ahead— only vague outlines of trees and tents—she knew where they were going as clearly as if it were a bright summer day. She'd taken this path many times over the last weeks, often with nervousness, but always with anticipation and happiness.

They were going to Nikolai.

Sini's boot slid again, and she nearly ran into the soldier, which prompted him to squeeze her arm even harder. Her body protested, and this time she couldn't prevent the stifled cry entirely. By morning, her arm would be colored with bruises.

At last they stopped moving. She shifted her weight and attempted to hold her coat closed with her free hand. She'd hurried to headquarters without buttoning her coat entirely, and they hadn't let her fasten it before leaving. Now she stood outside the dugout. Surely the soldier would loosen grip or at least adjust his hold; his fingers had to be cramping. He only tightened his grasp. She couldn't contain a gasp at the pain, which was now accompanied by burning tears that came from the physical pain as from her worry over Nikolai.

The group they'd been following spread out around the dugout. Two separate lanterns spilled enough light to give her a clear view of the door she'd opened and gone through so many times. She'd come to love and cherish that underground room—the place that held her dearest memories.

By the orange and yellow glow of flickering lanterns, she watched a line of men slowly approach the dugout, firearms at the ready. Nausea washed over her. She wanted to look away but couldn't.

This is it. The end.

Elomaa appeared and stepped to her side. The soldier finally released her arm. She rubbed it with her other hand as the major gestured toward the door in the ground. "You go first," he whispered to Sini. "Talk to him. Get him away from his firearm. Can you do that?"

She nodded miserably then withdrew her flashlight from her coat and turned it on. The weak beam spilled across the snow and finally landed on the handle of the door. She walked to it, the distance shrinking too fast. Standing in front of the door, she paused for just a moment. Elomaa cleared his throat in warning, so she unlatched it. She looked over at the major, who narrowed his eyes in silent threat.

She obeyed by opening the door. The darkness inside seemed deeper than any cavern, ready to swallow her whole. Nikolai was in there, waiting until he knew who was about to enter.

"It's me," she whispered unsteadily. No response. Maybe he was sleeping.

Or maybe he's too smart to be tricked. She'd never called his name without closing the door and securing it with the broom handle. As a precaution, he usually waited even after she'd called to him until she'd rounded the barrels and bags to his hiding place.

Maybe he'd heard them gathering around the dugout. Regardless of the reason, he remained silent. Sini shone the dying beam of her flashlight before her and carefully made her way to Nikolai's hiding spot. When she rounded the corner, there he was in his magnificence. He sat on a bag of wheat, shirtless. He'd been exercising.

He'll be cold outside without a shirt or coat.

His face lit up at the sight of her. "Hey," he whispered. "Didn't expect to see you again so soon."

He wasn't suspicious. Was that better or worse? She didn't dare draw any closer. If she tried, her legs would collapse beneath her. Besides, she needed to get him to come to her— away from his gun. She hoped the dim light obscured her wooden smile.

"I couldn't sleep," she said. Partial truth.

He stood and walked closer, arms extended for her. She stepped into his embrace and wrapped her arms around him, squeezing tight. Could he hear her pounding heart? If so, would he guess the real reason for it? Would this be the last time she'd ever be in his arms?

"Think I can help with getting you to bed?" he asked with a playful grin. He leaned in, and she waited, hopeful for one last kiss, the chance to whisper a farewell, an explanation. Ten more seconds. That's all she needed.

"Now! Go, go, go!" Elomaa's voice burst through the opening, and soldiers flooded the room like spiders.

"What—" Nikolai said. Before either of them could gather their wits, he was handcuffed, and Sini shoved into the corner.

"Where's the gun?" one soldier asked Sini.

She pointed, saying nothing as Nikolai's wide eyes looked from her to the men, to the soldier removing the pistol from the gap, and back to Sini. His initial expression of shock and confusion shifted as understanding seemed to dawn on him. She watched a myriad of emotions cross his face until finally, his jaw hardened, and his nostrils flared.

"Nikolai—"

"Hush!" a soldier said, hand up. "No speaking to the prisoner. Go outside. Your job is done here."

Sini reluctantly went to the door and climbed back up the incline, feeling Nikolai's stare on her back the entire time. Major Elomaa led her to a spot several meters away. "Wait here."

Voices came from below. "I have his sidearm."

"I have the knife."

"Prisoner searched. No other weapons."

And no gunshots. She let out a stuttered breath of relief on that count. Aside from some bruises on her arm, no injuries. Nikolai was alive.

He was shoved up the incline—first she saw his head, his shoulders, then his torso. He shuddered at the sudden chill, made worse, no doubt by his perspiration. He was yanked to the surface by waiting security officers, who grabbed him under the arms and restrained him while the others climbed out.

Sini's eyes burned. She yearned to hold his face between her hands. To kiss him one more time. To see her love for him reflected in his eyes.

I'm right here. Look at me, she thought, willing Nikolai to lift his face the slightest bit. They wouldn't let her speak to him, but if he'd only look at her, he'd know that she'd turned him in not because she'd betrayed him, but because she loved him. To save his life.

To save any hope they might have for a future together.

If he looked at her, they would exchange glances. He'd give her a sign of understanding—the slightest nod, the wisp of a smile, a surreptitious message mouthed toward her. Anything to carry her through whatever she would be facing for the remainder of the war. But Nikolai didn't lift his eyes from the ground. He kept his head down as the soldiers demanded information from him.

He answered in Russian, saying what Sini assumed were his name, rank, and serial number. No matter what question the officers demanded of him, that's all he said.

Speak Finnish, she wanted to yell, though would him speaking Finnish do any good now?

Elomaa ordered security to take him to the camp entrance, where a truck would be arriving any moment.

Flanked by a soldier on each side, Nikolai drew nearer. Soon, he'd pass close enough for her to touch his arm, if Elomaa weren't standing beside her. As he passed—and before she lost sight of his dear, beautiful face—she called to him with a strangled sob. "Nikolai!"

The guards stopped, making Nikolai's step come up short. He lifted his gaze directly to her, as if he'd known precisely where she stood. She was ready to say she loved him. Their eyes met—and for a flash of a second, they held.

Nikolai's expression turned into a snarl. He lunged at her like a rabid dog. "Whore!" he yelled, teeth bared.

Sini drew back, feeling as if she'd been struck. Elomaa stepped in front of her as the security detail wrestled Nikolai into submission. Sini peered around Elomaa's frame, her heart pounding from fear.

Fear of Nikolai—how was that possible?

A soldier held a rifle to Nikolai's back and forced him to keep walking. As he passed her, Nikolai glared at Sini one last time, then spat on her boots. The soldier shoved him roughly, the rifle now between his shoulder blades as they urged him toward the waiting truck, which had been started and now idled in the distance. Elomaa escorted them along the path, leaving Sini with other soldiers.

Before long, Nikolai's figure melded with the darkness ahead. Sini stared into the blackness, her world upended like a child's snow globe thrown across the room. Would she be arrested next and taken to a jail somewhere else? Would she see Leila again?

She'd saved Nikolai's life. But he'd spat on her. Cursed at her. *He loathes me.*

Her body went limp. A guard caught her, putting an arm around her waist to give her support. Everything blurred; she was vaguely aware that she should be grateful. For what, again? Oh, yes, for not having handcuffs slapped on her wrists—yet.

Nikolai, I love you. I didn't get to explain. I didn't say goodbye.

Her ears burned with the cold, and each breath of freezing air seemed to fill her lungs with ice. Her coat still hung open, but she was too weak to hold it closed anymore.

I'll get hypothermia if I stay out much longer. Freezing would be an easier death than what the army will do to me. I should take the coat off.

Tears built up and escaped, feeling hot against her chilled face. She had no strength to wipe them away. Tears didn't matter anyway. Nothing did.

Her heart folded in on itself, the pain so intense that her body seemed ready to crumble into pieces. Tears should have been a relief; they should have released some pain. They didn't. When more and more tears came, building and building until her body shook uncontrollably, she dropped to her knees in the snow, keening. Elomaa left her be.

I betrayed Nikolai. I betrayed my country. Even Leila will think I'm a traitor. Nikolai hates me. But I love him. Oh, God, don't let him hate me.

CHAPTER TWENTY-SIX

January 4, 1940

Marko hefted his duffel and left his tent. He headed for the camp entrance to meet the truck that would take him away from the Tolvajärvi sector and down to the Mannerheim Line. Soon he'd be operating in a bigger hospital behind the Mannerheim Line, where he'd wanted to be from the start. But as his boots squeaked in the snow, he felt a pull back to camp. At the side of the road, he joined a couple of other men waiting for the bus to take them to their next assignments.

"Forgot something," he said, dropping his bag beside one of them. "Watch my stuff? I'll be right back."

"Sure."

"Thanks." Marko turned around and weaved his way through the snowy paths to say goodbye to Leila. He listened for any sounds of an approaching bus engine but heard none. At her tent, he knocked a few times.

Her shift started in an hour. Even so, she'd be awake, and likely dressed and about to come eat.

Leila answered and broke into a smile. "I didn't expect to see you this morning. I'm not late for my shift, am I?" She checked her watch then looked back up with a question in her eyes.

"I'm leaving. My ride should be here any minute."

Her shoulders drooped a bit. "Already? I've enjoyed having you around."

He took her words as encouragement to say what he'd wanted to ever since seeing the pretty girl sitting across the classroom. This camp was the first time he'd seen her in a professional setting, and while it hadn't been long, he admired her skill. She assisted in the OR so smoothly that he almost thought she could read his mind. He'd watched her comfort soldiers in recovery. She worked extra shifts even when she needed sleep as desperately as anyone.

He'd realized anew how amazing Leila was. His time here only reinforced his desire to spend his life with her, to have her be his.

His mother had often said you never knew a person's character until you'd seen them in the middle of crisis. If war didn't show one's true character, he didn't know what would. He toed some snow, unsure how to approach the subject. "War's a constant parade of hellos and goodbyes, isn't it?"

"But the goodbyes are awful." She lowered her head. He couldn't tell for sure, but she was probably crying. He silently cursed himself for being the cause. Talking about goodbyes made her think about Taneli.

You dolt. Sure enough, a bright tear fell down her cheek. He wanted to wipe it away, and though he'd done so in the past, this time felt different. They stood on a precipice, and he had to take one more step before he could enjoy such liberties again.

"You'll see Taneli soon," Marko ventured.

"I miss him so much."

"When this is all over . . ." He suddenly had no idea how to finish the sentence. He'd thought through where he wanted this conversation to go, but not how to phrase it. "Where will you live?"

"Maybe with Aunt Sisko, for a little while. I'd like to return to Viipuri, but that might not be possible. My building might be flattened by now, and who knows where the border will end up being." She loosely crossed her arms and leaned against the door. "What about you?" She looked at him, her gorgeous eyes making his chest grow warm. Nerve endings buzzed throughout his body.

Say it.

"I'll be in my same old apartment. If . . ." He cleared his throat and tried again. "If your apartment isn't livable, you and Taneli can stay with me. You'd be close to Sisko, and—"

"Oh, I couldn't ask that," Leila said. After a moment, her anxious expression softened with a chuckle. "But imagine the gossip if we did. Everyone would assume that you and I . . ." She laughed again.

Why was the idea so funny?

"Yes, there might be talk." Marko tried erase a scowl. He searched for words, knowing that this moment was his one opportunity to make his hopes a reality. "But would that be so terrible?"

"Rumors about us?" She tilted her head side to side. "I suppose not. After staring death in the face, nothing will scare me, not even gossiping old ladies."

The moment had arrived. The fear of losing Leila entirely urged him to speak up. A burning in his chest said he might never get another chance. He wanted to believe that if she moved in with him, that he'd have opportunities to woo her—romantic evenings by firelight, cuddling on a couch, talking over tea. Confessing his love for her. Kissing her. Fully claiming her as his own.

But none of that can happen if you don't say it.

Leila raised her eyebrows in concern. "You look pale." She pressed her hand on his forehead like the practiced nurse she was. "You're hot. Try to put off your orders for a day or two. You need rest."

"I'm not sick." He took her by the shoulders and soaked in every feature, memorizing them. "What I meant before . . ." God, she was beautiful.

"What?" Her eyes searched his.

"Would it be so terrible . . . if the rumors were . . . true?"

At first, Leila didn't understand, but then his meaning dawned on her. She shook her head rapidly and broke away from his touch. "Don't."

"What if we were a couple? Husband and wife?" It was out. Or almost. He had to lay all his cards on the table to smooth the deep furrow in her brow. "Leila, for as long as—"

"I'll manage. *We'll* manage, Taneli and I, just as you said."

"But Leila, I—"

She opened her mouth to reply, but Marko hurried on before she could speak. "Stop," he said. "Listen to—"

"No, *you* stop," Leila said.

Her words surprised him into silence.

She breathed out heavily and put on an obviously fake smile. "You have a fever. Ask for another day or two. Don't try to be all manly like that summer when you broke your arm playing baseball at the park."

She was trying to lighten the mood—and change the subject. And it was working; a flood a memories returned in a rush. "Remember ice skating at that park?" he asked. He could still picture her pale pink hat and matching gloves. Her purple coat.

Leila relaxed, probably thinking he'd given up on the other thread. "The three of us had some good times."

"We did." Why did the conversation always have to include Jaakob?

"We're lucky," Leila said. "Our fifth-grade friendship has lasted into adulthood. How many people can say the same?"

"Fourth." The correction popped out. He remembered every year, every detail. She'd worn a white coat in fifth grade, one with a fur-trimmed hood. That was the winter he'd noticed how the tip of her nose turned red in the cold. Her nose had been red for the better part of the last week. He'd wanted to lean in and kiss the tip at least a thousand times.

"Fourth. My mistake." Her voice sounded deliberate, pushed, as if she had to think through each word before saying it. She'd keep deflecting unless he blurted the rest, so he had to say it fast.

"I've loved you as long as I can remember. Always will. I stepped aside for Jaakob, but he's gone now. You and I—we'd make a good match. He'd want you to be happy, and who better to make you happy than his best friend?" At the end of the speech, he inhaled and then let the air out unevenly, waiting for her answer.

For several seconds, Leila stared at the snowy ground. He'd imagined this scene through the years. Sometimes in his mind, she rejected him because she didn't feel the same way. More often, he pictured them embracing and kissing after she'd finally recognized her love for him, a love that had been right there in front of her all along. However it ended, the scene in his mind always began with Leila being surprised. But now, the scene wasn't going at all as he'd imagined it.

She raised her face to his and looked . . . sad. "I don't know what to say."

What did that mean? What was she thinking? What did she feel? He couldn't infer anything but a touch of sadness and perhaps pity.

Pity can't be good.

"Just think about it." Marko stepped back and put one hand up to stop her from speaking. "Don't answer yet. Maybe Jaakob, wherever he is, arranged for us to be together during the war—like a heavenly matchmaker. What are the chances that we both ended up here?"

"Why are you bringing heaven into this?" Leila asked. Blame filled her eyes. "You don't believe that Jaakob is anywhere, thinking anything, or doing anything. How dare you try to manipulate me like that?" She folded her arms tighter, closing herself off from him.

"I'm sorry," he said, stepping forward. She leaned backward, away. "I didn't mean to upset you. This whole thing must have come as an unpleasant shock."

She didn't nod in agreement. She pressed her lips into a line as if holding back emotion and stared past his shoulder.

Realization struck him like a punch in the stomach. "You . . . already knew."

239

A tear snaked down her cheek. She swiped it away. For the space of four heartbeats, he waited for her to speak. The only answer he got was a slight nod. She had known. For how long? Without another word, he turned and stalked away toward the idling truck.

Leila called behind him. "Marko, I . . ."

His step slowed. He turned his head slightly to hear her better—but not so much as to see her face. He braced himself.

"I'm sorry. I can't." Her words were a bullet to his chest. He gritted his teeth and took another step, but she spoke again. "You've always been one of the dearest people in the world to me. Closer than a friend—a brother."

A brother? His nostrils flared.

Snow squeaked with her footsteps, and then she spoke from right behind him. "Even if I felt the same way, I would still say no." He felt her touch on his shoulder.

Against his better judgment, he put a hand possessively over hers and turned around.

"My priority must be Taneli. Can you understand that?" She studied his face, hoping for understanding he could not give. "When the war is over, my son and I will have plenty to muddle through. I can't make room in my life for any man. Not now."

The following silence echoed the unspoken words, *Not ever with you.*

Marko dropped his hand from hers and walked away.

Her voice called out one last time. "I'm so sorry."

CHAPTER TWENTY-SEVEN

At last Marko reached his new hospital behind the Mannerheim Line. He waited for the thrill of ambition. This was what he'd wanted. But he didn't care anymore. He felt hollow. In a way, he thought he understood soldiers who'd asked him to take their lives. No procedure or bandage or medication could take this pain away.

Leila didn't love him.

Within an hour of his arrival, he was put to work, and glad for the distraction. He was one of a long row of doctors at tables, operating on a seemingly endless stream of severely wounded. Having to focus on gruesome injuries meant that he didn't have to consciously keep his emotions at bay. He felt as if he'd left his heart and everything it felt back in Tolvajärvi with Leila. He moved like an automaton. He stopped bleeding. Patched bodies. Picked out shrapnel. Treated burns. Stitched wounds. Watched too many men die on the table.

He simply moved to the next one.

His life consisted of the operating room, meals, and sleep. He didn't take his turns in the sauna, something he never would have believed himself capable of.

Two orderlies carried a patient off his table and out of the room as another set carried the next one in. Marko contemplated the never-ending stream. Would he operate until he dropped from exhaustion? How long had he been in here today?

The bright lights nearly blinded his weary eyes, making his head pound. The litter was laid before him.

"Faint pulse," his nurse said.

He had the urge to make a sarcastic remark. Of course the pulse was faint. Every single wounded man had a faint pulse from either blood loss or the freezing temperature.

Mental fog threatened to take over. He had no earthly idea which affected him more—hunger or fatigue—only that he doubted his ability to use a scalpel with precision much longer.

Leila knows how to wield a verbal scalpel. She cut out my heart.

"What are we looking at?" he asked.

The nurse consulted the hastily written chart resting at the foot of the litter. "Burns and shrapnel," she said over the man's moaning. "Mostly to the face and torso."

With a pair of shears, she cut away the man's uniform and exposed the raw, red wounds that under normal circumstances would be flowing with blood. These weren't. Marko would never get used such sights. Winter casualties contradicted everything he'd learned in medical school. He'd been taught to check sutures for leaks, but in the field, finding a leak became almost impossible until blood flow was restored by a return of body heat, when it might be too late anyway.

The man was put under, stilling his incoherent moans. Marko's nerves remained on edge. He envied the soldier the chance to sleep. A nap sounded as intoxicating as vodka.

He examined the damaged tissue. This one had a perforated lung. Not as rife with potential complications as—

He swore under his breath. "Perforated bowel."

This soldier would probably die. Not from bleeding out or hypothermia, but of sepsis.

I'll do my best.

But he couldn't do his best. Time spent creating perfect sutures could mean someone else dying while waiting their turn. How could he hurry on a bowel resection? He was about to perform that operation while so exhausted that he wouldn't dare drive a car. Everyone else in the room was in the same situation. He had to function.

An explosion in the distance pounded the operating room with a sonic concussion, followed by debris raining against the walls. Overhead lights flickered off and back on. Everyone stood paralyzed, waiting for a bomb to hit them directly, ending all of their lives in one quick moment.

After thirty seconds, another explosion went off, farther away. More Russian artillery rounds exploded in the distance. Noise from Molotov cocktails, the Finns' weapon of necessity, didn't carry this far. He returned to operating as shelling continued, far enough away that it didn't disrupt the room again, but he could no longer tell if the sounds were receding or approaching.

The hospital stood near a main road, so it could get steady supply shipments, but that also made it a target. Russian tanks, normally unable to drive up to most Finnish camps directly, could reach this hospital if the Line fell.

What if they're already here?

Then we're all dead.

Marko's ears rang as he stared at the wall, trying to make out any sounds of nearby enemy fire.

"BP is dropping." The nurse's terse voice brought his attention back to the table.

He shook himself awake. How long had he been standing there, staring at the clock? His heart rate increased as he tried to remember what he'd been doing, what was wrong with this soldier. Based on the look on the nurse's face, he'd die if Marko didn't act fast.

But he just stared at the patient. The man's clothing was already cut, revealing severe wounds. Marko's mind blanked as if his years of training had been wiped from the slate of his brain.

Marko's eyes traveled up and down the man's body, taking in tears and holes, burned flesh, shrapnel. Bile rose in his throat. He'd never been squeamish around bodies or blood. This wasn't a cadaver. This wasn't a hunting or skiing accident. This wasn't even a real hospital; it was living hell.

"Doctor?" The single word pierced through the fog. The nurse's volume increased. "Doctor!"

He couldn't answer. His eyes burned. From exhaustion? Cold? Tears? All he knew was that this man's life depended on him. So the man was as good as dead.

Marko shook his head back and forth. He backed away from the table. "I—I can't . . ."

He bumped into the table behind him. A tray of instruments fell to the floor. At the metallic clatter, a hush came over the room. Surgeons, nurses, and orderlies alike stopped everything to stare. But all he could feel was a cold sweat breaking across his forehead.

Maybe I'm sick. Leila said I was. Oh, Leila.

He used the table to hold him upright as he stumbled to the end and from there, clung to the counter on the long wall as he made his way to the door. All the way, he tried not to faint or vomit. The coppery smell of blood was everywhere; he had to escape it.

But first, he needed air. A sharp pain pressed on his chest. He clenched his fist and pressed it to his breastbone. His lungs wouldn't inflate.

A voice called from somewhere, one Marko vaguely recognized as one surgeon addressing another. "Leppänen!"

"Take Linna's spot! Nurse Liljeström can finish closing for you."

"Yes, sir," Leppänen said.

You're pathetic, Marko told himself. *You call yourself a surgeon.*

He put out a hand to push the door open, but he nearly collided with an incoming litter as it pushed the door toward him. The time it took to pass through felt eternal. With every second, terror and pressure built in his chest. He had to get out, find fresh air, or he'd die.

Another explosion rocked the tent. Marko covered his head as dust rained on him. He ran through the triage area, completely ignoring the calls of orderlies and moans of the wounded and didn't stop until he reached the room beyond the OR.

There, he cowered on the floor against a row of lockers, knees raised to his face, arms around his legs. He waited for the next blast, which would surely turn him into a pincushion for shrapnel. His surgical mask was suffocating him, so he pulled it down, but the ties might as well have strangled him. He reached up to take it off, but his fingers refused to work the ties. In frustration, he pulled it over his face and off his head, then gasped for welcome air, but his lungs were like lead, heavy and immovable.

He shuddered, sweating, as he waited for the next bomb. Soon it would be his body on the table, his life in another man's hands.

Another boom.

And another.

He leaned his face against a cool, metal locker, and a sharp edge dug into his temple. The resulting pain confirmed that he wasn't dead quite yet.

Breathe, he ordered himself. *In. Out. In. Out.*

What was the point, when he was about to die? Ever since he'd deployed, at any moment, day or night, he could have taken his last breath before being blown to pieces. And he'd thought he could make a difference.

The idea that they could succeed against Stalin's endless supply of soldiers—rows and rows of thousands and thousands, an endless river—was insanity. No matter how many Russians the Finns killed, more kept coming.

In several places, a handful of Finns had taken down thousands of Russians, but it didn't matter. Stalin just replaced them with a trainload of fresh men. The Finns had no more men to send, fresh or otherwise.

Russian soldiers often marched on, stepping over the still-warm bodies of their fallen comrades. When the abandoned bodies froze, the Reds used them as shields from machine gun fire. The whole war was barbaric—and hopeless.

Why hadn't the Allies helped as they'd promised?

Sisu can't win this war. We're all going to die.

He closed his eyes and pressed them into his knees, trying to block everything out, but grisly images flashed through his mind anyway, always returning to the same horrific vision.

245

His body on the metal table. He wore an infantry uniform cut open to reveal thousands of pieces of embedded shrapnel, dozens of bullet wounds, and random burns. His chest didn't rise or fall. Someone draped a sheet over him.

And through it all, he heard Leila's voice. *You're a brother. I can't.*

He gripped his hair with both hands and pulled as hard as he could, screaming as if an angel of death stood above him. Leaning against the locker, his entire body shook like an aspen tree in a windstorm.

CHAPTER TWENTY-EIGHT

"You won't get a second chance," Elomaa warned her. "And I'm not giving you an easy job. You'll face far harsher duties than peeling potatoes and washing bedpans. You'll see the war up close, in ways you've never imagined."

If he'd meant to scare her, he succeeded.

"One more slipup," he added, "and you will have far more serious consequences."

"I understand, sir. Thank you for the opportunity to continue serving." She bobbed at the knee in respect and was relieved when she was excused to eat lunch and then pack her things.

A transfer. That was Sini's entire punishment. Elomaa must have believed everything she'd said about intending to report Nikolai. Maybe he thought she was too naïve or immature to grasp the nature of the crime and figured the easiest way to deal with her was to pass her on to someone else. And maybe all of that was true.

However it had happened, she was leaving the hospital today, and not in shackles.

She'd eaten a small lunch, then, as ordered, returned to her tent to pack, which didn't take long. After weeks of constant work, being shuffled between the kitchen, infirmary, and operating room, she found being still rather unsettling. The tent seemed bigger somehow, cavernous. She had nothing to occupy her time with except her thoughts. Technically, yes, she could have been knitting, but one glance at her bag—and the remaining blue wool inside—made her heartsick. She doubted she'd ever knit again.

The tent flap opened, and an unfamiliar Lotta stepped inside. "Sini?"

"Yes?"

"Your transport leaves in twenty minutes."

"Thank you." Sini stood. "Do you know where my assignment is?"

"You weren't told? You're going to Suomussalmi."

"Oh." She hadn't heard much about that location except that there were horrors along Raate Road.

The rumors were true, then, if that's what Elomaa thought would be a fitting punishment. The Lotta turned to leave, but Sini had to know more. Much of the war had already included battles that seemed impossible, Finnish troops that had overcome unthinkable odds, battles won that made no logical sense but were true.

"Wait." She had to know if the tales about Raate Road were embellished. "Is what they say about Raate Road . . ." Her voice trailed off.

The woman had turned to leave, but she looked back, her hand on a tent pole beside the flap opening. "All true—it may end up being our greatest victory yet."

"Goodness," Sini said, and dropped to her cot, needing to sit again. The Russian slaughter, brought on essentially by an improvised siege that killed with cold and hunger, was unparalleled in war, or so they said.

"It's amazing," the Lotta said, and then left.

Sini tried to remember all she'd heard, things she'd dismissed because they'd seemed insane even in a war with so many surprises.

From what she remembered, Soviet division number forty-something was stretched out over several kilometers along Raate Road in the Suomussalmi area. Finnish skiers had blocked the road in both directions, halting the division's progress in both directions. The Soviet division was stuck, locked in by thick forest on both sides of the road.

The Finnish forces, in four groups, made surprise attacks, appearing out of the forest out of seemingly nowhere, then cutting across the road. They'd broken the Soviet line into smaller and smaller cells, which they could destroy relatively easily. Some already called the strategy the *motti* tactic, referring to cutting up logs into cords of firewood.

"So it's true, then?" Sini asked.

"The latest report I heard said that some of the cells are a kilometer or more away from others, and Russians are starving and freezing to death as much as being shot. Thousands of Russians are dead, or so they say, but the numbers I've heard sound impossibly high."

An inkling of relief waited in the corners of Sini's mind. "The battle of Raate Road is over, then?"

"The worst is past," the Lotta said. "But it's not over yet."

That probably meant that not all of the cells were under Finnish control, and that their troops would need more supplies to hold their advantage. Her job would be to deliver supplies to the men hiding in the woods lining Raate Road.

She'd probably get a white snowsuit. The fact that she'd be so close to the enemy that she'd need to wear camouflage every day made a wave of nausea pass over her. She pressed a hand to her middle and tried to stop picturing herself ducking and hiding as bullets splintered trees, sending woodchips flying around her head.

I deserve no less. I betrayed Nikolai. I should have at least told him what I was doing—and why—before reporting him.

The facts didn't matter. Not even how she'd been so sure that he'd be discovered and killed if she didn't act right away. That she'd reported him to save him. All she could think of, aside from the very real possibility that she might soon be killed by a Russian sniper, was that if Nikolai had once loved her as she'd thought—as she'd loved him—he no longer did. He despised her.

Over and over, her mind insisted on returning to the moment he'd given her that look of disgust. When he'd snarled and spat at her feet.

He hates me. Everything we had is gone.

Had he ever cared for her? Or had he merely been using her—first for food and shelter, then for pleasure? The last thought made her stomach turn even more. She'd reveled in being the center of someone's world for once, but that had been foolish of her. The actions of a girl. How could she have been so weak, so gullible, so desperate, that she'd believed the first man to show her real attention?

Was any of it real? She would have given anything to know. Feeling shaky and lightheaded, she put her head in her hands. In a way, Nikolai had been untrue to her.

She had been betrayed, too, in a way. She couldn't quite believe that, though she wanted to. Her stomach lurched again, and she could tell that this time, she might not be able to keep down what little breakfast she'd eaten. She hurried to the tent flap and climbed out half a second before she covered the snow with remains of bread and coffee. As Sini clung to a tent pole, panting in the freezing air with no coat, Leila appeared.

"What's wrong?" She felt Sini's forehead. "No fever, but you're definitely unwell—you look almost green. Go inside and lie down."

Sini grabbed a handful of snow to wipe her mouth then silently obeyed, returning to the tent and walking to the foot of her cot with small steps. She slowly lowered to her cot. She felt a little better already, though she didn't know if it was because she'd emptied her uneasy stomach, she was horizontal again, or because having Leila nearby was a comfort.

"I'm getting transferred," she said, eyes closed. She tried to breathe slowly and shallowly to avoid another trip to the snowbank. "In just a few minutes."

"That's why I hurried over," Leila said, dropping onto her own cot. "Päivi mentioned it—how she knew, I have no idea—but I left the infirmary and ran over, hoping I didn't miss saying goodbye."

"I'm glad you made it." Sini felt an additional measure of relief over the fact that Leila didn't seem to be aware that Sini's transfer had anything to do with the Russian spy found in the food-storage dugout. Hopefully that meant Elomaa hadn't spread the word. Leila didn't despise her—yet.

"I'll miss you," Leila said.

"I'll miss you, too." An enormous understatement.

"I was hoping to be with you for the duration." Leila didn't need to clarify the duration of what.

Not long ago, Sini would have welcomed the chance to leave. Her first days here had each lasted an eternity, and then all of a sudden, everything had changed. And then changed again.

She had a best friend in the form of the one woman she'd once imagined to be an enemy and the one obstacle standing between her and Marko. But Leila wasn't competition—never had been. Rather, Leila was kind and understanding. Sisterly. Genuine. Sincere.

Hearing about him from Leila's point of view had been a balm for Sini, offering healing she couldn't have had any other way.

All of these thoughts, and the emotions behind them, built up in her chest and spilled over. The tears came slowly at first, but soon they turned into a full-on crying jag. Leila left her cot and urged Sini to a sitting position, sitting beside her. They embraced as Sini wept.

"Everything will turn out," Leila whispered. "We'll see each other again. The war will end soon."

"I never had a sister," Sini said between sobs. "Until you."

"Me, neither. I'm so glad we found each other."

Leaving would be pure torture. Elomaa must have known how much a transfer would hurt.

Leila pulled back and smiled through tears, sniffing and wiping her cheeks. She reached forward and wiped Sini's cheeks as an older sister might. "We won't lose each other." She then turned to her footlocker and rummaged around, pulling out a book, an envelope, a notepad, a pencil, and a few other things.

She set most of the stack on her cot and began writing on the notepad with the pencil.

She tore off the paper and held it out. "This is Aunt Sisko's address and telephone number in Helsinki. No matter where I end up, she'll know how to find me, and you'll have a place to stay."

Sini took the paper and memorized the address—not that she'd lose the paper, but as a precaution. "That's not far from my place," she said, a tiny smile pulling at the corners of her mouth. "If you live with her after the war, we could see each other often."

"I'd like that." Leila pushed the notepad and pencil toward Sini. "Now I need your address and telephone number."

Sini complied, returned the notepad, and they held each other again. Sini didn't come from an affectionate family, so this moment felt both strange and wonderful. She might never know whether Nikolai had pretended to love her, or whether his hateful reaction stemmed from shock and hurt. But she knew one thing: Leila cared. The notepaper in her hand was proof.

Provided she never learns about Nikolai.

Leila slipped the notepad back into its home, then picked up the envelope and held it in her hands as if weighing it. "I don't have much family. Did I ever tell you that?" She glanced up and shrugged. "Of course, you already know about Jaakob's death."

"You have Aunt Sisko and Taneli."

"Yes, I do," Leila said with a thoughtful nod, staring at the envelope. "But Aunt Sisko is old. My parents are gone. I have no siblings." Her blue eyes pierced Sini with a hopeful expression. "Taneli has only one godparent."

"Marko."

A nod. "But he hasn't been involved in Taneli's life as a godfather should be." Leila dabbed the back of one finger to one eye and then the other. "Taneli needs more family, and so do I. So, I took the liberty of, well, here." She held out the envelope. "I don't want to pressure you at all. This is only if it's something you want to do."

Curious, Sini accepted the envelope. She peered inside the unsealed package then removed several official-looking papers—official, but not military.

"I'd like you to be Taneli's godmother," Leila said.

"You want—" Sini put one hand to her mouth in surprise, not daring to hope for such an honor. "I've never been religious."

"Were you baptized as a baby?"

"Yes, but I don't know who my godparents were. I'm not close to any relatives."

"Being a baptized Lutheran is the only requirement. How often you pray or attend services doesn't matter." Leila leaned forward. "I have a feeling you'd be far more involved in Taneli's life than Marko has been or ever will be. It would mean the world if you said yes and made us all family."

Family. Sini had never belonged to one, not really. Here she was being asked to join Leila's. Tears pricked her eyes. "You're sure?" She wanted this more than she could have ever imagined, but only if Leila wanted it, not if it was a gesture of pity.

"Absolutely. Taneli has already lost his father. Aunt Sisko can't have many years left, and I don't know if Taneli will remember her. I doubt Marko will ever be in our lives. Taneli needs more than I can give him." Leila placed a hand on Sini's. "He needs a godmother." Her voice broke as she added, "And I need a sister. I didn't know that before, but now I can't imagine life without you in it." She pointed at the papers. "Don't feel pressured. It won't be official without your signature."

Sini could hardly form a sentence. "How? How did you do this?"

"I wrote my pastor asking permission, and he granted it. He was never happy with Taneli having only one godparent. This is unorthodox, but exceptions can be made in uncertain times. Taneli won't need special gifts or any of that. I just want you to be part of our family."

Sini hadn't met Taneli, but she already loved him and wanted to give him everything she never had. She'd be the best aunt a little boy could hope for. "I'd be honored. Truly."

253

"Taneli will adore you," Leila said. "I know it."

"I'll spoil him rotten," Sini threatened with a laugh.

Leila's voice grew somber. "Promise?"

"I promise," Sini said. "You're stuck with me, and so is my godson." She took the pencil from Leila, signed the papers as if a delay might make them evaporate into mist. If needed, she'd sign them again with ink.

She looked at her signature and felt a warmth in her chest. Their relationship would continue until the grave. She had a firm place to stand when the rest of her world crumbled around her. *Family* with Leila meant far more than it ever had through blood.

Maybe, in seeking love from Marko and then from Nikolai, she'd been seeking belonging, someone to love her unconditionally. She'd assumed that the hole in her heart could be filled by romance and stolen kisses.

Such a foolish idea—she could see that now. Men and romance had their place, but she'd be happiest as Leila's adopted sister and Taneli's godmother. Not as any man's anything else.

Leila pulled carbon copies from the back of each page and handed them over. "Yours."

Sini carefully folded the pages. "I'll treasure these."

"Me, too," Leila said.

A soldier stuck his head into the tent through the flap and called for Sini. "Transport's loading."

"Coming." Sini slipped the papers into her duffel, stood, then did her best to keep her eyes dry when faced with saying goodbye to her new sister.

"We *will* be in touch," Leila said. "Before you know it, we'll be shopping for dresses at Stockmann, and you'll be buying Taneli too much ice cream."

"Soon," Sini said.

"Soon," Leila agreed.

As Sini lugged her bag to the bus, she did her best to freeze her emotions so she wouldn't think about missing Leila. Or about losing Nikolai. She missed so much about him—his smile, his voice, his kisses . . .

Yet any happy memory was quickly followed by that of his accusing eyes and their accusation of disloyalty.

Better to think of Leila, of how life would be better after the war. Unless she ever learned about Nikolai. Why did Sini's thoughts always return to him? He was like a bright flashlight beam shining in her eyes, incapable of being ignored.

I saved you, she wanted to tell him. *Because I love you.* If she saw him again, would he believe her? Forgive her? Would he be sent back to the Soviet Union before the war ended?

And would she ever know what had really happened between them?

She boarded the bus and took her seat, feeling only half alive, but that was better than wrenching sadness. As the bus lurched forward, Sini nearly cried out for it to stop, to let her run back to the dugout, to kiss Nikolai one last time.

But he wasn't there anymore. He'd been taken way.

And he hated her.

The frozen shell she'd built around herself kept the emotional frenzy inside; by looking at her, no one would have known that she had a war going on in her chest.

The bus drove on and on; and as the journey stretched, her tears finally fell, one by one, as if the ice shell she'd constructed were melting. The pain she'd held in pushed into her heart, and this time, she couldn't stem the tide.

When the bus stopped, she got off and transferred to a railcar headed for Oulu. She moved silently, like a sheep bound for slaughter. She was done crying. In fact, she wondered if she could cry anymore; she felt wrung out.

From Oulu, she had one last leg by car before reaching Suomussalmi. Whatever duties awaited her, at least they wouldn't involve the sights or smells of the infirmary.

The train pulled out, and she rested her head on the window. *I have a godson. Now he has two godparents.*

255

Sharing that responsibility with Marko would be the closest thing to a relationship she'd ever have with him—ironic, now that she cared nothing for him. Life certainly had an odd sense of humor.

In Oulu, she disembarked into darkness and found the vehicle that would be taking her to the camp. The truck was open to the elements in the back, with only a flimsy fabric cover and benches lining the back on both sides.

Sure enough, she was directed to climb into the bed of the truck. She took a deep breath through her nose to steel herself—a mistake. The cruel temperature nearly froze her nostrils together, and the cold air cut her lungs. It had to be negative thirty centigrade, or nearly.

We'll be lucky to reach camp without frostbite.

She moved along the bed of the truck, hoping to sit near the cab, where the wind might be less intense. She found a spot and sat on the bench. The truck bed had some wool blankets, but they reeked and were wet, lying in several centimeters of muddy slush. She tucked her skirts tight around her legs, then braced herself as the truck jolted forward.

CHAPTER TWENTY-NINE

January 6

After Sini had worked for two days as support for the large group the military referred to as Task Force Kari, she had yet to see Raate Road. No doubt Elomaa would be disappointed if he ever learned that so far, she'd avoided what thought would be her punishment.

Her assignments had consisted of cooking meals for the men returning from patrol and preparing meals for other Lottas to take to men along the road, hiding in camouflaged dugouts every five hundred or so meters along Raate Road.

Whenever a patrol group returned, the soldiers looked almost as bad as some of the men Sini had seen in the infirmary—including some who'd died. The men ate, slept for a few hours, and went on duty again. Some got to have a sauna turn during rotations, which might have been the one thing keeping up morale.

On the afternoon of Sini's third day, halfway through her shift, she was given a new assignment to drive a supply truck. That would be unnerving enough; the snow and ice and identical forests were all treacherous. But her stomach soured for another reason: she would be driving supplies to Task Force Fagernäs, the division assigned to destroy the enemy line on Raate Road. She prayed she wouldn't have to see the road itself.

Alone, she drove the dark, icy roads. The truck was equipped with a radio, and in some spots, the road had been sprinkled with pea gravel for traction. But with newly fallen snow, she had to grip the steering wheel hard and focus to avoid sliding off the road, head-on into towering pines.

She radioed ahead to Task Force Fagernäs, so when she drove up and came to an unsteady stop—sliding a meter or so before coming to halt—several men and two Lottas were waiting to unload the truck. Fifteen minutes later, the engine still warm, Sini climbed back into the cab. She couldn't help but think about how the Lottas were likely stacking food in their own dugout.

Everything returned to Nikolai.

Once more, Sini put the truck into gear. Daylight had fled, and the thick darkness made the road ahead hard to see. She wiped condensation from the windshield using her sleeve and sat forward, peering through the windshield and trying to make out the road ahead, which was barely visible in the beams of the yellow headlights.

At long last, she reached the turnoff to camp, and she breathed shakily with relief. The adrenaline that had kept her alert during the drive began to wane, and a wave of fatigue threatened to wash over her. She parked behind another truck, but as she pulled out the key, nausea rushed over her. The paper sack that had held food for the trip was almost empty. She didn't dare waste time dumping the remaining crackers out, and instead held the sack in front of her to catch whatever it could. Ever since her transfer, she'd felt as if she had the flu, except she had no fever, so she couldn't plead illness to avoid work.

She'd spent so much time focusing on driving that it had to be the cause of her fatigue. Clutching the paper bag, she gingerly climbed out of the truck and began to wonder what else was wrong with her. It wasn't the flu, and it wasn't only fatigue. Something felt *off*. She couldn't pinpoint how, but her body didn't feel like her own. Perhaps this was her body's way of responding to war.

With her boots on the icy ground, she stood still a moment to wait for the lightheadedness to pass. When she felt stable, she shoved the truck door hard so it would close all the way, but the force threw her off balance. She scrambled and barely managed to keep herself from hitting the ice. Her vision swam with dizziness, making the nausea worse. Both had hovered at the periphery for hours. If she didn't get somewhere soon, she'd pass out and freeze to death before someone found her.

Closing her eyes, she swallowed hard and tried to breathe deeply. That only made the nausea worse. Her stomach contracted, and she could feel the crackers coming up. With one hand on the truck, not daring to let go, she turned to the snow in time for her stomach to empty itself, contracting again and again until she was dry heaving.

At least it was dark; no one had seen her get sick on the snow. She fumbled for her flashlight and struggled to free it from her coat pocket. She shined the light on the mess, made a face, and kicked snow over it. Then she weakly made her way into camp. She'd come to hate the sight of the white, eight-sided tents and their uncomfortable cots. For the moment, she couldn't wait to reach hers and sleep.

But first, she needed to report at the camp office and check the truck in. Then she could officially go off duty. She dreaded seeing Kaisa, the head Lotta. The woman looked as if she'd been born with lips pulled down at the corners. Her tight bun pulled the corners of her eyes. Sini had been on the receiving end of several of Kaisa's lectures and doubted whether the woman was capable of smiling. An attempt might shatter her face altogether.

Kaisa refused to believe that Sini was genuinely sick and needed rest. Sini needed sleep, but she didn't dare push back or look weak, or she'd face a dishonorable discharge or another punishment. At least, that's what Elomaa had said. He hadn't been specific, but her imagination provided plenty of possibilities.

In the office, Sini recorded the time of her arrival, the details of the delivery, then checked in the truck key, all with no sign of Kaisa. Hoping for several hours of sleep, Sini dragged herself to her tent and collapsed onto her cot, lying on her side without taking off her boots or coat. The world began spinning again, but at least she could close her eyes. Plus, no one was yelling at her.

Somewhere in the back of her mind, she remembered that she'd meant to get some food. She should have checked to see when her next shift was scheduled, too. But now that she was on her cot, she couldn't move. Not for a few minutes, at least.

She must have fallen asleep, because the next thing she knew, the tent was gray instead of black. The tent flap flew open, bringing with it a swirl of cold air and snow. Sini opened one eye, wincing at the temperature and noise. A dark silhouette appeared, hands on her hips. She cringed and waited for Kaisa's reprimand.

"Toivola. *What* are you doing?" she demanded. "You're about as useful to the country as a pile of potato skins."

"After I checked the truck in, I came here to rest," Sini said groggily. How long had she been asleep? It felt like only a few minutes, but her scratchy voice and the dim daylight coming through the tent walls indicated at least an hour or two must have passed.

"You were not relieved of duty." Kaisa strode over and gruffly pushed a hand onto Sini's forehead. She grunted. "No fever, of course. Get up."

"I'm so sorry," Sini said, sitting and struggling to wake fully. "I thought my shift was over when I returned the truck key. But I think something is wrong—" She covered her mouth and looked about for something to throw up into, but then ran outside and, without a second to spare, vomited onto the snow beside the path. Only stomach acid.

She stood there, hands shaking, dreading having to face Kaisa's reaction. With her boot, Sini covered the mess with snow, then used a handful to wipe her mouth. When she turned back, Kaisa lifted one eyebrow into a doubtful arc.

"I am so sorry," Sini said again. "I sincerely want to do my part."

What was wrong with her? Sini had no fever or chills or any other typical signs of illness besides exhaustion and nausea. If only Leila were here and could help her figure out what was wrong.

At the thought of Leila, of how nurturing and kind she was—like a mother—Sini's eyes went wide.

Could I be . . . She swore under her breath.

Fraternization alone was grounds for dismissal. A pregnancy would send her home in disgrace. And a pregnancy from a Russian spy? She shook her head, trying to chase away all sorts of consequences her imagination insisted on inventing.

What would Nikolai think if he knew? In her mind, she could see the warm smile he always gave before kissing her. But that memory was quickly replaced by the look of hatred he'd thrown at her before spitting at her feet.

She might have a part of him inside her. His hatred. His disdain. One hand instinctively went to her middle. She might be carrying a Russian's child. An enemy's child.

And my child, too, she reminded herself.

She couldn't ever tell anyone who it belonged to. If she was pregnant.

Kaisa sniffed, bringing Sini's attention back to the moment. "You were to have eight hours to eat and rest, but Kukka got sick—actually sick—and can't make the meal delivery on Raate Road."

Meals to the road were done by kick sled; one couldn't get there by truck. And Kaisa expected Sini to be able to make the journey? How many kilometers was it there and back?

"Fia will go with you; she knows the way. Two kick sleds will be loaded and ready in just a few minutes. Hurry."

"Yes, ma'am." Sini imagined balancing on the runners, propelling herself through uneven forest, a load of food sitting on the seat in front of her, sloshing around, maybe spilling. What if she vomited on the food? Or fell off the runners from exhaustion?

"Maps will be left on your kick sleds. They're already getting loaded. Report in five minutes."

Sini bobbed respectfully. "May I get a bite to eat first? That might give me some strength."

Kaisa considered it for a moment, then nodded with a jerk of her head. "Very well. But be quick about it. Report in *ten* minutes."

"I will. Thank you." Would she be able to keep food down if she ate it fast? She hurried to the mess tent, where she sipped a little broth and filled a thermos with more for the trip.

All too soon, Sini and Fia were heading through the trees on their kick sleds, compasses resting atop their loads in front of them. Most likely, Sini would be seeing the *motti* cells of Russians up close. She hoped not. She wanted to find the soldiers' camouflaged barracks off the road, feed them, and be on her way.

When soldiers rotated through camp from the dugouts to patrol to camp, they often spoke of the surprise attacks and the resulting *mottis*, executed with such speed that the Russians hadn't seen the white-suited Finns until they were upon them. The brilliant strategy was true of the Finnish tradition and made her proud of her country.

The Russians had fought hard, but their firepower wasn't helpful; the Finns had been able to get too close for a tank to lower its guns to fire at them. Armed Russian troops had been too shocked to react at all.

The gaps between *motti* cells had been broadened, with stretches of snow separating the groups of Russians. Someone had said that the result must look like links of sausage from the air. As some *motti* cells shrank, others broke out in fights. Some had been completely destroyed, one man at a time, by Finnish snipers tied high into trees.

Thousands of Russians were already dead along the road, and the remainder were starving, freezing, or so paranoid that they were on the edge of madness. A couple of Soviet planes had attempted food drops, but hardtack hadn't been nearly enough to stave off the hunger of more than a few men for couple of hours.

The whole thing sounded like a tall tale from someone's imagination. Surely some of the stories she'd heard were exaggerated.

She and Fia pushed their kick sleds for at least half an hour, with Fia in the lead. Sini was grateful for one thing: traveling through the forest during daylight hours felt much safer than driving a truck at night.

"How much farther?" she asked, keeping her voice low in case any Russians were near.

"We're almost there." Fia let her sled slow, and then pointed. "Over there, up the hill."

Hill? Sini groaned.

About ten minutes later, Fia stepped off her sled and announced that they'd arrived. Sini couldn't make out a camp or men anywhere, but then again, that was the point of camouflage. On Fia's direction, they hid their sleds beneath a group of pines then headed out to find the hidden dugouts and a few men to come get the food.

Fia paused, searching for a landmark. She checked her compass. "They should be right here." Had they gone the wrong direction? One area of the forest looked pretty much the same as another.

"That way," Fia said, walking ahead. "I know we're close."

The only sounds were their feet crunching on the snow, and the sound of their snowsuits swishing with each step. Sini was grateful to be walking; kicking the sled was more exertion than she could take. Walking was slower, and she could rest more.

"Are we lost?" Sini whispered after a while. What would they do if they got totally lost? Would they be able to find their way back to the sleds? Or would they die, as Nikolai would have if she hadn't helped him?

No, they would be fine. They were dressed for the conditions, Sini reminded herself, and Fia had a small backpack with provisions as well as a radio. They'd be fine. If they could only find the hidden dugout. Fia stopped so suddenly that Sini bumped into her. She expected the Lotta to keep going, but her eyes had grown wide, and her mouth hung open as she walked forward.

"What?" Sini scurried to keep up, climbing toward a clearing, which turned out to be a road. A burned-out panzer came into view.

"Raate Road," Fia whispered.

Strewn along the length of the road were more burned-out vehicles—artillery, trucks, and more. This was probably an abandoned *motti*, maybe last in the line.

They stopped at the edge of the road and waited. Fia seemed to be straining to hear, but when no sound reached them for several minutes, she gestured to Sini and said, "Come."

They walked along the edge of the road, alert and wary. Silence was no comfort; Russian snipers could be lying in wait. Dim voices came from somewhere in the distance. They might be speaking Finnish, but she couldn't be sure.

Fia paused and stared at the road nervously. "Is anyone out there?" she called—not loudly, but more than a whisper. Enough to carry to a nearby dugout.

Sini turned to look at the burned and abandoned vehicles. She saw no sign of human life. Together, curious as much as anything, they stepped into the remains of the *motti*. More destruction—not just vehicles but boxes and trunks overturned, their contents strewn about.

But now that they'd come into the center of the road, they saw more than just supplies and vehicles. The dead were everywhere, frozen in place, looking like gray statues.

One man held a long-since spent match to light a cigarette hanging from his blue lips. Another hugged himself, hands under his arms for warmth he'd never feel again. In one area, she noted animal hair and realized she was looking at a horse's mane. She drew closer. The horse was stiff as stone. She looked away, but something caught her eye, making her turn back—the flank looked wrong. A closer look revealed chunks of flesh carved out.

Sini covered her mouth in horror; what little broth that remained in her stomach threatened to come back up.

"They were . . . starving," Fia said. A hand went to her mouth, matching Sini's. They shared the sadness and horror.

These men had come to their country to kill and to conquer. They were the enemy. But Sini couldn't suppress the tears threatening to form in the corners of her eyes. She turned away, aching for the victims' families.

She'd heard the *motti* tactic praised and celebrated. She'd quietly celebrated the ingeniousness of the Finns in fighting a Goliath with the equivalent of a David army. But seeing the reality . . . Elomaa was right.

Her stomach convulsed. Bile rose in her throat. She held her breath and locked her knees so she wouldn't drop to the ground from weakness.

Sisu. *I have* sisu. *Be strong.*

Her vision slowly narrowed until she felt as if she were staring into a tunnel. The world closed in on her and went dark right before Sini's body hit the snow. Her last thought was of Kaisa.

I'm a disgrace for being weak.

CHAPTER THIRTY

Six weeks later—February 18, 1940
The Mannerheim Line

Marko hunched inside a snowy trench on the Intermediate Line, assigned as infantry, a humiliating position to be in as a man with his background and education. But after January's breakdown in surgery, he could no longer be trusted to wield a scalpel, apparently. But a rifle? Oh, yes.

Artillery shells whistled overhead day and night, without a break. He'd thought that at the Intermediate Mannerheim Line, he wouldn't see much action, but that turned out to be wrong, too. The front line had fallen back, so now the Intermediate Line was the front line trying to hold off the enemy.

Shells exploded everywhere, sending wave after wave of concussion. He felt like a trapped animal in that trench. He pressed his back against the wall, as if that would provide shelter, but the frozen earth only dug into his back painfully.

A round hit closer than usual; Marko covered his ears with his hands. Nothing could entirely block out the sound, but he needed to dull the pounding somehow. He braced his boots against the muddy ice of the trench floor, elbows on his thighs, eyes closed.

More rounds exploded nearby. He sucked in a breath and waited for the ground to stop trembling. Even his boots shook. The moment one tremor ended, another began.

The earth was never still, the air never silent. Neither had been for over two weeks now.

Though this section of the line had been largely abandoned, the Soviet assault continued. Marko and a handful of others were left behind to delay Timoshenko's offensive push. Marshal Mannerheim had ordered most of the Intermediate Line to fall back to the third section of the Mannerheim Line.

There was no fourth line.

If Timoshenko's forces broke through, he *would* reach Helsinki. The war would be over in a matter of hours, and they would all be Stalin's subjects.

When Marko's hands didn't muffle the explosions enough, he grabbed his white-painted rifle, which he'd leaned against the side of the trench. He held the stock tighter, hoping the waves of sound and trembling would ebb, as if his weapon were a sign of security—something that could protect him, something permanent.

It wasn't either of those things, of course. Nothing was permanent anymore.

The metal felt foreign in his hands, big and awkward beneath his fur-lined gloves. He missed the precision involved with using a scalpel. He'd done a lot of good in operating rooms. But he'd been sent to a trench away from the rest of the army, given this ugly rifle, which he was told to use to kill.

This wasn't supposed to be how he helped the war effort. As heinous as the first-responder station had been, he wished he could go back, patching up wounded Finnish soldiers instead of trying to kill Russians. But with more than half of the Finnish army dead, more men were always needed at the front.

Only a handful of medical personnel remained, and supposedly he wasn't stable enough to be one of them. Besides, if the Line fell, stitching the wounded wouldn't matter.

Marko looked along the trench at the men left behind on the Intermediate Line with him. Their orders were to delay Timoshenko, not defeat him. To buy the rear line some time. Timoshenko would march on. They'd almost certainly die here, in this barbed-wire-covered terrain, without a person nearby who knew or cared about him.

More thundering sounded overhead. The ground shook again. Thin sheets of dirt and snow tumbled into the trench, some making tinkling noises bouncing off his helmet. He reached up and brushed it off, not that doing so mattered. His helmet, like his uniform and rifle, didn't match the others'. So much of what they wore and used was pieced together however it could be. His helmet was one of several thousand purchased cheaply years ago from some other country. Germany? He couldn't remember, and it didn't matter anyway.

Marko wanted to stand, to look above ground, to see something besides the claustrophobic trench. Maybe search the sky in the distance to tell whether the artillery attack was almost over. But lifting his head even a few centimeters could mean getting his head blown off. Not even his cheap helmet could prevent that.

One explosion after another rocked his body to the bone. Trees in the distance groaned and creaked, falling into the snow. Soil and pieces of rock burst into the air, leaving craters in the already pockmarked earth.

Gradually, the booms of shells grew farther apart. He began to breathe a little more regularly. Unbelievably, the artillery slowed . . . and then it stopped. It actually stopped.

An eerie silence permeated the air, pressed on his ears almost like the sound had before. No one moved except to look at one another. They all knew what came after an artillery barrage: an infantry attack.

Leap Day is soon, he thought, dimly aware that it was an odd observation under the circumstances. Would he be alive to see it? Or any other Leap Day?

He checked his magazine then pressed his back into the trench wall again. His pulse pounded so hard that his ribcage felt like an anvil, fear striking his heart again and again. The Mannerheim Line *would* fall. That was the reality.

Yet it should have fallen two months ago. How had it hung on so long, without many supplies, weapons, or support?

Since November 30, the Russians had breached the Mannerheim Line in various spots along its one hundred twenty kilometers stretching across the Karelian Isthmus. Each time, miraculously, the Finns rallied and repaired each breach. The Line held.

But then, beginning on the first of February, the Russians had begun a nonstop artillery attack, weakening the already crippled Finnish forces. Even small breaches could no longer be repaired.

So the first row in the Mannerheim Line had fallen back. Then most of the Intermediate Line had, too. The Rear Line now held on by the thinnest of threads. They needed Marko's sad group of fifteen to give them more time to prepare.

Every soldier he'd seen was haggard, running on two or three hours of sleep a night. What little sleep they got was hardly restful, punctuated as it was with explosions. Some men managed to sleep deeply from sheer fatigue, not even flinching at the sound. Marko envied them.

But even those men would probably be dead soon. He doubted those at the Rear Line were doing any better.

The post-artillery silence lengthened. Ten minutes passed. Fifteen. Twenty. Each increased the dread in his chest. When would the infantry advance? He didn't want them to come, but they would, and he'd have to shoot. The waiting was unbearable. The quiet period was nothing more than the calm before the storm.

March on us already.

He knew what would come after the infantry attack: another artillery salvo, or perhaps an air raid. The attacks never ended, day or night; the type just changed. Which made this ongoing silence so unnerving.

Marko's leg muscles had knotted from crouching in one position too long. He moved that leg, stretching it and moving it into another position and winced at the pain. More silence. What was taking the Russkies so long? They never waited.

The group in the trench, exhausted from staying alert, tried to be ready to fight at any moment, but a full hour passed, and then another, with no indication of an infantry advance. No sound of any advance or other attack.

As he often did, Marko distracted himself by reviewing what he needed to do. Don his white cape. Rest his rifle on the edge of the trench. Stay as low in the trench as possible. Take out advancing Russians. The thoughts curdled his stomach, despite knowing the actions were necessary.

I've killed before, he thought. *I've killed several men in the last six weeks.* And he'd kill again. He knew he had to, and soon. Even more sickening, the number would likely reach double digits today. He gritted his teeth and swallowed back bile.

He'd killed eight men so far on the Line. The Russians hadn't come for their fallen, so those men's corpses were still out there. At least he couldn't tell which snow-covered lumps had his bullets in them. A small mercy.

The silence stretched on. One soldier in the trench moved, making everyone look at him. Instead of using the periscope, the man slowly raised his head above the trench's surface. Marko expected him to be shot in the forehead by a sniper, but after a moment, he lowered back down, unharmed.

"Nothing," he whispered, confused.

The others exchanged equally perplexed looks, but didn't move. Their job was still the same: kill off as many Russians as they could to give the rear more time to prepare.

They waited, the tension mounting. How long had it been since the artillery barrage had ended? An hour? More? What game were the Russians playing? Were they hoping the Finns would die of fright?

Marko couldn't stand the suspense. Crouching, he got to his feet, then did what the other soldier had done before: slowly straightened so he could see for himself. With his eyes barely above the trench, he scanned left, right, and straight ahead. For hundreds of meters, the ground was dotted with overlapping craters, evidence of the unrelenting February attacks.

In comparison, January had been if not a vacation, at least a lull. That's when the Soviet forces had backed off a bit, mostly to decide how best to wipe out their enemy. Turned out that destroying small Finland hadn't been as easy as Stalin had anticipated.

He saw no movement, nothing indicating an attack. No Russian vehicles. No men. Nothing but evidence of past tanks and explosions in no-man's land.

Here and there, he made out stumps—the remnants of trees blown to bits. Unlike the hospital in Tolvajärvi, the Karelian Isthmus wasn't protected by thick forests, something he'd known intellectually before, but seeing it was another thing altogether. He'd never seen Finnish land with such a scarcity of trees, but now, even those trees were gone, splintered and fallen. The land would never heal.

But where were the Russians?

Yesterday, he'd watched a Finnish soldier run into no man's land to throw Molotov cocktails into the air vent of a Soviet tank. The man hadn't gotten back to the trench, but he was too close to the tank for it to lower its gun enough to fire at him, so it chased the soldier. Marko hadn't been able to look away, sure the man would be flattened any moment by the huge treads.

The soldier sprinted but couldn't outrun the panzer. He looked about frantically, searching for escape. Then he darted suddenly and jumped into a small crater, hands over his head. The tank had rolled right over the crater—not *into* it. A moment later, the soldier had popped up, climbed out, and raced back. The sight had been enough to send Marko into a panic attack, but the others cheered when their brother in arms dropped into the trench.

He was about to duck below the surface again, but a faint sound stopped him. Was it a voice? He wasn't sure. He strained to listen. Had he imagined it, or was someone moaning? Was it an animal?

There it was again. Definitely a human, a man, and he wasn't just moaning, he was saying something, repeating the same two syllables. At first all Marko could make out were two vowels lingering in the air. He strained to make out the rest. Finally, he recognized the word.

271

"Sta . . . lin . . ."

He scanned the landscape, searching. Where was the man who was crying out the name of the Soviet leader?

"Stalin . . ." The man was clearly crying now.

Ducking, Marko trotted to the some of the others farther down the log-lined trench. "Do you hear that?" he whispered, jabbing a finger toward the surface. "A Russkie is out there alone, calling for Stalin. He sounds wounded."

Antero, a soldier a few years Marko's junior, folded his thick arms. He had broad shoulders and cords of muscles, like fishermen at a pier selling his wares. "Sounds like a trap to me."

"We need to help," Marko said. "If he's wounded, his own men aren't going to come for him. We know that."

A man behind Antero snorted. "Sure. We climb from safety to go help a Russian."

Antero nodded. "Say one of us does go help. The Russkies may be heartless, but they aren't stupid. They're hiding and waiting for us. That guy out there is probably faking it, waiting for one of us to be stupid enough to help. And they'll shoot *us* dead."

Put that way, it did sound like a trap.

But I can't just sit here. I'm a doctor.

"Who has binoculars?" Marko asked.

One of the men dug around a metal supply box and produced a pair. Marko slung his rifle over his shoulder and took the binoculars, then slowly straightened. He put the binoculars to his eyes, searching the landscape. A few more cries helped him pinpoint the man some ways off, tangled in barbed wire.

The Finnish army had strung many lines hoping to stop or at least delay the invaders, hiding some in snowbanks.

The Russian's face looked white and pinched, and the snow beneath him was stained red. His chest rose and fell in shallow, quick breaths. His uniform was torn, exposing skin with deep scratches, as if he'd struggled against the sharp wire that held him fast. He'd lost the strength to fight, and now he was slowly dying, calling Stalin's name.

Marko set the binoculars aside then crouched and ran along the trench to the spot where they'd put a stone as a stepping stool. He'd scarcely put one boot onto the stone before a hand slammed against his shoulder and whipped him around.

"What do you think you're doing?" Antero demanded, crouching, too.

"Someone has to help him," Marko snapped.

"It's a trap, you idiot. Go out there, and they'll shoot you, then come for the rest of us."

"No." How could he make Antero understand? "He's been out there for an hour now. Why would the Russians set a trap like that? They'd likely kill one of their own, and for what benefit? Killing off a few of us in a trench?"

"Staaa-liiiin!" Again came the haunting call from the surface, more haunting now, more desperate.

The sound twisted Marko's insides. "He got caught in *our* trap, not the other way around. I'm sure of it."

"You think they'd just leave one of their men—alive—like that?"

Marko lifted one shoulder in a shrug. "They leave plenty of others on the ground, not knowing if they're dead yet. Something's different. They should have begun an infantry push."

"Exactly," Antero said. "A change in tactic could be a trap."

"If so, it's a pathetic excuse for a trap," Marko said.

When Antero spoke again, he addressed the entire company. "If they send out a patrol to get him, we hold our fire. But no one will go out there to be a hero to that Russkie and risk the lives of everyone else."

As much as Marko hated to admit it, Antero was right; this probably was a trap. A change in tactic could mean anything, and that climbing out of the trench now could be tantamount to suicide. If the last three months had taught them anything, it was that Stalin was ruthless. Marko reluctantly sat on the rock. The others returned to their positions, each waiting out whatever this day had in store.

He rested his arms on his thighs and tried to relax, maybe nod off for a few minutes. But he couldn't sleep. The calls of "Stalin!" didn't stop. They got weaker and farther apart, but the Russian was still out there, dying.

None of this made sense. Not that war made any sense. All he knew for sure was that he wanted to help that man but couldn't.

After another hour or two had passed, there was enduring it no longer. He made his way to Antero, who had dozed off. Marko touched his arm, and Antero jolted awake, reaching for his weapon.

"What's—" The wild look on his face calmed when he realized it was just Marko, but then his expression turned to one of annoyance. "What do you want?"

"We have to do something."

"We've been through this, Linna," Antero growled, closing his eyes again.

Marko jerked his head in the direction of the weak voice. "If we can't save his life, then let's end it, so he can stop suffering."

That would be the humane thing to do. It would also be the only thing to keep Marko from wanting to scream and pull out his hair to make the voice stop.

Antero thrust his jaw forward as the suggestion tumbled about in his mind. He turned to his right. "Ilkka," he called to another member of the company.

The man jogged over, hunched. "Yeah?"

"You've still got rounds in your machine gun?"

"Yes," Ilkka said. "Some."

"Use them to take out the Russkie," Antero said, his voice void of emotion.

Ilkka's eyes flicked to Marko then back to Antero. "Sir? He's dying anyway."

"That's the point," Antero said. "Put him out of his misery."

"Yes, sir," Ilkka said. He turned to fulfill the order but moved slowly, going to his machine gun, where he got into position. The man was too far away for anyone but a trained sniper to end this quickly, unless they used a machine gun.

Marko turned his back to Ilkka. Nothing could drown out the sound of the gun, but he didn't have to see the moment Ilkka fired. Rapid gunfire burst through the winter air. Seconds later, though it felt like an eternity, it was over.

Everyone in the trench held their breath and listened.

"Got him," Ilkka whispered, as if sensing the need to be quiet. "Now what?" he asked Antero.

"We wait and keep watch," Antero said. "If we see no sign of the enemy by noon tomorrow, I'll confirm with the Rear Line that our job here is done, and we'll withdraw."

Even knowing he was about to pose a potentially insane idea, Marko found himself proposing it anyway. "Before withdrawal, could we send a small patrol to see what's going on? What they're planning? Maybe go tonight, in the dark?"

Antero considered it, then blew out, sending a puff of white into the air. "That would give us a more complete report in the morning. Good thinking, Linna. Let's do it now. Sun's already going down. It'll be dark enough soon." He turned to the company. "I want three men on patrol. Stay on the edges, avoiding this section of no-man's land as best you can. See what you can find of the Russians." He held out a radio to Simo. "Go quickly. Radio when you have something to report."

"Yes sir," Simo said, reaching for the radio with a hand that trembled slightly.

He must think this was part of a Russian trap.

Simo and the other two men gathered their skis and climbed out. Marko straightened and watched the patrol head off with quiet swishes. Soon they blended into the snow.

Those left behind in the trench boiled water with a small portable stove and made their dinner. As Marko ate his porridge, he kept checking his watch. The patrol seemed to have been gone so long. But no, his watch showed that time simply moved slower than a frozen river.

Without the cries for Stalin's help eating at his nerves, Marko finally nodded off. But at the first sound of a crackling radio signal, he sat bolt upright. He made his way to Antero and listened.

"What are you seeing?" Antero asked.

"Russians everywhere," Simo said. "All dead. We don't dare go much farther, because we'd be skiing over corpses."

"Come on back," Antero said. "We'll send another patrol in the morning."

"On our way."

Dead Russians? Marko tried to fathom an explanation. Could a crippled Finnish artillery have taken out an entire Russian infantry regiment without knowing it?

CHAPTER THIRTY-ONE

Morning dawned a hazy gray. Marko asked to be on the second patrol, and Antero granted the request.

Breakfast: hardtack soaked in weak coffee. Not at all satisfying, and with only a suggestion of flavor beyond dirt. He never thought he'd miss the meals from the kitchen in Tolvajärvi—usually soups and meat sauces over potatoes, sometimes fish. He would've paid a lot for a hot meal no fancier than pea soup. He'd eat bowls of it now, if given the chance.

"Patrol, head out," Antero called. "Let's get this over with. The withdrawal orders will be confirmed as soon as you report."

Marko raised his skis above the edge of the trench and pushed them onto the ground before climbing out. Soon he and the rest of the patrol were skirting the edge of this section of no-man's land, again led by Simo. Gradually, the patrol moved quicker, and Marko felt himself relaxing, getting used to skiing. Being able to move at his full height felt freeing. The worst of the winter was past, but the earth wasn't out of its frosty clutches quite yet. Weak sun warmed his face slightly, so he tugged his scarf down to his chin. February provided more sunlight, and a little more warmth—or, rather, a little less cold.

Eventually, Simo held out an arm to halt their progress. "There. That's what we found last night."

Acting on their training, the men hopped off their skis and dropped low. Marko scanned the area, trying to make out anything ahead.

Dead Russians everywhere, he remembered hearing. Where were they, and why?

He spotted several Russian vehicles—jeeps and trucks. From what he could tell, this looked like an infantry's staging area, where they'd gather before an attack. Had an infantry unit been ordered to advance after the artillery barrage, as usual, but then some of them had died? If so, how? And where were the rest of them?

Marko lowered his gaze from the vehicles to the bumpy ground, expecting to see a man here and a man there. But he wasn't looking over hilly ground. He wasn't seeing boulders or shadows. The ground was covered with piles of the dead. Marko's scientific mind tried to make sense of it. The arrangement looked as if men had been standing in ranks and files, but had then collapsed on top of one another in overlapping, semi-organized rows. Dead.

Simo waved the patrol forward, bringing him back to the moment. They stepped back onto their skis and approached the horrific scene. When he stopped, Marko instinctively put the back of his hand to his nose, as if the stench of decaying bodies would overwhelm him.

Frozen corpses don't smell, he reminded himself, and lowered his hand. *But if this happened in summer, the stench would knock a man over.*

Instead, the frigid temperatures had preserved soldiers' expressions. Marko paused at the edge the area, trying to gather strength before stepping across an invisible line that would show him a kind of destruction and loss of life he'd never be able to forget. He paid no mind to the rest of the patrol; the dead held his attention like an irresistible magnet he both dreaded seeing and felt compelled to see.

Some of the Russian dead were nothing more than lower-body stumps. Their torsos must have been blown off. He stepped over arms and legs, trying to maintain a mental and emotional distance—to not feel too much or think too much. He wasn't succeeding very well.

Angry red neck stumps contrasted against white snow. The gray Russian uniforms looked brand new. Clean and pressed. The men's faces were freshly shaved.

Drawn forward by an unseen power, Marko walked on, deeper into the staging area. He found more dead, though not as tightly packed as those who'd fallen while lined up. One of the dead sat on a log, a metal box open on his lap. Marko walked over and peered inside, spying a can of fish, a small bottle of vodka, and another can he couldn't identify. The man still clutched a chunk of bread in one hand. His mouth was partway open, likely with a frozen bite of bread he'd been chewing.

What had happened here?

Marko raised his head and looked around to see his fellow patrol members pawing through the uniforms of the dead. They pocketed handguns, bullets, and Russian money, both paper and coin. Simo strode about the area, which encompassed about two acres. Simo spoke into the radio as he counted and then reported vehicles, weapons, and other details.

The whole scene felt fake, like a surrealist painting. This nightmare couldn't be real. Marko walked on in a stupor, whether in a straight line, a circle, or meandering path, he didn't know. He was trying to take it all in and keep it all out at the same time. Alone, he reached a spot apart from the main staging area. Maybe he could find relief here from seeing so much death.

A jeep stood alone in an open field. Gaps and craters surrounded the jeep, the tell-tale signs of artillery fire.

This entire area had experienced heavy fire.

Then why hadn't his company heard about a Finnish assault here? How had the Finnish army gotten the kind of ammunition required to create this kind of damage?

He approached the jeep, where a man sat on a stool in the back. He had the same stiff, pale appearance as the other dead. Marko didn't want to see more but felt pulled forward. One step at a time, he moved forward until the dead Russian was so close that he should have been able to speak.

A pair of binoculars hung from the dead man's neck. A large paper was spread open on his lap. In one hand was a telephone receiver, the cord severed and dangling. Unable to help himself, Marko climbed into the jeep and peered over the dead man's shoulder. The paper was a map of the Isthmus with various writings and marks in Cyrillic.

A section of the map had two areas circled in pencil. The first he recognized as the Intermediate Line—a Soviet target, no doubt. The second had to be this staging area, which had received the brutal assault intended for the Finns.

A possible explanation clicked into place. This man had likely been trying to call his commander when artillery fire reached them.

This attack was not the result of Finnish fire. It was from the Russians' own artillery.

With uneasy legs, Marko got out of the jeep and stumbled away. He had to escape the gruesome scene, but his mind refused to let go of the details he'd learned. With each step, he grew more certain of what had happened—of why his company had waited and waited for the Russian infantry, and why they'd never come.

The answer was horrifyingly simple: they'd been destroyed by their own artillery.

Marko walked past the mounds of dead soldiers and headed around them to find his skis, unable to look at them again, especially now that they were easily visible, with their uniforms raided by the patrol.

I have to get out of here, Marko thought. *Get far from the dead man with the telephone, who'd surely been making a frantic call as he died.*

Every sight pressed on Marko like a weight—the man forever eating his lunch, young soldiers in new uniforms with their bodies blown apart.

He was about to ask Simo for permission to go ahead, but he couldn't get enough air. He dropped to the snow. Images bombarded his mind like unforgiving artillery.

Images of blood and death and hell.

CHAPTER THIRTY-TWO

March 13

After more than a month of relentless Soviet artillery attacks, a treaty had finally been signed. A ceasefire was imminent, yet shells continued to fall onto the pocked ground, making old craters larger, ragged, deeper.

When the ceasefire took effect and the shelling stopped for good, thousands of acres would be permanently scarred. Tens of thousands of trees had been turned into matchsticks, but it was the granite bedrock that bore some of the deepest, rawest evidence of destruction.

All of it stood witness to the punishment leveled at Finnish forces at the Isthmus for six weeks straight.

What would the world sound like when the shelling stopped? Marko couldn't remember silence. The last he'd heard silence was the day they'd had to kill the poor wretch caught in the wire fencing.

Now Marko sat in a small muddy pillbox, waiting for the ceasefire to begin but unable to fathom its reality. It seemed as if he'd always been hearing explosions, many so loud that some of the old bunkers had collapsed from the concussion. Men had gone deaf.

This small pillbox had nine men cramped inside. Everyone was jumpy, as if they'd had liters of black coffee. Some sat on stools; most sat on duffels or other makeshift seats. He hated the cramped space but had to remind himself again and again that it was better than the mud- and ice-filled trench.

Those with watches kept them in the open so others could track the minutes ticking oh-so-slowly toward eleven o'clock, when the ceasefire was to begin. Noon Moscow time.

More than once, Marko thought his watch had stopped, so he put it to his ear, but that didn't help. With the explosions, and likely ear damage, he couldn't hear something as quiet as a ticking wristwatch.

He leaned toward the working radio—a rarity in the area— hoping to hear news. The volume was already as loud as it could go, but making out words was still hard. Updates always included the time and how many minutes remained until the ceasefire.

I'll be home soon, he thought. *I'll go to my apartment, make a cup of fresh coffee. I'll add milk and sugar—luxury. Then I'll sit at the table and stare out the window, drinking it as slowly as I want to.*

The image of Leila pouring his coffee came to mind. He smiled—and then gritted his jaw, trying to chase away what he now knew was a fantasy. He had no chance of being with her. She didn't love him. Not as he loved her, anyway.

Where was a beer when you needed one?

At last, the radio announcer counted down the last few seconds to eleven o'clock. Eleven dongs rang out to mark the hour. Static followed, so someone switched the radio off. Everyone waited. No one spoke, but everyone anticipated the silence.

It fell all at once like a heavy cloak, almost suffocating with its weight. One soldier stood from the duffel he was sitting on and unlatched the door of the pillbox. He pushed it open to reveal a sunny day. No shelling. No explosions.

Marko peered outside. In the distance, other men poked their heads out of dugouts and trenches like groundhogs, their faces lifted skyward as if soaking in the light. He sat in place, unmoving but listening, wanting to believe. Others around him did the same, only a couple of the men moving to the door and going outside.

Maybe Marko and the rest of them were too tired to celebrate.

In the corner, a soldier named Korvanen lowered his head to his hands and wept. "It's over. I can't believe it's over."

Others nodded soberly. Several sniffed and wiped their eyes with the backs of their hands. Most stayed in place as if reverencing the moment, honoring the dead, and perhaps, like Marko, getting used to the idea that the war was finally over.

Someone came to the door and ushered them outside. "Come! It's sunny, and it's over! Celebrate!"

The movement got him to stand, but after weeks of explosions and tremors, both the silence and the solid ground felt disorienting. Maybe this was what sailors felt with sea legs after a long voyage. Marko reached for the wall to steady himself.

Korvanen lowered his hands, stood, and followed him. The two waited as three others left first. The two men exchanged glances, nodded, and walked out, one after the other.

Marko squinted at the bright light. He shielded his eyes. Dappled shadows were cast by a few shrubs remaining on the ground.

Slowly, more soldiers and Lottas emerged, all blinking like prisoners seeing the sun for the first time. Marko walked forward, toward no-man's land, drawn to the sight of so much carnage, so much death he couldn't prevent, feeling an obligation to stand on the ground where so much blood had been spilled.

Behind him, men and women alike wept. Some fell to their knees, keening or holding their heads, shaking with tears of grief—emotion they'd held inside for too long.

To honor the fallen, Marko tried to commit every detail to memory. His eyes burned with tears, and soon he felt them on his cheeks. Snow dripped from somewhere—maybe from a bunker or a tree branch or a tent—with a steady plink-plink.

Water was a sound of spring. A sign of hope. Of life.

He took another step and another, through snow and hardened mud, over tree roots and splintered rocks. Now that he'd left the pillbox, he had an urgent need to see for himself that the war had ended. To know it.

Several minutes later, the trenches of the rear line far behind him, he paused beneath a tall pine that had somehow survived the shelling, and pushed a branch aside to see better. He'd crossed much of no-man's land. Now he looked over the expanse. This place would always be hallowed ground. The thousands who'd held the Mannerheim Line so long against impossible odds had made it so.

Those who'd resisted, day and night, with little to no ammunition and few supplies, had consecrated this ground.

If he'd been a praying man, he would have knelt right there to speak to God, knowing that no other spot on earth could be so close to deity. As a boy he'd once believed such tales. But any seedling of faith that might have survived to adulthood had been ripped from his soul on his first day at the aid station.

He looked back toward what had been the last of the Mannerheim Line. More soldiers emerged from trenches, dozens now standing at their full heights for the first time in days, if not weeks, lifting their faces without fear to the sky. Holding their arms out and laughing. Embracing one another tightly, parting with heavy thumps on the back.

Others dropped to the ground and wept.

We're still free.

He could scarcely believe it. Yes, the terms of the ceasefire were harsh; Stalin required sanctions to punish his puny neighbor who'd had the audacity to resist him.

But even with sanctions, even losing some land, Finland hadn't fallen. Estonia had fallen. Latvia had fallen. Many others still would. But not Finland.

A sudden boom rocked the ground. Marko ducked and raised an arm to block—what? A celebratory gunshot? When the boom ebbed, he remained hunched over, and he looked around, searching for the source. Was it an accidental discharge as the Soviets pulled back?

Another explosion came. And another. Shells rained from the sky again as the volley renewed.

Had they gotten the time wrong?

Everyone who'd emerged from safety now raced for cover. Many dropped to the ground, some bracing themselves, others falling because they'd been hit with shrapnel or impaled by falling metal. Once more, he witnessed men staining the snow beneath them with their blood.

Heroes who'd survived the hellish war, who'd only begun celebrating their survival, were now dying.

With each shell, more men collapsed where they stood. Some fell, screaming in pain while bleeding out. Marko, somehow not hit, couldn't move. He saw but couldn't comprehend. His brow furrowed in confusion even as his heart clenched with terror.

Run! His brain ordered, but his legs refused. He checked his watch. It was half past eleven. The ceasefire should be in effect. Yet the renewed attack dragged on.

He couldn't think. The wounded and dying were at a distance, but he thought he saw hundreds of bloodied stumps, gaping wounds, anguished faces. Did he? Or was his mind playing tricks?

Run! His mind yelled again. *As fast as you can!*

You'll never make it, a second voice said.

And a third—the quietest but most sinister voice of all: *You're weak. A real doctor would run to those men to help them.*

The voices argued, back and forth. Marko remained frozen, unable to tear his gaze from the devastation. His feet felt rooted to the ground as if he were a century-old pine.

Blow me to matchsticks too.

After what could have been seconds or hours, the volley ended as suddenly as the ceasefire had begun. Once more the eerie silence fell, pressing against his ears, but this time it was punctuated by cries of pain.

This time, no one emerged to look at the sun. Those who'd returned to safety stayed there. The only movement came from the dying as they shifted, their cries getting louder.

He tilted his face to the sky and waited for the next attack. Where was he now? Who was his commanding officer, and where to find him? What to do?

He couldn't think past this moment. Not when a vise was closing, ever tighter, across his chest. His heart fluttered like a hummingbird's wings.

Is this what it feels like to die? The thought flitted past his consciousness. So did curiosity about how he'd been injured. Or had he? Was this all dream? Maybe he was sleeping and would wake up. Yes. That made the most sense because none of this felt real. He couldn't even feel his legs. Maybe they'd been blown off.

From the corner of his eye, Marko saw someone approaching. The figure stumbled, limping with each step. Several others appeared—injured soldiers making their way somewhere? Had they received orders? Was he imagining the line of men? The first man passed by. More followed in a rag-tag column, dragging rifles, holding their helmets by the strap. No one lugged a machine gun or pulled a sled with one on it; those were too heavy, surely left behind.

Many men were bleeding. Others had broken bones— some sticking through flesh, others distorting the shape of an arm or leg. All looked like death walking. Most said nothing, just dragged one foot after the other.

Here and there, a few men cursed Stalin for that final artillery volley after the ceasefire.

The sight reminded Marko of the legend of Lemminkäinen from the *Kalevala*. After the mythical hero died, his mother used a rake to gather his body parts from Tuonela, the river of death, and reassembled him.

That's who we are: the dead, like Lemminkäinen. But we lack a bee with godly honey to bring us back to life. This field is our river Tuonela. We are its dead.

Marko fell into line, not because anyone told him to, but because he sensed he belonged with the other walking dead. He followed the line mindlessly, unaware of the passage of time, blocking out everything but the march he was on. He left behind the nightmares he'd witnessed, letting his mind fade into a welcome haze that was little more than a blur.

At some point—hours later, the next day, he didn't know—he found himself standing indoors. What was this place?

"What's your name?" a woman asked. She wore a gray dress, and her blond hair was pulled back.

For a moment, his heart leapt, but then his face scrunched up again. He felt he should know his name, and that he'd once known a woman in a gray dress with hair like that.

The haze obscured so much. The only memory he could conjure was of dead men walking and walking. He lifted his chin and spoke to the wall.

"Lemminkäinen. We are Lemminkäinen."

CHAPTER THIRTY-THREE

March 25

Sini was home, lying in her same old apartment, in the same lumpy bed. She had the same couch, the same bookshelves, the same pictures on the walls, the same dishes in the cupboard. The same clothing hung in the closet, including the dress she'd worn the night she'd made the uneaten dinner.

Nothing here had changed. She'd been back from the war for weeks, and everything felt different. If her apartment hadn't changed, she had. This place had belonged to a different person. She'd never be that woman again.

One difference she didn't imagine was the silence from Marko's apartment above hers—no footsteps on squeaky boards, no doors opening or closing. The building directory in the lobby still read *Linna*. Marko hadn't been on any casualty list; she'd looked. While she didn't feel toward him as she used to, she did wonder why he hadn't returned to his apartment nearly two weeks after the ceasefire. She wondered if he'd made it.

Another wave of nausea came over her. She rolled off the bed and stumbled to the bathroom, where she knelt by the toilet. Several dry heaves later, she shakily sat back and leaned her forehead against the tub. The cool porcelain felt good. She hadn't seen a doctor, but she had no doubt that she carried Nikolai's child. She had all of the symptoms, including the weeks since her cycle should have come. She breathed shallowly, glad no one in the field ever knew. After her collapse on Raate Road, Kaisa had simply determined that Sini was too weak for duty and sent her home.

Sini didn't remember much of that day. After fainting, her next memory was waking with a jolt and finding herself being dragged on a wool blanket behind two skiers. On the right, Fia kicked her sled, and in front of her, another soldier kicked Sini's sled. She must have fainted after that, because she remembered nothing more of returning to camp.

But she did remember Kaisa's reaction after they arrived, standing with her hands on her hips, her tight bun making her look particularly ornery. Sini braced herself to be yelled at, but Kaisa just snorted.

"You *fainted*? I don't know what the matter is with you," Kaisa said, looking at Sini still huddled on the blanket. "Maybe you're ill, or maybe you lack character. Whatever the reason, you're incapable of serving as a proper Lotta." When Sini tried to speak, Kaisa interrupted. "You're going home. Today." She turned on her heels and stomped off, probably thinking she'd leveled a blow.

Sini cried, and Fia dropped to her knees, trying to comfort her, not knowing that they were tears of relief. The trip home was largely a blur of riding busses and transferring to trains, all colored with exhaustion and nausea.

Now, as Sini lay in bed day after day, hardly able to care for herself, memories of the starved, frozen men of the *motti* resurfaced, giving her nightmares both awake and asleep.

She couldn't help imagining starving Russians cutting into a dead horse for meat. Biting the raw flesh. Her stomach lurched. She got to her knees again and gripped the sides of the toilet, heaving. Only a little stomach acid came up. She wiped her mouth with a bath towel and leaned against the tub again. She had to find something else to think about.

I need to buy food. Crackers and milk, at least.

But even when the sickness ebbed, she dreaded going out. No matter how brief the errand, the moment she returned and opened the door to the building, the familiar scent washed over her, and with it, memories of the old Sini.

Whenever she reached her floor, she paused out of habit and looked up toward Marko's place. She no longer felt sadness or yearning for him. She felt nothing toward him but a curiosity and neighborly concern.

That was the one good thing in her life—no longer hoping for him to love her. How could she now? Not after knowing Leila. Not after loving Nikolai.

She'd spent the last weeks of the war listening to the radio and learning just how close the country had come to losing everything. How much Stalin would be sure they paid for his humiliation on the global stage.

They were safe and free. Sini focused on that thought. *Free.*

The telephone rang in the kitchen. She debated whether to stand and risk vomiting on the floor or letting the call go unanswered. Who could possibly be calling her anyway? Then again, her stomach had nothing to get rid of. And it could be Leila. She'd promised to call after the war.

Sini forced herself to stand. With one hand over her middle, she made her way to the telephone and answered it. "Hello?" she said, sitting at the table with the receiver to her ear.

"Sini?"

"Yes." Sini closed her eyes against the bright light coming through the window; it made her headache worse.

"It's Leila. I'm in Helsinki, visiting Aunt Sisko."

"Oh, I'm so glad you're safe."

"So are you! I worried when I didn't hear anything after you left for Suomussalmi."

"I've been home for a little while," Sini said vaguely.

"We both made it," Leila said. She let out a happy sigh. "It's over, and we're alive."

Sini's hand rested just below her navel. Being alive definitely mattered.

But she still had so many worries and questions. What about Nikolai? Would he contact her? Did he still hate her?

Would she ever be able to explain why she turned him in? And what about their baby?

She'd been able to confide nearly everything in her heart to Leila, but she couldn't broach those questions. "Will you be staying with Aunt Sisko permanently?" The other questions would be answered in time.

"For her sake, I hope not," Leila said. "She insists on being the hostess, and I can tell she's getting tired. But I can't stay in Viipuri now that it belongs to the Soviets. Did you hear that they're calling it by its old Swedish name? It's Vyborg now."

Sini cringed. "That seems so wrong."

Leila sniffed. "We have a few days to go back for belongings, but they gave the city such a pounding that I don't know if anything is left of our apartment building."

It wouldn't have been beyond Stalin's cruelty to kick out any Finns who hadn't yet evacuated and then prevent anyone from coming across the new border. So it was good news that Leila would be able to go back briefly. Hopefully she'd salvage a few things. Perhaps a wedding picture or Taneli's baby book. Assuming, as she said, that her building hadn't been flattened.

"If I can't find a place in the next week, I'll find a room at a hotel to give Aunt Sisko a break. I might not be much of a burden, but a young boy would wear her right out."

"Live with me." The words came out before Sini had thought them through, but they felt right and created a flutter of happiness in her chest. She looked around the apartment and smiled at the idea of Leila and Taneli living here. Space would be tight, but being with them would be worth it.

"Oh, Sini," Leila said. "I wasn't—"

"I want you to," Sini said, feeling more animated than she had in weeks. "It's about time we got to be together in a way besides trying to keep soldiers alive and our toes from freezing." She liked the idea more and more. "Say yes. I'd love to have the two of you with me."

With me and the baby.

"Are you sure?" Leila sounded hesitant. "It would be lovely—"

291

"I'm positive." Having Leila and Taneli here would be as much for Sini's sake as theirs. Sini needed her best friend.

"I'd like that," Leila said. "I could still check on Aunt Sisko without being a burden. And it really would be wonderful to spend time together under different circumstances."

"Then it's settled." Sini debated whether to tell Leila about the baby now. The news had to come out eventually, but she wasn't showing yet. Some clothing fit tighter than usual, and she was losing her waist, but all of that was easy to hide or explain away.

Just like hiding Nikolai. But I couldn't keep him hidden forever, either.

Where was he? Did they kill him? Send him back to Russia? Everything circled back to Nikolai and the baby and around again.

Leila could assume that the father was someone Sini met after discharge, or that it was the man Leila had assumed Sini had a flirtation with at camp—a Finn. No need to correct the assumption.

"So when can I see you?" Sini asked. She hadn't called Meiri about resuming work at the yarn shop; she was still on leave. As long as her nausea cooperated, she could see Leila any time.

"That's why I called. Taneli comes home today. His ferry from Stockholm docked at Turku this morning, and he'll be arriving by train this afternoon." Pure joy came through Leila's voice. At long last, she'd hold her boy again.

Sini stroked her stomach with one thumb, imagining feeling the same fierce devotion toward her own child. *Am I capable of loving a baby that much? When I look into my child's eyes, will I always see Nikolai's hatred there?*

"Let's meet before he arrives," Leila suggested. "Then you can come to the station with me."

"Oh, I couldn't intrude on your reunion," Sini said.

"Nonsense. He needs to meet his new godmother," Leila insisted. "How about lunch in about an hour?"

Sini glanced at the clock. If the pattern held, the worst of her nausea would be over then. "Sounds great. Where should we meet?"

"How about the Havis Amanda statue?"

"See you there in an hour." Sini hung up then walked about her apartment, excitement overcoming any upset stomach. She mentally added another adult-size bed in the other corner where Leila and Taneli could sleep, and a cradle beside her mattress. Soon the place would be filled to bursting with warmth and love.

Sini sat on her bed and imagined the walls ringing with laughter, the patter of small feet, drinking tea in the evening with Leila as their children played together on the floor. This space, once one of sadness, would have happiness and meaning. She took a deep breath and let it out, feeling peace and contentment.

When she went to get ready for lunch, she took extra care with her appearance. She liked feeling pretty. As a Lotta, she'd never been able to try, and most days since coming home, she'd felt too sick to bother.

Now as she curled her hair and put it up with combs, she wondered about Leila. What did she wear, and how did she style her hair when she wasn't donning a Lotta uniform and a bun? What if they didn't recognize each other at first? Sini grinned at the idea, then applied a layer of lipstick. No more thinking of the war. No thoughts of Russia. Not even of Nikolai.

In spite of the late-spring chill in the air, she put on a sunny yellow dress, added her coat and scarf, then headed outside to the harbor. There she sat on the short wall surrounding the Havis Amanda statue.

The worst of the winter had passed, but the harbor hadn't entirely melted yet. It had dark lines of water surrounded by ice. Last time it was entirely melted, her life had been dramatically different. Last time she'd been by this statue, too.

Today, she was waiting for someone she had reciprocal relationship with. Someone who she knew would come.

The flurry of excited butterflies in her middle was tinged with worry that their friendship had been based on the war. What if it wouldn't survive outside camp? No, even if war had first brought them together, they'd become friends over matters of the heart.

Church bells rang, marking the hour. Sini watched passersby more carefully, holding her breath, biting her lip. One, two, three women walked by. One approached the statue but greeted a young man to Sini's left. Several more passed.

And then there was Leila.

She approached from Sini's right, looking around. Sini stepped forward, grinning. She raised an arm and waved. "Leila! Over here."

Her friend's head turned, and her face broke into a wide smile. Clutching a shiny red purse—very un-Lotta-like—Leila hurried toward Sini. They threw their arms around each other and hugged tight—very unlike Sini.

"It's over," Leila whispered as they embraced. "We're back. We're *back*!"

Sini fought tears. Hitler was far from being stopped, and Stalin might renege on the treaty. But for now, their country remained free.

Leila and Sini both cried, then laughed, then cried again. They wiped their cheeks, smiling widely. "Let's go eat and catch up," Leila said.

By some miracle, Sini had a real appetite and couldn't wait for a nice sandwich or salad followed by a pastry. Fortunately, her savings hadn't been entirely depleted, and she'd spent precious little on food lately, so she could enjoy an occasional treat.

They walked along, talking as if they'd known each other for years and had shared hundreds of lunches. Every moment felt easy and natural.

A few blocks into their walk, they waited at a corner for the light to change. Two men behind them spoke to each other in Russian. Nikolai jumped to Sini's mind, and an empty ache filled her chest. She surreptitiously peeked over her shoulder to see if one of the men was him.

Leila spun toward him, eyes blazing with fury. "Get *out* of our country!" Her index finger jabbed sharply to the side. "The war is over. You failed to conquer us. Now get the hell out!"

The men stood there, stunned into silence.

Leila threw one arm to the side again, pointing. "Go!"

The men backed away, hands raised. Leila held her stance, fuming, until they'd turned a corner and were out of sight. She finally lowered her arm, but her nostrils still flared, and she breathed heavily. A small crowd had stilled to watch the spectacle.

Sini flushed at the sudden attention. "Excuse us." The light had changed, so she grabbed Leila's arm and hurried across the street with her. On the other side, Leila marched along the sidewalk. Her face was red, her jaw set. Sini had to hurry to keep up.

After a couple of blocks, Leila stopped and whirled on Sini. "How *dare* they?"

Sini stood there, unsure what to say, but knowing one thing, at least—she couldn't tell Leila about Nikolai. Ever.

"One of them might be a Finn who speaks Russian—"

"Don't make excuses for the animals." Leila stalked down the street.

Sini followed, too stunned to speak even when they passed the café she'd hoped to eat at. Leila's feelings were understandable. A lot of things would be different if not for the Russians.

If not for them, I never would have met Nikolai. I wouldn't know what it is to love a man. I wouldn't be carrying his baby. She wished she could also think that at least she knew what it was to be loved in return, but the truth was, she might never know.

Eventually Leila let out a weary sigh and slowed her step, coming to a stop beside a women's clothing store. She leaned against the brick building, looking wrung out. "I'm sorry." She rubbed her forehead with one hand. "I don't know what came over me." She shrugged helplessly.

"I know," Sini said quietly.

"I was at a hospital on the Mannerheim Line those last weeks. The fire kept coming and coming. Sometimes I still hear the shells, and I look for cover." She closed her eyes and shook her head. "Most nights, I can't sleep, and if I doze off, I have nightmares. I'll never forget this one boy on the table. He was only sixteen . . ." She pressed her eyes and lips closed.

Sini put a hand over Leila's, a silent comfort. They both understood one thing: no one escaped war unscathed.

Leila stared at the sidewalk. Her eyes were rimmed with red. "The worst was that final barrage after the ceasefire. It was as if Stalin were a spoiled child throwing a final tantrum because he didn't get his way. The screams when our men realized what was happening . . ." Furrows etched her forehead. "The OR collapsed."

Sini drew her friend into her arms. "It was unspeakable," she whispered into Leila's ear. "All of it."

"I'll never forgive them," Leila said. "Never."

Sini pulled back and put an arm around Leila's shoulders, urging her to walk. "Let's get you some good, hot coffee and a meal. Taneli will be here soon. Everything will be better then."

"Yes. Yes, it will." Leila nodded several times, quickly. "Right. Thank you. I can't be a crying mess when I see him. No letting him see anything but happy tears." She pulled a handkerchief from her coat pocket, then dabbed her eyes and wiped her nose. After tucking the cloth away, she smiled—only a little at first, but then more as they kept walking.

"I'm sorry for what I did back there." Leila seemed to have shaken off the heavy load of hatred. She looked like her usual self.

"No reason to apologize," Sini assured her. "Not after what you've been through."

"I didn't know I was capable of such ugly feelings. I let some of it out, and it *all* came out like a hate bomb."

They went to another café, where they both ordered vegetable soup with rye bread. Leila chuckled when she got her bowl. "Why did I order this, when I can finally eat anything I want?"

The soup had a variety of vegetables—and surely more flavor—than what they'd eaten during the war, but still, it was soup.

Sini laughed too, then took a sip of coffee and sighed with pleasure. "Much better than any from a field kitchen."

For the first time in weeks, her stomach calmed enough to enjoy a meal. Maybe she was past the worst of the morning sickness, or maybe seeing Leila had lifted her spirits above the nausea. Whatever the reason, Sini was grateful for the respite—and that meant she had more time to find a way to tell Leila about the baby and invent an explanation for the father.

Toward the end of the meal, Leila seemed antsy. She pushed her bowl away and checked her watch. Her index finger tapped the table as if she was vainly attempting to keep still.

"How about we head to the train station?" Sini suggested, sliding her bowl away to show that she was finished—which she wasn't, but she'd had enough, and Leila mattered more than some unfinished soup.

"You're not done." The relief in Leila's voice belied her words. She was eager to get to the station.

"I've had enough—honest." To emphasize the point, Sini stood, put on her coat, and tied her scarf. "Let's go. We don't want to be late."

"Definitely not," Leila said. As she buttoned her coat, she spoke quickly, smiling the whole time. "We should be early. If the train arrives ahead of schedule, and I'm not there—" Sini reached out and touched Leila's hand, which stilled over a button. Leila looked up.

"We'll be there on time," Sini said.

Leila's face glowed with anticipation. "I get to see my baby soon."

They pushed through the doors and headed toward the train station at a fast clip.

CHAPTER THIRTY-FOUR

The whole world felt fuzzy, just like Marko liked it—all of his senses dulled, turning everything into a comforting haze. It helped dim the constant shelling still ringing in his ears.

He took a swig from his paper-bag-wrapped bottle, anticipating the promise of a warm buzz. A miracle drink if ever there was one. Not only did it mute the shelling, but it also blocked out the wind, which bit his fingers through the holes in his gloves and nipped his ears through his equally ragged knit hat. Sometimes his nose and cheeks still stung with the cold, his chin less so now that his beard had grown out.

Why the commanding officers hadn't gotten on his case about shaving, he'd never know. Maybe a beard kept him less noticeable to possible spies. After all, he wasn't in uniform anymore, either. No one had come for a report recently; he should ask about his dress next time they did.

Sitting near an intersection, he looked left, then right, but his head moved sluggishly. This was his job now: looking for spies embedded in the capital. He'd had to be ready at all times to intercept threats. He'd seen nothing suspicious today. The cold granite beneath him seeped through his clothes, so he downed another gulp.

An unsettling but recurrent feeling settled over him; he didn't remember much about his past. Probably because of the Russkies. They'd done something to his brain. He squinted into the distance as if that would help him remember. It didn't. Maybe more medicine would help. His bottle always made things better.

He tried to raise the brown bottle to his mouth, but his arm wobbled, and a few drops spilled out. Panicked over losing even a little of the precious drink, he slammed the bottle to the ground with a clank. He'd spilled it too many times already, and if he didn't keep taking it, the shakes got worse. Then he couldn't haul boxes at the dock to earn enough for a few more bottles of medicine and maybe a meat pie or a sausage from a street vendor. Some days he got lucky and had a little left over for cigarettes.

Someday, his CO would come. He'd report, and he'd be rewarded. He imagined a hot bath, trays of sumptuous food, new clothes. And a medal, of course. Until then, he had to survive on the streets and watch for spies.

Marko pushed his back against the building to steady himself. The cold stone now seeped into his spine. But sometimes, steadying himself like this was the only way to drink from the bottle. He wrapped both hands around the paper bag and slowly brought the opening to his lips. The liquid gold burned as it went down. Some dribbled onto his chin, but that couldn't be helped.

The smell and taste were enough to make him relax; in a few minutes, the medicine would do its job, and he'd feel even better. He leaned back and searched the intersection for spies again. They'd gotten awfully sneaky, blending in as locals. Some spoke perfect Finnish—they could even say *höyryjyrä*.

The military needed a new test. They'd underestimated the Soviets, if they'd found men who could say that word correctly. He'd tell his commander as much in his next report, which he hoped would be soon. He'd been finding spies in all kinds of unexpected places. Not only men, but women and children, too. The Reds had no shame. None at all.

His head listed to the left, and his body slowly followed, nearly falling to the sidewalk, stopped only when the words of a nearby woman pierced his consciousness.

"I worried so much that Taneli would forget me."

He jerked to attention, catching himself before his cheek hit the cobbled sidewalk. Slowly, he pushed himself up, head sweeping left and right, trying to find the speaker. The voice sounded so familiar. If he hadn't been trained so well, he would've thought it belonged to a friend. He knew better. This was another spy.

"He hasn't been gone nearly long enough to forget his mother," another voice answered. "He'll still be your little boy."

That voice sounded familiar too. Were two spies walking around together? Those sneaky Soviets.

"Yes, he'll still be my little boy." That was the first voice again.

The sound stung his chest with the cut of betrayal. Clearly, she was the more dangerous of the two, but they both had to be stopped. The country depended on him to root out Russkies before they infiltrated the entire country.

Stalin sends women to do his dirty work, he thought with disgust. He used the building for support as he got his feet under him. And there the women were, only steps away from him, waiting for the light to change.

"In a few years," the first woman continued, "he might not remember us ever being apart." She sounded *happy*. Marko scowled.

Both women wore nice coats and scarves, while he got by with layers of old clothes so dirty he wasn't sure of their original colors. Those Russian women were getting their fine things at the expense of Finnish labor and sacrifice.

He spat on the ground, but they didn't even notice. "Go back!" he yelled. A couple of passersby glanced his way and hurried on. "Back to Russia!" The female spies glanced over curiously but turned back to the crosswalk. Other people nearby increased their distance. Good. Let them fear an officer of the army.

He pounded his chest then pushed off the building. "Look at me, you dirty Russkies!" He staggered toward the women at the crosswalk, but the ground rose and fell like ocean waves. He reached for the building, but he'd moved too far from it; all he found to grasp was the shoulder of a middle-aged woman, but she scurried away, clutching her purse to her chest.

He approached the spies. The one he'd heard second tapped her foot, looking anxious for the light to change. The first spy looked at him again, this time studying his features. The light changed, and her partner tugged on her coat sleeve. Like fools, they headed for the other corner. As if they'd lose him so easily.

"Hey, I'm talking to you girls in the fancy dresses. You don't fool anyone."

In the middle of the street, the first spy froze and looked at her partner. They were intimidated by him. Good. He grinned. After another swig, he strode their way.

"Hurry," the nervous spy said. "We can outrun a drunk." She tugged harder on her friend's sleeve. The light had changed again, but they were still in the middle of the street.

"Wait," the first spy said. Against protestations, she turned around and leveled her gaze at him.

That's right. He lifted his chin and looked down his nose at her. *Face me like a man.* With bravado, he chugged the rest of the bottle and threw it onto the pavement. The shattering glass, even dulled by the paper bag, made him grin wider.

The second woman paled and reached for the one staring at him. "Let's go! Leila!"

The name jolted him. He stopped walking as a flash of pain shot through him.

A traitor. Definitely.

"Come on." The second girl tugged her friend's arm. "We can't be late for the train."

But the first spy kept looking at Marko, brow furrowed with a mixture of emotions he couldn't read. What he'd thought was fear might have been worry. A car honked, but she held up a finger as if telling the driver to wait.

Chest out, he stood tall to further intimidate her. Several people looked hesitant and wary. He was doing something right.

"You dirty, filthy Russians," he muttered. "Go to hell, all of you, and live with the devil!"

He stepped off the curb, but what looked like snow and ice gave way, and his foot caught in a puddle. He pitched forward onto the cobblestones. He scrambled to his feet, knowing the urgency of regaining his dignity, but slipped on tram tracks. This time he landed on his hands and knees. Both palms stung, and pain shot through his knees. His body was too weak for him to hop back to his feet as he used to before the war. He breathed in and out, trying to gather strength.

The first spy—Leila was her name, if the second one could be believed—knelt beside him. Fool. If she'd run when her friend had suggested it, they might have escaped his tail. Russians always were fools.

Leila laid a hand on his shoulder. "The war's over." Her voice was soothing, but he resisted its comforting tone. "The Russians are gone." She sounded so confident, so understanding. In spite of his training, he couldn't help but listen. He almost believed her.

Was the war over? Could a kind, soft voice like that belong to the enemy? Maybe he hadn't heard from his commander because everyone thought he'd been told that the war was over. That they'd forgotten him.

Bewildered, he lifted his face to hers. "What do you mean?"

"The armistice went into effect almost two weeks ago." She smiled at him—a beautiful smile that penetrated deeper than his medicine, awakening something that had long slept.

Leila moved her hand to his cheek. At first he flinched, but when she kept smiling, he sank into her touch. He moaned at the delicious softness of her hand. Its warmth seemed to thaw his very soul.

She peered into his eyes, searching. "Marko, it's you, isn't it? You're Marko Linna."

He heard a gasp, and his attention snapped over to see the friend on the far sidewalk, with both hands to her mouth. Still on the cobblestones with Leila, he glared at the other girl. He wanted to return to the safe haven of Leila's touch, warmer than any sauna. Cobwebs gradually cleared from his mind as if someone brushed them aside, revealing memories from another life.

He knew this face—this angel. He'd known and loved her his whole life. This was no Russian spy. This was Leila. *His* Leila. His true love.

His face twitched with emotion bubbling from beneath a hardened shell, which she'd managed to crack. Tears threatened to build in his eyes, and he couldn't stop them. "You came back to me." Awe coursed through him. Joy. "I knew you'd come back. I knew you loved me."

He threw his arms around her. Leila stiffened slightly and caught her balance against the cobblestones with one arm. He hung on, and she didn't pull away. The fear, hurt, and anger melted, leaving grief and sadness he could hold back no longer. He sobbed into her shoulder.

"It was horrible," he said, clutching her coat with his fingers. "The shelling never stopped. Men were torn to—"

"I know," she said, patting his back. "I know." After a minute, she leaned away enough to hold his face. "Let's get you out of the street, okay?"

"Okay. Anything for you." He nodded several times. He had to put his weight on her shoulder as he pushed himself to his feet. She got up too, and he leaned on her to stay on his feet. She nearly fell but righted herself and continued to comfort him. Everything about her was a balm soothing his raw soul.

The world swam about him. The street undulated. He didn't care. Nothing mattered but the happiness making his head feel stuffed with cotton. The joy wiped away his pain.

"I love Leila," he murmured, holding fast to the one truth he knew for sure.

"Take a step with your left foot. Good." She gently urged him forward to her friend—Sini, he now remembered—on the other side. How he knew that name, he couldn't remember. But that didn't matter.

"Leila loves me," he told Sini.

"Take another step," Leila said.

His vision blurred, and the world kept shifting. Holding tight to Leila, he threw his head back to look at the sky. Surely *it* wouldn't move. There. Pale blue. Storm clouds above the tall buildings. He smiled and sighed with happiness.

The sky never left. Leila had come back. His one true love. Against daunting odds, she'd found him.

"Leila," he said. "Leila, Leila. Mine. *My* Leila."

His boots felt heavy and awkward. He paused to rest. "We're getting married." He looked at her dreamily. "We'll be happy forever. Let's get married right now."

Leila looked at her friend and swallowed. "I have an appointment right now, but I'll see you again very soon. Let's keep going. Cars are waiting for us to cross the street." She patted his arm. "You're doing well."

He was vaguely aware of cars stopped in both directions. Let them wait. He planted his boots in place. "We'll get married after your appointment?"

"Let's go sit on that bench by the tram stop over there," Leila said, gesturing with a nod. "Then we'll talk."

He pulled away. "We're getting married *now*."

Leila moved in front of him and took his hands in hers like a mother helping a child on ice skates for the first time. "We need to get off the street before anything else. Come. One step at a time." She pulled, walking backward. He followed. Of course he'd go anywhere she asked. One step, then another. One lane of cars moved again.

"Good," she said. "That's right."

Her name slipped away from him, like snow melting through his fingers. He stopped. He couldn't remember how he'd gotten into the middle of the road, or who this woman was.

"What's your name?" Maybe she was a spy.

"I'm Leila, remember?"

Leila. Leila, he repeated. He looked at their hands and remembered. Pigtails. Snowball fights. Boating on the lake. "It's you."

"Yes."

He took in her smile, her eyes, which looked at him with pity. Something was wrong. Indistinct thoughts swam in his mind. Had something happened with Leila that he'd forgotten?

Bystanders began yelling. He angrily waved a shushing arm; he couldn't think with such noise. They had to be Russians; Finns weren't loud and obnoxious in public. The noise grew louder, with more voices, louder ones.

Then another sound—screeching metal.

Marko looked toward the noise, but registered only a tram barreling his way. Time stretched, suspending every movement in frames like a slideshow of surreal photographs. Each had oddly bright and colorful pictures.

The tram struck, wrenching Leila from him. He felt a rush of air as the tram passed. The high-pitched screech continued until it shivered to a stop half a block away. Leila lay on the cobblestone, unmoving. Crimson covered one side of her head. A matching pool spread under her, filling the cracks between cobblestones.

He stared. What had happened? Dazed, he searched the crowd of stunned onlookers. Through the confusion battling in his brain like enemy fire, he could tell that his left arm felt strange. He raised it, meaning to make a fist and stretch his fingers. Turn it around to check for injury.

But he had no left hand.

Something tore through his insides and escaped his throat. Something loud. So loud. He told it to stop, but it only grew louder. He couldn't look away. Couldn't stop screaming. He stood in the middle of the street, his vision tunneling into blackness. He didn't see anything around him anymore.

Only two things felt real: The scream clawing from his throat, and the bloody stump at the end of his arm. The wailing of sirens grew louder. Of course, he recognized the noise as the alarm of an incoming air raid.

The war *wasn't* over. Marko searched the sky for bombers but found none. Yet. They had a little time.

Someone called, "Anyone a doctor or nurse?"

He raised his hand—or rather, his stump. "I'm a doctor. A surgeon."

But they ignored him. Dirty Russians, all of them.

The skies opened, dropping some kind of shell—small and wet, but growing in number by the second. One hit his forehead. He swiped at it with his good hand, sure he'd see blood from a new head wound. His fingers came away with nothing but clear liquid. A new kind of poison?

Best to take cover right away. Who knew what the Soviets had come up with? He hunched over and hurried to the other victim.

Devilish Russians, he thought with a snarl. *No better than animals to attack a civilian.*

But before he could touch the patient, another woman kneeling beside her raised a hand, palm out. With her mouth drawn into a tight line, she spoke sharply. "Back off."

"I can help," he said.

She leaned over the victim, shielding her from him. "I won't let you touch her!"

The poor girl was in shock. That was the only explanation. She needed someone with a firm hand and calm demeanor. This must be a frightening situation for her.

The air raid siren grew louder, only now there seemed to be several of them. Marko searched the sky again. Still no bombers, but they'd be here any minute. If officials had activated additional sirens, the incoming attack must be big.

What had he been about to do? He shook his head and looked around. Oh, yes. The wounded woman on the ground and her terrified friend.

"No time to explain." He held out his hands to calm the hysterical girl. But his left hand wasn't there. He stared at where it should have been.

"Go. Away!" the friend said.

"You have to trust me," he told her. "I'm a doctor."

Why are civilians in no-man's land? He brushed the thought away like an annoying bug. He needed to focus on the moment, on tending to the wounded. He took another step closer, and the girl's nostrils flared.

"Marko, listen to me," she said, oddly calm but firm.

How did she know his name? He slowed his step and cocked his head.

"Good. Stay there. An ambulance is coming. Can you hear it?"

"That's an air raid siren." He shook his head fiercely. "Don't you understand? Help isn't coming. The whole world promised help, but they never sent it." His face crumpled. "It never came."

Suddenly the tiny droplets were falling everywhere, bursting onto the ground and against his skin like cold darts. More of them fell out of the sky from invisible Soviet bombers. His skin seemed to burn. His training kicked in: it was time to get out of no-man's land.

"Back to the trench!" He looked around frantically then found a dark line in the middle of ice. He pointed to that spot in the distance. That was the safety of the trench. He grabbed a nearby young man who was strong, if inexperienced. "You. Carry the wounded. Everyone else, follow me!"

He spun around, and his wounded arm began to throb. He looked down and saw blood all over his clothes. That didn't matter now. He raced toward the trench, still yelling for the others to follow, ordering the young man to hurry and carry the casualty to the trench, to safety.

Marko ran as hard as he could, but it felt slow, like running through water. He ignored the bomber pellets hitting his face, focused entirely on the dark line of the trench ahead. He refused to succumb to the new Russian weapon, to fear, or to fatigue.

At last he reached the trench. And jumped.

CHAPTER THIRTY-FIVE

Sini watched in shock and confusion as Marko jumped right into the harbor, into a ribbon of dark water where an icebreaker had cleared the path for boats.

He was yelling about running to a trench. Sini tried to piece together the confusing tangle of the last few minutes and started to realize what had happened to Marko's sick mind, what he'd thought was going on. Several men ran to the spot he'd jumped from, so she turned her focus to Leila.

Despite the tram's impact, Leila's chest rose and fell, but barely. Her eyes lacked the blank stare Sini had feared—the one she'd seen in the operating room, and worse, on the faces of the *motti* dead.

"Leila, stay with me. I'm here." Sini pressed two fingers to her neck to find a pulse, as Leila had taught her. Cold fingers made it hard to know if she'd found the carotid artery—and, most likely, made it hard to feel a heartbeat if she had the right spot. "Hold on, Leila." She repeated her name, knowing that doing so would increase her chances of staying conscious. "You're going to be fine, Leila. Help's coming."

What else had Leila taught her? Sini tried to remember every moment they'd been together, everything from the cottage with the doctor who'd lost his hand to changing bandages in the infirmary to helpful guidance in the operating room. But no matter how much Sini tried to remember specifics about nursing, all she could think of was that her best friend might die.

Breathe, she ordered herself. *Stay calm, for her sake.* With her fingers still pressing against the side of Leila's neck, Sini closed her eyes and focused. There. She felt a beat. Two. A third. The heartbeat was weak but definitely there.

Now what? Sini looked around, hoping to find a police officer or ambulance medic—anyone who knew more about injuries than she did. She pulled off her scarf and pressed it to the wound on Leila's head in an effort to stop the bleeding— she was pretty sure that was the right thing to do.

The scarf may introduce bacteria and cause an infection.

But without the pressure, Leila might bleed to death. She knew that head wounds bled particularly heavily, but this seemed to be too much. She no idea how big the wound was; there was too much blood to tell.

"You're doing great." The words were ones Sini had heard Leila say to comfort patients. Something in Sini's heart twisted, and her eyes blurred. She blinked to hold back the tears, ordering herself to be emotionless. If she'd learned anything from Leila, it was that in an emergency, a cool head must prevail.

What would Leila do if she came across this type of accident? Still pressing the scarf to the head wound, Sini scanned Leila's figure, deliberately replaying the hideous accident in her mind and trying her best to be objective. That meant thinking of Leila as a patient, a casualty, not as a friend.

Her body and head had both gotten the brunt of the tram's impact. *Blunt-force injuries. Possible internal bleeding.*

A soldier came to mind who'd had similar injuries. He'd deteriorated quickly, and they'd discovered a little too late that he was bleeding to death from the inside.

Nothing I can do about internal bleeding right now. What else? If Marko were here—and lucid—he'd know what to do. She glanced toward the harbor and allowed herself a split second to say goodbye to the man who'd been her friend, the man who'd had such a bright future, now gone.

Leila moaned, and Sini's mind went on high alert. "Leila. It's Sini. Stay with me. You're doing fine."

Leila swallowed—something that took effort—and looked at Sini. "T-Taneli."

Oh goodness. The chaos of the accident had made Sini forget about the reason they'd been on the street in the first place.

"Will your aunt be there to meet him?" Sini asked.

A tiny shake of the head seemed to be Leila's answer, but Sini wasn't sure if the movement was intentional or a sign that her friend was about to lose consciousness. Leila opened her lips to speak. They looked dry, almost unreal in how pale they were. "You go."

Sini shook her own head. "I'm not leaving you."

Somehow Leila got the strength to reach out and touch Sini, who wrapped her free hand around Leila's, still pressing the scarf to her head with the other. "He needs someone there when he arrives."

"Yes, but—" Sini couldn't think clearly, couldn't speak clearly.

"He needs a mother." Leila's voice grew weaker with each word. "You're his mother now."

"No." Sini sat back on her heels in shock. "You aren't leaving. Stay with me. You'll be fine. You'll see."

"Promise me." Leila, weak as a baby, looked right into Sini's eyes with the strength only a mother's love could create. Tears fell from her eyes, down her temples, and into her hairline.

Sini felt her own tears spilling down her cheeks. "I promise," she said. "But you have to promise to fight."

The paramedics pushed their way to Leila, making Sini stand and back away. She watched them take her vitals and do other things that she wouldn't have recognized a few months ago. Instruments and techniques Leila had taught her.

The drizzle had stopped, and a chilly breeze kicked up in its place, sending gooseflesh along her arms and making her feel cold to the core, colder than she'd been at any time during the war.

Will I ever feel warm again? The thought flitted through her mind as an idle curiosity. The answer didn't matter.

The accident had happened so fast it was over in a blink, but now, each moment replayed itself, stretched out like an elastic in her mind, the individual images hanging in the air like a slideshow, her mind running through the horrors again and again. The sound of Leila's body being struck. Her body hitting the cobblestones. The brakes' high-pitched screech as the tram stopped. Marko gaping at his injured arm. Blood pooling around Leila's head and filling the cracks between the cobblestones.

Trying to shut out the images was useless. They kept playing like a film, often stopping at particularly awful moments.

"Miss?" A man's voice broke through the haze.

Sini blinked at the sound and realized that a blanket had been drawn over Leila's face. The scarf still lay on the cobblestones beside her body. A sob escaped Sini's throat, and she covered her mouth. "No. No, no, no. Keep trying! You can't give up."

The man who'd spoken a moment ago now stepped in front of her to block the way. He wore a police uniform. "I'm so sorry."

"But she can't be—"

Leila's final words echoed in Sini's mind. *You're his mother now.*

Sini's own words returned too: *I promise.*

The police officer held a notepad and pencil stub in one hand—just like the pencils she and Leila had used while doing inventory. "I'm Officer Korhonen. I can get you a blanket and some coffee. You're probably going into shock. When you're feeling better, I'll need to ask you some questions."

She shook her head back and forth rapidly. "I have to go. Now." She took his notepad and scrawled her name, address, and phone number. "I'm sorry, but I have to go. Her son is about to arrive at the train station from Sweden. I have to meet him."

"You were the female victim's friend?"

His question made Sini's step come short. How could she answer that question? Leila and Marko had both been her friends. They were both victims. How could she possibly make this officer—or anyone—understand what roles those two people had played in her life?

Those things mattered. Every piece of their combined histories had led to this moment. But there was too much to explain, almost too much for Sini to comprehend.

"I knew them both." She held the top of her coat together at her neck.

"Did they know each other?"

Sini's eyes burned. "They did, very well." She was dimly aware of another hot tear.

I can't do this. I have to go.

"What were the victims' names?" Officer Korhonen asked.

A giant rock seemed to press on Sini's chest. Eventually she managed to speak, but her voice sounded like that of a thirteen-year-old boy. "His name was Marko Linna. Dr. Marko Linna." The other name would be harder. "Her name . . . is . . . was . . . Leila. Leila Kallio. I don't know her maiden name."

"Do you know how we can contact her husband?"

Sini shook her head, her eyes unable to tear themselves away from the stretcher with Leila's body. "He died a few years ago." Sini swiped at her tears angrily. "The war is *over*. All three of us made it back. We were supposed to be safe." Her tears came faster and heavier, and she couldn't stop them. "But the war still killed them both."

Korhonen nodded somberly in a way that told her he understood. He'd likely served, too, and knew plenty of others who would forever bear the scars.

You're his mother now. Leila's voice rang in Sini's head, repeating itself.

She could practically feel Leila looking over her shoulder, pouring maternal worry and urgency into Sini's heart. She'd be able to cry more later. For now, she had a promise to keep. She straightened her shoulders and wiped her cheeks. "You have my number," she told the officer. "I have to go. I'm his only family. I'm his—" A new shock settled over her. "I'm his godmother."

Hearing herself say the words made their weight settle on her shoulders. Leila had done the paperwork to make Sini part of her family. That was the reason Leila had given, but what if she'd wanted to be sure her son would be cared for if his mother didn't return from the war?

I have a family. Taneli is mine. The film in her head changed to images she'd seen throughout her life. Being moved from one relative's apartment to another when she became an inconvenience. Christmas celebrations where she got fewer gifts because she wasn't "really" part of whichever family she was staying with. Starting over in yet another school. Not daring to make friends because she'd probably be torn from them soon.

Those images were quickly replaced by new possibilities, the things she didn't get that she could give Taneli: a home he could always count on and the knowledge that he'd never be sent away again. She could give him holidays where he mattered as much as anyone else in the room. Christmases he opened gifts he'd longed for—and that she'd provided. He'd be able to make lifelong friends. He could finish school and go on to a trade school or a university—do whatever he wished.

"May I go?" Sini asked, already walking backward.

Korhonen nodded. "I'll call this evening or tomorrow morning for an interview."

"Thank you." Sini slung her purse over her shoulder. "So much."

She raced off, determined to be the guardian that Leila would want her to be. To do that, she had to succeed at her first duty as Taneli's godmother. The holes left in her heart from her childhood might never be healed, but she could prevent similar ones from being made in his.

Sini hurried through the streets, feeling the late March wind stinging her face. She reached for her scarf, only to remember that it was gone, used in a vain attempt to save Leila.

Taneli, she thought, dodging slower pedestrians. *Think of Taneli.* The words became a mantra as she ran, as her lungs burned with effort. She had to be strong—and fast—for his sake. For Leila's.

She hadn't met Taneli, but she knew his face from Leila's photograph, and she'd heard enough about him that she felt as if she knew him. She already loved him. How much older did he look now than in the black-and-white photograph Leila had kept by her cot? Even a few months since that picture was taken could have lengthened his face and lessened the roundness of his cheeks.

Help me recognize him, she prayed as she increased her pace. *Help me. Help him to know he's loved. That he's safe with me.*

Sini ran north as fast as she could, racing across streets and dodging cars when the light was red. By the time she entered the train station courtyard, her legs felt like rubber. She slowed and gasped, trying to get enough air. In spite of her wobbly legs, she kept moving, though spots appeared in her vision.

No fainting, she demanded of her body. Wreckage from past air raids had been cleared, so she didn't have to weave around debris or worry about tripping over piles of bricks. Yet as she reached the doors flanked by two giant statues of men holding globes, a deep-seated fear burned at the base of her throat, and her step slowed slightly.

I'm not really a mother. She placed a hand to her swelling middle, as much to ease her nausea as to remind herself that she would be giving birth in the fall. She would be a real mother then.

I know nothing about caring for a three-year-old. Would he still be in diapers? What did he eat? How well could he speak? Had he turned four during the war? *I love him, but he is a stranger. And I'm a stranger to him.*

Sini stood before the big wooden doors, knowing that walking through them would mean walking into a new life. She took a breath and grabbed one of the hefty handles on the door and pulled it open, then stepped inside. She did her best to ignore the fear of an uncertain future gripping her heart. Her shoes clicked on the smooth floor as she hurried to the other side of the building, where she exited. She scanned the signs to find the correct platform and found it on the far end.

No train yet. Still walking briskly, she checked her wristwatch—a quarter past. She was late. Had the train come and gone? Body shaking from fatigue, she approached a woman sitting on a bench. "Has the train from Turku arrived?"

"The one arriving at ten after?" the woman asked. "It's late, as usual."

"Thank you." Sini breathed a sigh of relief and tried to calm her hammering heart. She found an empty bench and dropped to it. Now that she'd stopped running, and the rush of panic began to fade, a confusing, overwhelming mix of emotions pulled in different directions inside her.

What should she say when the train did arrive and Taneli got off? What should she do? What would he think when he didn't find his mother? Would a hug from an unfamiliar woman be comforting or frightening?

A loud whistle sounded. Sini stood expectantly, waiting as if the fates were about to issue a decree. The engine belched as it entered the station. The railcars gradually slowed, then lurched to a stop. The train sighed with the release of steam as if letting out the breath Sini had been holding.

Before long, passengers began to disembark, and Sini's worry shifted to something new: Taneli would be traveling with a guardian of some kind. What if they wouldn't let her take Taneli? A fierceness rose in her breast. He belonged to her, and she'd do whatever it took to make sure he had the home Leila had intended for him. He would not be taken to someone who didn't love him.

I know nothing about children, but I love him. That must count for something. If someone challenged her claim, she knew what she'd do: fetch the paperwork Leila had so carefully prepared before their transfers. Sini could prove that she was Taneli's legal guardian.

Leila planned this all along, just in case.

That's why Leila had gone to the trouble of making it official in the middle of the war. She couldn't wait on an uncertain future. If the decision had been only from sentimentality, it could have waited. Sini felt a small measure of lightening from the pressing burden.

Leila trusted me, and she was an excellent judge of character. I can do this.

She looked up at the sky and whispered, "You knew what you were doing, didn't you?" Perhaps, if there was life after death, Leila heard her.

Adults passed by, carrying suitcases, some looking for loved ones. Businessmen hurried along, checking their watches and weaving through the throng. Then a little towhead appeared, followed by small, brown shoes and a chubby little hand holding a woman's slender one. The little boy wore a rucksack and clung to a stuffed bear. A yellow tag was pinned to his coat.

For the second time that day, time slowed. Sini took in every moment—every sight and sound—as Taneli was guided along the platform, his sweet face searching every woman he found for his mother's face. For every step the woman took, his short little legs took at least three; he practically trotted at her side. His gaze passed right over Sini.

This has always been about family. Go. Be his family. She lifted her chin, determined to do right by him and Leila.

The thought had the effect of a gentle shove. Sini stepped forward and called to the woman. "Excuse me," she said with a nervous smile. She glanced down at herself, hoping she looked presentable. The hem of her dress had a blood stain, but it was dark, so it might pass for mud.

The woman stopped. "Yes?"

The little boy eyed Sini. His pale blue eyes had long, blond lashes. His card, as Sini knew it would, read *Taneli Kallio.* The lines below identified Leila Kallio as his mother and his hometown as Viipuri.

His innocent gaze melted Sini's heart and filled it with a warmth she'd never known. A desire to protect and care for Taneli, to teach him and love him, filled her being. She would be there to cheer him, comfort him, praise him.

The woman tilted her head. "Can I help you with something?"

"Yes, I'm his guardian." Sini cleared her throat, buying time as she tried to find the right way to explain without her cacophony of emotions getting in the way. She bent to Taneli's level and held out a hand. To her delight, he released the woman's and held his out to Sini, but still clutched the bear in his other arm. She took his hand, with its soft, perfect skin and gently shook it. She blinked several times to hold in welling tears.

"Taneli, it's very nice to meet you. I'm Sini. Your mother sent me for you." She had to gather herself before going on. Her lips quivered, at first refusing to form words, but at last she managed, "I'll take care of you now."

CHAPTER THIRTY-SIX

Fifteen months later—Saturday, June 25, 1941
Helsinki

"It's time you expand your circle," Sisko said one morning over breakfast at the kitchen table. She sipped her tea and returned to her knitting—a Christmas stocking for Taneli. She lowered her chin and peered at Sini over her glasses. "And by that, I mean that you need more lady friends. A man friend couldn't hurt, either."

They'd had this conversation, or variations of it, many times since Aunt Sisko had moved in. Since *Grandma* Sisko had moved in, as Taneli called her.

Sini spooned applesauce into baby Leila's mouth. The little girl grabbed the handle of the spoon and tried to navigate it to her own mouth, but managed to get her fingers covered in applesauce instead, which she proceeded to wipe in her hair.

"You mischievous little *tonttu*," Sini said, leaning in to kiss little Leila's forehead. With a damp dishcloth, Sini wiped Leila's sticky fingers, but glanced at Aunt Sisko, who was still eyeing her. "I don't need a lot of friends."

Or a "man friend."

Clucking her tongue, Aunt Sisko shook her head. "I'm not suggesting you make friends with a flock of pigeons." She finished the stitches on one needle and punctuated her next words with the now-empty needle. "Say what you will, but you do need a good friend. At least one. I remember what being a young woman is like." She tapped her hair with the side of the knitting needle. "Even if my gray leads you to believe otherwise."

Her insistence made Sini smile. It also made her wonder anew whether Marko's and Leila's deaths had left a hole that Aunt Sisko herself filled by pouring maternal affection into Sini and the children. Whatever the reason, Sini welcomed the prying and poking. Even Aunt Sisko's stern looks were signs of concern and affection.

Baby Leila, almost nine months old, kicked and squealed in her highchair, knocking the bowl of applesauce to the floor. At the clatter, she froze, stared at the messy floor, then covered her mouth with her hands and giggled uncontrollably. Her chubby legs pumped with glee.

"Silly girl," Sini said, moving to clean the mess.

Aunt Sisko tugged on her skein of red yarn and raised her eyebrows at Sini as she walked to the sink to rinse out the dishcloth. When Aunt Sisko didn't look away, Sini wrung out the cloth, turned off the faucet, and faced her. "What?"

"You know." Only then did Aunt Sisko look away and return to her knitting.

"Yes, I know." Sini carried little Leila, face out, to the sink. Washing her face and hands off with the faucet would be easier.

"Women need community and closeness," Aunt Sisko went on. "You need someone who is like—well, like a sister."

Sini's hand paused under the running water for a few seconds. The one person who'd been like a sister to her was gone. The reminder was a physical ache. "I had that kind of friend once," Sini said quietly, washing the last of the food from Leila's face. She turned off the sink, dried Leila's hands and face, then sat her on the floor with some wooden spoons as toys to play with while Sini did the dishes.

She returned to the sink with several cups and plates. When she began scrubbing them, Aunt Sisko couldn't see the welling tears in Sini's eyes. She did want a friend—someone to have a

319

coffee with or go to the park with while watching their children play. But she couldn't fathom ever having another friend as dear as Leila.

"No one will ever replace her," Sisko said, as if reading Sini's mind.

Neither spoke Leila's name; they both knew. Sini stared into the water and suds, tamping down the grief these thoughts always brought with them.

"Not even her namesake can replace her," Aunt Sisko said.

Sini nodded agreement, not trusting herself to speak for fear of sobbing the moment she opened her mouth. She silently placed the last of the dishes into the drying cupboard above the sink and closed the cupboard doors.

In a ball of excitement, Taneli raced into the kitchen, dressed for the day. His hair, however, stuck up in all directions. "I'm dressed! Can we go to Karl's now?" He hopped on his toes, wearing stocking feet. Each day, Taneli looked more and more like his birth mother, especially in the eyes and mouth.

"Not until you brush your teeth and I comb that mop on your head."

Taneli zipped to the bathroom, and a moment later, the sounds of running water carried to the kitchen as he likely tried to wet and comb his hair himself.

Karl was Taneli's best friend and lived upstairs. They'd moved in shortly after Marko's death. Karl's mother, Tuuli, was widowed by the war and had two young children close in age to Taneli and Leila. The neighbors traded off tending the other's children about once a week so the other could complete errands or simply have some alone time.

Laughter and a thump of some kind came through the ceiling from Tuuli's apartment. Sini imagined Tuuli and her boys playing up there. Sini caught Sisko's eye—and raised eyebrow, followed by faux-innocent, "Hmm."

Sini knew what she meant—that Tuuli could very well become a friend. Maybe not as close a friend as Leila had been— or maybe she could be. No way to know without exploring that path.

Before she could think too much about it, she walked to the telephone and called Tuuli, who answered after two rings.

When she heard Sini's voice, she asked, "Are you still bringing the children this morning?"

"I am," Sini said. Her fingers played with the spiral of the telephone cord. She glanced at Aunt Sisko, who smiled back knowingly as her knitting needles clicked. Sini cleared her throat. "I was wondering if you'd be interested in going out for coffee sometime . . . just the two of us."

"That would be delightful," Tuuli said. She sounded sincerely excited. "I need the chance to talk to an adult about grownup things. How about a week from today?"

Sini made a note on the calendar hanging by the table. "That sounds lovely. Let's plan on it."

"Great," Tuuli said, then chuckled. "The children shouldn't be the only ones who get to play with friends. See you in a few minutes."

After Sini replaced the phone in the cradle, she let out a big breath. Sisko, for her part, had dropped her knitting into her lap and applauded.

"Well done." She winked, then took up her knitting again. "See? That wasn't so difficult."

"What would I do without you?" Sini said the words lightheartedly but meant them. Aunt Sisko was the grandmother and mother she'd never had.

Baby Leila smacked the legs of the highchair with a wooden spoon and grinned, reminding Sini to finish getting the children ready for their playtime. She fetched Leila's shoes from the basket by the door, scooped Leila into her arms, and brought her to the couch to put them on. Leila kicked and squirmed, trying to keep her feet away from the shoes—laughing the entire time, of course. A minute later, with the shoes finally buckled, Sini lowered her daughter to the floor. Little Leila twisted around, wobbled, and caught herself from falling on her diaper by gripping Sini's knee.

"You okay?" Sini stroked her daughter's golden hair.

A grin of gums, save for two teeth on the bottom met her, followed by Leila reaching for Sini's face and pressing her open mouth onto her cheek in a big, slobbery kiss and, "Aaaah!"

Sini kissed Leila's downy head, and said, "I love you too, my golden treasure."

Taneli emerged from the bathroom with mostly wet hair. It stuck out in only a couple of spots now. "I brushed my teeth and combed my hair!"

Good enough. "Then let's go," Sini said.

She set the baby on the floor, where Leila crawled to Taneli's side, and clung to his pant leg to pull herself to standing. Sini nudged the government-issued baby box back into the corner by her bed with her toe. She'd applied for a box a few months before Leila was born, and it came filled with cloth diapers, baby clothes, blankets, and more.

The boxes were a relatively new innovation by the government, only a few years old now. They were provided to expectant mothers in financial need. The sturdy cardboard had a pretty paper design and doubled as a crib—something else Sini couldn't afford to buy. She'd be able to provide more for her children after finishing nursing school, but her classes didn't start until fall.

"She's pulling my hair!" Taneli yelped. He'd leaned over to play with Leila, who had a handful of hair clasped tightly in her little fist.

Sini had to keep herself from laughing as she gently pried Leila's tiny fingers off his hair. Most people would have seen the scene as commonplace, hardly worth noting. For her, it was everything. She had two children and an "aunt" who loved her. She had a family.

She also had a purpose—her family was her purpose. Each person within these apartment walls owned her heart with a depth she hadn't known it was capable of. Every decision, every day, was made and colored by how it would affect her little family.

Her feelings for Nikolai . . . even they paled compared with what she felt for her children. Or so she tried to convince herself. She'd drunk him in as if he were water and she a nomad in a desert, desperate to feel alive—to stay alive. She'd loved him. Still loved him.

Would her love for Nikolai have burned out if they'd been able to stay together? She didn't know, and speculating on what might have been did nothing but hurt. Since she'd last seen Nikolai, she'd learned one big thing: love didn't heal old wounds so much as it increased the size of your heart. Never once had she yearned for her children's love, desperate to feel needed and cared for. No, they already loved her wholeheartedly, without reservation. Their love had no requirements, no exceptions.

When Sini had raced to the train station fifteen months ago, she'd thought she loved Taneli. And she had. But within a matter of days—hours, really—he'd captured her heart and sealed it in his. She had no desire to ever get it back.

"What will you be doing today?" Sisko asked. "Anything enjoyable?"

Usually Sini used her time away to handle errands easier done alone, and on the rare times she didn't have any urgent errands, she'd take a long walk, read a book, or visit a museum. Once she'd attended a concert. Another time, she'd tried a new dessert at the Fazer café. Finding pleasurable things that didn't cost a lot was relatively easy—she'd missed so many simple pleasures of life during the war.

Today's outing, however, wouldn't be one of those pleasurable things, and it wasn't a typical errand like going to the outdoor market or paying a bill.

"Nothing exciting today," Sini said, slipping on her own shoes and taking her purse off a hook. "Today, I'm going to the Lotta Svärd office to remove myself from active status."

"I'm so relieved to hear that." Aunt Sisko's knitting dropped to her lap. "This isn't a safe time."

They'd both heard rumblings of more war with the Soviets. The subject was discussed on the radio at night, in all of the newspapers, by people on the street. Only the most oblivious didn't recognize that the Soviets weren't done with them yet.

ative.

Worse, the Finns were caught between two dictators: surrender to Stalin's rule, or fight the Soviets along the border again, this time for Germany. If they did the former, they'd never again be free. If they refused Hitler, he'd cut off the country's outside transportation and destroy the domestic lines, making them all starve to death. He had the capability, with little more than a snap of his fingers.

How could a small country still recovering from a brutal beating just over a year ago hope to contend with two world powers at the same time? No amount of *sisu* could change the fact that the future looked bleak.

"Don't worry," Sini said. "I have no plans to go anywhere as a Lotta."

"Good." Aunt Sisko's needles resumed, though they moved much more slowly than even a few months ago. Her knuckles were swollen, her hands spotted with age. She loved knitting and insisted on doing it even though it hurt because creating calmed her soul.

Sini hoped the Lotta Svärd wouldn't ask her to turn in her uniform; she wanted to keep it. The irony wasn't lost on her. The scratchy, ugly thing was now steeped in experiences and people and memories she never wanted to forget. It hung in her closet, and every so often, she pulled it out and inhaled. The smell always sent waves of memories through her.

Aunt Sisko gave an approving nod. "Lottas might not be needed again, but it's best to be safe." She lifted her eyes to Sini's, and the look they exchanged said more than words could have: that any war effort would require thousands of Lottas. This time, Sini couldn't be one of them. She'd stay behind and hope her children would still have a Finland to grow up in.

Sini had a horrid feeling that if war broke out against the Soviets again, the conflict wouldn't be over nearly as quickly as it had been in the 105-day Winter War. With so many already dead, and many survivors crippled, where would the Finnish army find any soldiers to fight? They'd already used their reserves and beyond, sending old men and young teen boys to fight.

A second war might end in a matter of days, as Stalin thought his first invasion would. If so, the Finns would be soundly slaughtered, and their homeland—the Maid of the North—would be absorbed by Stalin's communist machine. Would anything of Finnish culture or language survive?

"We'll be back in a couple of hours."

Sini lifted Leila onto her hip then opened the apartment door. Taneli raced past her but then tripped on the threshold and landed on the hard tile floor with an *oof*.

"Are you hurt?" Sini quickly knelt, sitting Leila beside her, and assessed the damage.

"Ouch." Taneli pushed himself to his knees and rubbed his forehead. He might have a goose egg, but otherwise seemed no worse for the wear.

Sini was about to stand when she heard heavy footfalls on the stairs, which made her pause. For the briefest flash, she thought it was Marko coming home, but of course it couldn't be.

Before she could stand, a pair of men's shoes appeared in her vision and stopped right in front of her.

Both curious and nervous, she looked up to see who this person was—dark slacks, a button-up shirt, a light jacket. And a familiar face with startlingly blue eyes and hair so pale it was nearly white.

The clothing could have belonged to anyone, and she'd never seen civilian clothing with that face. Could it be?

He didn't speak, and she didn't either. Hardly able to believe her own eyes, she slowly stood, lifting Leila as she did so. Taneli instinctively huddled close on her other side.

Sini and Nikolai stared at each other—for how long, she didn't know. She wanted to cry. She had a thousand questions. But she didn't dare speak, not without finding out from him first why he was here and what he thought of her.

These eyes didn't hold hatred. But they did once. Angry, bitter hatred. That mouth, which now looked vulnerable, and had said *I love you*, had also cursed and spat at her.

After a terribly long silence, Nikolai swallowed, making his Adam's apple bob in his throat. He looked at baby Leila. His eyes widened slightly and became glassy. He nodded at her then finally spoke.

"Is she . . . ?"

Sini nodded, unable to speak as tears welled in her own eyes too. What should she say—what *could* she say? Months ago, she'd imagined a blazing lecture she imagined blasting at him if she ever saw him again.

Now, though . . . she couldn't say those things. She could hardly speak at all. And a big reason was that the love she'd once felt for Nikolai roared back to life like a dried spruce going up in flames. Her affection had been made of drop after drop of love, creating a lake of the soul, and she'd long believed the lake to have dried.

This moment, she realized that those drops didn't make a lake. They weren't made of water, but of fuel. The reservoir had waited inside her so long for this moment, and now it had been struck with a match, which was dropped into her heart, bringing the fire back bigger and hotter than ever.

"I, uh . . ." Nikolai lowered his gaze, and Sini realized he was holding an envelope. He looked at her then back at the letter. "I came to bring this to you. To explain."

"All . . . right." Sini reached for the envelope, and he handed it to her. Their fingers brushed, as they had when she'd given him the chocolate bar so long ago. And just as she had then, she felt an electrifying zing go through her at his touch.

"I didn't expect to see you," he said. "I don't mean to interfere in your life. I just . . ." He shrugged, brow furrowed, jaw working with emotion. "I needed to explain. I know you can't possibly love me anymore, but maybe you won't hate me."

Another thousand questions filled her mind. Every word he spoke raised more.

He took a step backward and lifted a hand in a wave. "I memorized your address, and I wanted to be sure it arrived . . ." He took another step toward the stairs but then looked at Leila again as if he could hardly believe she was real. "I won't want to be a burden, but I can help with money, and with . . ." Nikolai looked at Sini again. "I'll stay away. You have my word." He turned and reached for the bannister.

"Nikolai." Saying his name felt foreign and familiar at once.

He stopped and looked back at her, but his hand remained on the bannister.

"Would—would you come with us on a walk? Maybe tell me what you wrote?"

Something like hope flashed in his eyes. "If you're sure."

"I'm sure." Sini slipped the letter into her purse. For a moment she debated whether to bring the children to Tuuli after all or to have them come along so that if she felt the need to cut this conversation with Nikolai short, she could use naptime or a diaper change as an excuse. She opted for the latter, so she turned to the apartment and called to Sisko. "Would you call Tuuli and tell her the children aren't coming today?"

The floorboards squeaked as Aunt Sisko walked. She peered around the corner from the kitchen and nodded. "Is everything all right?"

I certainly hope so.

"Just fine," Sini said, glad that Sisko's vantage meant she couldn't see Nikolai. There would be plenty of time to explain later.

CHAPTER THIRTY-SEVEN

She and Nikolai took the cramped elevator to the bottom floor, easier with two small children than navigating several flights of stairs. As they left the building and turned onto the main street, Sini adjusted Leila on her hip and reminded Taneli to hold her hand.

"I could hold . . . the baby," Nikolai said. His tone was questioning, not demanding. Vulnerable, even. "If you'd like me to, that is."

"Thank you. I should have thought to bring the stroller."

Nikolai reached for Leila, who leaned toward him with a grin. He took her into his arms, and she settled there happily, with two fingers in her mouth as they walked along. She seemed to enjoy being taller than her mother.

Sini had always thought that Leila took after her father, but seeing them together was stunning; the resemblance was uncanny. Leila was a miniature, feminine version of Nikolai. She had the same eyes and even the same chin. They'd walked nearly a block before Sini managed to speak. "Her name is Leila."

"Leila," he repeated. "After your friend?"

"Yes." Sini smiled, surprised he remembered. "And this is Taneli, her, well, now my son."

Nikolai paused on the sidewalk and held out his hand. "Nice to meet you, Taneli," he said. "I've heard good things about you."

"You have?" Taneli asked, tentatively shaking Nikolai's hand, then looking up at Sini with questions in his eyes.

"This is my good friend Nikolai," Sini said. She glanced at Nikolai, who smiled back, seemingly pleased with how she'd described him. He was far more than a good friend, of course. He was her first real love. He was the father of Taneli's little sister. "We, um . . . met during the war."

"Neat," Taneli said, then skipped ahead, stopping only when he reached an intersection, where he waited as Sini had taught him to do.

A tram passed. She watched it, mesmerized until it turned a corner. She'd never ride one again.

When they entered a small playground, Taneli ran off, climbed up the ladder of a slide and hooted with glee as he went down it. "Mommy, look!" he called over and over as he went down a second time headfirst and then another time feet first but on his stomach.

She and Nikolai, with Leila on his lap now, sat on a park bench. Between them hung an invisible barrier of fifteen months and a storm of unresolved emotions.

What had he come to tell her? Perhaps she should just pull out the letter and read it. But when he stayed quiet for several minutes, she could bear the silence no longer. "Did you come to visit from Leningrad?" She had no idea what crossing the border was like for Finns and Russians right then, but the question was the only thing she could come up with what to say.

"No, I've been living in Oulu with my aunt and her son. And my mother."

Sini turned to him with surprise. "I'm so glad you got to be with her."

"Me, too. She managed to get out shortly after I was called up. She kept her Finnish citizenship, so she was able to stay here."

"And you? How . . ."

"After the war, I was released to my aunt. Apparently, my parents wanted me to be accepted in Russia completely—my mother wasn't, often seen as second-class because she was an immigrant—so they never told me that I was born in Oulu."

Not even Taneli's calls for Sini to look could penetrate her shock. "Does that mean you're . . ."

"Yes. I'm a Finnish citizen. Thanks to you, I was a sorry excuse for a spy. I didn't send the Soviets any information about the Finnish army, so I'm not considered a threat."

"Goodness." Sini could hardly grasp the details. They seemed to come at her faster by the moment.

"To be on the safe side, though, I changed my last name to my mother's maiden name, Lehtinen."

"Are you still Nikolai?"

"I am." He smiled at that. "I should have written earlier, but—"

"No need to apologize," Sini said. She still feared whatever he'd meant to tell her.

"I would have, but my mother was very ill, and she passed away a few months ago. And now . . . I'm going to do what she wanted me to—what you said I should do." He'd spilled so many surprises already that Sini could not fathom what he referred to.

"What's that?" she asked.

"It's why I'm in Helsinki now. I moved from Oulu because, well, I'll be attending Aalto University in the fall."

"That's wonderful news," Sini said, genuinely happy for him. "I always said you had a talent for art."

"You did, but how could you really tell when my art supplies consisted of little more than pencil stubs, charcoal, and occasionally leftover sauces?"

He grinned as if cracking a joke, but Sini was serious. "I knew."

"You really did."

The moment had a sweetness to it, but soon the silence returned. Nikolai rubbed his mouth with a hand. He handed Leila back to her then wiped his palms on his thighs. "I had to tell you . . ." He stood and paced. "It's all in the letter, but—"

Once more he scrubbed a hand down his face, then stilled his feet and looked right at Sini. "I know why you turned me in."

Despite the warm June day, the night he'd spat at her returned in full force. Tears sprang to her eyes. "You . . . do?"

"You saved me."

A hot tear escaped. She nodded and tried to say, *Yes.* More tears fell, and she covered her mouth with one hand to hold back the sobs threatening to come out.

Nikolai hurried to her, concern in his eyes. He dropped to the bench again and reached for her. She fell into his embrace as best she could with Leila on her lap, and she cried. The sobs would not be contained.

"Sini," he said, holding her close, stroking her hair, as he'd done so many times in the dugout. "How I acted wasn't real. I had to protect *you*."

His words pierced the sphere of grief. She sniffed, caught her breath a couple of times between sobs, and raised her head. "What?"

"You saved me. I had to be sure you'd be safe, and the only way to do that was to pretend that I . . ." He shook his head. "I can't even say it."

The sobs were evening out as Sini tried to think through everything he was saying, tried to reimagine that horrible night and view it through his eyes. Tried to grasp that he'd loved her. Really loved her. And *that* was why he'd acted so hatefully. *Because* he loved her.

"You loved me?" she finally managed. She wiped her tears with one hand then smoothed some of Leila's hair.

"I never stopped loving you." He reached out and smoothed back some of Sini's hair then rested his hand behind her neck and stroked her cheek with his thumb. She leaned into his touch, into the warmth of his skin on hers.

A shrill noise cut through the air. Fear clenched Sini's chest. She straightened, and Nikolai released her, sitting at attention as well. They both recognized that sound.

Air raid.

A young mother from across the playground scooped her toddler from the swings and ran. The little girl had both hands over her ears, and she started crying, her lower lip thrust out, as her pale-faced mother ran.

"Where's the nearest shelter?" Nikolai asked.

But Sini was already halfway across the playground to Taneli, who looked up at her. "What's that noise?"

Nikolai had followed on her heels. He picked up Taneli. "Want to ride my back?" he asked, but swung him around without waiting for an answer.

Sini threw him a grateful look. She hadn't asked him to do that; he'd just stepped in. "A shelter is that way." She nodded to the right, then, clutching Leila to her chest, Sini ran with Nikolai and Taneli at her side.

They ran until the movement of the crowd forced them to slow to a walk. After what was probably two or three minutes, but felt ten times that long, they reached the entrance. She and Nikolai both glanced at the sky—still no planes—and he urged her to enter first. He followed behind as they and dozens of others hurried down the steps into the basement shelter.

Tuuli will help Sisko get to safety, Sini told herself.

Behind them, a man yelled, "I see a bomber!"

A little boy somewhere ahead burst into tears. Furious at the man, Sini turned around and yelled, "Hush!" She continued down the stairs. At the bottom, she took Nikolai's hand, and together they found a spot on the floor to wait out the raid.

In one corner, the scared boy sat on his mother's lap. "Everything will be fine," she repeated, rocking side to side and stroking his hair. The shelter vibrated from a strike.

Taneli startled and looked about, eyes wide. "I don't like it here."

Sini reached out to comfort him, but Nikolai spoke instead. "How high can you count? Can you count to a hundred?"

"Yeah," Taneli said, brow still furrowed with worry.

"Let's see how high we can count until the next boom. One, two, three . . ."

Taneli looked from Nikolai to Sini, who joined in. "Four, five, six . . . you know what's next." She put a hand on Nikolai's knee, a wordless gesture of gratitude for comforting her son in a scary situation.

"Seven." The number came out sounding like a question.

"Good job," Nikolai said. "Let's count. "Eight . . ."

All three counted quietly together, reaching thirty-five until the next strike. That one shook the shelter harder than the first. Sini schooled her features so Taneli and Leila would remain calm.

"Do we start at one again?" Taneli asked. The tension from before was no longer in his voice.

"We do," Nikolai said. "Do you think we'll get higher than thirty-five this time?"

"Let's find out," Taneli said. "One, two, three . . ."

Next to Sini, an older man grumbled. "Knew this was coming. We'll get our land back from greedy Stalin."

Hitler was using threats to force Finland into helping Germany invade the Soviet Union, but every Finn knew that he wasn't getting the support he thought he'd secured. The Finns had no desire to conquer anyone; all they wanted was their freedom, and if they could get back the land they'd lost in the Winter War, they would.

Hitler had given them a Hobson's choice: fight for their land or starve to death. But Finnish soldiers wouldn't invade beyond their original border. Germany might expect the Finnish army to invade Leningrad, but he'd be sorely disappointed. Stalin had learned about *sisu* the hard way. So would Hitler.

Another man replied to the first, and the two went on talking about making Stalin pay, as if that were possible.

The room shuddered again.

"We didn't get to one hundred," Nikolai said cheerfully. "Let's try again."

Taneli was leaning against Sini now, clearly nervous and needing comfort, but he counted along with Nikolai all the same. After another boom—this one after Taneli had reached only twenty—Sini closed her eyes and pulled into herself, trying not to cry, trying to be strong for her children. Her shoulders shook as she tried not to cry.

As if he could tell what she felt and what she needed, Nikolai put an arm around her shoulders, and she leaned in close. The children adjusted positions on what was essentially Sini's and Nikolai's combined lap. She settled her cheek against his chest and listened to the steady thrum of his heart, a sound she'd missed more than she'd realized.

"It'll be all right," he whispered in Sini's ear, then kissed her hairline. "It'll be over soon."

The rest of the time in the shelter, she never stopped praying—for her babies, for her country, for peace in a world where war raged. That somehow she could raise her children in safety and freedom.

The war had made some people reject the idea of God, but the opposite had happened for her. She didn't yet know what she believed, only that she found comfort and strength in prayer. Her children needed her to be strong and at peace. So she prayed.

Sini reached for Nikolai's free hand and interlaced her fingers through his. He kissed the top of her head, and she breathed out deeply, her worries easing ever so slightly. As they once had under very different circumstances, Sini and Nikolai were seeking safety underground. This time, with two children who relied on them, Nikolai's own child among them.

Years ago when she'd dreamed of a future with a man she loved, of having a family, this was not what she'd pictured. Not even almost. But she would be grateful for every day that Nikolai was part of her life, for every moment of being a mother.

No matter what the years ahead held, they would be trying, no question. The unrest in the world might not end for years to come.

Would war tear her little family apart? Would Nikolai be sent back to Russia someday? Forced to fight for the Soviets again? Or called up to fight for the Finns? Would the nation fall to Stalin after all? Would her children have a free nation to live in? Would they survive whatever war brought them?

Amidst the worried thoughts, a voice pricked her heart—God? Leila's spirit? She didn't know, only that it spoke in a whisper, barely more than a breath.

Your family will live.

She let out a deep breath, held Nikolai's hand a little tighter, and joined in the counting once again. She repeated the voice in her mind.

Your family will live.

For now, that was enough.

Soldiers! I have fought on many battlefields, but never have I seen your like as warriors! . . .

After sixteen weeks of bloody combat, with no rest by day or night, our army stands unconquered before an enemy whose strength has grown in spite of terrible losses . . .

That an army so inferior in numbers and equipment should have inflicted such serious defeats on an overwhelmingly powerful enemy, and, while retreating, have over and over again repelled his attacks, is a thing for which it is hard to find a parallel in the history of war. But it is equally admirable that the Finnish people, face to face with an apparently hopeless situation, were able to resist giving in to despair, and instead to grow in devotion and greatness.

Such a nation has earned the right to live.

—Field Marshal Gustav Mannerheim

HISTORICAL NOTE

The Winter War began with the invasion of the Soviet Union on 30 November 1939 and ended with the ceasefire 105 days later, on 13 March 1940.

Stalin lied, claiming that Finland fired the first shots, and insisted that he had to invade because the Soviet Union "needed" much of the southern part of Finland, including the archipelago off the coast, as a buffer between the Soviet capital of Leningrad and German forces. Of course, in reality, Stalin wanted to take over yet one more country, as he already had with Latvia, Lithuania, and Estonia, and the world knew his true motives and condemned them.

The casualties of the Winter War are estimated to be about 70,000 Finnish soldiers (~29,000 dead) and about 350,000 Soviet soldiers (~167,000 dead), though the Finns were heavily outnumbered and outgunned.

Finland retained its independence, but at a cost: they lost the entire Karelian Isthmus, land north of Lake Ladoga, and a more, totaling more than 10% of pre-war Finland and 30% of pre-war industrialized Finland, including Viipuri (known today as Vyborg), a major economic city. Soviet losses were so large that a joke among Russians was that they gained just enough land from Finland to buy their Soviet dead.

Fifteen months after the ceasefire, Hitler saw an opportunity to invade the Soviet Union via Finland. He gave them an ultimatum: help him invade, or he'd cut off Finland from other countries and cripple the nation's own transportation lines, which essentially meant that Finns would starve to death.

Finland made an uncomfortable and reluctant alliance, with one objective: to regain the land they lost in the Winter War. Finnish troops really did refuse to go beyond the original border. Of course, that meant they also refused to help German forces invade Leningrad, which enraged Hitler.

The Winter War was far more complex than a single novel can portray, so I had to decide what areas of the border and fighting to show, at the expense of many other significant locations and events not being mentioned at all.

Aaro Pajari, who led the raid Marko participates in, was a real military leader and is considered to be one of the greatest World War II heroes of the country. The raid happened as it is shown in the story, including a feint attack in the distance, the Russian camp burning logs that essentially turned themselves into sitting ducks, and so on, as shown in the novel.

Pajari took the assignment despite a heart condition because he knew the landscape better than anyone else, and he collapsed from a heart attack on the way back. As a lieutenant colonel, he was the leader of the broader Tolvajärvi campaign. After victory in that sector, he was promoted to colonel. By the end of World War II, he was a master general. He received the Mannerheim Cross of Liberty twice.

Baron Carl Gustav Mannerheim, head of the Finnish army, was a real figure, as was Colonel Talvela. The other military and medical characters are the author's creation.

Molotov cocktails were relied upon by Finnish forces, who had very few weapons, and the improvised explosives, known around the world today, got their name during the Winter War, thanks to Molotov himself being one of the Soviet military leaders involved in the conflict.

Finnish ingenuity helped keep the country from falling quickly, as shown in the novel. These elements included understanding how to live in the bitter cold, make stoves that produce little smoke, wear white camouflage snowsuits, use skiers for ambush-type attacks, and more. Medics did thaw ampules in their mouths or in their armpits. Vehicles had to be turned on regularly so the engines wouldn't freeze. Finnish forces used different combinations of fuel that had lower freezing points than those the Soviets used.

Lottas drove supply trucks and helped the war effort in dozens of other ways, including "general support," as Sini does. One unit of Lottas were stationed at a look-out post watching for incoming Soviet planes, and some sources say they were the only armed women in World War II.

Finnish *sisu* and creativity in holding on as they waited for international aid was, in part, why they never got much aid: journalists reported one amazing battle after another, with small numbers of Finns taking out thousands of Soviets. As a result, the world looked on, impressed by the plucky Finns who, they assumed, had the conflict under control.

Some minor aid came here and there, often in the form of food rather than in men or weapons. Some men from various countries went to Finland on their own to fight. Sweden sent quite a few. Many children of Finnish immigrants in the U.S. went to help. Small numbers of volunteers came from other countries came as well, including actor Christopher Lee, known best today as Saruman from the Lord of the Rings movies.

Some events depicted in the book that are directly from the war include the motti tactic and resulting horrors along Raate Road in the Suomussalmi area (something reportedly taught at West Point), the Soviet soldier stuck in barbed wire along the Mannerheim Line and how he was finally shot to be put out of his misery, the Soviet infantry unit destroyed by their own military's artillery, the volley of artillery after the ceasefire, and more.

The Tolvajärvi area field hospital where most of the story takes place in is my invention, as is the border town of Kivilä where Leila and Sini ski to help the wounded doctor. Kivilä is based on many border towns that were evacuated, largely burned down, and then boobytrapped, though Kivilä itself fictional.

The role of the Winter War in World War II is largely unknown, but it had far-reaching effects, two of which I feel are worth mentioning.

First, the Winter War revealed many weaknesses in the Soviet army, from communication to supplies to techniques. Following the Winter War, the Soviet Union regrouped and was able to prepare their military so that when Hitler invaded from the European mainland in Operation Barbarossa just over a year later, Soviet forces were in a much better position to be able to hold off the German forces longer and more effectively than they would have been able to without the harsh lessons learned during the Winter War.

The second significant element comes from an unlikely place: The United Kingdom. Prime Minister Neville Chamberlain promised aid to Finland but never sent it. Every election is complicated, and one event can rarely be pointed to as a single reason for any result. That said, Chamberlain's lack of follow-through in sending aid did not sit well with his fellow Brits. That was one reason his popularity dropped among UK citizens. He lost the next election. The man who beat him? Winston Churchill. (I cannot imagine World War II without Churchill!)

Finland is the only European nation bordering Russia to never fall to Soviet rule. When the Soviet Union collapsed in 1989, the Finland-Russia border became the path that economic activity, tourism, humanitarian aid, and more entered Russia.

Thanks to remaining independent, Finland was able to support such endeavors. However, to this day, many Finnish baby boomers hold resentment toward Russians due the Winter War and Continuation War

Such resentment isn't a surprise, as few families escaped serious injury or death, and the nation not only lost land (and with it, thousands lost their homes), but was also saddled with a heavy burden. The Soviets demanded heavy financial reparations for their international humiliation: $600 million, which is $5.3 billion in 2018 U.S. dollars.

One specific fact reveals much about Finns' *sisu* and their commitment to doing what is right: Finland remains the only nation on earth that has paid its World War II debts.

Despite my attempts to make the story as accurate as possible, errors may have slipped through. The responsibility for any errors is mine.

ABOUT THE AUTHOR

Annette Lyon is a *USA Today* bestselling author, an 8-time Best of State medalist for fiction in Utah, and a Whitney Award winner. She's had success as a professional editor and in newspaper, magazine, and technical writing, but her first love has always been fiction.

She's also half Finnish thanks to her mother, who was born and raised in Helsinki. Her father has spent many years in Finland, and in the U.S. taught Finnish literature courses on the university level. Her family spent three years in Helsinki during her youth, which led her to love Finland, its language, and its culture. She's been writing for years, and turning to her Finnish heritage for inspiration was bound to happen!

She's a cum laude graduate from BYU with a degree in English and is the author of over a dozen books, including the Whitney Award-winning Band of Sisters, a chocolate cookbook, and a grammar guide. She co-founded and was served as the original editor of the Timeless Romance Anthology series and continues to be a regular contributor to the collections.

She has received six publication awards from the League of Utah Writers, including the Silver Quill, and she's one of the four coauthors of the Newport Ladies Book Club series. Annette is represented by Heather Karpas at ICM Partners.

Read more about the Winter War in the first chapter *War of Hearts*, a novella, below.

WAR OF HEARTS
CHAPTER ONE

December 10, 1939—Finland

Anna didn't realize she'd fallen asleep until the freezing, bumpy train screeched to a halt and jolted her awake. She opened her eyes and tried to regain her bearings. The sky outside was pitch black; she couldn't see anything through the windows, not even stars. She stared at the windows—blacked out to avoid detection by Soviet aircraft. A shudder went down her spine.

That's right. I'm in a war zone. Her mind came fully awake. This wasn't California. She'd traveled across the entire U.S., took a ship to Sweden, and finally, this train on her way to a non-combat encampment north of Lake Ladoga.

Dill, her boss at The Star had planned to send Keith, another, more senior reporter to cover Stalin's invasion of neighboring Finland, but his appendix ruptured, so he'd be in the hospital for the foreseeable future. While Anna would never wish bad fortune on a colleague, if Keith had to get sick, she was quite happy to take his place at the last minute. She'd convinced Dill she was the right reporter to cover the so-called Winter War in Keith's absence.

"I've worked harder than any of the other writers on staff," she'd told him. A staff of almost all men—just one other woman. "I deserve the assignment."

He'd agreed, so she'd gone home to pack, relieved to be traveling. She hadn't told Dill her biggest reason for wanting the job, because it had nothing to do with being a journalist. Simply put, Anna needed some distance from Pete, from the torrent of emotions that seeing him every day in the newsroom meant.

Now she had her distance. She was far from home in the dark and cold, and most definitely alone in this frozen wasteland. She'd done some research on the war so far and knew the basics, including the geography of cities she'd only just heard of. She'd build on that knowledge after she arrived in camp.

Stalin wanted to take over ports and other areas of land he viewed as strategically good for Russia as a whole and for Leningrad in particular, almost certainly taking over the country entirely in the process so it would fall to Communist rule. When he'd first invaded, he's planned for the exercise to be over almost as quickly as it began. A few days, ten days at most. About two weeks into the fighting, the Finns had proven to be far greater adversaries than Stalin ever expected from his miniature neighbor, and all the political experts now said that the war was just getting started.

Anna stood and buttoned her new coat as she waited to exit. She bought it in New York City en route for this assignment—no finding one like this in southern California. When the car door opened and a whoosh of frigid air swirled inside, Mother's voice came to Anna's mind. "You're leaving one kind of difficulty only to ask to enter another, far more horrible kind."

"I'll be safe," Anna had told her. "They aren't sending me to a conflict area."

What Mother hadn't known was that Anna wouldn't mind physical suffering; it would be much easier to endure than the emotional turmoil she faced every day. No, whatever this war held for her, Anna would much rather be near the Tolvajärvi battlefront in the deepest winter than walking through Santa Monica, seeing the palm tree beneath which Pete had first kissed her.

As Anna waited in the short line to get off the train, her mother's words repeated in her mind.

Perhaps I am a little crazy, but I had to get away.

Arctic weather, soldiers with powerful stories to tell, a foreign landscape: it would all help distract her from the bitter breakup she'd gone through the night before Thanksgiving. The humiliation of that evening still stung.

The humiliation part was your own fault, she chided herself.

In her defense, she'd thought Pete was going to propose that night three weeks ago—a lifetime ago. When he'd arrived at her parents' home to pick her up for their usual Friday date, his surprised expression said that he hadn't remembered her parents offering to have him over for dinner, not until he saw them standing in the dining room beside an elaborately set table.

He'd leaned in and whispered, "Anna, there's something important we need to discuss. Can we go somewhere private?"

"Of course, darling," Anna had said, her heart speeding up at the prospect of wearing Pete's ring. "Come meet my parents first." Like a silly schoolgirl, she'd blushed with anticipation as she'd led him to the dining room and introduced Pete to her mother and father. Looking back, Anna remembered Pete looking a bit pale.

Turned out that Pete was nervous—just not for the reason Anna assumed.

Throughout dinner, he'd remained uncharacteristically quiet, even when Anna hinted that he broach the topic on his mind. "So what's the important thing you wanted to discuss?" she asked as she buttered a roll. She sent her mother a smile; they both just knew it would happen tonight.

Pete swallowed a bite of meatloaf, his eyes moving nervously from Anna, to her father, to her mother. He cleared his throat uncomfortably. "Could we please speak in privacy?"

Anna set down the roll and patted his arm playfully. "Come now, Pete," she said, in hopes of easing his jitters. "If you have something important to say, you can say it in front of my family."

They'll be your family soon too.

He pushed away from the table, placed his cloth napkin beside his plate, and stood. "I, uh…"

Anna licked her lips and clasped her hands, ready to say yes.

"I—I need to go." Pete headed for the front door.

"What?" Anna said, her voice going up an octave as she flew to her feet.

Pete's step paused, and he turned around, but he avoided her eyes—and Father's, and Mother's—seeming unable to find a place to look until he settled on the rug. "I came to say goodbye, Anna. I'm not ready to be tied down." His eyes met hers briefly. "I'm sorry." His cheeks had spots of pink in them. Their gaze held, and she sensed pain and regret in his before he looked away, muttered "Excuse me," to her parents, and strode away. The front door shut hard behind him as if he couldn't wait to escape.

Now Anna stood in a train car with support staff for a battlefront a world away from that dining room. How could she have been so foolish as to think he cared about her—was about to propose to her?

You came here to forget. Stop thinking of him.

She hefted her suitcase and clutched her purse, making sure that her notepad and pencil were easily accessible; one never knew when one would find a golden nugget worthy of reporting. Along with the other passengers, she shuffled closer to the exit and peered outside but found almost total darkness, save for a few lamps and the light of the full moon reflecting off the snow.

What time was it again? She checked her wristwatch, tilting it toward the light inside the car. Ten o'clock at night. Of course it was dark. She'd heard of Finnish winters, how the days had only a few hours of sunlight. She looked forward to seeing that for herself tomorrow.

A plane buzzed in the sky overhead. For a moment, everyone in her car stopped moving and held their breath—a secretary, two nurses, a few soldiers, and others, all frozen as one. Only when the plane passed without a strike did they breathe a sigh of relief and keep moving toward the door.

The moment Anna reached outside air, the shock of the frigid air made her gasp involuntarily. One step outside the train car was miles colder than inside it. She descended the remaining steps and reached the platform, where she quickly lifted her coat collar to protect her face. Her nose was already starting to tingle with pain. She set down her suitcase and searched her pockets for the thick gloves she'd bought, also in New York, and put them on.

Heavens to Betsy. She'd known she was coming to a cold place, but she hadn't expected to be chilled to the marrow after only seconds. And men lived and fought in this weather?

The things we do for freedom and our families.

That's exactly what the Finnish soldiers were doing, against all odds. That's what she was here to do: show American readers of The Star what was really going on in this small nation.

I'll have to actually be able to see something first. She hated the dark already. This assignment would be a bigger challenge for a California girl than she'd assumed. On her way, she'd braced herself for cold, for pine trees instead of palm trees, for snow. For things to be different. But this was beyond different. Back home, even in December, winter, such as it was, mostly meant it wasn't hot out—not that your lungs felt as if they were freezing your body from the inside out.

"Miss Miller?" a deep voice called from behind her, one with a thick accent, making the I's sound like long E's, and rolling the R at the end of her name: Mees Meellerrr. She turned to see two men striding toward her, one much larger than the other. The taller looked to be in his mid-forties.

The other was shorter and much younger, twenty at most. He wore civilian clothes—leather boots, a warm coat and hat, but nothing official-looking, yet he was clearly a soldier. He carried a rifle and walked like he'd recently come out of military training.

With a start, Anna realized he probably had just come from training.

The two men stopped before her, as the elder shook her hand. "Welcome to Finland," the older one said in accented but clear English. "I hope we can make your stay comfortable." He spoke like a concierge at a hotel.

"Thank you." This was Anna's first chance to really see the young man up close, and she couldn't help noticing his obviously worn coat and boots. Word was that the Finnish army was low on almost everything, but especially on ammunition, guns, and artillery. They had virtually no tanks to speak of, and their men had never been trained for what to do when confronted with them, which had been a disaster the first day of the war. They had a limited number of men, and even an even more limited number of uniforms. So the rumor about uniforms was true.

The young soldier reached for her suitcase, which she surrendered with a smile. She turned back to the older man. "Are you Commander Talvela?"

"No, no. He's over this area, but he's not visiting our camp today. I'm Kuusinen, by the way. No relation to the fake president." He shook his head, clearly disdainful of the puppet government Stalin had erected for the Finns.

"I'll remember that," Anna said, and followed them through the snow, picking her way behind them toward a jeep. She could hardly see where she was stepping. If she reached the car without slipping and falling on her face, it would be a miracle, even though she'd bought a pair of sensible boots to go with the coat and gloves instead of the pretty boots with the high heels she'd eyed in a Manhattan department store. Even so, Anna had to scurry to keep up.

They finally reached the jeep, which was parked near a snowbank. The young man hefted Anna's suitcase into the back then hopped behind the wheel. Kuusinen gestured toward the back seat. "For you. The back is a somewhat gentler ride."

"Oh, okay. Thank you," she said, taking his hand as he helped her up.

Climbing up in a skirt was tricky business, but as she settled into her seat, she was extra glad for the thick long johns she wore underneath. Otherwise, her limbs would have frozen right off.

She clutched her purse on her lap and made sure her suitcase was steady. "Has my photographer arrived yet?" The magazine promised to send a photographer along, but they had different itineraries. As Anna was a last-minute replacement for Keith, she didn't know when the photographer would be arriving or even who it was.

"Yes. He came yesterday morning," Kuusinen said as he lifted himself into the jeep.

Whoever he was, he'd gotten almost two full days' worth of experience ahead of her. She hoped he was a team player, that he'd share his information so his pictures and her stories that went with them would be good—award-worthy good.

"Let's go," Kuusinen said after Anna scooted back in her seat. The younger man nodded and started up the engine.

They were off, bouncing along icy roads, the headlights looking like two slashes cutting the way before them. The darkness felt so all-consuming and unfamiliar that Anna wished herself back home in her apartment with a cup of peppermint tea.

At least someone from home was in camp; a little bit of the familiar would be welcome, particularly when the "little bit" was simply a fellow American. Not for the first time during this journey, Anna wished she'd gotten a chance to meet her photographer and get to know him so she could get a feel for how he worked and how best to utilize their skills.

The jeep slid around a corner, just missing an animal, which pranced off through some trees.

"Was that a—a reindeer?" Anna stammered. Her arms shot out, griping the jeep for dear life.

"Yes," Kuusinen said. "We mustn't hurt the animals, of course."

Of course? How about we keep ourselves alive first? Her grip tightened. Oh, if I ever get safely back on solid ground, I'll need a good laugh.

What she wouldn't give for her cozy bedroom with the yellow glow from her lamp as she read a novel under her comforter. She'd done so the night before she left three days ago, but it felt like another world, another lifetime now as the jeep hurdled her through the inky, never-ending blackness.

At least this will keep me from thinking about Pete.

"I hear it's this dark in the day as well." she called to the front seat, determined to keep Pete out of her head. The cold air bit her throat and lungs. "Is that right?"

Kuusinen turned to talk to her over his shoulder, one arm resting on the driver's seat. "This time of year, yes." He looked as relaxed as if he were strolling down Hollywood Boulevard. "We get a few hours of light each day. Three or four, maybe."

"Three?" Anna repeated, incredulous. People lived this way? How?

"Or four," Kuusinen said. "Oh, but just wait six months, and we'll have so much light, you can hardly sleep at night. That's when we have three or four hours of darkness a night."

"Goodness," Anna said, shaking her head as she tried to grasp what such a life would be like. She wouldn't mind seeing a Finnish summer, but she was rather glad she wouldn't be here anywhere near long enough to find out what they were like.

"It's a beautiful country and a beautiful life," Kuusinen said. His face grew more serious. "A wonderful life we will not lose to Russia."

She nodded. "I believe you." The intensity in his eyes said that no matter what, he and his people would never give in, even against the giant Soviet army.

"I don't know how you do it," Anna said.

"*Sisu*," Kuusinen said without missing a beat.

"I'm sorry. I don't know that word." Anna's forehead crinkled. "See-sooh? What does that mean?"

"There is no good English word. Some say it means 'guts,' but . . ." He made a face and shook his head, showing his disdain for the translation. He pounded his chest. "*Sisu*. It's what makes us strong. Determined. Brave even when things look bad. We get through anything. We keep going no matter how hard. The Russians thought they could come take over with their tanks and cannons and hundreds of thousands of men against our small numbers. But we don't surrender. This is what we learn from living with these winters and defeating them every year."

As he spoke, puffs of white escaped his mouth. He leaned closer to Anna and narrowed his eyes. "*That* is *sisu*."

Made in the USA
San Bernardino, CA
20 July 2020